THERE'LL
be BLUE
SKIES

There'll be Blue Skies is Ellie Dean's first novel.
She lives in Eastbourne, which has been her home
for many years and where she raised her three
children.

THERE'LL
be BLUE
SKIES

Ellie Dean

arrow books

Published by Arrow Books 2011

2 4 6 8 10 9 7 5 3 1

First published in Great Britain in 2011 by
Arrow Books
Random House, 20 Vauxhall Bridge Road,
London SW1V 2SA

www.randomhouse.co.uk

Addresses for companies within The Random House Group Limited can be found at:
www.randomhouse.co.uk/offices.htm

The Random House Group Limited Reg. No. 954009

A CIP catalogue record for this book
is available from the British Library

ISBN 9780099560463

Typeset in Palatino by Palimpsest Book Production Limited,
Falkirk, Stirlingshire

The Random House Group Limited supports The Forest Stewardship
Council (FSC®), the leading international forest certification organisation.
Our books carrying the FSC label are printed on FSC® certified paper.
FSC is the only forest certification scheme endorsed by the leading
environmental organisations, including Greenpeace. Our
paper procurement policy can be found at
www.randomhouse.co.uk/environment

Printed and bound in Great Britain by Clays Ltd, St Ives PLC

Acknowledgements

There'll be Blue Skies is set in a time before I was born, so I have had to pester many people to help me make the story as authentic as possible.

Edie Brit, you're a star! Thank you so much for giving me the many insights into how life was in a seaside town during WW2. Your input was invaluable. Thanks too, to Brian Putland for introducing us.

I would also like to thank my mother-in-law, Kathleen Cater, and her friend, Jean Lane, for answering all my questions, and to Paul Nash for the information on southern RAF stations, life on the south coast during WW2, and the many hours you must have spent trawling through your extensive library. To Mick Barrow at the Hastings Fisherman's Museum, the staff at the Eastbourne Lifeboat Museum, and the curator at Newhaven Fort, I am most grateful for your time and your generosity in sharing your vast knowledge. A huge thank-you also goes to the hundreds of people who have posted their war memories on the Internet. I've pinched a few comic – and not so comic – incidents I hope you don't mind.

Lastly, I would like to acknowledge the unswerving loyalty of my literary agent, Teresa Chris, and the support, faith and guidance given by my editor, Georgina Hawtrey-Woore. Without these two brilliant women, this book would never have been written.

THERE'LL
be BLUE
SKIES

Chapter One

October, 1939

The threat of war had been the talk of the East End and, although Sally Turner had little idea of what it would really mean, she'd heard enough of the old men's tales to know it would probably be the most frightening thing she could ever experience. After the rumours and fears had been confirmed in Chamberlain's declaration, she could see the changes in the narrow streets and alleyways of Bow, for many of the children had already been sent to the countryside. Now it was her turn to leave with her little brother, and the thought of being taken far from the sights, sounds and smells of the only place she knew was terrifying.

She carefully placed the birthday card on top of their clothes, closed the battered suitcase, and secured it with one of her father's old belts. It was the only card she'd received and, as it had come from her father, it was extra special, and not something to be left behind. Harold Turner was already at sea when war was declared, and she had no idea where he was – but he'd remembered she'd turned sixteen a month ago, and it made her adore him even more. Her mother, Florrie, had forgotten as usual.

'Where's Mum?' Ernie was sitting on the end of the sagging couch which pulled out as a bed. He and Sally slept there every night unless Florrie was entertaining – then they went downstairs to Maisie Kemp's. 'I want Mum.'

Florrie hadn't come home last night and Sally could have done with knowing where she'd got to, but she had her suspicions. The pubs, clubs and streets in the East End were heaving with servicemen looking for a bit of fun – and Florrie liked a good time. 'She's probably gone off to work early,' she said, calmly.

'Mum never goes to work early,' he muttered.

Sally wasn't willing to get into an argument over their mother's whereabouts. Ernie was only six. 'There's a war on,' she said, instead. 'Everyone's got to do their bit – including Mum.'

Ernie's clear brown eyes regarded her steadily. 'Old Mother Kemp says Mum's doing 'er bit all right, and that Dad wouldn't like it. What did she mean by that, Sal?'

Maisie Kemp should learn to keep her trap shut around Ernie, thought Sally. 'I don't know, luv. Now, sit still and let me sort you out or we'll never be on time.' She tucked her fair curls behind her ears and picked up the special boot which she eased carefully over Ernie's misshapen foot. Once the laces were tied, she began to buckle the leather straps round his twisted, withered leg.

The polio had struck just before Ernie's second birthday, and it had left him with a crippled leg and weakened muscles – but, despite his disability, Ernie was like any other six year old – full of cheeky mischief and far too many questions.

'Do we 'ave to go, Sal?'

She made sure the callipers weren't too tight and patted the bony knee that jutted from beneath the hem of his short trousers. 'The prime minister says we 'ave to get out of London cos it ain't safe. All yer mates are going, and you don't want to be left out, do ya?'

Ernie shrugged and pulled a face. 'Why can't Mum come with me?'

'Because she can't – now, where did you put your school cap?'

He pulled it out of his pocket and rammed it on his head before tugging on his blazer. 'Will I 'ave to go to school? Billy Warner says there ain't no school in the country, just cows and sheep and lots of poo.' He giggled.

Sally giggled too and gave her little brother a hug. 'We'll have to just wait and see, won't we?' She made him a sandwich with the last of the bread and dripping. 'Eat that while I tidy up, then we must be going.'

It didn't take long to strip the bedding off the couch, finish the washing-up, and collect the last

3

few things to take with them. Their home consisted of two rooms on the top floor of a house, which was in a sooty red-brick terrace overshadowed by the gas-works and Solomon's clothing factory, where she had worked for the past two years alongside her mother.

Florrie had the only bedroom; the sitting room, where Sally and Ernie slept, doubled-up as a kitchen, with sink, gas ring and cupboards at one end. There was no bathroom, water had to be fetched from the pump at the end of the street, and the outside lav was shared with four other families. Baths were once a week in a metal tub on the strip of lino in front of the gas fire.

Sally had lived there all her life and, as she helped Ernie on with his mackintosh, she felt a tingle of apprehension. The journey they were about to begin would take them far from London, and although she'd run the house and raised Ernie since his illness, she was worried about the responsibility of looking after him so far from the close-knit community which could always be relied upon to help. She had never been outside the East End, had only seen pictures of the country, which looked too empty and isolated to be comfortable – or safe.

Putting these doubts firmly away, she covered the precious sewing machine with a cloth and gave it one last, loving pat. It had been her grandmother's, and the skills she'd taught Sally had meant she could earn a few extra bob each week. But it was part of

4

a heavy, wrought-iron table which housed the treadle. It had to be left behind. She hoped it survived – and that Florrie didn't take it into her head to sell it.

With a sigh, she squashed the worn felt hat over her fair curls, pulled on her thin overcoat and tightly fastened the belt round her slender waist. She then gathered up handbag, gas masks and suitcase before handing Ernie his walking stick.

'I ain't using that,' said Ernie with a scowl.

'It 'elps you to keep yer balance,' she said, tired of this perpetual argument. 'Come on, luv. Time to go.'

He snatched the hated stick from her and tucked it under his arm. 'Do I 'ave to wear this, Sal?' He plucked at the cardboard label hanging from a buttonhole on his school mackintosh. 'Makes me look like a parcel.'

'Yeah, you do. It's in case you get lost.'

'I ain't gonna get lost, though, am I?' he persisted. 'You're with me,' he retorted with the blinding logic of the young.

She smiled at him. 'Just wear it, Ernie, there's a good boy.' She locked the door behind her and put the key under the mat before helping him negotiate the narrow, steep stairs that plunged into the gloom of the hall.

'Yer off then.' Maisie Kemp had just finished scrubbing the front step, her large face red beneath the floral headscarf knotted over her curlers. She groaned as she clambered off her knees and wiped her hands down the wrap-round pinafore, before taking the ever-present fag out of her mouth. 'Give us a kiss then, Ernie, and promise yer Auntie Maisie you'll be a good boy.'

Ernie squirmed as the fat lips smacked his cheek, and he was smothered in her large bosom.

'No sign of Florrie then?' The blue eyes were knowing above the boy's head, the expression almost smug.

'Mum's meeting us at the station,' said Sally, unwilling to admit it was highly unlikely she'd even remembered they were leaving today. 'Cheerio, Maisie, and best of luck, mate. See you after the war.'

She clutched the suitcase with one hand and Ernie's arm with the other. Maisie could talk the hind legs off a donkey, and if they didn't get away quickly, they'd be later than ever.

Their slow progress down the cracked and weed-infested pavement was made slower as the women came out of their houses to say goodbye, and the remaining children clustered round Ernie. Not all of them would be leaving London, but Sally and her mother had been forced to accept that Ernie's incapacity meant he would be more vulnerable than most once the bombing started. It was also why he had to be accompanied – and as Florrie had flatly refused to leave London, Sally had no choice but to give up her job at the factory and go with him.

Ernie let go of her hand, and abandoned the walking stick as they came in sight of his school. He hurried off to join the swarm of chattering children, the calliper and thick special boot giving an added, stiff swing to his awkward gait.

Sally kept an eye on him as she joined the cluster of tearful women at the bus stop. If he got over-excited, his muscles cramped, and it would do him no good just before their long journey. With this thought she had a sharp moment of panic. Had she remembered his pills? She dipped into her coat pocket and let out a sigh of relief. The two little bottles were snug and safe.

'I wish I were going with you,' sobbed Ruby, her best friend. 'But what with the baby to look after and me job at the factory . . .'

Sally rubbed her arm in sympathy. 'Don't worry, Rube. I'll keep an eye on the boys for as long as I can – and we'll all be back again soon enough. You'll see.'

Ruby blew her nose, her gaze following the eight-year-old twins as they raced around the play-ground. 'I'm gonna miss the little buggers and that's a fact,' she muttered, clasping the baby to her narrow chest. 'The 'ouse ain't gunna feel the same without 'em, especially now me old man's gone off to war.'

Sally knew only too well how tough it was without a man in the house, but she could only imagine how hard it must be for her friend to have to send her children away. She was rescued from

7

having to reply by the arrival of three buses. They pulled to a halt and a large, well-fed woman in a tweed suit and laced-up brogues climbed down from the leading bus. She took in the scene at a glance and clapped her hands before her plummy voice rang out.

'Mothers, say goodbye to your children, and make sure they have their gas-mask boxes and identification discs, as well as their brown labels firmly attached to their clothing.' Her stern gaze swept over the tearful, defeated faces. 'I do hope you've managed to pack everything on the list. We can't expect our host families to provide any more than they already are.'

Sally thought of the long, impossible list she'd been given, and knew she wasn't the only one here that couldn't manage to get even half the stuff the government seemed to think was necessary. After all, who could afford spare shoes and two sets of underwear when it was hard enough to put food on the table?

She stood back as the other women gathered up their children, kissing them, holding them tightly until the last possible moment. None of them knew when they would see each other again and, as realisation set in, the older children quietened, their fear and distress almost tangible as the little ones began to cry.

Sally battled with her own tears as she hugged Ruby, kissed the baby and ordered the twins to hold

Ernie's hands. She was aware of the envious glances of the others, and tried not to feel guilty. It wasn't as if she'd had any choice in the matter.

'Children,' the woman called. 'Form a line here, so I can check your labels.' She shot a glance at Ernie's calliper. 'You must be Ernest Turner,' she muttered, going through the list pinned to her clipboard. Her gaze travelled over Sally and a thick brow rose in disdain. 'Are you his mother?'

Sally didn't like the way the woman made her feel, and she returned her stare. 'I'm 'is sister,' she said firmly, 'and we're together. I'm also looking after these two,' she added, indicating the twins who were jostling one another and sniggering.

'This is most irregular.' She sniffed her disapproval, took their names and executed large ticks on her list. 'Go to the back of the first bus, and hurry along. We don't want to be late, do we?'

Sally felt as if she was five again, and being reprimanded by her headmistress. Her face was burning with embarrassment as she helped Ernie and the twins clamber up, and struggled down the narrow aisle with the suitcase, walking stick, handbag and gas-mask boxes. Settling the boys by the window, she watched the tearful goodbyes on the pavement. The bus was already filling up, the younger children snivelling as they clutched an assortment of brown paper parcels, cardboard cases and gas-mask boxes – the older children more thoughtful, their wistful eyes gazing out of the windows for sight of their mothers as the truth sank in.

There was still no sign of Florrie, and she suddenly felt very young and vulnerable. If it hadn't been for Ernie, she'd have got off the bus and headed for the factory, where at least she knew the routine and everything was familiar – but Ernie needed her, so she reluctantly stayed put.

The fat woman finally clambered aboard with her clipboard and ordered the driver to get going. As the buses slowly trundled away from the school, the women walked alongside them, touching the windows where their children's tearful faces were pressed against the glass, calling out last-minute instructions and loving endearments to their little ones.

It was almost a relief to Sally when the buses picked up speed and left them behind. The guilt was growing by the second, and she couldn't look those women in the eye any more – but the sound of wailing children just emphasised the finality of it all and made her want to cry too.

As their bus made its grinding way through the streets, Sally kept Ernie and the twins occupied by pointing out the preparations for war. There were sandbags piled in front of government buildings and public air-raid shelters; white tape criss-crossed windows, and tank emplacements were strung all along the river. Signs over shop doorways declared support for Chamberlain, exhorting their customers to do their bit for the cause, whilst recruiting stations were busy with long lines of men patiently awaiting their turn. London's parks had been dug up to provide even more shelters, and every available strip of land was being planted with vegetables. They smiled as they saw men painting out the street signs – that would confuse the enemy and no mistake, for London was a warren of streets and alleyways.

The entrance to Victoria Station was surrounded by vast piles of sandbags which were guarded by armed soldiers. As the buses ground to a halt, the fat woman took charge again. 'You will form up in pairs in a straight line and follow me,' she boomed. 'Everyone hold hands with the person next to you and make sure you have everything with you.' She stepped down and was met by three more women who looked just like her.

Sally and Ernie were the last to leave the bus, and she gripped tightly to his hand as the long, snaking line headed into the gloom of the great station. The twins were nearby; she could hear their loud voices above the almost deafening chatter of hundreds of children pouring off similar buses.

There was little time to look around, but the impression Sally got was of a vast domed ceiling, endless platforms and giant steam engines. The noise and bustle of hurrying men in uniform, of crying women, wailing babies and excited children was overlaid with clouds of smoke and steam and the strong, pungent smell of burning coal. As neither of them had been on a train before, she and Ernie stared in awe at their surroundings and Sally realised they were both experiencing a tingle of expectation for the coming adventure. Perhaps it wouldn't be so bad after all.

Their labels were checked again, and then they were being led down the platform, past the great iron wheels to where porters helped them climb aboard. Sally slid back the door to the empty compartment, placed the gas masks and suitcase in the luggage rack and helped the other children settle in.

Once Ernie was made comfortable by the window, she tugged on the leather sash and leant out, scouring the bustling platform for sight of their mother. Just one glimpse of that peroxide hair was all she needed – just one fleeting sight of that familiar, brightly dressed, energetic figure cutting a swathe through the kitbags and suitcases that littered the platform was all she asked for.

'She ain't coming, is she?'

Ernie's pinched little face revealed his disappointment, and it twisted Sally's heart. She sat down and clasped his hand. 'No, luv,' she said softly beneath the hubbub of a hundred children's voices and the shouts of the porters. 'She's probably too busy at the factory and forgot the time.'

Ernie looked at her solemnly through the tears. 'I wish you was me mum,' he sniffed, burying his head into her side.

She put her arm round him and silently cursed Florrie for being so thoughtless. If her Dad had been here things would have been different. And as she sat consoling Ernie, she felt tears welling, and hurriedly blinked them away. She missed her father terribly – was as lost and frightened as her little brother, but it would do no good to let Ernie know that.

The train jolted alarmingly as a great shriek of steam and smoke billowed along the platform. The clank of the huge iron wheels slowly gathered pace and they left the gloom of the station and began to roll with a clickety-clack past the rows of red-brick terraces, the rooftops, spires, bridges and factories of London.

Sally's fear fluttered in her stomach. For, as the wheels picked up speed and settled into a rhythm, they were taking her away from home and everything she had ever known.

Peggy Reilly was glad Bob and Charlie were at school, and that her husband, Jim, was at the Odeon, where he worked as a projectionist. Her father-in-law, Ron, was making enough fuss as it was, and his lurcher wasn't helping by getting in the way and trying to cock his leg on everything.

The two men from the council had arrived at Beach View Boarding House an hour ago with the Anderson shelter – a large, ugly sheet of curved corrugated iron which they proceeded to erect over the four-foot-deep hole they'd dug at the bottom of the long back garden.

'We might have had to pay seven quid for that,' muttered Ron, 'but you'll not be getting me in it. The damp will have me shrapnel on the move again, and I'm a martyr to it already, so I am.'

Ron's shrapnel was a regular topic of conversation, along with his war stories. Anyone who didn't know him would have thought Ronan Reilly had won the First World War single-handedly. 'You'll be pleased enough of a bit of shelter when the bombs start dropping,' Peggy replied, her smile soft with affection for the cantankerous old man. His bark was always sharper than his bite, and she was used to hearing his complaints.

Ron pulled a face, grabbed the shaggy-coated Bedlington cross by the scruff and ordered him to sit. 'They didn't get me in the last war, and if they manage it in this, then it'll be in me own bed, so it will. I'll not be sleeping in that.'

He tied a length of string to the dog's collar, patted the pockets of his voluminous poacher's coat and stuck his unlit pipe in his mouth. 'Harvey and me are goin' off to find a bit of peace and quiet,' he announced. 'We'll be back for our tea.'

Peggy took a deep breath and let it out on a sigh. Ron was a widower and, at sixty-two, a law unto himself, with strong opinions and set ways. It wasn't that he was impossible to live with – just difficult. And yet he had a lot of good points, for he was masterful at telling stories, a knowledgeable countryman, skilled hunter and forager, who loved nothing more than taking his grandsons with him when he roamed the nearby hills that he knew so intimately. She just wished he wouldn't keep his ferrets in the scullery and let Harvey sleep on his bed. It was most unhygienic.

'That's it, missus. Thanks for the tea.' The foreman broke into her thoughts and handed her back the mugs. The men tipped their caps and hurried through the back gate. They had another eight shelters to erect before it got dark.

Peggy eyed the Anderson shelter with deep suspicion, and realised she agreed with Ron. It didn't look a terribly welcoming place to spend the night, and she rather hoped they would never have to. She took a few hesitant steps towards it, noting the rough wooden door they'd put on the front, and the sods of grass they'd placed over the roof. It looked as if it had grown out of the ground like a giant and rather menacing molehill.

She moved closer and gingerly followed the muddy steps down to the door. There was a dank pool beneath her feet, and the back wall and tin roof were already coldly damp to the touch. As she tried to imagine what it would be like to sit in here for possibly hours during an air raid, the door swung shut behind her, plunging her into earthy, smothering blackness. It was like being buried alive.

With rising panic, she fumbled her way out and

took deep breaths of the clean salty air that blew off the sea. If she was going to persuade anyone to spend time in there, she would have to get Jim to make it more habitable. Though getting her rogue of a husband to do anything practical around the place was something she hadn't yet managed in their twenty-three years of marriage. Jim was always far too busy getting into mischief, and she suspected he was rather looking forward to the prospect of doing even more shady deals now war had been declared.

Peggy firmly dismissed her suspicions. She'd known he was a scallywag when she'd married him, and had long since learnt to turn a blind eye to his nefarious ways. As long as it didn't affect her family, or her marriage, she was prepared to accept he would never change, for she still loved her dark-eyed handsome husband whose smile could make her feel fifteen again.

She pulled her meandering thoughts into order and made a mental note that the steps and floor would have to be concreted, a bench fixed to the wall so they had somewhere to sit, and a hook placed on the roof to hold a lantern. She could bring down the old oil heater to chase away the damp and chill, and put together some blankets and pillows which they could take in with them when needed. It would be a terrible squash, though, with so many people in the house – for, apart from her own family of seven, she had two lodgers, with an evacuee due to arrive later today.

With that thought, she glanced at her watch. The day was half gone, and there was a lot to do before she had to be at the station. She walked down the path that ran through Ron's vegetable garden, and hurried past the outside lav, concrete coal bunker and ramshackle shed until she reached the double doors that led into the two-bedroom basement flat, which Ron shared with twelve-year-old Bob and eight-year-old Charlie.

On passing, she shot a glance into the bedrooms, noting they were untidy as usual, and that the ferrets were absent from their cage beneath the scullery sink. Ron must have them in the pocket of his poacher's coat.

She quickly made the beds, tidied up and scrubbed the stone sink in the scullery before climbing the concrete steps that led into her kitchen on the first floor.

Beach View Boarding House had been in her family for three generations; when Peggy's parents retired to a bungalow in Margate, she and Jim had moved to Cliffehaven and taken it over. Peggy had run it as a successful bed-and-breakfast establishment until the news came from Europe. The impending declaration of war had put an end to holidaymakers coming to the seaside.

Money was tight and now only two of her five guest rooms were occupied. The Polish airman whose name she could never pronounce was in one, and dear little Mrs Finch was in the other. The evacuee from London would go in the smallest of the three rooms in the attic, next to that shared by her two daughters.

Beach View was a tall Victorian terraced house set on a hill three streets back from the promenade. Surrounded by many similar terraces, there was only a glimpse of the sea from the top right-hand window. Arranged on four floors, the large rooms had been divided up to provide five guest rooms and a bathroom on the top two floors, her bedroom on the hall floor, along with the kitchen and guest dining room. The square entrance hall led through a glass-panelled front door to a flight of stone steps which overshadowed the basement window and ran down to the pavement.

Peggy bustled about her kitchen, aware of the time passing as she peeled carrots, onions and potatoes for the stew they would have tonight. Rationing hadn't started yet, but she'd already registered with the local butcher and grocer, and the ration cards were sitting on the mantel above the fireplace where the Kitchener range warmed the kitchen.

It was her favourite room, which was a good thing, because she spent a lot of time in there. The window overlooked the garden and the backs of the houses behind it; the lino was worn, but colourful, and matched the oilcloth she'd spread over the table, which could seat eight at a pinch. There was a picture of the King and Queen on the wall, shelves were laden with crockery, and hooks above the range held pots and pans. The wireless stood proudly on top of the chest of drawers where she kept her best linen tablecloths, and the kettle was set to one side of the hob, filled and ready to put on to boil. There was always time for a cup of tea.

'I'm hungry,' whined Ernie, as he jealously watched the other children eating the sandwiches their mothers had packed so tearfully that morning.

Sally was hungry too, but after Ernie's breakfast of bread and dripping, there had been nothing left in the larder to bring with them, and no time or money to buy something on the way. 'Sorry, luv. You'll just have to wait until we get to wherever we're going.'

'But I'm hungry now,' he muttered.

'I know,' she sighed, the guilt flooding through her again. He was so small and skinny and he relied on her for everything. She'd let him down. Then she remembered the toffee in her coat pocket. She'd been given it the day before at work – one of the girls had brought in a big bag of them and she'd popped it into her pocket, meaning to enjoy it the night before. Rummaging, she found it, and brushed off the fluff. 'Suck it slowly,' she advised as she unwrapped it. 'It will last longer if you don't chew.'

Mollified and content, Ernie closed his eyes and savoured the sweet.

Sally folded her hands on her lap and looked out of the window. She reckoned they'd been travelling for at least an hour, and the sights of London were far behind them now, replaced by endless fields, narrow lanes, thatched cottages, sprawling farm-houses and big open skies.

She looked down at the fast-running river as they clattered over a bridge, gazed in awe at the sight of the great rolling hills that seemed to tower over the tiny villages nestled beneath them. She had never seen such emptiness before, and wondered how people managed without shops and neighbours close by. What did they do all day? How did they make a living?

The sound of the door to their compartment sliding open made her turn. It was the bossy woman again.

'We shall be arriving in ten minutes,' she said. 'Don't leave anything behind, and that includes your rubbish,' she said, with a pointed glare at the sandwich wrappings on the floor. Her gimlet gaze settled on Sally. 'I will hold you responsible for the children in here. Make sure they are ready to alight once the train comes to a standstill.' She shut the door with a sharp click and moved on down the swaying corridor to the next compartment.

'I don't like her,' mumbled Ernie through the toffee. 'I 'ope she ain't staying with us.'

'I expect she'll be going back to London,' replied Sally, as she pulled down the cases and parcels from the luggage shelf. Having checked that each child had been reunited with the correct items, and that the wrappers and sweet papers were tidied away in an empty paper bag, she slipped on her coat and hat and hid the bag in her pocket. She didn't want the fat woman finding fault – it could make a difference to where they were billeted.

She fussed with Ernie's blazer, mackintosh and school cap, and held his squirming chin in a tight grip as she gave his face a quick clean with her handkerchief and tugged a comb through his tangled hair. Satisfied he looked reasonably presentable, she glanced in the mirror above the opposite seat, and had to admit she looked tired. The felt hat and draughty coat looked tired as well in the light that streamed in through the window, but there was nothing she could do about it. She sat down again and clutched the handbag on her knees, wondering where they were going, and what the people there would be like.

The train slowed to a crawl and chuffed its way along until it reached the platform. Sally was joined at the window by the excited children, and she looked for some clue that might tell her where they were. But all the signs had been taken down and, as the train took them deeper into the gloom of a large station, Sally realised that wherever they were, this was a fairly big town.

As the train came to a halt and billowed smoke, she clutched Ernie's hand and steered the other children in front of her as they joined the crush in the narrow corridor that ran alongside the compartments. The noise was deafening as everyone talked at once and the three women in charge bellowed out their orders.

Sally found the twins in the melee and kept them close as they followed the women across the concourse to an area that had been cordoned off with bunting. Beneath the large welcome sign there was a long trestle table manned by an army of smiling women in WRVS uniform.

Sally's mouth watered and the children's eyes bulged at the sight of so much food in one place. There were cakes, sandwiches and rolls, milk and cordial and, at the end of the table, a vast urn promised hot, sweet cups of tea. Her stomach rumbled loudly and she hoped no-one had heard it. 'See,' she said, turning to Ernie. 'I told you we'd be fed soon.'

She found him a seat in the rows of chairs that had been set out, and left him in charge of the case and gas masks to join the queue. The older children helped the little ones as the women behind the table served huge slices of cake and iced buns, their cheery smiles making them forget just how tired and frightened they all were.

When Sally had loaded his plate and settled him with a mug of tea, she went back for her own. The hot tea was the best she'd ever tasted – full of milk and sweet with sugar, it slipped down and revived her no end – and no-one minded when she asked if she could have another cup.

The cake, sausage roll and two sandwiches were delicious, and she could have eaten more, but she didn't want to appear greedy. There were a lot of children to feed. But Ernie had no such inhibitions. He'd polished off his plateful and gone back for more. 'I don't mind the country if the food's like this,' he said, through a mouthful of chocolate cake.

'You'll make yourself sick,' she warned, hastily wiping chocolate off his blazer. 'And do mind what yer doing, Ernie. Yer supposed to eat the cake, not wear it.'

He'd finally eaten his fill, and Sally polished off the discarded sausage roll before returning the plates to the nice WRVS ladies. As she returned to the seat beside him, she became aware of a crowd of people standing on the other side of the cordon. She guessed they had to be those who'd volunteered to take in the evacuees, and she studied them carefully as, one by one, the children were led away.

She noticed that siblings were kept together, and that some people took three or four of the kids, while others only took one. Some of the people looked very smart in good winter coats and polished shoes, and she rather hoped that one of them would take her and Ernie.

The twins went off happily enough with only the merest wave goodbye, and Sally noted the pleasant-faced woman who led them away. They would be all right.

As the numbers dwindled, Sally realised she and

Ernie were being scrutinised closely before being passed over. So, she thought, that's the way of it, is it? Well, if they don't want us, we can always go back home, and good riddance. She held Ernie's hand and tried not to care that she and her brother were being muttered over as if they were on a butcher's slab – and found wanting.

'Miss Turner. Mr and Mrs Hollings have kindly offered you a place in their home. Please bring your belongings with you.'

Sally gathered everything up and helped Ernie to his feet.

'Just you, dear. Your brother has been assigned another billet.'

She shot a glance at the middle-aged couple, caught the way she was being ogled by the husband and sat down again. 'I ain't going nowhere without Ernie,' she replied, 'and especially not with them.' She glared at the man, who at least had the decency to redden and look hurriedly away.

'Your brother will be hard to place, Miss Turner, which is why we have made arrangements for him to go to the local orphanage.'

Sally felt a chill run down her spine as she leapt to her feet and stood in front of Ernie. She didn't trust this woman not to grab him and try to haul him away. 'He ain't no orphan, and he ain't going nowhere without me.'

The woman shrugged and turned apologetically to the couple, her voice loud, the tone scathing. 'This is what you get for trying to help. Really, these East End girls have no manners at all. I do apologise.' She hustled them away.

'What's an orph . . . orphan . . . ?

'Nowhere you need worry about, luv.' Sally grimaced as she returned to her seat and held him close. If this was an example of what she could expect in this place, then she and Ernie would be better off in the Smoke. At least people didn't judge them there.

She was battling with her angry tears, trying to remain in control of her emotions for his sake. Being so young he, thankfully, didn't understand what was going on. She looked around her. Most of the children were gone now, and soon they would be the only ones left. It was galling to be unwanted – and shaming. Nothing like this had happened to either of them before.

Mrs Finch had come into the kitchen and, wanting a bit of company, had chattered on over several cups of tea. Peggy felt sorry for the poor old duck – after all, she'd reasoned, Mrs Finch was a widow whose sons had migrated to Canada many years before, and rarely wrote to her. She was, to all intents and purposes, alone in the world. It did no harm to gossip as she worked. But my goodness she could talk.

Peggy had glanced at the clock and almost left her in mid-sentence as she tore off the apron and headscarf, grabbed her coat and bag and rushed off.

To make matters worse, she'd missed the trolleybus, and the old car had taken longer than usual to get started.

As it groaned and complained up the hill to the station, she was aware of the passing time – and that now she was very late. She parked haphazardly, slammed the door and hurried on to the concourse.

One glance told her everything, and her heart went out to the skinny girl who was sitting so stoically beside the frail, crippled little boy. They were poorly dressed and looked half starved, and the boy's pinched little face made her want to bundle him up and carry him home.

'Mrs Reilly? You're late. I'm afraid there's only those two left, and the girl is a troublemaker. Perhaps you'd be better off waiting until the next train?'

Peggy tore her gaze from the girl's large hazel eyes and regarded the woman coldly. 'In what way has she caused trouble?'

She lowered her voice. 'She refused to let us place her brother in the orphanage – and turned down the chance of staying with a very nice family who live in Havelock Gardens.'

It was a leafy street on the better side of town, and Peggy held no illusions about the snobs who lived there. Her sister Doris was one of them. 'Havelock Gardens isn't all it's cracked up to be,' Peggy answered with the withering look she'd perfected over the years of running a boarding house. 'And why should the boy go to the orphanage?'

'He's a cripple,' she said, making it sound as if it was something contagious, 'and therefore rather difficult to place.'

'I'll take the pair of them,' said Peggy, adjusting the ancient fox fur that hung around her neck.

'Really, Mrs Reilly, I don't think . . .'

'No, you don't do you?' Peggy's look was scathing as she turned away. The girl and her brother were watching her, and she thought she could see the hint of a smile touching the girl's mouth as she stood to greet her.

'My name's Peggy Reilly, and I'd like you to come and stay with me. How do you feel about that?'

The girl's smile faltered, her gaze darting between Peggy and the woman in charge. 'Ernie too?'

'Of course,' she said firmly. 'I have two boys of my own, and I'm sure he'll settle in just fine.'

'What'ya think, Ernie? Would you like to go with this lady?'

Ernie was eyeing the fox round Peggy's neck with some suspicion as he slowly nodded. 'That's a dead fox, ain't it?'

'It most certainly is,' she said with a warm smile, 'but back home, Granddad Ron has some real live ferrets – and a dog. Would you like to see them?'

'What's a ferret?'

Peggy laughed. The little boy might look wan and half starved, but he was as inquisitive as Bob and Charlie and, she suspected, as mischievous. 'It's long and furry and likes nothing better than going down holes after rabbits.'

'Why's that fox biting 'is tail?'

'Shut up, Ernie.' Sally shot Peggy an apologetic glance, her smile hesitant as she introduced herself. 'If you're sure you can put up with all 'is questions, Mrs Reilly, then, yes, we'd like to come with you.'

'That's settled then.' Peggy was not one to hang about. She picked up the case and took Ernie's little hand. 'Come on, Ernie, let's get home and see if Granddad Ron has got back with those ferrets.'

Chapter Two

Anne Reilly was almost twenty-three and felt blessed that her first post since qualifying was at the local primary school where she'd once sat enthralled by the things she could learn. Her smile was soft with contentment as she collected the exercise books and stacked them on her desk. She loved teaching, and the children had been well behaved today, even her little brother, Charlie.

The bell began to ring; classes were over until Monday. 'Don't run,' she called out to the stampeding children, 'and stop pushing, Charles Reilly. You'll get home soon enough.'

Her youngest brother shot her his cheeky grin and eased through the door before tearing down the hallway with an enthusiastic yell of freedom. At eight years old, Charlie had far too much energy – but he was bright and absorbed his lessons like a sponge. Anne had high hopes for Charlie.

She cleaned the blackboard, put away the chalk, rulers and pencils in the desk and set about tidying the classroom. The arrival of so many evacuees had swelled the numbers at Cliffehaven Primary, and there was very little room to manoeuvre around the desks and benches. But that wasn't the most pressing problem, for space could always be found somewhere – it was more the fact that the majority of those evacuee children could barely read and write, let alone knew the names and dates of the English Kings and Queens or recited their tables. It seemed the East End children were needed to earn money, not waste time at school – and it was extremely difficult to run a classroom efficiently when half the children had to have special coaching to get them up to scratch.

Anne sighed as she stowed the reading books away in the cupboard. The headmaster was aware of how hard things were getting, but with a shortage of books and more evacuees scheduled to arrive over the next few weeks, the situation could only get worse. There had been talk of dividing up the lessons – the local children in the morning, evacuees in the afternoon – but that would mean only half an education for all of them, unless they worked through the holidays as well.

She stuffed the exercise books into her briefcase, pulled on her warm woollen coat and scarf and shut the classroom door behind her. Everyone had to do their bit, and if it meant shorter holidays and longer hours, then that was what she would do.

Her thoughts were disrupted by Dorothy who was emerging from her own classroom across the corridor. She and Dorothy had known each other all their lives and had attended the same teacher-training college. 'You look as if you've had a bit of a day,' Anne said with a smile.

'You should try teaching that lot,' Dorothy replied, sweeping back her wavy ginger hair. 'Half of them can't sit still for more than a couple of minutes, and it's the devil's own job to keep order. I can't say I'm sorry it's the weekend.'

Anne took her arm and gave it a sympathetic hug. Dorothy had several disruptive children in her class, and she fully understood how hard it was to keep them quiet and focused on their lessons. 'What are your plans for the next two days? Are you seeing Greg?'

Dorothy drew the bulging briefcase to her chest and gave a rueful smile as they headed for the front door. 'Marking this lot will take up most of the evening, but, yes, I'm meeting Greg for a drink later. Want to join us?'

Anne shook her head, making her dark curls dance. She didn't fancy playing gooseberry with Dorothy and her Canadian soldier. 'I've got other plans,' she replied, knowing there was a twinkle in her eyes.

Dorothy raised an eyebrow. 'It's like that, is it?'

Anne could feel the blush rise up her neck and into her face. 'We've only known each other a few weeks,' she protested. 'Give us a chance.'

'Martin Black is a bit of a catch, though, you have to admit,' said Dorothy. 'He's handsome, single *and* an RAF pilot – what more could you want?'

'I'll have to wait and see,' murmured Anne, as Dorothy collected her bicycle from the shed and they walked to the gate. 'Martin got his orders last night. He'll be moving to a permanent base within the next two weeks. He can't tell me where it is, of course, but it could be miles away, and we might not get the chance of seeing each other quite so much.'

Dorothy's smile was knowing. 'Oh,' she said, with all the wisdom of a twenty-three year old who'd had a string of admirers, 'I'm sure you'll find a way.' She settled her briefcase in the bicycle basket and pedalled off, wobbling slightly as she turned her head and waved goodbye.

Anne pulled on her gloves and tightened her scarf as the bitterly cold wind buffeted her. The gulls were wheeling overhead, filling the air with their angry cries. The fishermen must just have returned on the high tide with their daily catch.

It was a fairly short walk home, past the local shops and pubs before turning north and up the hill away from the seafront. But, as she hurried out of the school gates, her mind wasn't really on gulls, fishermen or classrooms. Her thoughts were full of Martin, and the worrying possibility that their fledgling romance would simply peter out once he was posted. She had no illusions, for she'd seen it happen to some of her friends – but life was uncertain for everyone, and she was determined to remain optimistic.

* * *

Sally trailed behind them across the concourse. Mrs Reilly was a small, wiry woman whose every step spoke of a boundless energy, but Sally was a little disconcerted by the way she had taken charge of Ernie, and of how willingly he'd taken his walking stick and gone along with her. She seemed nice enough, and she'd clearly put that awful woman in charge in her place. And yet Mrs Reilly was a smartly dressed stranger who talked posh, was clearly used to being obeyed, and wore dead animals round her neck. Sally decided to reserve judgement until she got to know her better.

As they emerged from the station, which was at the top of a long, steep hill, she was immediately struck by how cold it was, the air smelling cleanly of salt – instead of soot from a thousand chimneys, like back home. She looked up at the large white wheeling birds that shrieked and squabbled over the rooftops, and then gazed down the hill, past the large shops, banks and hotels with their stacks of sandbags and taped windows to where she caught a glimpse of blue glittering between the big houses. 'Is this the seaside?' she breathed.

'Indeed it is,' said Peggy with a beaming smile. 'Welcome to Cliffehaven. I know you must be finding it hard to take it all in, but I hope you'll be happy here.'

'I ain't never seen the sea before,' she said, awestruck.

'Cor,' shouted Ernie, who was far more interested

33

in Peggy's car. 'Are we goin' in that?' His eyes were wide and shining as he fingered the Ford's running board, the huge headlamps and the shining chrome.

'As long as it starts,' said Peggy, as she opened the door and helped him clamber on to the back seat. 'Otherwise it's the trolleybus.'

'Careful, Ernie. That's real leather, that is, and Mrs Reilly don't want you scratching it with yer calliper.' Sally's stern look was wasted, for Ernie was too busy leaning over the front seat to examine the dials and switches on the dashboard.

'I shouldn't worry too much,' laughed Peggy. 'This old car has withstood four children and more besides. Let him have his fun.'

Sally gave Ernie another furious look as she put the suitcase on the seat beside him and closed the door before warily joining Mrs Reilly on the front seat. The car smelled lovely, and it reminded her of the market stall in Petticoat Lane where Alf Green sold the gloves and handbags he made with the leftovers from his cobbler's shop. She could feel the cool leather against her bare legs, and the way the seat cushioned her, but she sat ramrod stiff, terrified she might damage it. Mrs Reilly must be very rich to own such a car.

'Off we go then. Hold on tight. This old girl gets a bit temperamental, but she'll be fine once we get going.'

Sally pressed back into the seat and held on as the engine spluttered into life and they jerked their way down the hill. But as the car slowly rattled and backfired its way past Woolworths and the Odeon cinema, she forgot to be nervous, for the patch of blue at the bottom of the road had captured her full attention.

They reached the crossroads at the bottom of the hill and Peggy drew to a halt. 'There you are,' she said, with obvious pride. 'That's the English Channel.'

'So it's not the sea then?'

'Well, it is, but only the bit that divides us from France and the rest of Europe.'

'Cor,' breathed Ernie. 'It's big, ain't it?'

Sally gazed in awe and disbelief, unable to voice her agreement. It was enormous, stretching from the towering white cliffs at one end of the promenade to the rolling hills at the other – and as far as the eye could see to the horizon where it seemed to melt into the sky. The blue was laced with white frothy waves that splashed against the shingle and the enormous concrete blocks that had been placed haphazardly across the bay. Gulls swooped and swirled overhead, flags fluttered, and the people walking on the promenade had to hold on to their hats and bend into the October wind.

She thought how envious her friends back home would be, but as she eyed the thick coils of barbed wire, the warnings that the beach had been mined, and the concrete gun emplacements that lined the promenade, she realised that, even if she did get up the nerve, she would never be able to actually get down on the beach, or dip her toes in the water.

Peggy seemed to have read her thoughts. 'It doesn't look its best at the moment,' she said, engaging the gears with a clash. 'Even the pier has been closed off for the duration. The army came the other day and dismantled half of it to prevent enemy landings.'

She turned the steering wheel and they headed east along the road towards the high white cliffs that were topped with grass, and the occasional gun emplacement. 'If you want to go on the beach, then the only place is down there where the fishing fleet comes in – but it's a busy place with the boats in and out, and not very safe.'

Sally stared up at the cliffs and back to the sea. She took in the black boats with their sails and ropes, and the men who clambered over them in their thick jumpers and sturdy rubber boots. She could even see the nets hanging out to dry in the wind, and the lobster pots stacked on the shingle. The nearest she'd ever come to seeing fish was in Billingsgate Market.

'I feel sick,' muttered Ernie.

Peggy slammed on the brake and Sally rushed to get him out of the car. 'Oh, Ernie,' she sighed, as he vomited copiously down a nearby drain. 'I told you not to eat so much,' she scolded softly.

Ernie's little face was green-tinged as she cleaned him up with Mrs Reilly's spotless handkerchief, and gave him a hug.

'Too much excitement and chocolate cake, by the look of it,' Peggy said, as she helped him back to the car, told him to lie down, and gently tucked a blanket round him. 'We'll be home soon,' she soothed.

'I'm so sorry, Mrs Reilly.' Sally's face felt hot and she couldn't look the woman in the eye. 'He's ruined yer 'ankie, an' all. I'll get you another one as soon as I'm earning.'

'Nonsense,' said Peggy, taking the offending article and stuffing it in her handbag. 'All children are sick at one time or another and the handkerchief can go in the wash with everything else.' She clashed the gears and the car stuttered along the seafront. 'If I had a penny for every time Bob and Charlie had been sick, then I'd be a rich woman.' She smiled at Sally and patted her knee. 'Don't worry, dear,' she murmured. 'We're nearly home, and he'll be as right as rain after a cup of tea and a bit of a lie-down.'

Sally didn't know what to make of Mrs Reilly. She seemed really nice, and had been very kind about Ernie making a show of himself – but what did a woman as rich as her want from them? She'd met do-gooders before, and they always wanted something in return for their favours; like the lady in the bakery back home, who wanted her ironing done in exchange for the few stale rolls she handed over begrudgingly at the end of the week.

Her doubts and suspicions multiplied as they

turned from the seafront and began to climb the steep hill lined with row upon row of grand terraced houses. There were no factories or gasworks overshadowing them; no cracked pavements or littered streets with kids playing football, and women leaning in their doorways having a gossip. The windows were clean, the paintwork shining in the autumn sunlight, steps scrubbed, railings clear of rust. The gardens were neat and even the smoke from the chimneys was blown away by the wind coming off the sea.

She spotted two pubs down a side street, and a row of shops – but no sign of Goldman's Clothing factory where she was supposed to start work in two days' time.

'That's the local shops,' said Peggy, slowing the car. 'The big building at the far end is the hospital, and the one opposite it is the primary school where my daughter Anne teaches. Bob started at the secondary school this term, but Charlie goes there, and so will Ernie.'

'But Billy said there weren't no school in the country,' wailed Ernie from the back seat. He was obviously feeling better.

Peggy laughed. 'This is the seaside, and there *is* school,' she said before resuming the drive.

Ernie opened his mouth to express his fury at having been misled, and Sally hurriedly changed the subject. 'How far is it to Goldman's factory?'

Peggy frowned. 'Goldman's? Is that where you'll

be working? How did you manage to organise that?'

'Me boss at 'ome arranged it. Mr Goldman's 'is brother-in-law.'

'I see.' Peggy changed down gears as the hill steepened. 'You don't look old enough to be working at all,' she said, glancing at her, 'and Goldman is a hard taskmaster, by all accounts. I'm sure I can get you something a little less—'

Now it was Sally's turn to be indignant. 'I'm sixteen,' she replied, 'and I've been 'olding down me job at Solomon's for near on two year now. I know the work, and I'm good at it.'

'I see,' sighed Peggy. She seemed to pull her thoughts together. 'Goldman's is past the hospital and primary school at the end of that road,' she said, with a nod of her head. 'It will be a bit of a walk every day once winter really sets in, but there's a spare bicycle in Ron's shed. You can borrow that once it's been mended.'

Sally was feeling rather ashamed of her outburst. Mrs Reilly was only trying to be helpful – but she didn't have the first idea of how to ride a bike, and was reluctant to admit it. 'I don't mind walking,' she replied.

Peggy glanced across at her. 'Well, if you change your mind, Anne or one of the boys will show you how to ride it. It's a bit of an old bone-shaker, but it'll get you there and back all right.' She pulled into a side street and brought the car to a halt halfway along. 'This is it,' she said, turning off the engine. 'Welcome to Beach View.'

'I can't see the beach,' grumbled Ernie, who was kneeling on the seat, looking out of the back window.

Sally was about to admonish him for being rude when Peggy intervened. 'You will from your bedroom window,' she said cheerfully. 'Come on, let's get you indoors. Anne and the boys will be home from school by now, and we can all get acquainted.'

Sally looked up at the terraced house, and felt even more uneasy. It was really smart, like one of the mansions near Hyde Park, with its portico and wide, white steps leading up to a smart door that had coloured panels of glass which caught the sun. There was a brass knob, and a knocker in the shape of a lion's head, and at the end of the sweeping white steps were lanterns set into sturdy concrete pillars. She took in the frothy white net curtains at the taped windows, the tubs of flowers beside the door, and knew she and Ernie could never really fit in here.

'Don't let outward appearances fool you,' said Peggy, who must have noticed her uneasiness. 'It might be big, but that's because it used to be a guesthouse. Now it's just a home – a home for me and my family, and any poor soul who needs somewhere for the duration. Now it will be home for you too.' She put her hand on Sally's arm, her brown eyes expressive and sincere. 'Don't fret, Sally. We might be different to what you're used to – but we don't bite.'

Sally wasn't at all sure how to react, for Mrs Reilly was like no-one she'd ever met before – and yet she seemed to have a warm heart, despite her forthright manner and, unlike Florrie, appeared to really care about her home and her family. She gave her a hesitant smile, for the doubts were still there. Mrs Reilly seemed all right now, but she might not be quite so friendly when Ernie had one of his terrible attacks of the cramps in his back and legs which had him screaming through the night.

Sally hitched Ernie on to her hip and carried him up the stairs as Peggy took the suitcase and opened the front door.

She could hear someone talking in a soft Irish accent as they stepped into the hallway, which smelled strongly of beeswax polish and cooking – scents that reminded her of her grandmother's house and made her nostalgic for the days when the old lady had been alive. She set Ernie on his feet, aware of his little hand clutching her as they gazed in awe at the sweeping staircase and high ceilings. This was a world away from Bow, and she suspected he felt as disorientated and uncertain as she did.

'That'll be my father-in-law, Ron, telling the boys one of his outrageous stories,' said Peggy, as the voice continued to drift out to them from somewhere at the back of the house. 'No doubt he's forgotten he's supposed to keep an eye on the stew. Come on, no time like the present to meet some of the family.'

Ernie looked up at Sally, his big brown eyes fearful. 'I'm nervous too,' she whispered, as they reluctantly followed Mrs Reilly down the hall. 'Just hold my hand, and we'll both be all right.'

'Well, and it's about time too. Me stomach thinks me throat's been cut, so it does.' Ron turned from the sink where he'd been skinning a brace of rabbits. 'Hello,' he said, his piercing blue eyes boring into Sally and Ernie. 'Who do we have here then?'

From the doorway, Sally took the scene in at a glance. The old man had a weather-worn face and thickset, sturdy figure which was encased in a misshapen sweater and baggy old trousers. The young woman sitting at the table before a pile of exercise books was pretty with creamy skin, dark eyes and hair and elegant hands. The two boys were tousle-headed, with clean faces and bright, intelligent eyes which were studying her and Ernie with unmasked curiosity. A large shaggy dog was stretched in front of the black range. It eyed them disinterestedly and went back to sleep.

'This is Sally and Ernie,' said Peggy, drawing them forward. 'They're going to be living with us for a while until it's safe to go back to London.'

'Are they now?' Ron wiped his bloody hands down his trousers, his eyes twinkling. 'And here's me thinking you were only taking the one, Peggy.'

'I changed my mind,' she retorted.

Sally stood in the warm, homely kitchen with its heavenly smell of stew and held tightly to Ernie's hand as Peggy eyed the gutted rabbits with disfavour and made the introductions.

'My younger daughter, Cissy, should be home from work soon, and then of course there's Mrs Finch and the Polish gentleman who you'll meet at teatime,' she finished. She smiled and added confidentially, 'Don't ask me to pronounce his name – it's virtually impossible.'

Sally was finding the whole thing daunting, and she was aware of Ernie's hand clutching her fingers. 'Pleased to meet yer, I'm sure,' she said, and only just managed to stop bobbing a curtsy, like her gran used to when she worked as a ladies' maid in the big house in Hyde Park.

'Nice to meet you, Sally.' Anne half stood and shook her hand. 'I hope you'll excuse me, but these books have to be marked before I can go out.'

Bob shook hands solemnly before returning to his comic, but Charlie had fewer inhibitions and swung from the table, making a beeline for Ernie. 'What's that on your leg, Ernie? Are you a pirate?'

Ernie tried to melt against Sally as he shook his head.

'I've got a bad leg too,' said Charlie, pointing to a graze on his knee. 'Got it wrestling a shark.'

'Charlie, don't fib,' said Peggy, as she took off her coat, fur and hat and tied on her apron. 'And leave poor Ernie alone. Can't you see he's tired and out of sorts?'

'Aw, Mum. Can't I show him my treasure?' He didn't wait for a reply, and turned back to Ernie. 'D'you like pirates? I've got a whole box of treasure downstairs. Want to have a look?'

Ernie relaxed his hold on Sally's coat. 'Pirate treasure?'

Charlie nodded. 'I've even got a skull,' he breathed. 'D'you want to see it?'

'A skull?' Ernie forgot to be shy, and his eyes widened as he took a step towards Charlie. 'A real one?'

'It's from a dead fox,' muttered Bob. 'There're loads up on the hills. Granddad finds them all the time.'

Charlie rolled his eyes. 'I never said it was a *human* skull,' he said in exasperation. 'Do you wanna see it, Ernie?'

'I dunno.' Ernie shot a glance up at Sally, who nodded encouragement.

'Aw, come on. It's only downstairs . . .' He looked at Ernie's leg, suddenly not so certain of himself. 'I suppose I could bring it up,' he said hesitantly, 'but . . .'

'I ain't a cripple,' muttered Ernie. 'A few old stairs don't bother me.'

Sally was about to intervene when Ron took charge. 'But why walk when you can get a lift? Will you be trusting me to take you down there into the dungeon, Ernie?'

Ernie eyed him warily. It was clear to Sally that he was longing to see the skull, but was rather daunted by the old man who was now looming over him.

'Sure, and it'll not take a minute, and you might find you even enjoy it. Are ye man enough to sit on me shoulders, Ernie?'

Ernie giggled and took a hesitant step towards him. The last time he'd ridden on a man's shoulders it had been his father's.

Ron's eyes twinkled and he winked at Sally before bending down and swinging little Ernie on to his broad shoulders. 'Right, me hearties,' he cried, as the child squealed with a mixture of terror and delight and clutched at his hair, 'let's be going in search of Charlie's plunder.' He ducked as he reached the entrance to the basement steps. 'Mind your head, there, shipmate!'

'You'll have to excuse him,' said Peggy in a fluster, as Ron and the boys thundered down to the cellar. 'He means no harm, but I sometimes wonder if he's ever grown up.'

Sally's smile was nervous. 'He will look after him proper, won't 'e? Only Ernie ain't strong.'

Peggy set the kettle on the hob. 'Ron knows what he's doing, dear. Ernie will come to no harm with him.'

'Mum's right,' said Anne, closing the last of the exercise books with a thankful sigh. 'Granddad's the best playmate any child could have, but I should warn you, Sally, he'll get all of them into mischief.'

Sally had little doubt of it but, as she returned Anne's smile, she realised how nice she was, and wondered if they could become friends despite the differences in age and background. She glanced round the homely kitchen and took off her coat. It was wonderfully warm in here. 'Can I help with anything, Mrs Reilly?'

'Bless you, no. Everything's almost done, and once Cissy gets back, we can eat.'

'That's your other daughter, ain't it?'

Peggy nodded as she set out cups and saucers and filled the warmed teapot. 'Cissy's a year older than you, so I'm hoping you'll get on. But she's a strange one, and takes a bit of getting used to.' She sat down, pulled a packet of Park Drive out of her apron pocket and lit up the first of the two cigarettes she allowed herself each day.

Sally sat beside her, intrigued. 'Strange?'

Anne closed the bulging briefcase and set it on the floor before she too lit a cigarette. 'What Mum means is that although Cicely works in Woolworths on the High Street, she's convinced her destiny lies in Hollywood.' She laughed softly, and shook her head, making her shining hair bounce on her shoulders. 'She spends hours in front of the mirror and makes the house shake when she practises her dance routines.'

Peggy poured the tea. 'Cissy models herself on Judy Garland but, so far, she's had to be satisfied with the back row of the chorus.' She gave a deep sigh. 'Where she gets it from, I have no idea.'

'She must be very glamorous,' said Sally wistfully, as she dug her careworn hands into her coat pockets to hide them. The sight of Anne's manicured nails made her self-conscious.

'She likes to think so,' replied Peggy, clattering cups and pouring tea. 'Personally, I think it's time she settled down to something more sensible.'

Their conversation was interrupted by whoops and pirate yells from the basement.

'It sounds like Ernie's fitting in all right.'

'I hope you'll soon feel the same way,' said Peggy, her brown eyes speaking volumes. 'Go on, love, drink that before it gets cold, and then I'll take you up to your room so you can settle in before we eat.'

There were two flights of stairs, with a runner of carpet held in place by shining brass rods. She followed Peggy, noting the fresh paint and the ornate coving on the ceiling.

'I hope Ernie is going to be able to cope with these stairs,' said Peggy. 'Perhaps I should change things around and put you on the first floor?'

'He'll manage fine, Mrs Reilly. I can carry 'im up and down.'

'Well,' said Peggy, 'if you think that will be all right. I suppose you'll only be sleeping up here, and if you want to go out for the evening, I can always sit with him in case there's an air raid.'

'I won't be going out, Mrs Reilly.'

Peggy eyed her quizzically. 'But you're young. You have to have some fun.'

'Ernie relies on me,' she said firmly, 'and I'd never forgive myself if anything 'appened and I wasn't 'ere.' She didn't like to confide that, although this was true, she actually couldn't afford to go out. Ernie's medicines cost a lot of money, and if he got ill, then the doctor had to be paid too. What with his clothes and shoes and everything else, her wages were stretched to the limit.

Peggy seemed to accept her explanation and said no more until they reached the top landing. 'Here we are, dear,' she said, as she approached the middle door of three. 'Anne and Cissy share the other room, but the third is empty for now.' She unlocked the door and pushed it open. 'I'll get my Jim to bring up another bed for Ernie. I wasn't expecting to have two of you, you see.'

'It's all right,' said Sally hastily. 'Me and Ernie are used to sharing, and I expect 'e'll feel a bit strange for a while till he gets used to it 'ere.'

'I'll get Jim to bring up another bed anyway,' said Peggy, with a determined glint in her eye. 'He can use it when he's more settled.'

Sally stepped hesitantly into the room, expecting a gloomy attic, bare floorboards and a lumpy bed. What she discovered was a bedroom fit for a princess and, carefully putting down her case, she stared around her in awe.

Square and sunlit beneath a gently sloping roof, it was furnished with a single wrought-iron bed which was made up with crisp white linen and a floral eiderdown that matched the curtains. There were three rugs scattered over the polished floorboards, a mirror above the gas fire that stood in the small hearth next to its meter and, under the window, was a dressing table and soft armchair. A sturdy wardrobe and chest of drawers completed the furnishings, and through the window she could see over the rooftops to a glimpse of the sea.

'It's lovely,' managed Sally, hardly daring to believe this was to be hers for as long as she stayed. It was a palace compared to the dingy two rooms in Bow.

'You can ignore the old gas lamps,' said Peggy, 'we've got electricity up here now.' She flicked the brass switch next to the door and the central light came on to prove the point. 'You'll need some sixpences for the gas fire, but I can always let you have some to be going on with. I change the sheets and towels once a week, and meals will be in the dining room now there are so many of us. Breakfast is at seven, lunch at twelve, and tea at six thirty after the boys have listened to *Children's Hour*.'

Sally's happiness and awe disappeared like fog as she suddenly realised she would be expected to pay some kind of rent for all this luxury. 'I won't be able to pay you no rent until I get me first wages. 'ow much do you charge?'

'Goodness me, Sally,' breathed Peggy, clearly shocked. 'You don't have to pay your board and keep, dear. The government gives me a grant for that. All I ask is for you to hand over your ration book, keep the room clean and tidy, and perhaps help a bit round the house like my daughters do.'

Relief flooded through her as she reddened. 'I didn't realise,' she murmured.

Peggy cocked her head. 'Didn't you get the leaflet they sent out when the arrangements were made for you and Ernie to leave London?'

'I might have,' she hedged, knowing full well she had – but she wasn't about to admit she could barely read well enough to have made sense of it.

'Oh, well, never mind. You're here now.' Peggy smoothed the creaseless pillowcases and checked the blackout lining on the curtains. 'Just remember to keep these shut once it's dark,' she murmured, 'we don't want Wally Hall round here throwing his weight about.' She smiled as Sally frowned. 'He's the ARP warden, and a proper little Hitler.' She gave a sniff of derision. 'Actually, he's just a jumped-up post office clerk with ideas above his station.'

Sally grinned. 'Yeah,' she said. 'We got one of them at 'ome.'

They smiled at one another. 'Come on then, let me show you the bathroom and how to work the gas boiler. It's a bit fierce, and needs handling just right.'

The bathroom was one floor below. It was a large,

square room tiled in white, with polished lino on the floor, and a claw-footed bath taking centre stage. There was frosted glass in the window, and against one wall stood a heavy iron radiator – which, to Sally, was the height of luxury. Peggy showed Sally how to turn the tap on the gas boiler, hold the switch and aim the lighted match into the hole at the front. It came to life with an alarming bang before it settled to a soft roar.

'Just be sure you turn it off when you've finished,' warned Peggy. 'And if Cissy seems to have moved in for the duration, keep banging on the door until she comes out. That girl can spend hours in the bathroom.'

Sally was still overawed by the fact there was a proper bathroom in the house and could only nod.

'I'll be in the kitchen if you need me, and don't worry about Ernie, I'll keep an eye on him. Tea's in about an hour, so you've plenty of time to settle in. Have a bath if you want.' She hurried downstairs.

Sally eyed the deep tub with misgiving. A person could drown in that. She returned to the bedroom and softly closed the door behind her. Not even in her wildest dreams could she have imagined sleeping in such a wonderful place and, as she touched the crisp linen and breathed in the scent of fresh air and Omo soap powder in the fluffy towels, she was tempted to climb on top of the thick, downy eiderdown and go to sleep.

Then she caught sight of her reflection in the

dressing-table mirror. She had felt quite smart when she'd left Bow, but now she could see that her felt hat and travel-stained overcoat looked scruffy: there was a smudge on her cheek and her hair was a tangled mess. The thick woollen skirt she'd finished making the night before had bagged and looked dowdy, and her best cream sweater was worn and shabby compared to the lovely one Anne had been wearing. Her shoes were sturdy enough, but even they could have done with a bit of a polish.

'You don't belong 'ere, Sal,' she muttered, the stress and strangeness of the day finally crumbling her resolve. She sank into the soft armchair and burst into tears.

Aleksy Chmielewski had seen the girl moving like a shadow along the corridor before she hurried upstairs. He'd been coming out of his room on the first floor, and she hadn't seen him, but he'd watched her until she disappeared on to the top floor.

He was thoughtful as he made his way to the bathroom. She reminded him of his little sister Danuta, and seeing her so unexpectedly had brought back the memories he'd tried so hard to put to the back of his mind.

Striking a match, he lit the boiler, turned the taps until the water gushed into the deep tub and stood staring into space as the steam rose and misted the windows. He had last seen Danuta in Warsaw.

It had been the spring of 1938 and he'd been due

to rejoin his squadron which was fighting in the Spanish Civil War. The picnic had taken place in the park near their tenement apartment on the poorer side of the city. None of them had realised then that their way of life in the ancient, beautiful city was about to come to an abrupt and bloody end.

Aleksy turned off the taps, stripped and sank into the hot, soothing water. He closed his eyes, the memories as sharp and haunting as always. He could see Danuta sitting next to Anjelika, his lovely wife, who had their baby Brygida on her knee. They were laughing with the little girl as she clapped her hands in delight at the flitting butterfly that eluded her.

The tears seeped from beneath his lashes as he sank further into the water. Anjelika had looked so beautiful that day in her floral dress, with ribbons in her dark hair and his locket around her neck. He could hear her laughter and that of his sister and child – could see his elderly parents and read again the anguish in their eyes as they tried to pretend they weren't concerned that their only son was leaving once more to fight a war they didn't understand. Could remember so painfully how he'd tried to imprint every moment of that day in his memory so he could carry the images with him. For now, they merely served to haunt him.

Aleksy angrily smeared away the tears, washed thoroughly and clambered out of the bath. Wrapping a towel round his waist, he cleaned the steam from the mirror and studied his face. It was a strong face – like his father's – and although he was not yet forty, he now had the same wings of grey at his temples.

He looked away, the anguish in his eyes too hard to bear. Warsaw had fallen before he could reach his loved ones – and there had been no word from them since.

Chapter Three

They had all gone into the garden to inspect the Anderson shelter before it got too dark. The boys considered that sleeping in it would be a ripping adventure, and had to be forcefully made to understand it was for emergencies only. The adults were less enthusiastic, and there was muttering about seeking shelter in the basement or under the stairs until Peggy put her foot down and told them in no uncertain terms that they had no alternative.

She told Jim what needed to be done to make it more habitable, and, so he wouldn't forget, handed him the list she'd made earlier before showing everyone where she'd stacked the spare blankets and pillows so they could be grabbed on the way down to the basement door. She had already placed the paraffin heater and Primus stove in the shelter along with a battered camping kettle and saucepan. A dozen candles and a big box of Swan Vesta matches were in an old biscuit tin to keep them dry.

Sally had watched in admiration as Peggy had organised everyone. Ron was to be in charge of the boys when the siren sounded, but the dog and ferrets would have to remain in the basement. She and Jim would take care of Mrs Finch, and the Pole would make sure everyone on the top floor had been accounted for, and that Sally could manage with Ernie. Once this was organised, they'd returned to the warmth of the house and the delicious aroma of stew.

The large dining room had an ornate fireplace and mantel, and bay windows hidden behind heavy velvet curtains that were lined with blackout material. Several small tables had been put together to accommodate them all, and these were covered with colourful cloths. The chairs didn't match, the cutlery was diverse, and Ernie had to sit on two cushions to reach his plate. But none of it mattered, for the atmosphere was warm and friendly, and Sally began to feel a little more at ease.

She had been content to watch and listen as the family chatted about their day, Ernie and Charlie tried to outdo each other with tall stories, and Ron continued his argument with his son Jim that if he was going to die, then it would be in his own bed, with his animals beside him – and not in some hole in the ground with a tin roof.

Peggy was a real mother, she realised wistfully. The sort of woman who would offer comfort and advice, even a hug if necessary, and would never dream of abandoning her family for the bright lights of the nearest pub. And yet she was fully in charge of her household and plainly stood no nonsense. It was clear she adored her handsome husband, Jim, who had the same twinkling eyes and soft Irish brogue as his father – and used them to full effect. Possessed with the sort of charm that made women look at him twice, Sally suspected Peggy didn't always have an easy time with him.

Mrs Finch was aptly named, for she was a tiny, birdlike woman who chattered away regardless of whether anyone was listening, her grey head bobbing as she consumed a surprising amount of stew and apple dumplings. The Polish airman who, to everyone's relief, insisted they called him Alex, was quietly spoken with lovely manners, but Sally thought he had sad eyes and wondered why.

Cissy had stuck her blonde head around the door to greet everyone before disappearing upstairs. The meal was almost over by the time she returned in a cloud of perfume to announce she didn't have time to eat because she'd be late for the theatre. Blowing a kiss to them all in dramatic fashion, she ran out of the house, slamming the front door behind her.

Anne had left soon after and, with a stiff little bow, Alex went back up to his room to study the English textbooks Anne had lent him. Mrs Finch settled down to her knitting by the kitchen fire, the dog lying across her feet until Ron took him out for his nightly walk to the pub.

As Sally had helped with the washing-up, she'd wondered what Martin Black was like. It sounded very romantic to be stepping out with a handsome and, no doubt, dashing RAF officer, and part of her wished that she too could go dancing or to the pictures. But as she said goodnight and carried a protesting Ernie upstairs, she realised that all the while she had him to care for, she wouldn't get the chance. She felt no bitterness – it was a fact of life.

Ernie hadn't wanted a bath; like Sally, he wasn't used to such a big tub or so much water, and at first it had been a struggle to get him into it. She was soaked by the time he finally allowed her to wash him and, once he was clean and dry, and tucked up in bed, she'd sunk into the warm, slightly grubby water and closed her eyes with a deep sigh.

The first day was over and she felt slightly easier now she'd met everyone. But it still felt odd to be far from home, and for the first time in her life she felt a pang of something close to yearning for those cramped rooms in Bow. The Reillys seemed to be a warm-hearted and welcoming family – but they weren't her family, and she must guard against the temptation to ever believe they could be.

Peggy had sorted out the boys, helped Mrs Finch to bed and finished the ironing. Now she was sitting beside the range with her knitting, listening to a concert on the wireless. Jim had gone back to work at the cinema for the evening session, Cissy was dancing in the revue at The Apollo, and Anne had gone to meet Martin. Sally and Ernie were upstairs, and no doubt Ron had taken Harvey to The Anchor, and was ogling the middle-aged landlady's magnificent bosom as usual.

She chuckled as she counted stitches and changed needles. Ron had been widowed for nearly thirty years, and who could blame him for lusting after the luscious Rosie Braithwaite? He'd been at it for years with no luck at all – it seemed her determination to keep him at arm's length was as strong as her knicker-elastic, for Ron had got no further than a peck on the cheek under the mistletoe at Christmas.

But then, she reasoned, the fun was in the chase, and perhaps they preferred to keep things as they were? She carried on knitting, but the music that poured softly from the wireless wasn't really holding her attention. Her thoughts kept drifting to Sally and her little brother.

The boy was settling in well, thanks to Charlie and Ron, but she was worried about Sally. She looked about fourteen and was too thin and pale, far too young to have the responsibility of looking after Ernie as well as holding down a job in a factory. What was her mother thinking of?

Peggy sighed and put down her knitting. The girl had put on a brave face during the evening, and Peggy admired her spirit, but it was clear she'd been crying beforehand, and was no doubt feeling homesick and disorientated. It would be hard for her until she found her feet, and Peggy fully understood why. This large house full of strangers must be daunting after what she suspected were a mean few rooms in Bow. At least there she would have been amongst her own people who looked out for her. She'd heard about the strong community spirit in the East End, and hoped for Sally's sake it was true. She couldn't bear the thought that she'd struggled alone.

She had tried gently questioning her as they'd washed the dishes and put them away, but Sally was a proud little thing and had revealed very little, other than that her mother worked in a factory and her father was a merchant seaman. Reading between the lines, Peggy suspected there was little love lost between mother and daughter, but Sally's face had lit up when she talked about her father. It was clear he meant the world to her, and was probably the lynchpin that held the little family together despite his long absences at sea.

She tucked the knitting away in its bag, turned off the wireless, and stared into the red heart of the fire. At least Sally had been given a stamped addressed envelope so she could send a note to her mother telling her where they were – but the girl's doubt that there would be a reply was an indication of the mother's lack of concern, and Peggy had had to resist the urge to add a strongly worded post-script. It wouldn't help anyone – least of all Sally and Ernie.

Peggy gave a deep sigh. They were a pair of waifs, and her soft heart yearned to make things right for them during the time they were with her – but she knew she must never overstep the mark and take on the role of mother to either of them, for one day they would have to go back to where they came from, and she had her own children to look after.

'Excuse please. I not disturb?'

Peggy gave a start. 'My goodness, you made me jump, Mr Chemy . . . Chemyes . . .'

'Please, you must call me Alex,' he reminded her gently, as he stepped into the kitchen. 'I am sorry to make you jump, but I not have the right money for meter in my room.'

She smiled up at him and got to her feet to reach for the tin on the mantelpiece. He had lovely manners and was probably the most charming guest ever to have set foot in her house. She would quite miss him when he left. 'That's easily sorted. Come and sit by the fire while I find some change. It must be cold up there.'

His smile creased the corners of his eyes as he perched on the edge of a kitchen chair. 'I am used to the winters in Poland, Mrs Reilly. But with no fire to give colour and life, it is a little bleak, I think.'

She wasn't sure if he meant the weather was bleak, or if he was referring to his room. Deciding it was just his being Polish that made it difficult for him to express himself properly, she gave him the benefit of the doubt. After all, she reasoned, he'd only arrived a couple of weeks ago. She took his pound note, stuffed it in the tin and gave him the right money back.

'You will please explain these coins to me?' He spread them on the table.

Peggy sorted through them. 'This is a shilling, what we call a "bob", and this is sixpence – that's half a shilling, but it's usually called a "tanner", and these are threepenny bits. These big ones are half-crowns – they're worth two shilling and sixpence. The sixpenny bits go in the meter.'

Aleksy frowned, clearly still baffled.

She tipped some pennies and farthings from the tin to help her explain more clearly. 'So,' she said, 'there're four of these farthings to the penny. Twelve pennies to the bob, and twenty bob to the pound – or what some call a "quid".'

He reached into the breast-pocket of his jacket and pulled out a small notebook and a stub of pencil. As Peggy went through it all again, he noted it down before returning the pad to his pocket. 'Thank you. It is most complicated, I think. I will learn like schoolboy, as with my English, eh?'

She liked his smile: it lit up his eyes and took the sadness away. He must be lonely so very far from home where everything from the language to the money was strange and confusing – but then her home seemed to be a magnet for the lost and dispossessed these days.

'Don't feel you have to go,' she said, as he

gathered up the coins and rose from the chair. 'I was just going to make some cocoa – it will have to be powdered milk, I'm afraid; the boys finished the fresh at teatime.' She smiled up at him warmly. 'Would you like some?'

'Ah, the famous English cocoa. I have heard of this. Thank you. I would like to try.' He sat down again, his long legs stretched towards the warmth of the fire as he lit a cigarette.

Peggy measured out the powdered milk and added water to the pan before setting it on the hotplate. Stirring in the cocoa powder, she was aware of him watching her closely. 'It won't really taste the same without proper milk, but needs must.'

'I am certain it will be delicious,' he murmured.

She waited for it to thicken and carefully divided it between the two mugs. To her annoyance, her hand slipped as she was carrying it to the table, and she splashed hot cocoa on to the cloth.

'I will clean.'

Before she could protest, he'd leapt to his feet, fetched the cloth from the sink, wiped away the spill, rinsed out the cloth and hung it over the tap. This was such an unusual sight that Peggy could only stare at him.

'I am sorry,' he said with a frown. 'You not like me to do this thing?'

Gathering her wits, she gave an uncertain laugh. 'You can do any job you like about the place,' she said. 'It's just a surprise to see a man lend a hand, that's all.'

His frown deepened. 'Your husband, he does not do these things?'

'It would never occur to him,' she muttered. Realising she was being disloyal, she swiftly added, 'But then he's good at other things.' What these were, she couldn't quite recall, and she covered her embarrassment by taking the proffered cigarette from the packet of Park Drive and letting him light it.

'I like this cocoa,' said Aleksy, after he'd taken a sip. 'It is very good.'

'That's good,' she replied, fishing a shred of tobacco from her tongue. 'You'll probably get quite a lot of it if you're staying in England a while.'

'I am here for as long as the RAF needs me,' he said. 'But of course I will not always be permitted to remain in your delightful home. I will soon be sent to the airbase barracks to help instruct the Polish fliers.'

She laughed and shot a glance over the battered furniture, worn lino and draughty windows. 'I'd hardly call this delightful,' she replied. 'The whole kitchen needs a coat of paint, new windows and lino – and I don't know what else.'

His handsome face grew solemn, his eyes darkening with some inner pain. 'It is delightful, Mrs Reilly, because it is a home. You have your family here – and that is the most important of things, I think.'

She nodded in agreement and thoughtfully puffed on the cigarette. She was certainly lucky she didn't have sons old enough to be involved in the fighting. 'Where is your home, Alex?'

'Warsaw,' he said quietly, gazing now into the depths of his cocoa. 'My family is still there. They did not manage to escape the siege.' He lifted his head, his eyes unnaturally bright. 'I do not know if they are still alive. But I pray each night that they are.'

Peggy felt terrible. 'Oh, Alex. And here's me moaning about a bit of paint and lino.' She took a sip of cocoa, her thoughts focused on the awful news reports that had come out of Poland in recent weeks. 'How did you manage to escape to England?'

He seemed to pull himself together, and even managed a wry smile. 'I was pilot in Spain during Civil War. I was shot down and taken prisoner. But I finally manage to escape and get back to my squadron.'

'You must have been very brave,' she murmured.

He gave a self-deprecating smile and shrugged as he threw the stub of his cigarette into the fire. 'I am very careless, for I was shot down again. I am in hospital for long time. When I am better the war in Spain is over, but Warsaw is under siege and I cannot go home.'

He scrubbed his face with his hands, the gold of his wedding ring glinting in the firelight. 'I try so hard to reach my family, but is impossible now my country is in enemy hands. Now all I can do is wait and pray that I may see them again.'

'I hope your prayers are answered,' she said softly.

'Thank you,' he murmured. 'It has been good to speak of them. When I am with other Poles we do not talk of families and home – it is not good for keeping mind clear for job we must do.' He dug into the breast-pocket again and pulled out a worn leather wallet. 'You would like to see photograph? I carry it for long time, but I look at it every night.'

She took the creased and faded photograph and regarded the sweetly pretty face of his dark-haired wife and smiling child who sat beside another young woman and an elderly couple in what looked like a sunlit garden. She felt tears prick as she handed the precious photograph back. 'You have a lovely family, Alex. Thank you for showing me.'

'It is I who am in your debt.' He finished the cocoa and stood. Taking her hand, he kissed the air above it as he clicked his heels and bowed. 'And now I return to my English books. I do not have my sister's skill with languages, so I must work very hard I think. Good night, Mrs Reilly.'

Peggy sat for a long while after he'd left, staring into the flames, trying to imagine how it must feel to not know if your entire family were alive or dead. She had so many things to be grateful for.

'Mum? I didn't expect you to still be up.'

Peggy emerged from her thoughts and smiled as Anne slipped off her coat and sat beside her.

'Did you have a good evening? Where did he take you?'

'We went dancing at the Regency Hotel.' She eased off her high-heeled peep-toed shoes and wriggled her feet. 'I don't think I've sat down all evening. Those RAF boys certainly know how to wear a girl out.'

'Well, it doesn't seem to have harmed you much,' said Peggy with a smile. 'Want some cocoa?'

Anne shook her head and sat forward, her expression suddenly serious. 'He wants to take me to meet his parents,' she said.

'Well, that's a good thing isn't it?'

'I suppose so, but it's all a bit soon, don't you think?'

'I suppose it is, but with the way things are at the moment, there's not much point in hanging about.' Peggy studied her daughter, seeing the battle of hope and doubt in her expression and wondered what it was that was holding her back. 'But if you're not sure about your feelings, I agree, it would be wise to wait a bit.'

'He got his orders today,' she said quietly. 'He's leaving Cliffehaven Monday week.'

'Oh.'

'He can't tell me where he's going, of course, but he promises it isn't too far away, and that he'll be able to see me when he's on leave or stood down.' She flicked back her hair and fidgeted with the hem of her sweater, her gaze not quite meeting her mother's. 'He says his parents want to meet me, and that they've invited me to lunch next Sunday.' Her brown eyes finally settled on her mother. 'I can't really refuse, can I? It would be terribly rude.'

Peggy had watched her closely and suspected she knew the reason behind her reluctance. 'You don't have to accept the invitation,' she began. 'If they still want to meet you in a few weeks' time, you can go then.' She touched her daughter's hand. 'Are you afraid that if you go, it will give out the wrong message?'

Anne nodded. 'We've only known each other a couple of months, and meeting his parents is taking things a bit too quickly.'

'Have you told him that?'

'Mmm. But he said he didn't want to wait any longer, and what with him already flying missions, he doesn't want to risk . . .' Her brown eyes were tear-filled as she looked at her mother. 'I don't know what to do, Mum,' she murmured. 'I do love him, really I do, and it would be simply awful if anything happened to him. But it's all moving so fast, and I feel I'm being pressured.'

Peggy stood and gathered her into her arms. 'Then tell him you'll see his parents another time, and that you need to be certain about things before you rush into them. If he loves you, he'll understand.'

There were questions Peggy wanted to ask, but was afraid to hear the answers, so she kept silent. She and Jim had met when he was on leave during the First World War. They had rushed into things and, before she'd known it, she was expecting Anne. Jim had done the right thing by marrying her, but those first years had been tough, and there had been many a time since then that she'd doubted whether he really loved her.

But then Jim had never been a man to turn down the favours of a pretty woman and, although it broke her heart, she'd had to live with that knowledge, and rein him in when things got overheated. They were happy enough, and she still adored him, but like his father, he was a man who walked his own path.

'We haven't . . . you know . . . Done anything,' said Anne hesitantly, her face reddening.

'Good,' said Peggy firmly. 'Just you make sure it stays that way until you get a wedding ring on your finger.'

Anne's blush deepened. 'But I do love him, Mum. So much. It's really difficult . . .'

'I think you and young Martin should do your courting here,' said Peggy. 'You can have the dining room after tea. I'll make sure you aren't disturbed.'

Anne visibly relaxed, as if a great weight had been lifted from her shoulders. 'Thanks, Mum.' She kissed Peggy's cheek. 'I'll tell Martin next time he telephones.'

'You do that, love.' She kissed Anne goodnight and began to clear away the mugs. But her hands stilled as she set the crockery in the sink. Her daughter was a vital young woman who was being forced to face a world in which nothing was certain. Perhaps she and Martin were meant for each other – perhaps it was just a momentary fling brought on by the excitement of war and the sense that every day had to be lived as if it was the last. Either way, Peggy didn't want her daughter to get hurt – and although she couldn't always protect her, she could at least help give her a bit of breathing space until she knew what she wanted.

Sally lay awake long after Cissy and Anne had stopped talking next door. She wasn't used to sleeping alone, and was alert for any sound of distress coming from Ernie. He had surprised her by willingly clambering into the narrow bed Jim Reilly had carried up earlier. At six, he'd informed her, he was old enough to sleep in his own bed like his new best friend Charlie.

Sally luxuriated in being able to stretch out, to have the pillow to herself, and not be kicked and nudged throughout the night. She snuggled beneath the eiderdown ready for sleep – but it was too quiet, and she found herself listening for some sign that there was life in the streets below.

Back in Bow she'd become used to hearing the men fighting outside the pub at closing time, and had learned to sleep through the neighbours' screaming matches, the banging of doors and the thuds of heavy boots on wooden floorboards. Those sounds had been her lullaby since childhood, and now the silence seemed to creep in on her, making her wakeful and restless.

Sally stared at the slither of moonlight that knifed across the ceiling from between the curtains, her thoughts on home and the life she'd left behind. The girls at the factory in Bow would be out on the town still, and looking forward to the weekend. She missed them, especially Ruby, and hoped she would find it easy to make friends with the girls in the factory down here. She wasn't usually shy, and could stand up for herself, but as the new girl she would have to keep her head down and her mouth shut, until she'd worked out the order of things.

Factory life had its hierarchy, just as everyday life did. The boss sat in his office high above the factory floor, his overseer marching back and forth along the lines of machines as he barked out the orders, and organised the cutters, packers and machinists. But the real power lay with the women who sat at their machines day after day, and although Sally had only been fourteen when she'd started working there, she'd quickly learned she must stand her ground, and prove herself if she was to survive that first week.

There were always those who led, those who bullied and formed intimidating cliques, and those who simply faded into the background. Sally had firmly avoided getting roped into the sometimes malicious gossip, had learned to laugh at the smutty jokes she didn't understand, and to get on with her work. For every item of underwear finished and passed earned her another few pennies.

She experienced a flutter of nervous excitement as she thought about her new job. Goldman's factory had once made underwear too but, according to her old boss, they had secured a licence to make uniforms. But the best news was that the wages were higher, set each week and not reliant upon how many garments were made. Not having to pay rent here, or give half her earnings to Florrie, would be her chance to save some money, rent her own machine and get her home dressmaking business up and running again.

It had just started to flourish in Bow when she'd had to leave, and she hoped it wouldn't be long before she could begin again, here, where people had more money. If successful, she could then look after Ernie and give him all he needed without having to rely on anyone else. With this pleasant thought, her eyelids fluttered and sleep began to claim her.

'Sal? Sal, I don't like it on my own. I'm cold.'

Sally dragged herself awake and reached for him. 'Come on, luv,' she murmured. 'It's toasty warm in here with me.' She lifted the bedclothes and he crept in beside her.

But as she cuddled him close, she came fully awake. He was soaking wet.

'Ernie,' she whispered fiercely, as she frantically

threw off the bedclothes and hauled him out of her bed before his sodden pyjamas could wet that too. 'Oh, Ernie, no wonder you're so cold.'

'I'm sorry, Sal. I didn't mean to.' He clung to her, his legs wrapped round her waist, his face buried in her neck.

'I know you didn't, luv,' she said, swiftly stripping off the borrowed pyjamas and bundling him in a towel. 'Sit on the chair while I clean up. If you want to go again – then use the po.' She pointed at the china chamber pot Mrs Reilly had placed under the bed, and hurried to strip Ernie's bed. The blanket was, thankfully, only slightly damp, but the sheets and mattress were soaked.

Sally was almost in tears as she used the dry corner of one of the sheets to try and get the worst out of the mattress. It would stain, she was certain, and it had looked brand new when Mr Reilly had brought it upstairs.

Having done her best with the wet patch, she hauled the mattress over to the gas fire and fed in one of the tanners Mrs Reilly had given her. It would take all night to dry and probably cost far more than a single tanner, but she dared not let the mattress ruin. Mrs Reilly would be furious.

Ernie sniffled and shivered as he huddled into the towel. 'I'm cold, Sal. I wanna go back to bed.'

Sally tamped down on the rising panic and dragged on her overcoat to cover the petticoat she used as a nightdress. Having gathered up the soaking sheets and pyjamas, she perched Ernie on her hip. 'I got to wash these, first,' she whispered. 'You too,' she added, wrinkling her nose. 'God, Ernie, you pick yer moments, don't yer? You ain't done this for years.'

'I wanna go 'ome, Sal,' he whined.

'Don't be daft,' she whispered back. 'I thought you and Charlie was getting on like an 'ouse on fire?'

He shrugged and buried his head in her shoulder. 'Will Mrs Reilly be cross with me, like Mum?'

'Course not,' she replied, fearing that Mrs Reilly would probably have them both out on their ears if she found out Ernie wet the bed. She tiptoed down the stairs to the bathroom and pulled down the blackout blind before turning on the light and locking the door.

Sitting him on the chair in the corner, she lit the boiler and flinched at the loud noise it made. Surely the whole house would be woken? She stood very still in the centre of the bathroom and listened. When she was satisfied no-one was stirring, she turned the taps just enough to quietly cover the bottom of the huge tub with a couple of inches of water. 'Now, Ernie,' she whispered with some urgency. 'You're not to make a noise. Not a word. You understand?'

'But I don't want another ba—'

'Shush. You'll have the whole 'ouse awake.' She slipped off her coat and hung it on the hook at the back of the door.

He sat sullenly in the few inches of water as she soaped him, but perked up when she bundled him back in the towel and plonked him on the chair. 'I'm thirsty,' he declared in his piping voice. 'Can I have a drink?'

'That's the last thing you'll get. Sit there and don't make a sound while I wash these.' The tone of her furious whisper seemed enough to silence him, and Sally dumped the sheets and pyjama trousers into the bath. She worked up a good lather and scrubbed them as hard as she could, rinsing them under the tap, checking there were no stains left before she wrung them out.

'I'm tired, Sal. I wanna go to sleep.'

'In a minute.'

The sheets were dripping, but there was nowhere she dared hang them. Frantic and tearful, Sally eyed the mop and bucket in the corner. She carried the bucket across the room to the sturdy radiator, tied a corner of the sheet to one of the pipes, and began to twist it tighter and tighter, squeezing as much water out of it as she could.

Some of it went in the bucket, but most of it puddled on the linoleum. She quickly mopped the floor and repeated the process with the other sheet. Satisfied she'd managed to get them as dry as possible, she hurriedly mopped the floor again.

'Can I go to bed now?' Ernie asked sleepily.

'Not until you've been to the lav,' she whispered back. 'I can't risk you doing this again tonight.' She put on her coat and carried him into the lavatory. When he was done, she didn't dare pull the chain, for the noise it made could wake the dead.

Once back in their room, she dressed him in his pants and vest and settled him back in his bed, using a dry folded towel as a mattress. Covering him with the eiderdown, she kissed his cheek and smoothed back the lick of hair from his brow. He was a dear little kid, and it wasn't his fault he'd wet the bed. But Sally feared Ernie's bedwetting might continue – and, if it did, then Mrs Reilly was bound to find out sooner or later. It was vital she could think of some way of stopping him.

After a hasty check on the steaming mattress to make sure it wasn't getting scorched, she hurried back down to the bathroom. Gathering up everything, she checked the bathroom was clean and tidy, and that there was no sign of the night's escapade before closing the door softly behind her.

Returning to their room, she opened the doors on the big wardrobe and hung the sheets over them. The pyjama bottoms were suspended from the mantel above the gas fire, held in place by her heavy shoes. It smelled like a laundry, she realised, and quickly opened the window a few notches to let the cold night air in.

Ernie was fast asleep, curled like a cat on the folded towel, and seemingly undisturbed by the trouble he'd caused.

Sally took off her coat, climbed into her bed and

pulled the eiderdown and blanket round her. She was cold to the bone and exhausted, but her heart still raced and she couldn't dismiss the thought that tonight might only be the start of her worries.

Chapter Four

Sally woke with a start, disorientated and confused by her surroundings and the unfamiliar sounds coming through the open window. It took a moment to realise she was in Cliffehaven, and that it was the murmur of the sea and the screech of gulls she could hear. Then the memory of the previous night returned and she hurried out of bed to check the mattress.

The gas fire had gone out, the meter was empty, but the mattress had dried sufficiently, and there was only a small stain in the middle which she hoped Mrs Reilly wouldn't notice if she put it back upside down. The pyjama trousers had dried well above the fire, but the sheets were still slightly damp. With a deep sigh of relief, Sally took the sheets from the wardrobe doors, and dragged the mattress away from the hearth.

It was almost seven, so while Ernie slept on, Sally dressed quickly in the skirt and sweater she'd worn the day before. She didn't possess such finery as stockings, not even the thick lisle ones, so she pulled on knitted ankle socks and slipped her feet into the sturdy lace-up shoes. Running a brush through her tangle of fair curls, she attempted to keep them in order with two plastic combs firmly planted either side of her middle parting.

But her hair would not be tamed, and the curls sprang in all directions about her face. With a grimace of impatience, she glared at her reflection. There were dark circles under her eyes, her skin looked pale and blotchy, and her eyelids were still swollen from the tears she'd shed during the night. 'There's no doubt about it, Sal,' she muttered. 'You ain't never gunna be an oil painting, so why bother?'

She put down the brush and went to open the curtains. Bright sunlight poured in, making her blink. The sky was pale blue, and there were two seagulls making a terrible racket on the roof across the street. She breathed in the clean, salty air, bracing herself for whatever the day had in store before she went to wake Ernie.

'Come on, sleepy 'ead,' she said softly. 'Time for breakfast.' She slipped her hand beneath him. The towel was still dry.

Ernie grumbled and fidgeted as she fixed the calliper and finished dressing him. After a trip to the bathroom, she carried him back upstairs and hurried to remake his bed. Not wanting a repeat performance of the night before, she decided he should have only one small drink with his tea and no more before bedtime. Once he was asleep, she would put the folded towel underneath him, and hope for the best.

If that didn't work, then she didn't know what she could do, other than keep waking up in the night to carry him to the lav. And, if she did that, then she was asking for trouble. No-one could go without that much sleep and, once she started working, she'd be dog-tired to begin with.

She carried Ernie downstairs, and stood in the hallway wondering if she was supposed to go in the kitchen or the dining room.

'Good morning, you two,' said Anne brightly, as she came out of the kitchen carrying bowls of steaming porridge. 'Come and sit down before this gets cold.'

Sally followed her into the dining room and found that almost everyone was already at the table. To a chorus of greetings, she settled Ernie on the cushions and tucked in his chair before taking her place next to him.

Anne put one of the bowls in front of Ernie. 'Now,' she said, with a smile. 'I expect you to eat all of that up so you'll get big and strong.'

Ernie looked up at her with adoring eyes and nodded. It was clear he was smitten, and Sally had to bite down on her smile.

The porridge was like nothing she'd ever tasted before, and Sally relished every mouthful as Mrs Finch chirruped like a sparrow, the boys talked about the local football team and Ron carried on what appeared to be a well-worn argument with his son.

'There's no government order to put animals down,' the old man said grumpily, 'and there's no man on this earth who will make me murder mine. I've seen the queues outside the vet's, and it's wholesale slaughter, that's what it is.'

'But it's not fair to expect them to suffer when the bombs start dropping,' said Jim Reilly, throwing down his napkin with impatience. 'The poor things will go half crazy with fear.'

'Harvey and the ferrets are used to loud noises,' muttered Ron through a mouthful of toast and marmalade as he stirred four spoonfuls of sugar into his tea. 'They've been out with the guns often enough.'

'It's not the same, and after going through the last war, you should know that,' Jim persisted. He pushed back his chair. 'You'll see I'm right, Dad.' He grabbed the newspaper from the table and left the room.

'No-one tells me what's best for my animals,' mumbled Ron.

Sally realised this was a long-running argument between father and son, and wasn't surprised when Peggy changed the subject.

'What are everyone's plans for the day?' she asked brightly.

Mrs Finch wanted to finish the book she'd been reading so she could return it to the library; Alex had to report to the Royal Air Force headquarters on the other side of town; Cissy was still in bed asleep, and Anne had some washing to do before she helped Peggy with her shopping.

'What about you, Sally?' Peggy's smile was warm, but her eyes were concerned.

'I thought I'd see how far it is to Goldman's. I don't want to get lost and be late on me first day tomorrow.'

'I'm surprised they want you to start on a Sunday,' said Peggy. 'Even though there is a war on, it's still the Sabbath.'

'They're upping production according to Mr Solomon,' she explained. 'We'll be working in shifts through the week, including Sundays.' She didn't add that it would mean extra pay if she worked Sundays.

'It's over a mile and a half, and will be a bit of a trek for Ernie,' said Anne, thoughtfully. 'He could stay here with me for the morning.'

Sally did a quick calculation. The walk would certainly be too much for Ernie, and she doubted she could carry him that far – but she didn't want to cause the family any upset by leaving him behind more than she had to. As it was, she would have to ask them to look after him when she was working. 'If we walk slowly, we'll be all right,' she said without much conviction.

'You'll not be taking the boy that far,' said Ron. 'He'll come with me and the lads up into the hills. Put some colour in his cheeks, so it will, and he can learn about Cleo and Delilah, and how they work with Harvey to catch rabbits.'

Sally had visions of Ernie getting lost or injured, perhaps even being bitten by something. She'd seen those ferrets and they had sharp-looking teeth and a vicious gleam in their eyes she didn't trust. 'Oh, I don't know,' she stuttered. 'Thank you, but . . .'

'That's settled then,' said Ron, as he pushed away from the table. He ruffled Ernie's hair as he passed. 'Eat up, young feller. There's rabbits to be caught, perhaps even a hare, and the day's wasting, so it is.'

Sally saw the eagerness in the boy's face and looked to Peggy helplessly. 'Will 'e be all right, Mrs Reilly, only 'e's never been in no 'ills before, and 'e ain't strong enough to go climbing, and . . .'

'It's all right, Sally, really,' said Anne. 'Granddad will look after him as if he was his own. Safe as houses, he is, and it will do Ernie good to get out and about.'

'She's right,' said Peggy softly, rising to clear the table now everyone had finished eating. 'You look as if you could do with some fresh air as well,' she added, piling up the plates. 'Didn't you sleep well?'

'Ernie was a bit restless,' she replied quickly before the boy could say anything. 'I'll be fine once I know where the factory is, and can find me way round. I shouldn't be gone long.'

'There's no need to hurry back. Ron will be out for hours, and I'll pack sandwiches and biscuits, and put in a big flask of tea to take with them. They won't starve.'

83

'That's very kind of you, Mrs Reilly. Are you sure 'e won't be no bother?'

Peggy shrugged off her thanks. 'One more small boy is no more trouble than the two I already have,' she said firmly. 'And I suspect you'll want us to look after him while you're at work, so he needs to get used to us.'

'I *was* going to ask . . .' she began.

'No need, dear,' she said comfortably. 'I'll gladly look after him when he comes home from school, and if you work a late shift, then I can put him to bed.'

Her kindness was overwhelming, and Sally felt close to tears. No-one had ever helped like this before without wanting to be paid.

Peggy smiled. 'Why don't you take a bit of time for yourself while you can? Perhaps have a walk along the prom, and get some good sea air into your lungs before you get stuck in that factory every day.'

Sally felt a surge of pleasurable hope. It would be nice to get her bearings, and to look at the sea for a while. To walk and not worry she was going too fast for Ernie, and spend a few minutes looking in shop windows without having to rush back. 'Really? You wouldn't mind? But what about the 'ousework? Don't you want an 'and?'

'Anne and I have it all under control,' she said, carrying the plates to the door. 'You go and enjoy yourself. We'll manage just fine.' Without further discussion, Peggy and Anne headed for the kitchen.

As Ernie finished his third piece of toast, Sally hurried upstairs to fetch hats, coats, scarves and gas masks. She took a long look at the room, checking that everything was neat and tidy and, when she ran back down to the kitchen to help with the washing-up, there was a lightness in her step she'd rarely experienced before.

'I've drawn you a map,' said Anne, once everything had been dried and put away. She spread the piece of paper on the table. 'This is us here, and this is the seafront. I've put in the names of the roads, and some of the big buildings you'll pass and, of course, marked where the public air-raid shelters are just in case. There haven't been any raids yet, but there's no guarantee they won't start any minute.'

She smiled and returned to the map. 'That cross is where the factory is situated. From there, you can walk into the main part of town and back to the seafront. In essence, you'll be walking in a large circle. If you get lost, just ask for the pier, then take the third left up the hill from there.'

'Thanks, ever so,' breathed Sally, who was very impressed by Anne's drawing.

'It's no problem at all,' she replied, her brown eyes warm and friendly. 'And if you find yourself anywhere near the Daisy Tearooms in the High Street at about four o'clock, Mum and I will treat you to a cup of tea and a bun.'

Sally blushed at her kindness and could think of nothing to say.

Ron broke into the awkward moment by appearing at the top of the cellar steps. 'Where's that boy, Ernie?' he said. 'I need him to carry me nets.'

Ernie could barely keep still he was so excited, and Sally had a job to get him into his mackintosh, cap and scarf. She couldn't fit the wellington over his special boot, but Charlie's cast-off fitted his other foot perfectly.

She smiled nervously as Ron took charge of the gas-mask box and stowed the packets of sandwiches and the flask into the deep pockets of his ankle-length coat before carrying Ernie off under his arm like a sack of potatoes.

Ernie didn't seem at all put out by this strange behaviour; in fact he was laughing fit to bust and urging the old man to go even faster down the cellar steps.

Sally followed them and stood in the basement doorway to watch as Ron whistled up the dog, checked his pockets and then swung Ernie on to his shoulders. He set off down the garden path to the gate, surrounded by boys.

With a huge grin and barely a wave, her little brother was soon out of sight as they went down the alley that ran between the backs of the houses. Ernie seemed to have forgotten all about her.

It was bitterly cold despite the bright sun, and the wind that came up from the sea tugged at Sally's hat and tore at her coat. Squashing the hat in her pocket, she battled to cover her hair with the brightly coloured square she'd bought for tuppence from a second-hand clothes dealer who had a stall in the Portobello Road.

With it tied firmly beneath her chin, she hitched the handbag and gas-mask box over her shoulder and walked down the hill. Turning into the first street on the right, she passed two pubs and a small parade of shops. Rationing hadn't started yet, but the shortages were beginning to be felt and there were long queues of patient housewives outside the bakery and grocer's.

The hardware store seemed to stock everything from a nail to a wheelbarrow and, through the butcher's shop window, she could see rabbits and chickens hanging from hooks. The little corner shop supplied cigarettes, newspapers and magazines alongside shelves of canned and bottled goods. Behind the counter there was one entire shelf reserved for large jars of sweets.

She eyed the gobstoppers, sherbet dabs, farthing chews and liquorice bootlaces and breathed a sigh of relief that Ernie wasn't with her. She had no money, and she hated having to deny him such special treats.

She passed the school where Ernie would start on Monday. The building looked in a better state than the one in Bow, and the playground had swings and slides in one corner, and part of it was marked off for football. The hospital opposite the school was large and grey and looked a bit forbidding, and she hurried on until she found the factory. That looked forbidding too, but then factories, in her experience, were never very attractive.

Goldman's took up an entire block. Built of red brick, there was a high wall round the perimeter, which was topped with coils of barbed wire, and a pair of impressive iron gates barred entry. Walking a bit further on, she found a smaller entrance and passed through into a large concreted yard where several lorries were parked by a series of loading bays. She headed for the door which had 'office' written on the glass, and followed the clattering sound of a typewriter down a long, gloomy corridor.

The office was square and would have seemed larger if there hadn't been such a big desk in the middle and so many shelves and cabinets lining the walls. Behind the desk sat a dark-haired woman with bright red lipstick and rather alarming eyebrows which seemed to be arched permanently in surprise. Dressed in black, with the white collar of her blouse peeking at the sweater neckline, she was thudding the keys of the Olivetti with some vigour, and didn't seem to notice Sally standing there.

'Excuse me,' Sally said above the clatter.

The typing continued until she reached the end of the page. Ripping it out of the machine, she placed it in a metal basket on the desk and finally looked up. 'Yes?' Dark eyes coolly regarded Sally from head to toe.

Sally squared her shoulders, unwilling to be cowed. 'Is Mr Goldman in today?'

There was the hint of a sneer to those red lips. 'What do you want with Mr Goldman?'

'My name's Sally Turner, and I'm due to start work here tomorrow. I have a letter for him from Mr Solomon.'

She put out her hand, and Sally noted the nails had been painted to match the lipstick. 'You can give it to me. I'll make sure he gets it.'

Sally held firm. 'Mr Solomon asked me special, to give it straight to Mr Goldman.'

The woman took a deep breath and reluctantly left her desk. Her skirt was pencil-slim, reaching to just below her knee, and her shoes were high-heeled, showing off slim ankles and shapely legs encased in fine stockings. 'I'll see if he's in,' she said smoothly. 'Don't touch anything while I'm gone.' She tapped on the door behind her desk and eased round it and out of sight.

Sally stood by the desk, hands in pockets, not daring to move.

A huge man emerged from the other room and instantly made the office even smaller. He had a large cigar wedged into the corner of his thick lips, his eyes were small but sharply intelligent, and his three-piece suit looked as if it had been specially made to restrain his girth.

He looked down his bulbous nose at her, his head wreathed in cigar smoke as he stuck his thumbs into the pockets of his straining waistcoat. 'You have a letter for me?' His deep, gravelly voice told of years of cigar smoking.

'Yes, sir.' She handed it over and shuffled her feet, not sure what to do next.

A diamond ring winked on his little finger as he took the letter and stuck it into an inside jacket pocket. 'Marjorie tells me you start here tomorrow.' At Sally's nod, he scrutinised her from head to toe, just as his secretary had done. 'You look a bit young and skinny for my liking. I need my workers to be robust. How old are you?'

'Sixteen, sir. I been with Mr Solomon for two year now, and 'e's never had no reason to complain about me work.'

'Hmph. We'll see,' he muttered. 'Give her sixpence for her trouble, Marjorie, and then get me a cup of tea. I'm parched.' He gave Sally another fleeting glance and left the room, shutting the door firmly behind him.

Marjorie sniffed as she dug into a tin box on her desk, and almost grudgingly handed Sally the sixpence. 'Mr Goldman is a fair employer, but he doesn't hold with tardiness. If you're not on time tomorrow, you will not be hired.'

Sally had no intention of being late. She wouldn't have taken the sixpence either if she hadn't needed it. She gave a sharp nod and quickly left the office, which reeked of Marjorie's sharp perfume and Goldman's cigar. It was quite a relief to get back in the cold, fresh air.

Following Anne's map, Sally headed for the High Street. After a leisurely stroll, during which she'd explored every shop window and market stall, she bought a penny's-worth of humbugs for Ernie to share with Bob and Charlie, and headed back down the hill towards the seafront. The town hall clock was striking two, and she was amazed at how quickly the morning had passed.

She reached the seafront and settled out of the wind on a concrete bench that had been set inside an ornate, open-fronted shelter. Her first, awestruck impression of Cliffehaven had been interrupted by Ernie being sick; now she had time to take it in and get a real feel for the place.

The pier must have looked lovely before the army ruined it. Now the once-elegant attraction had been boarded up and festooned in barbed wire. It stretched into the sea rather forlornly, stranded like some forgotten island far from shore. But the sea still sparkled and softly splashed against the great iron feet of the abandoned pier, and Sally hoped it wouldn't be too long before it was open again, and she could have the chance to explore it.

She turned her attention to the way the town sprawled along the edges of the crescent of shingle that ran between jagged white cliffs to the east, and softly rolling hills to the west. It wasn't anywhere as big as London, of course, but it was a fair size, with houses thickly massed nearest the sea, thinning out beyond the town centre and dotted among the hills that ran behind it like protective arms. She could imagine it in peacetime, with lots of families walking the promenade, children splashing in the sea, music coming from the pier, and colourful stalls selling cockles and whelks and candyfloss.

Sally let her gaze drift over the large hotels and private houses that lined the seafront. They were mostly boarded up for the duration, but it was clear from the different flags that fluttered from turrets and poles that some of them had been taken over by the forces. She could even see servicemen rushing back and forth or lounging on the balconies and terraces with pints of beer.

She turned her attention back to the promenade which had been closed off with rolls of barbed wire and heavy artillery emplacements, There was still a strip of pavement to stroll along and, although there were no deckchairs like in the postcards she'd seen in the corner-shop window, the bright winter's day had brought people out of their houses to stroll, or watch the Australian soldiers play a noisy game of football in the street.

Soldiers, sailors and airmen in the uniforms of many countries strolled in groups along what was left of the promenade. They were whistling and calling out to the giggling girls, who pretended not to be watching them. Sally smiled wistfully, and felt strangely distanced from it all.

She moved away from the bench and pulled up her coat collar as she headed into the east wind. The London streets were full of servicemen as well, and she'd come to recognise the nasal twang of New Zealanders, and the slow drawl of the Australians, which was so different to that of the Yanks, who seemed to think they owned the place, regardless of the fact they weren't even part of the war yet.

She shyly walked past a group of whistling sailors, keeping her chin tucked into her collar, and her gaze firmly on the pavement as they tried to coax her into talking to them. She wished she knew how to react without giving them the come-on – wished she could laugh, and flirt, and treat the whole thing as a bit of harmless fun. But she was too inexperienced and unsure of herself. Unlike her mother, who always had an answer, a smile, or a flirtatious look to throw back at them. It would have driven Dad wild if he'd caught her behaving the way she did when he wasn't around.

The sailors finally gave up and she was left in peace to continue her walk towards the fishing boats that sheltered beneath the cliffs. There were several moored on the narrow strip of shingle that was free of barbed wire and hidden mines, and the fishermen were doing a roaring trade as the housewives jostled to buy a share of the day's catch.

It was all very different to Billingsgate, and even the smell wasn't quite so bad because of the sharp sea wind.

The blood-chilling wail of the air-raid siren filled the air at the very moment an aeroplane dived out of the sun. It swooped below the barrage of gunfire from the Bofors guns on the cliffs, the rat-a-tat-tat of its bullets strafing the promenade.

Sally couldn't move – and couldn't think. The plane seemed to be heading straight for her, its spew of deadly bullets flying ever nearer. She was mesmerised.

A hand grabbed her arm, yanking her off her feet. She cried out as she was thrown to the ground and rolled unceremoniously beneath a concrete bench. Bruised and shocked, she was about to protest when his weight squashed the breath out of her.

She fought against him, but found she was imprisoned, strong arms holding her against a thick woollen coat-front that smelled vaguely of moth-balls. 'I can't breathe,' she managed, struggling to escape him.

'Keep still, woman,' he growled, even as he shifted his weight slightly.

She could breathe now, but her cheek was pressed intimately into his neck, her lips almost touching his ear lobe.

'He's coming back. Hold on tight.'

The roar of the enemy plane grew louder as it came nearer and nearer, and Sally forgot her discomfort as terror flooded through her and she clutched the stranger's coat.

She flinched as bullets thudded into the bench above their heads and sprayed them with needle-sharp shards of concrete. Tried to burrow into his chest, as they clattered along the pavement, pinged off railings and lamp posts, and embedded themselves deeply into the grassy kerb. The down-draught of the Fokker's low-flying passage above them threatened to blow them out of their hiding place – and he pressed harder against her, anchoring her to the ground.

The noise was deafening as the Bofors guns fired from the cliff-tops and along the promenade. The enemy plane roared over them again, still firing its deadly hail of bullets. And then it was gone.

Sally lifted her head as the welcome sight of two Spitfires came roaring over the headland. She could see them giving chase out into the channel and watched in awe over the stranger's shoulder, as they did battle with the enemy plane. Diving, twisting, turning, they seemed to be taunting the Fokker. It was a deadly, almost graceful ballet against the clear blue sky.

The Fokker took a direct hit, burst into flames and nose-dived into the sea, and a ragged cheer went up as the Spitfires executed a victory roll above the seafront before disappearing back over the hills.

'They'll get into trouble for that,' muttered the man. 'Victory rolls are a definite no-no, especially so close to civilians.' He gave a sigh. 'But that's the boys in blue for you – never know when to stop showing off.'

Sally tried to wriggle from under the stranger, but he was too heavy to shift. 'Get off,' she protested. 'You're squashing me.'

He didn't move. 'The name's John Hicks, by the way. What's yours?'

'Sally Turner,' she replied through gritted teeth. 'Now, will you get off?'

He kept hold of her and rolled them both out into the open.

Disconcerted, Sally found she was lying on top of him in full view of everyone on the promenade. She looked down to find she was being regarded by a pair of laughing blue eyes that were fringed with long dark lashes. 'You can let go of me now,' she said stiffly, to hide her embarrassment.

'I rather like the view,' he replied unrepentantly. 'Are you sure you want to leave?'

She tore her gaze from those bright blue teasing eyes and pushed away from him. Staggering to her feet, she brushed down her coat and took in the aftermath of the attack. There were several wounded people lying on the pavement and in the street, windows had been shattered by bullets, and someone had crashed their car into a lamp post. There were already two ambulances pulling up and lots of people rushing to help.

Realising she wasn't hurt, and couldn't do much

to help anyone, she searched for her handbag and gas mask. To her dismay, she discovered they'd been blown into the coils of barbed wire and were stuck fast. There was no sign of her pretty headscarf.

'I'll get them.' John Hicks sprang to his feet and within minutes was back with her belongings. 'I'm afraid there's a bullet-hole in your handbag, and it's got a bit scratched on the wire,' he said. 'You must let me buy you a new one.'

'This one will do fine,' she said firmly, eyeing the damage with despair. It was the only one she had, and now it was ruined. But she wasn't about to accept presents from a stranger – she wasn't that kind of girl.

She looked up at him. He was very tall, with broad shoulders and the manner of a man used to getting his own way – but there was no sign of a uniform, and she wondered at that. 'Thanks for rescuing me,' she said.

'At least let me buy you a cup of tea. I know a very nice place . . .'

'Oh, my Gawd. Ernie!' Sally snatched her gas mask from him. 'I gotta go,' she breathed, 'me little brother's . . .' She didn't have time to talk, so she turned and started running.

'Can I see you again, Sally Turner?' he shouted after her. 'Where do you live?'

She didn't answer him. Her heart was racing, her mouth dry and tasting bitter. Ernie was up in the hills where the enemy plane had come from. She could only pray that Ron had brought the boys home long before the attack – if he hadn't, then she couldn't bear to think of the consequences.

Ron had spotted the enemy plane long before the sirens had gone off. He'd swiftly ordered the boys into the circle of gorse, and had sat with them in its deep shadows, chewing thoughtfully on his unlit pipe as they'd watched the dogfight from the cliffs.

When the enemy plane exploded and fell into the sea, he'd given a grim nod of satisfaction and patted the lurcher's soft, shaggy head. 'That'll teach 'em to disturb decent folk going about their business, Harvey,' he muttered.

The dog looked back at him and wiggled his brows. Nothing much fazed Harvey, for he was used to the sound of gunfire – but he wasn't at all sure about low-flying aircraft and air-raid sirens. He'd dug himself deep beneath the gorse throughout the attack, now he'd edged out his nose, waiting for the all-clear to sound.

'That was terrific, Gramps,' enthused Bob. 'Did you see how quick the Spitfires were to shoot him down?'

'I saw,' said Charlie, his eyes gleaming with excitement. 'And when me and Ernie are grown up, we're going to fly a Spitfire just like those.'

'I probably won't be allowed,' said Ernie, 'but I could fire one of them guns easy enough.' He mimed turning the wheel that moved the huge anti-aircraft guns into place, and pretended he was firing at the enemy.

'It'll all be over by the time we're old enough,' said Bob gloomily.

'Let's hope so,' muttered Ron. 'But if the last war was anything to go by, you might get your wish yet.' He eyed his grandsons with a scowl that hid his deep affection. All three boys were wearing school caps, belted gabardine coats, wellingtons and short trousers, their faces ruddy with the cold, eyes sparkling with excitement – and Ron hoped with all his might that this war would end soon and they would never be called to fight.

With a deep sigh, he checked that the two ferrets were happily ensconced in their separate inside pockets of his poacher's coat, scratched the greying stubble on his chin, readjusted his cap and got to his feet. 'Come on. It's time to collect the purse-nets and get home.'

'Do we have to?' groaned the three boys in unison.

Ron didn't bother to argue. They had enough rabbits for the pot and to sell to the butcher, it was a long walk home, and his orders would be obeyed. His grandsons knew the penalty for disobedience – a clip round the ear and no hunting trips for at least a week.

As he balanced Ernie on his hip and pushed his way through the spiny ring of gorse, his ankle-length coat caught on the thorns, hampering his progress. With a soft oath, Ron freed himself, set Ernie on the grass, and turned his face into the biting wind that came off the sea.

The boys and the dog scrambled after him and, as little Ernie watched enviously, Bob and Charlie raced off through the long, windswept grass – the dog in search of rabbits, the boys pretending they were Spitfires.

Ron watched them for a moment, glad of their innocent pleasure in a world gone mad. No doubt people were killed or injured in that surprise attack, but all the boys had in their heads were thoughts of the daring adventures they read about in their comics and the Biggles books they borrowed from the library. Please God, he prayed silently, don't let them ever learn what it's really like.

He remembered his own enthusiasm for war, and how he'd so naively enlisted in search of adventure, only to face the shattering reality of the trenches and the horrors of the Somme. He'd been forty – and really too old for enlistment – but his two sons, Jim and Frank, had barely left school when they'd joined the Royal Engineers to fight alongside him. It was only a matter of chance they'd all survived to come home – and now, a mere twenty-two years later, they were at war again.

He thought about his sons, and the rift that had grown between them. They had once been so close, but Jim and Frank lived very separate lives now, and hadn't spoken to each other since they'd been demobbed. He'd never discovered what had caused the quarrel and, as they both refused to discuss it, he had to accept he never would.

Setting the dark thoughts aside, he ignored the twinge in his lower back – a reminder of the shrapnel still embedded there – and lit his pipe. He might be regarded as past it by some, but he'd joined the local Defence Volunteers, carrying the old Enfield rifle he'd kept after being discharged from the army. To his mind it was only playing at soldiery, and his skills were going to waste. He had little respect for Colonel Stevens, who led the platoon; he was only a librarian, and had spent the better part of the last war well behind enemy lines in the catering corps.

Ron hawked phlegm and spat before surveying his kingdom of windswept grass and arthritic trees. The softly rolling hills above Cliffehaven were as familiar to him as the back of his hand, and a welcome escape from the claustrophobic confines of the basement rooms beneath Beach View. From his vantage point, he could see the great sweep of farmland and pastures to the north, the sparkle of the sea beyond the white cliffs, and the tiny farming hamlets in the valleys. It was a green and pleasant land and a priceless legacy for these young ones to inherit – and although he was no spring chicken, he was determined to defend it to his last breath.

The pipe smoke drifted behind him as he called the boys to help retrieve the dozens of nets he'd laid over the rabbit burrows. Once they were all gathered and tucked away in one of his many pockets, he whistled the dog to heel and set off for home with Ernie on his shoulders, the other boys racing ahead of him.

Sally was out of breath as she fumbled with the key and stumbled through the door into the hall. 'Ernie? Ernie, where are you?' she cried out desperately.

'It's all right, dear,' said Peggy, hurrying to her. 'They'll be back any minute, I'm sure.'

'They haven't come 'ome?' Sally covered her mouth with her hand to hold back the anguished tears. 'Oh, my Gawd,' she sobbed. 'I knew I should never 'ave let 'im go with Ron. Now 'e's injured or dead or . . . or . . .'

'Now, now, that's enough of that my girl,' said Peggy firmly as she steered her into the kitchen. 'You're letting your imagination run away with you. I'm sure Ernie's absolutely fine.'

'How *can* you be sure?' Sally demanded. 'They ain't back, and I saw people lying in the road, dead or dying, and the plane kept coming back and back again, and there was bullets and . . .' She fell into Peggy's arms and sobbed against her shoulder.

'Anne,' ordered Peggy, 'go and get the brandy.'

'I don't want no brandy. I want Ernie. Oh, Gawd, I'll never forgive meself if 'e's been 'urt.'

Peggy gently stroked the hair out of Sally's eyes and held her face. 'Stop it, Sally. You'll make yourself ill. Ron is with the boys and he'll make sure they're safe. They'll be home in a minute, you'll see.'

'But the plane come from up there where they've gone. I saw it.'

'It was too busy shooting at everyone down on the seafront to bother with an old man and three boys,' she soothed, taking the glass of brandy from Anne with a nod of thanks. 'Drink this, Sally. It will make you feel better.'

Sally took a sip and screwed up her face. It tasted horrible – but the shock of it seemed to calm her.

Anne came and sat beside her. 'Did you get caught in it all, Sally? Is that why you're so frightened?'

Sally nodded and sniffed and had to borrow yet another of Mrs Reilly's handkerchiefs to blow her nose. 'It were awful,' she hiccupped. 'It come out of nowhere and just started shooting everyone. Some bloke grabbed me and shoved me under one of them seats, otherwise I'd've been killed too.'

'Whatch'a crying for Sal? Yer ain't 'urt, are yer?'

'Ernie? Oh, Ernie.' Sally flew across the room and grabbed hold of him. 'I thought you was shot,' she said against his neck. 'I was out of me mind with worry.'

He squirmed away from her grip. 'Granddad Ron made us all hide in the bushes,' he said. 'I weren't frightened,' he added defiantly.

'Thank you, Mr Reilly, for looking after 'im. I were that worried.'

Ron shrugged off her thanks, muttered something about feeding the ferrets and went back to the basement.

Ernie was frowning as he tugged at Sally's arm. 'What 'appened to yer coat, Sal? It's all dirty and yer got a cut on yer knee and all.'

Sally hadn't noticed. 'I fell over,' she said, smoothing back his hair from the little face that was still rosy with fresh air and excitement. 'Weren't looking where I were going, as usual.'

'Cor,' he yelled. 'Is that a real bullet-'ole in yer bag? Is the bullet inside? Can I 'ave it?'

She took her bag from him, eyed the neat hole in the side, and realised there was another in the bottom. 'It must 'ave gone right through,' she said. 'Sorry, Ernie, there ain't no bullet.'

His little face looked mournful as he stared at the handbag. 'Are you sure?'

She realised she had to distract him. 'Look what I got, Ernie.' She pulled the bag of humbugs out of her coat pocket.

'They're all squashed,' he complained.

'Sorry, luv, I must have fell on 'em. But I reckon they'll still taste all right. Mind you share 'em now.'

She watched him sit on the top stair to the basement and bump his way down on his bottom before she sank into the chair by the fire. Her legs were shaking, and she felt as if the stuffing had been knocked out of her.

'How can I go to work and leave 'im?' she asked Anne. 'What if there's another attack and I can't get to 'im? I thought we was supposed to be safe 'ere.'

Anne put her arm round Sally's shoulder. 'We

can't stop going to work, or keep the children from school, or not have any fun, and just sit about waiting for the next raid, just because there's a war on,' she murmured. 'If we do that, then we're letting down all those brave boys who're risking their lives for us.' She gave a deep sigh. 'Like those pilots today. They knew what had to be done, and they did it with no thought for their own safety.'

'I saw a poster today.' Peggy put the kettle on the hob and rattled teacups. 'It said something like, "Your Courage Will Bring Victory", so that's the attitude we're going to have in this house,' she said, with quiet determination. 'No matter how bad it gets, or how frightened we are, we will keep our heads high, roll up our sleeves and keep going until this war is won.'

Sally nodded, calmer now. 'I'm sorry for making such a fuss,' she said, balling the handkerchief in her hands. 'But Ernie's all I got till Dad comes 'ome, and I promised I'd look after 'im.' She looked at the two kind faces and felt the tears rise again. 'I'm frightened,' she whispered.

'We all are,' soothed Anne, 'but there's nothing like a nice cuppa to perk us all up. I don't know about you, Sally, but I'm parched.'

Chapter Five

Ernie had helped Ron and the boys feed the animals, groom the dog and fetch fresh vegetables from the garden. He was still overexcited about the adventure of the day, and talked non-stop through tea until he abruptly fell asleep with his head resting on the table.

Sally had carried him upstairs, woken him enough to use the lavatory, and put him to bed, the towel firmly tucked beneath him. She returned downstairs to help clear the dishes and put the kitchen straight, but the trauma of the day had taken its toll and she'd gone to bed soon after, clutching Peggy's spare alarm clock.

Sleep came swiftly, but it wasn't restful. The possibility that Ernie might wet the bed again was always with her, and the knowledge she dared not oversleep because of work in the morning kept waking her. Yet even her dreams made her restless, for they were of enemy planes, of small boys lost in the wilds of the hills and of bullets whining and thudding all around her – but, most disturbing of all, were the dreams of strong arms holding her, and of a pair of laughing blue eyes that seemed to know her every thought.

When the alarm clock startled her awake, she lay for a moment, groggy from lack of a proper sleep and loath to leave the warmth and comfort of her bed. She'd been up with Ernie twice in the night to ensure his bed remained dry but, as she clambered reluctantly out of bed and checked on him, she felt the dampness and sighed with weary despair. She simply didn't have the time or energy for this, but she supposed she should be thankful it was only the towel and his pyjama trousers she would have to wash this time.

Swiftly pulling on her clothes and brushing her hair, she carried him, protesting, down to the bathroom where she gave him a quick wash. While he dressed, she rinsed out the towel and the pyjama trousers. The radiator was hot, but she wouldn't have dared to use it anyway. Peggy Reilly would take one look and know what had happened, and she couldn't afford to upset her.

'I'm hungry,' he said, as she fixed his boot and calliper. 'Can I go down and 'ave me breakfast?'

'Are you sure you can manage?'

'Course I can,' he said indignantly. 'I got me bum, ain't I?' He slid from the chair and made his way out of the bathroom and on to the landing, where he grabbed hold of the banister to help maintain his balance as he hobbled towards the stairs. With a wide grin, he sat and bumped and slid his way down.

Sally grinned back at him and, on hearing a door

open nearby, hurried back to their room. With the towel and pyjama trousers draped over the top window, she closed it just enough to anchor them firmly, and pulled the curtains together to hide what she'd done. She just had to hope no-one from the house looked up from the pavement.

Deciding she should try and make a good impression on her first day, she changed into the pencil-slim skirt and white blouse she'd finished sewing two nights before she'd left London. The blouse had been made from an old tablecloth she'd found in Petticoat Lane. The body of the blouse was linen, hand-sewn with pin-tucks that emphasised her slender figure. From the sweetheart neckline, the rest of the blouse was lace, with tiny pearly buttons at wrist and throat, and a Peter Pan collar. The skirt was plain navy blue, cut from a dress her mother had discarded as too dowdy.

With a dark blue cardigan to keep her warm and protect the blouse, she parted her hair down the middle and anchored it with combs before eyeing her reflection in the full-length mirror on the wardrobe door. She looked very smart, but it was a shame about the shoes and socks – they didn't look right at all, but as they were the only ones she had, they would have to do. Grabbing her coat and gas mask, she went downstairs.

Everyone else seemed to be having a Sunday morning lie-in, but Peggy was already eating breakfast when Sally sat down next to Ernie and tucked into the porridge and toast. She ate quickly, for it was after seven, and she had to be at the factory by eight fifteen.

'I'll be back around four,' she said, when she'd finished. 'Are you sure it's all right to leave Ernie for so long?'

'Of course it is,' said Peggy, folding the newspaper. 'We've already discussed what we will do, haven't we, Ernie?'

Ernie nodded, looking a little uncertain. 'I'm going to 'elp Mrs Reilly peel the veg and make the pastry for the rabbit pie. Then I got to wash me face and 'ands and get ready for church.'

'Church?' In Sally's experience, church was for christenings, weddings and funerals. Poor Ernie.

'That's right. We always go to church on Sundays, and Father McCormack gives all the boys and girls a sweet if they've been good during the service.'

'What kinda sweets?' Ernie looked at her suspiciously.

'Toffees, usually,' she replied with a smile, before rising from the table. 'I've made some sandwiches and a flask of tea for you to take with you, Sally. It's only Spam, I'm afraid, but you've got to eat something.'

'That's ever so kind, Mrs Reilly, but I can last out till . . .'

'Don't be silly,' she said briskly. 'You're far too thin as it is, and I'm determined to get some flesh on those bones and some roses in your cheeks. There will be sandwiches and tea every day from now on – and I won't have any arguments.' As if to emphasise the point, she left the room.

Sally looked at Ernie, who licked porridge from his chin and grinned back at her. 'She's bossy, ain't she?' he said. 'But I like 'er – a lot. She makes good porridge.'

It was another bitterly cold October morning, the sun only just emerging over the horizon to struggle against the thick, low cloud. The sea was as grey as the sky, and the gulls sounded mournful as they floated on the wind and called from the rooftops and lamp posts. But, despite the bank of cloud, the air was fresh and clean – unlike the thick, choking smog of London, where thousands of factory chimneys belched their filth over everything.

Sally had sponged off the worst of the damage to her coat and stitched the tear at the side so no-one would know it had ever been there. The handbag was beyond repair but, as she didn't need it today, it didn't matter – yet she mourned the loss of her pretty headscarf, and wondered if it had been blown out to sea, or was lying somewhere, trapped in a tangle of barbed wire.

Accepting that it was gone forever, and there was little she could do about it, she hitched the gas-mask box over her shoulder, and swung the string bag from her wrist, feeling the weight of the flask and packet of sandwiches. She usually had a crust of bread and cheese, and a cup of water from the street standpipe when she was at work, and although she'd eaten her fill at breakfast, she was looking forward to the luxury of Spam sandwiched between slices of soft, fresh bread.

She arrived at the factory with ten minutes to spare and saw women hurrying towards it from all directions. Following them through the side gate, she realised most of them were her mother's age, or older, and spoke with a strange, drawling, rolling accent that was hard to decipher. There were a few younger ones, and she was pleasantly surprised to hear the welcoming sound of the East End coming from a group of three who were arm-in-arm and chattering nineteen to the dozen. It would be nice if she could get to know them, she thought. It would make her feel more at home.

As they walked across the vast concrete yard, another swarm of women emerged from a door at the far end of the building, and Sally realised this must be the night shift clocking off. It paid really well, but Sally had had to forget even trying for it – she couldn't leave Ernie all night with Mrs Reilly, especially if he was going to wet the bed.

Sally followed as the women swarmed into the building, grabbed their work-cards and, with the careless ease of long familiarity, slipped them into the machine that would mark their time of arrival with a small puncture hole, before taking it out again and sliding it back to where it had come from.

She took a moment to find hers before she could do the same. Then she let herself be carried along by the chattering, laughing stream into the workroom where the BBC Home Service radio programme blared out from two huge speakers strung from the rafters.

She let the river of women flow round her as she stared in amazement. It was five times bigger than the factory in Bow, and cavernous, with row upon row of long tables supporting dozens of heavy, industrial sewing machines. There were windows in the roof, but they were so grimy that very little light penetrated them – but this was counteracted by banks of lights hanging from the ceiling.

Huge rolls of khaki material lay beside rolls of air-force blue on the specially made shelves that took up the whole of one end of this enormous space. In front of them were the numerous tables where the paper patterns would be outlined in chalk before the skilled cutters got to work and each section of uniform began to emerge from the expensive cloth.

At the other end of the building, Sally could see the packers loading the finished uniforms into boxes, which were then hauled away on special trolleys to the loading bays at the top of a short concrete ramp. The height of these loading bays had been calculated to match the height of the lorries' storage space, so the boxes could be loaded quickly and efficiently.

Sally turned and regarded the long wooden stairway that ran behind her to a broad balcony high above the factory floor. Built into this balcony was a room with a window that took up most of one side. This was where the manager could watch every worker's move. He was as powerful as the factory owner, for he was king of all he surveyed – and had the livelihoods of his workers in the palms of his hands.

'We don't pay you to stand about gawping.'

Sally looked up and swallowed. 'I'm new,' she managed. He was an unattractive man in, Sally guessed, his late thirties, with bad skin, greasy hair and a mean-looking expression. He had thick glasses and wore a long, dun-coloured duster coat, buttoned over his clothes, which did little to enhance his pallor.

'And I'm the shop-floor supervisor, Mr Simmons.'

'Sally Turner, sir,' she replied, playing up to his undoubted ego.

He sniffed and looked at the clipboard clasped awkwardly in his withered hand before pointing vaguely to the other side of the cavernous room. 'Row nine, machine fifteen.' His pale eyes bored into her from behind the thick lenses of his glasses. 'We expect the highest standards here, or you're out,' he warned. 'You'll have fifteen minutes for lunch. Tea will be available at eleven and four and must be drunk at your station. The cost will come out of your pay-packet.'

'I don't need tea,' she replied. 'I brought me own.'

He obviously didn't approve of his routine being changed and glared at her before putting a mark beside her name on the piece of paper in his clipboard and eyeing his watch. 'Get to work, Miss Turner.'

Sally quickly walked down the rows, counting them as she went. Row nine was about halfway down, her machine two from the end. She slipped behind the two gossiping women, shrugged off her coat and hung it with the string bag and gas-mask box over the back of her chair.

She grimaced as she sat down. The chair was wooden, the legs at different lengths. No doubt it had been rejected and passed down the line – and now, being the new girl, she was the unlucky one to have it. Making a mental note to bring in a cushion tomorrow, she looked round for something to jam under the leg.

'Hello, ducks. The name's Brenda. Welcome to hell.' The woman had a cheerful face despite her words, and she continued to smile as she covered her curlers with a scarf and tied it firmly at the front.

'It can't be that bad, can it?' Sally was still trying to find her balance on the chair.

'You wait until Hitler Simmons over there starts having a go,' Brenda said grimly, cocking her head towards the supervisor and folding her meaty arms over her vast bosom. 'Thinks he knows it all, strutting about like a cockerel in a hen house – all puffed up and full of himself.'

She reminded Sally of Maisie Kemp – right down to the curlers, and the fag hanging out of her mouth.

'Here you go,' said Brenda, reaching for the empty cigarette packet in her apron pocket. 'Double that up and stick it under the leg, or else you'll be lopsided all blooming day.'

Sally tested the effect and discovered it did the trick as long as she didn't wriggle about too much.

'Yeah, y'wanna watch Simmons,' confided the girl on the other side, giving Sally a nudge and a wink. 'Gets a bit 'andy, if yer know what I mean. Thinks 'e's Gawd's gift.' She gave a snort of derision, tossed back her fair hair, and tugged the ratty cardigan more tightly over her narrow chest. 'As if any of us would give 'im the time o' day.'

Sally perked up as she recognised the Cockney accent. 'We 'ad one of them in Bow,' she replied. 'Someone told 'is missus what 'e were up to and we never 'ad no trouble again.'

The girl's blue eyes lit up. 'Bow? We're almost neighbours. I'm from Stepney, just off the Mile End Road. Pearl's the name.'

'Sally.' They grinned at one another in delight.

'I love your blouse,' said Pearl, wistfully. 'Where'd you get it?'

Sally unbuttoned her cardigan to show it off, delighted Pearl liked it. 'I made it out of an old tablecloth.'

'You made that?' Brenda eyed it keenly, and ran a finger over the tiny pin-tucks. 'That's lovely work,' she said admiringly.

'Me gran was a seamstress. She taught me to sew.'

Pearl leaned in closer to inspect the workmanship. 'You could make a bob or two doing stuff like that,' she murmured. 'Especially when them clothing coupons come in.'

'Yes,' said Brenda. 'Make do and mend is what we'll all have to be doing from now on, and there will always be repairs and alterations – as well as clothes for special occasions.' She nodded as if to confirm this statement. 'I'll put the word out for you, ducks. These can use machines, but when it comes to real sewing they don't know one end of a needle to the other, let alone do fine work like that.'

Sally's smile was warm as she thanked Brenda. She was so glad she'd worn her blouse this morning – perhaps this was to be a lucky day. 'I can only do the 'and stuff for now,' she warned her. 'I ain't got a machine yet.'

Brenda nodded and began a conversation with the woman on the other side of her, so Sally turned back to Pearl. Within minutes they were chatting like old friends, finding places and people they both knew and reminiscing about the King's Coronation two years before and the street parties everyone had had to celebrate. They agreed he sounded lovely on the wireless, but it was a terrible shame he stuttered.

Then the runner dumped the piles of cut fabric beside each of them and, before she was halfway down the line, the whistle had gone to begin work. 'We'll 'ave a chinwag later,' shouted Pearl above the racket of over eighty machines.

Sally swiftly and expertly checked her machine was properly threaded and working, then picked up the wad of material that had been pinned together at one corner. It was a pair of khaki trousers, with seams, pockets, zip and waistband to be sewn together before it went to another table for the hem, buttonhole and button to be done by hand.

It felt good to be back at work again – and good to know she had someone her own age, and from a similar background, to chat to in the breaks.

The whistle went at noon and there was a stampede for the back door. They poured out into the large rear garden which had been concreted over and furnished with a collection of battered tables and benches. The air was cold and made them pull up their coat collars, but it was good to be out of the noise and stale atmosphere of the factory.

The promised canteen would be finished by the end of the month, and the workmen on the scaffolding whistled and called down to the women offering everything from a kiss to a bite of their sandwiches. When they clambered down to join them, there was a great deal of laughter as they exchanged sandwiches and flirted over cigarettes and teacups.

Pearl tugged at Sally's hand. 'Quick, over there.' They jostled through the melee and managed to grab a sunlit space on a low wall. Grinning at each other, they unwrapped their sandwiches and began to munch.

'So, what you doing all this way from 'ome, Sally?'

She explained about her brother and described the family she'd been billeted with. 'They're ever so kind,' she confided, 'and Ernie's 'aving the time of 'is life, so I reckon we landed on our feet.' She regarded the china-doll face with the big blue eyes, and the slender figure wrapped in a threadbare coat. Pearl was aptly named and, despite the fair hair and Alice band, was probably older than she looked. 'What about you?'

Pearl wrinkled her delicate nose and tossed back her long fair hair. 'I'm eighteen and shouldn't be 'ere at all,' she said, through the last of her jam sandwich. 'But I come down with me little sister who 'as the asthma something chronic.' She shrugged. 'What with nothing 'appening in London – no bombs and such – Mum wanted her 'ome again. I already got this job, so I stayed on.'

'What's yer billet like?'

'They're an old couple what expect me to clean and cook for 'em. But at least I get good grub and a comfy bed, so I don't mind.' She giggled and blushed. 'They even let me use the front room when Billy comes round.'

'Billy?'

Pearl nodded with a dreamy expression. 'He's lovely, is Billy. Works on 'is dad's fishing boat.' The softness faded and she frowned. 'But they got a letter the other day from the Admiralty which will change things.' She sighed and sipped her tea. 'They're going to requisition the big trawler to use as a minesweeper, and Billy's planning to join the Royal Naval Reserve so 'e can captain it. It's all a bit worrying, really.'

Sally didn't know what to say. Everyone's lives were upside-down at the moment and nobody knew what the future held.

Pearl's expression suddenly hardened. 'Watch out, Sal,' she hissed. 'Here come the cats.'

Sally followed her gaze. The three women she'd seen ahead of her in the queue this morning were making their way towards them. They looked pleasant enough, but Pearl obviously knew them better. 'Cats?' she murmured.

'Mmm. With claws. Don't for one minute think they'll be your friends. That Iris just wants to be Queen Bee and lord it over us cos we're from London.'

Sally watched them cut a swathe through the gathering, noted how many of the women turned their shoulders, their gazes sliding away as they passed. One was blonde, one brunette and the other a redhead – they made quite an impression – and Sally guessed they were in their mid-to-late twenties.

'Who's this?' said the brunette, who was clearly the ringleader.

'This is Sally from Bow,' said Pearl. 'Sally, this is Iris.' She pointed to the redhead and the blonde. 'Jean and Pat.'

Sally smiled, taking in the smart clothes, the make-up and fashionable hairstyles.

'What you doing over 'ere?' Iris's dark eyes bored into Pearl. 'You know I don't like you mixing with this lot. We London girls gotta stick together.'

'It's sunnier over 'ere,' said Sally quickly, 'and after sitting inside all morning, it's nice and cheerful.' She held Iris's steady gaze. 'There's room on the wall. Why don't you join us?'

Iris glared at her before giving a nod to the other two, and sitting down. 'Got a fag, Pearl? Only I've run out.' Iris screwed up the empty cigarette packet and threw it to the ground in disgust.

'You know I don't smoke, Iris.'

'What about you, Sal?'

'I don't either.'

'Blimey,' muttered Iris. 'You're a pair of right little goody-two-shoes, ain't yer?' She sniggered and nudged the redhead. 'What you reckon, Jean?'

'I reckon they're just a couple of kids and not worth our time,' she replied, her expression scornful.

'You could be right. Come on Jean, give us a fag. The whistle'll go in a minute, and old Simmons will be on the warpath.'

Sally had met her type before and wasn't impressed

or cowed by her. She finished eating her delicious sandwiches and watched as the cigarettes were lit and the three women began to talk amongst themselves – patently ignoring Pearl and Sally, who didn't mind a bit, but who would have preferred to carry on their own conversation in private.

It soon became clear to Sally that, although they were all from the East End, she and Pearl had very little in common with the other three. They were married, for a start, but with their husbands away with the forces, they'd come down to the coast to find work and have a good time.

Sally poured tea from the flask and shared it with Pearl as she listened to their conversation. It was full of bitchy remarks about the other women to begin with, but this soon turned to comparing the generosity and allure of the foreign servicemen who were stationed in and around Cliffehaven. The general consensus seemed to be that the Yanks were the most generous, the French the most romantic and the Poles were real gentlemen but almost impossible to understand.

From there, the talk continued to the local dances, the pictures they'd seen and the conquests they'd made. It was a boastful, coarse exchange, interspersed with shrieks of raucous laughter that had people turning their heads and made Sally wince. They sounded just like Florrie and her mates when they got together.

She glanced at Pearl who merely shrugged and

drank her tea. It seemed the other girl was similarly unimpressed and had nothing to bring to the conversation either, and that made Sally like her even more. But Pearl had obviously gone along with Iris and the others before today, and she hoped there wouldn't be any fallout over her standing her ground.

'You must come with us tonight,' said Iris, suddenly turning to Sally. 'We're going to the dance at the Pier Hotel. The Yanks come into town from their base nearby, and they know 'ow to splash their money about.' She reached into her handbag and pulled out something wrapped in tissue paper. 'Look what I got last night,' she breathed.

Sally eyed the silk stockings. They were beautiful, but she could imagine how Iris had come to have such a gift. 'Not tonight,' she replied pleasantly. 'I got things to do.'

'Nothing's more important than 'aving a good time. The blokes will pay, it won't cost yer nothing.'

'Don't make no difference,' replied Sally. 'I still got other things to do.'

'What about you, Pearl?' The brown eyes were daring her to refuse.

'I got a date already,' she said.

'I ain't one to take no for an answer,' Iris said evenly. 'Bring 'im along, if you must, but I expect you and Sal to meet us outside the Town Hall at seven.'

Sally glanced at Pearl and could see she was

wavering. 'We already gave you our answer, Iris,' she said quietly.

'So you're refusing to come out with us?' Iris put her hands on her hips as she stood and viciously crushed the cigarette beneath the toe of her fancy shoe.

'That's right,' said Sally. 'I got a little brother to look after, and Pearl's got a date.'

'Then get a babysitter,' snapped Iris.

'I already left him all morning. I ain't leaving 'im again.' She stood and tipped out the dregs of tea from the cup and screwed it back on to the flask as the whistle signalled the end of the break.

Iris sniffed with derision as she eyed both girls. 'You'd only cramp our style anyway.' Her sneering gaze swept over Sally's shoes and socks, and Pearl's threadbare coat. 'Your bloke can't be up to much, Pearl Dawkins, cos no-one *decent* would want to get within half a mile of you and your smelly clothes. As fer you,' her eyes bored into Sally, 'you'll regret this. And that's a promise.'

She linked arms with the other two and headed for the factory door. A muttered exchange between them had them shrieking with laughter again.

'Blimey, you got some nerve, Sal,' breathed Pearl. 'No-one says no to Iris.'

'Then it's time someone did.'

'You're very brave,' said Pearl, as they hurried indoors. 'But you'd better watch yer back from now on. That Iris is a spiteful piece and no mistake.'

'I've met 'er kind before,' said Sally, 'and she don't frighten me.'

'Well, she does me,' muttered Pearl, as they weaved their way back to their work-station. 'She can be a right cow when someone upsets 'er – and the other two are just as bad, cos they do what she tells 'em.'

'If you're up for it, what you say we stick together?' said Sally, as they took their places in front of the machines. 'There's strength in numbers, and if we keep firm, and make friends with some of the other girls, then they'll just 'ave to accept we don't want to get involved.'

'Yea, why not?' Pearl smiled. 'I'm glad you came to work 'ere.'

Sally smiled back. 'So am I,' she replied – but she was all too aware of Iris on the other end of a far table, shooting her hostile glances. Pearl's advice was valid; she'd definitely have to watch her back.

Aleksy had been at the airfield all morning, struggling like the others with the English language. The teacher was a retired college lecturer who liked the sound of his own voice, and Aleksy had spent most of the lesson staring out of the window at the grey skies and the windswept grass, his thoughts drifting.

There were no planes as yet, for they were all still based at the old airfield on the other side of the hills. This new airfield had been sited on a requisitioned farm which sprawled across the broad, flat lands that swept northward for many miles beyond Cliffehaven. It would soon be operational with a proper runway, flight-tower and hangars. The barracks were almost completed, the offices, canteen and workshops at the point where they were being fitted out. There was a great deal of activity outside as men from the Royal Engineers dug and built and hammered and sawed, but he missed the roar of the Spitfires and Hurricanes.

He was restless and on edge, impatient to be in the thick of things instead of hanging about. All this inactivity gave him too much time to think and fret over the lack of news coming out of Poland. The new group of Polish airmen had nothing to add to what he already knew, but at least it meant he had something to do. He'd made a start at getting to know them, and to gauge their capabilities. Many of them were boys who'd managed to escape Poland by making the long, hazardous journey across Europe to be here, but they were inexperienced and poorly trained, their English non-existent. He would have his work cut out to get them through the rigorous demands of the RAF examinations.

But there were older, battle-hardened fliers, like himself, who simply wanted to get on with the job. In his role of senior officer in charge of the local Polish contingent, he understood only too well how they felt, but it was the devil's own job to keep discipline when they drowned their sorrows and their impatience with the prodigious amounts of vodka they always seemed to have stashed away.

The lesson was over at last, and Aleksy pulled on the sheepskin-lined leather flying jacket and stepped out into the grey drizzle of an English winter. He could smell the delicious aroma of *bigos* – a traditional Polish hunter's winter stew of cabbage, meat, sausage, tomatoes, honey and mushrooms – coming from the cookhouse, and his mouth watered. Though he doubted there would be honey, bay leaves and smoked plums in the stew, or the heavy, dark bread his mother had always made to accompany it, it was still a link with home and family.

He loaded his plate with stew, potatoes and the soft English white bread, and found a seat with some of the other veteran pilots. He was enjoying the stew, even though it wasn't a patch on his mother's, when he saw the padre come into the cookhouse. Not taking much notice of the man, Aleksy carried on talking and eating.

'Aleksy Chmielewski?'

The soft voice was at his shoulder and he looked up into the calm face of the elderly padre and lost his appetite. 'What is it?'

'There is a letter for you,' he said, reaching into his pocket. 'From Poland.'

Aleksy had to resist snatching it from him, but he sat and stared at it as the padre placed it on the table. He was vaguely aware of the silence that had fallen amongst his comrades, but all he could see was the familiar writing.

'I will leave you to read it in peace,' the padre murmured. 'May God go with you.'

'And with you,' he muttered automatically. Aleksy stared at the envelope, which had been sent to several places before it had reached him here in the south of England. He softly touched the familiar writing as he tried to decipher when it had been posted – but with so many stamps and markings, it was impossible.

With barely a muttered apology to the others, he left the cookhouse in search of somewhere he could read this precious letter without interruption. In the far corner of the airfield he found the ruins of the farmer's barn and sat down on an abandoned bran tub. With his back pressed to the great oak beam that held up one sagging corner of the barn, he took a deep breath and opened the letter with trembling fingers.

It wasn't long, merely two sides of one sheet of thin, cheap paper, the words small and neat, the style fluid and poetic as only a Pole could write.

My dearest brother,
I write this in the hope it will find you, and that
you are safe and in good health. We heard you
had been injured again, and were in hospital in
Spain, but despite having written many times,
there has been no word from you. We can only

*pray you have found sanctuary in England like so
many of our brave friends. This letter is carried
by a friend who has promised to send it on for
me.*

   *I know the war in Spain is over for you, but
for us, my dearest Aleksy, there is much sad news
and my heart is sore that I must tell you, but it is
right you should know what has happened. My
tears fall, for it is hard for me to write of such
things, so I will do it swiftly.*

Aleksy's sight blurred with tears and his heart
thudded painfully as he stopped reading. He didn't
want to see the words he'd dreaded ever since he'd
left Spain. Didn't want to know what terrible things
had happened to his loved ones during his absence.
But he knew he had to – he owed them that much.
With a deep and trembling breath, he returned to
his sister's news.

*Our family is scattered and our apartment
building is destroyed. There is much hunger here,
and the winter is cruel, but I managed to find
shelter with Mamma and Papa in a tiny basement
on the other side of the city. The siege meant there
was very little food, even though I was willing to
sell everything for just a crust of bread or a
turnip to make soup. Mamma and Papa fought
bravely to survive, but they were too old and frail.
They fell asleep in each other's arms one bitter*

*night, and I carried them back to our old home
one by one and managed to bury them in the
garden. If you should return, there is a rough-
hewn cross to mark their resting place, and I stole
some holy water from the nearby church to bless
the earth that now covers them.*

Aleksy wept, the tears rolling down his face as the
pain seared through him and threatened to tear him
apart. But the agony was not over, for Danuta's
letter continued.

*Anjelika and Brygida moved into the basement
with me, and for a while we managed to survive
on what we could forage or steal. I was out trying
to find wood for the fire when they were taken.
The neighbours tell me they were forced into
trucks with many others and driven away. No-one
knows where they have gone, and no-one dares to
ask – but the rumours here are of labour camps. If
that is where they have gone, then at least they
will be fed and sheltered, for what use is labour if
it is too weak to work?*

*My dearest brother, my heart is heavy for you
and my prayers are offered daily – but in this
terrible place it is hard to believe there is still a
God, for no-one is listening to our cries for
freedom from this tyranny. We live like animals,
hiding in the darkness. The world we once knew
and the friends we once had are gone.*

I have left the basement for it is no longer safe. I wander the streets, hiding in the shadows as the tanks and trucks go past, making my way to the far side of the city where a friend has promised to get me out of Warsaw so I can fight in the Resistance. If you do not hear from me again, it is because I have failed.

May God go with you, sweet brother, and hold the memories in your heart of those days when the sun was shining and we thought our world would never change. I love you, and pray we shall all be together again – if not in this world, then in the next.

Your loving sister, Danuta

Aleksy bent his head, the tears coming from the depths of his soul.

'See ya tomorrow morning.' The shift was over and she and Pearl went their separate ways home. Pearl was billeted in one of the houses behind the town and, as it was a long uphill walk, and Billy was due to visit at six, she was in a hurry.

Sally waved and headed into the wind. She wasn't as tired as she usually was after a shift, and put it down to having eaten properly for once. It was good she'd made a friend, and there had already been three enquiries from other girls about doing alterations. Apart from the run-in with Iris and her cronies, it had been a good day, and she

130

was feeling positive and happy as she came to the end of the long climb and opened the front door to Beach View.

She could hear the boys making a racket in the back garden as she ran up the stairs to their room, and it made her smile. But as she opened the door her smile froze and her spirits tumbled. The curtains were billowing in the wind that came from the open window. There was no sign of the towel, or the pyjama trousers.

'I put them on the washing line.'

Sally whirled to find Peggy standing on the landing. For the first time since her arrival, there was no smile on the other woman's face. 'I . . . I . . .'

'You should have warned me Ernie wets the bed,' she said evenly.

'He don't usually,' stammered Sally, 'but with all the up'eaval . . .'

'That's understandable,' said Peggy as she came into the bedroom, 'but you should have told me. Then you wouldn't have had to go through all this subterfuge.'

Sally was uncertain what that meant, but suspected Mrs Reilly was accusing her of hiding things from her. 'I'm sorry,' she murmured. 'But I was frightened you'd chuck us out, and Ernie's beginning to settle, really 'e is, and 'e only done a tiny bit last night and—'

'It's all right,' she cut in softly. 'I do understand, and of course I wouldn't throw you out. But I would appreciate honesty, Sally. If there's anything you think I should know, then you must tell me.'

'I'm so sorry, Mrs Reilly. I only done what I thought were best.'

'I realise that, but you could have saved yourself a lot of bother by coming to me straight away instead of washing sheets in the bath in the middle of the night, and hanging things out of the window.'

She looked at her aghast. 'How did you know?'

'Our room is right under the bathroom, and I heard water running at two in the morning. I got up to see what was going on, and heard you and Ernie. I realised at once what must have happened.'

Sally reddened. 'Oh.'

'I waited for you to say something, but of course you didn't. When I heard you get up twice last night, I knew I had to do something about it.' Her stern expression had lightened, but Sally could see she was still displeased. 'Ernie needed his coat and cap for church, and I came up to collect them.'

'And found the towel and pyjamas.'

'Silly girl,' she murmured, her demeanour softening. 'Am I so terrifying?'

'No,' said Sally hastily, 'of course you're not, but because you're so nice, I didn't want to upset you or make you angry.'

Peggy gave a deep sigh. 'Sally, you have to realise that I'm here to help. I applied to take in evacuees, and was fully prepared to look after them on my own. Just because Ernie is with you, doesn't mean you have to carry the full responsibility of looking after him. Any other evacuee would have to be fed and taken to school and entertained until bedtime – it will be the same with Ernie.'

'I'm sorry,' she said again. 'I didn't think of it like that. Only I've always looked after 'im, ever since 'e were a baby.'

Peggy patted her arm. 'Then it's time you let someone help you,' she replied. 'You're far too young to have such responsibilities, and you need to have time to yourself once in a while.' She didn't wait for a reply, and went to Ernie's bed to show her what she'd done.

'I've hunted out an old mattress and a rubber sheet, and put extra linen in the dressing-table drawer. I suggest Ernie has nothing to drink after five o'clock, and that you lift him to the lavatory just before you go to bed.'

'Of course,' Sally murmured. 'I'll do me best to make sure 'e don't do it again.'

'I'm sure you will, but don't make too much of it, Sally. Any fuss and the boy will take much longer to settle in and return to his usual routine.'

'In a way,' Sally confessed, 'I'm glad you found out. I couldn't have gone much longer without a proper night's kip.'

'Yes, you did look very tired this morning.' She brightened and dug her hands in her apron pocket. 'How did your first day go?'

Sally smiled and finally relaxed – she'd been

forgiven. 'The work's easy, and I made a friend. Her name's Pearl – then there's Betty who promised to tell everyone about me home-dressmaking work, and I already got three enquiries.' She realised she was babbling and came to an abrupt halt.

'You do sewing? What sort of sewing?'

'Alterations, hems, zips, patching and repairs. I can also draw patterns and make clothes.' She took off her coat and showed Mrs Reilly her blouse and skirt. 'I made these before I come down 'ere, but I 'ad to leave me gran's Singer back in London, so it'll just 'ave to be repairs till I get enough money together to rent one.'

Peggy eyed the pretty blouse and the beautifully tailored skirt. 'Well, well, you are full of surprises, Sally Turner.' Peggy chuckled and beckoned her out of the room. 'I've got something to show you, come on.'

Sally tried to quell the hope that soared through her, but it was impossible, and when Peggy opened the door to the cupboard under the stairs, she almost burst into tears at the sight of the Singer sewing machine.

'I don't know what state it's in, haven't used it for years; but if you can get it going properly, you can borrow it for as long as you want.'

'Thank you, oh, thank you, Mrs Reilly. You don't know what this means to me, really you don't.' She threw her arms round a startled Peggy and gave her a hug. 'I'll do all yer sewing in return for the loan,' she cried, 'everything from turning sheets to making you a lovely outfit. Just say the word, and it's yours.'

'Let's see if it works first,' said Peggy dryly. 'Come on, help me get it out, and mind, it's a heavy great thing.'

They got it into the hall and slowly trundled it into the dining room and placed it under the window with a chair. 'I've said Anne and Martin can use this room in the evenings, but you can use it the rest of the time.' Peggy dusted the cobwebs off the mahogany lid with the hem of her apron before she unclipped it. Then she stood back and watched as Sally checked the shuttle, the needle and the treadle.

'A spot of oil and she'll run smooth as silk,' breathed Sally. 'Oh, and look!' She'd opened the drawer at the side of the smart mahogany casing and discovered numerous coloured cottons, a thimble, a box of pins, tailor's chalk and replacement needles. In another drawer were strips of ribbon and lace, zips of varying sizes, and buttons. It was a treasure-trove.

'I've got some old paper patterns somewhere,' murmured Peggy. 'I'll look them out for you later, though you might find them a bit old-fashioned.'

'That don't matter,' breathed Sally, still starry-eyed. 'I can change 'em about, or even make me own.'

'Sal, Sal. Come and look what we made.' Ernie was hobbling as quickly as he could into the dining room and came to a halt, staring at the machine. 'What's Gran's Singer doing 'ere, Sal? I thought it was in London?' His eyes widened and he looked over his shoulder with joyful expectancy. 'Has Mum come? Is she 'ere?'

Sally gave him a hug. 'It's Mrs Reilly's Singer,' she said. 'Mum's not 'ere, Ernie, she's still in London.'

His little face was crestfallen. 'She ain't comin' then?' At Sally's shake of the head, he squared his shoulders and put on a brave face. 'I 'spect she's doing 'er bit, like Old Mother Kemp said.'

Sally couldn't meet Peggy's gaze as she bit her lip. 'I expect she is,' she said. She ruffled his hair. 'So, wot's all the excitement about, Ernie?'

His face lit up and he tugged at Sally's hand. 'Come and look, sis. Ron and Bob and Charlie and me made something, and you gotta see.'

She looked at Peggy questioningly as he dragged her towards the door, but Peggy just smiled and shrugged.

'We gotta go outside,' he said, bumping down the cellar steps. 'It's in the garden.' He paused at the back door. 'Shut yer eyes, Sal, and count to ten before you come out, or you'll spoil the surprise.'

Sally and Peggy exchanged smiles and she did as she was told. She counted slowly, listening to the urgent whispers and the giggles from the other side of the door. Whatever they'd been up to had certainly generated a great deal of fuss.

'Ready or not,' she called, 'here I come.' She stepped outside and took in a sharp breath.

Harvey was barking as he charged alongside Bob and Charlie who were pulling on a loop of stout rope that had been attached to an old orange crate fixed to two sets of roller-skate wheels. They were moving at some speed and Ernie was yelling encouragement as he clung tightly to the sides.

'It's a crate-car, Sal!' he shouted as they came to a slithering halt in front of her. 'Now you don't 'ave to carry me no more.' He spluttered and protested as Harvey slobbered all over his face and tried to climb into the cart.

'Get outta there, yer daft, heathen dog,' muttered Ron, grabbing his scruff. 'So,' he said, turning to Sally. 'What are ye thinking about this fine mode of transport for the wee lad?'

'It looks a bit dangerous,' admitted Sally, having visions of him going too fast and falling on his head. 'What if 'e can't stop it and it goes down'ill with 'im inside?'

'To be sure I've put a brake on it. See.' He reached into the crate and pulled on a sturdy handle that had the pedal of an old bike attached at the end which acted as a brake against the right front wheel. 'It will need some refinement, so it will, and he mustn't be trying the steep hills just yet – but he can get to school and about the place without you having to carry him. Tis a grand thing, so it is.'

Sally saw the sparkle in Ernie's eyes and the rosy

cheeks of a little boy who was having fun. She couldn't spoil it. 'Yes, Mr Reilly,' she murmured, giving him a fleeting kiss on his prickly cheek. 'It is a very fine thing. Thank you.'

'Hrrumph. Right then,' he blustered. 'Let's be testing this magnificent vehicle on the pavement.' With the barking dog and the two whooping boys running alongside, he towed Ernie through the back gate and swiftly disappeared down the alleyway.

Chapter Six

Eight weeks had passed since Sally and Ernie had come to live with them, and now it was almost Christmas. The pair of them had settled in well and, as Peggy regarded them as her own – even though she knew she shouldn't – she'd dispensed with the formalities and insisted they call her Peggy or, in Ernie's case, Aunt Peg.

She sat in front of the kitchen range, knitting yet another sweater as she listened to the BBC Light Programme. Her own boys were growing like weeds, and although Ernie could have their cast-offs, he too was beginning to fill out and grow stronger, and she liked him to have something new now and again, even if it was from an old sweater she'd unravelled. Good new wool was hard to find these days, just like most things, what with all the shortages.

She glanced across at the kitchen table. Jim was home for once as the Odeon was shut while the projector was being repaired. He and Alex were playing cards and drinking vodka. Nasty, strong stuff that burnt the throat and could do no good to the stomach in her opinion – she couldn't understand why they drank it at all. But it was good to see Alex at ease again; he'd been far too quiet since getting that awful letter from his sister, and she'd worried he'd never pick himself up from it. The human spirit never failed to amaze her.

He was out of the house more often now the airfield was almost fully operational, and would be leaving them in a week's time to move into the barracks. She would miss him terribly, but knew it was what he needed. He'd been restless, hanging about the place, and now the planes had arrived he could teach the young, inexperienced pilots and feel useful again.

With her attention only partially fixed to the play on the wireless, she picked up the sound of the whirring sewing machine from the other room. Sally was busy filling the orders that had come from the factory as well as from some of the neighbours. Word had spread fast, and Peggy was worried the girl would work herself to a standstill. Yet she seemed energised now she knew Peggy was happy to look after Ernie. She'd settled in well, both here and at the factory, and had made new friends. Little Pearl Dawkins had become a fairly regular visitor now her sweetheart had joined the Naval Reserves, and Peggy had been delighted to hear them chattering like sparrows in the dining room after tea.

She gave a deep sigh as she counted the stitches. She just wished Sally would go out once in a while and have some fun – but it seemed she was determined to make her home-dressmaking business succeed. Which it would, thought Peggy with a certain amount of pride. There was no doubt the girl was talented, and the dress she'd made Peggy only last week from a bit of old silk counterpane was something to behold. She would wear it tomorrow night when her sister Doris came round for tea.

The thought of her sister stilled her hands. Doris was the eldest of the three Dawson sisters and, to Peggy's mind, had ideas above her station. She was married to Ted Williams who managed the Home and Colonial Store in the High Street, and they lived in a large detached house in Havelock Gardens on the smarter side of town. Doris didn't work at anything except on her clothes and her looks, and when she came to tea, she always made Peggy feel uncomfortable as she rolled her eyes at the faded, worn furniture and tired rugs.

Peggy got up from the chair and filled the kettle. She was parched and suspected Sally might be as well. Waiting for it to boil, she turned her thoughts to her other sister, Doreen, and couldn't help but smile. Doreen and Doris were chalk and cheese, and she supposed she was something in between – strange how that was.

'What are you smiling at?'

She turned, startled, to find Jim leaning back in his chair, his handsome face wreathed in a grin, blue eyes twinkling. 'I was thinking of how different we

Dawson girls are,' she replied. 'What with Doris being hoity-toity and Doreen being . . . well, Doreen, I suppose.'

'I like Doreen,' said Jim with a chuckle. 'There's no sides to her – you get what you see. As for Doris . . .' He pulled a face and shrugged.

She grinned back. Jim always flirted outrageously with Doreen whenever she visited, and it had become something of a game between them – a safe bit of fun that was never taken seriously. 'She's coming to tea tomorrow – Doris, that is.'

'Then I'll be finding something else to do while she's here.' He took a sip of vodka and picked up the cards Alex had dealt him.

'You could make a start on the list of jobs I gave you,' she said dryly. 'They're still here, pinned to the wall.'

'Jim and I will make start tomorrow morning,' said Alex, his voice slurring. He thumped Jim on the back. 'Is that not right, my friend? We must do all we can to help the little women, eh?'

Jim suddenly looked shifty. 'Well,' he began, 'I've a fair few things I have to be doing tomorrow. Perhaps after work on Monday would be better?'

Peggy caught Alex's eye. They both knew Jim wouldn't lift a finger, and that it would be up to Alex and Ron to complete the jobs that were now becoming rather urgent – like the broken guttering and cracked pipe, the loose tiles in the bathroom and the damp in the basement. Without bothering to offer them tea, Peggy poured water over the tea-leaves and left them to steep.

'Speaking of Doreen,' she said, after putting the knitted cosy over the pot. 'I'm surprised we haven't heard from her lately. You'd have thought she'd want the children out of London.'

'That sister of yours is a law to herself, so she is,' muttered Jim, eyeing his hand of cards without enthusiasm. 'She'll turn up if she needs you for anything – she always does.'

Peggy acknowledged the truth of this statement without ill-feeling. She loved Doreen and knew that her younger sister needed a helping hand now and again and didn't begrudge her. Doreen was divorced, with two young girls, and held down a secure job as secretary to the owner of a machine factory. She was a woman of the world, who enjoyed life and the company of many admirers, but she had always been a caring, loving mother who put her children first.

Yet Peggy fretted over their safety. Doreen had sent the girls to Wales before war was declared and then, several weeks later, demanded they returned home. If the war escalated – and there was no reason to expect otherwise – then the three of them would be in the thick of it.

Peggy poured the tea and sighed. No doubt Jim was right. She'd turn up sooner or later.

Sally carefully snipped off the loose ends of thread and held up the dress she'd made from a rather dreary outsized frock she'd found on a second-hand clothing stall in the town centre.

After she'd unpicked the seams, harvested the belt, buttons, collars and cuffs that would be useful for something else, she'd given it a good wash and iron before marking out the pattern. It was soft beige, and she'd tailored it to fit her customer's slim figure with discrete darts front and back, and a little kick-pleat that would show the cream lining when she walked. To liven it up, she'd added a cream Peter Pan collar and matching cuffs which came to the elbow, and had added cream piping down one side of the buttoned front. She'd managed to find eight buttons that matched the material perfectly, and had made a soft belt to finish it all off.

With a sigh of satisfaction, she leant back in the chair and stretched. There was only the hem to do now, and she could take it into work tomorrow afternoon to sort that out and get paid.

Thinking of the money she'd been saving in the jar under her bed made her feel even more satisfied. It was adding up, and when the jar was full, she would ask Peggy to help her open a savings account at the bank where it might even earn a bit of interest. She'd been talking to Mrs Finch, whose late husband had been a bank clerk and knew about these things.

She eyed the pile of clothes that were still to be finished and delivered. Brenda and Peggy had been brilliant at drumming up business, and life would have been very pleasant but for Iris.

Sally's success in making friends as well as a bit of extra money had had an unfortunate effect on Iris, who never lost an opportunity to spoil things. There had been the incident when ink had been poured over a skirt she'd left on her chair, broken needles in her machine, and scurrilous gossip – which, thankfully, no-one had believed. It was unsettling to have to keep watch for her next trick, and she hoped Iris was getting as tired of it as she was.

'Here you go, love. Get that down you.'

Sally smiled up at Peggy and took the cup. 'Thanks, I'm parched.'

She watched as Peggy admired the dress and began riffling through the pile of things on the chair beside her that still had to be finished. 'That's for Cissy,' she explained, as Peggy held up a confection of lavender tulle.

'It's a bit much,' Peggy sighed, turning it this way and that, and making the sequins sparkle in the electric light. 'Where on earth did she manage to find this much tulle?'

'She brought me a dress she'd worn for another show and I adapted it. The sequins take a bit of time though, cos she wants the whole bodice covered in them as well as sprinkled through the skirt.' She eyed it with pride and pleasure. 'She'll look ever so lovely in it,' she sighed.

'I hope she's paying you the going rate,' said Peggy sternly. 'She gets paid well at Woolworths, you know – and earns a fair bit prancing about on that stage.'

'Well, I give 'er a discount of course, cos she's your daughter, but yeah, she pays me.' She saw a look of mulish determination cross Peggy's face. 'Please don't say nothing, Peggy. I love making 'er pretty things.'

Peggy still looked mulish, but made no further comment.

The wailing siren shattered the peace, screeching like a banshee and echoing right through the house as it grew louder and faster and more chilling.

Peggy left without a word as Sally threw a sheet over the needlework and quickly slammed the lid over the Singer before racing upstairs to the bedroom. Ernie was already stirring – he knew the drill by now, and was trying to put on his coat.

'Come on luv, time we got into the Anderson shelter, even if it is another blooming false alarm.' She yanked on his coat and wrapped him in a blanket, grabbed her coat and their gas masks, and hurtled down the stairs.

Anne and Cissy were out, but she met Jim halfway up the stairs on his way to get Mrs Finch, who was as deaf as a post once she'd taken out her hearing aid and slept through everything.

'You're getting heavy,' she panted, running into the kitchen. Plumping Ernie unceremoniously on the chair, she rammed her feet into her shoes, tugged on her coat and reached again for her brother.

'I will take boy. You help Mrs Reilly.' Alex was dressed in his uniform, the leather and sheepskin flying jacket buttoned to the chin. He snatched him up and ran down to the cellar, their gas-mask boxes bouncing on his hip.

The siren was still wailing, filling the night like some demonic animal howling in pain. Sally tried to ignore it as she gathered pillows and blankets, and helped Peggy add extra tea and the milk to the box she always had ready to take with them. Everything they might need was in that box, from comics for the boys, to extra matches and cigarettes for the grown-ups.

Jim came hurrying into the room, tiny Mrs Finch in his arms, bleary and confused with sleep. 'Come on, girls, move, move.' He chivvied them in front of him, turned out the lights and shut the door before following them down the stairs and out into the darkness of the garden.

Ron was already opening the shelter door and bustling the boys inside. Sally could see the clouds of her breath as she ran down the path in that cold, starlit night. The siren sounded even louder now, and she could hear the ARP warden shouting at someone in the street to find shelter immediately. Searchlights cleaved the black sky, moving back and forth in great sweeps as they hunted for enemy planes.

She waited for Jim to carry Mrs Finch into the Anderson shelter and handed out the blankets and pillows. It was a routine they'd come to know, even though all the alarms since that strafing of the seafront had been false. She settled calmly beside Ernie, fully expecting the all-clear to sound any minute.

'I must go to the base,' said Alex.

'The warden won't let you on the streets while the siren's going.'

'I have my pass,' he replied. 'Goodnight. God be with you.' He pushed through the door and hurried through the gate to the air-force jeep he'd parked at the end of the street.

They looked at one another and smiled as they heard Wally Hall shout and the answering roar of the jeep's engine and squeal of tyres as Alex drove off.

'Da! Where do you think you're going?'

'I'm fetching me animals, so I am. I'm not leaving them in there.'

'You'll sit down, you silly old eejit,' shouted Jim above the wailing siren.

'Call me a fool if you want, boy, but I'm not leaving me animals.' Ron shoved his way out of the shelter.

Peggy had lit the hurricane lamp that swung from a hook on the metal ceiling. It threw eerie shadows over their faces and up the cold, damp walls, making their hideaway seem even more dank and cave-like. 'I hope the girls are all right,' she murmured, her eyes dark with worry.

'Of course they are,' soothed Jim, putting his arm round her waist. 'Sure, they've got to the shelters in time before. It'll be no different tonight.'

'I don't like them being away from home when the sirens go. You never know what might happen.'

'Now, Peg,' he said firmly, 'don't let that imagination of yours run riot. They'll be fine, so they will.'

She didn't look convinced, but she busied herself with sorting through the box of tins and jars, and found her knitting. But Sally noticed it lay untouched on her lap.

Ron returned wearing his poacher's coat and a tin helmet, the Enfield rifle slung over his shoulder. Harvey was howling as he crawled under the bench and licked the back of Charlie's leg. The ferrets were squirming and restless in the deep pockets of Ron's coat, and he sat down, pulled them out one by one and hypnotised them by softly stroking their bellies before he carefully put them back again.

'For the love of God,' sighed Jim. 'What the divil have you got on your head, old man?'

'It's me tin hat,' he retorted. 'Sure, and I'd have thought that was obvious.'

'But what good will it do if a bomb drops on you, tell me that?'

'I won't be caring if that happens,' he replied, fastening the strap under his chin and grinning at his son. 'But till then it'll keep me ears warm, so it will.'

'And what in heaven's name are you doing with that old t'ing?' Jim pointed to the rifle. 'It'll blow your head off, so it will – and then where will you be?'

'Without a head,' giggled Charlie.

Ron shot him a grin, and reached down to pat the dog's head and comfort him.

'Now we've got that settled,' Peggy shouted above the awful sound of the siren, 'would anyone like a biscuit?' She passed the tin round.

Ron settled down to munch his biscuits, Charlie and Bob on either side of him, the dog behind his legs foraging for crumbs.

Mrs Finch didn't seem to realise what was happening. She nibbled hers and asked if there was any tea to go with it, and why no-one had put on the electric light. She had the only chair – a canvas beach chair they'd managed to wedge into a corner to stop her falling out of it when she went to sleep – but it didn't always work, and Peggy had to keep a close eye on her.

Jim finished his biscuit and opened two bottles of beer he'd brought in his coat pocket, handing one to his father. Lighting a cigarette, he leant back on the bench and looked for all the world as if this was an everyday occurrence, and nothing to get het up about. But then he'd already survived the trenches in one war – he knew what to expect.

It was cramped even though the girls weren't here, and Sally was finding it hard to breathe – it was as if the walls were closing in on her, and the awful wailing siren didn't help one bit. She almost wished she could howl like Harvey.

* * *

The welcome sound of the all-clear came half an hour later. Stiff and cold they left the shelter, the heavy silence ringing in their ears. All the boys were asleep, and Sally carefully carried Ernie back to their bedroom and tucked him in with a stone hot-water bottle and an extra blanket. Weary and cold from the prolonged stay in the shelter, she was soon snuggled down and fast asleep.

The enormous explosion came without warning. It rocked the house, splintered glass, and sent clouds of plaster and dust raining down.

Ernie screamed and Sally rushed to him, dragging him from the blankets and on to the floor beneath the bed. 'They've come to get us,' he yelled, clinging to her, his tears hot against her neck.

Sally cowered under the bed, holding him beneath her to shelter him. 'It's all right,' she soothed, her voice betraying the terror that tore through her. 'They won't get us under 'ere.'

'I don't like it, Sal,' he whimpered, burying himself into her.

'Neither do I,' she murmured, kissing his cheek. 'We'll just have to be brave together.' But her thoughts were on Peggy and the others in the house. How bad was the damage? Had anyone been hurt? And why weren't the sirens going?

'Sally?' Jim came thundering into the bedroom, trousers and sweater hurriedly pulled over his pyjamas. 'It's all right, girl. It's not a raid, but a gas explosion.'

She crawled from beneath the bed, still holding a sobbing Ernie. 'Gas?'

Jim nodded as he drew back the curtains to reveal a smoke-laden sunrise. 'At the other end of the street.' He cocked his head at the sound of the fire engine bells. 'Looks like the fire brigade is on to it, but the neighbours are going to need help, Sally. Come down and settle Ernie with the other boys. Peggy's already gone to see what she can do, and it's all hands on deck.'

Ernie seemed to be over his fright and was quite happy to be with Bob and Charlie in the basement. Sally left them all wide-eyed and excited by the fuss and went to quickly check on her machine and the needlework. She was thankful she'd covered it all, for the dust was thick on everything.

Ron was in the kitchen – still wearing his tin hat – making tea and scraping margarine on bread. 'Where're Jim and Peggy?'

'Jim's gone to help clear the damage. Peggy's out rounding up everyone who might or might not need help, and to check on next door. I'm on cookhouse duty.'

Ron slopped boiling water into the teapot, and Sally stopped him pouring it into the cups until the leaves had steeped. She placed the cosy over the pot and gave it a bit of a swill to help it on its way. 'Is the damage very bad? Was anyone killed?'

'There's three of them in hospital, but only with minor injuries,' he replied, eyeing the empty milk bottle. 'Let's hope the milkman isn't late, or we'll have to go without.'

Sally hurried outside and was met by the stench of burning, and the pall of thick smoke that stung the eyes and the back of the throat. It was barely dawn, but even in this twilight, the scene was stark and made her gasp in horror and disbelief.

The two houses at the end of the terrace were gone – a gaping hole full of smoking rubble the only reminder they'd ever been there. Glass had shattered in most of the windows nearby, and the lovely lanterns at the bottom of the steps were ruined.

The end of the street was made impassable by the rubble that had fallen across it from the house opposite the explosion site. Its chimney stood like a forlorn sentinel over the exposed bedrooms and stairways where furniture stood incongruously in place and pictures still hung from the walls. There was even a vase of flowers on a table which was still covered in a cloth that fluttered in the breeze.

As she stood on the pavement and watched the frantic efforts of the firemen and wardens who were clearing rubble and searching for victims, she could see that a streetlamp had been bent by the force of the explosion so that it almost kissed the rubble that lay strewn beneath it, and black cables had been exposed which now twitched and sparked like fat electric snakes.

Sally wondered by what miracle no-one had been killed. The devastation was shocking, changing the streets for ever – but this must be nothing compared to the damage caused by an actual air raid, and the thought terrified her.

'Sally, can you help me, dear?' Peggy was clambering over the rubble, her arms around two women. 'They need to be indoors and getting warm.'

Sally could see that both women were in shock, and she gently helped them up the stairs and into the kitchen, settling them by the fire. 'Can you make more tea?' she asked Ron, who was sitting down cleaning his rifle. 'Only, Peggy's on a rescue mission and there's at least five more people to bring in – and that's without the firemen and the men helping to clear the rubble.'

She dashed back out again and coaxed the shell-shocked, bruised and battered people to leave the ruins of their street for the warmth and comfort of Peggy's kitchen.

'I'll set up a couple of trays of tea and take it out to the men. They must be exhausted.' Sally found as many cups and mugs as she could and poured the tea. 'We're out of milk,' she said. 'We'll have to use the powdered stuff.'

'We haven't any sugar either,' said Peggy, glaring at the empty bowl in front of Ron. 'How many times have I told you, Ron? The sugar's hard to come by – you can't keep putting four teaspoons in with every cup you drink.'

'Comes to something when a man can't have a decent cup of tea,' he grumbled.

'No sugar, you say?' Jim had appeared in the doorway, his face already streaked with soot and sweat. 'I've a solution for that.'

Peggy gasped as he returned from the cupboard under the stairs with two full bags in his hands. She snatched them from him before her neighbours could see and quickly stowed them on the marble shelf of her walk-in larder. 'Where did you get them?' she hissed, her tone furious, her glare accusing.

'Sure, and they were given me in return for a bit of a job I was doing,' he muttered, not quite meeting her gaze.

'And what job was that, Jim Reilly?'

'A bit of heavy lifting for old Mrs Smith down at the grocer's.' He winked at her and tapped his nose. 'It always pays to make friends in the right places, Peggy. Especially when there's a war on.'

'I hope you're not lying to me,' she whispered furiously.

'As if I would, me darlin' girl.' He grabbed her and planted a sooty kiss on her cheek.

She shook him off. 'If I believed that, I'd believe anything. I've got my eye on you Jim Reilly, so be warned.' She quickly topped up the sugar bowl and picked up one of the trays. 'Come on, Sally, let's get this tea outside before it grows cold.'

Sally saw the swift, knowing look pass between Jim and Ron, and knew Peggy was right to be suspicious. But she said nothing and, with the other tray of cups, followed her outside.

'Well,' breathed Peggy, 'that's what I call perfect timing.'

The milkman was at the end of the street, his large horse patiently waiting as he took the crates off the back of the dray and carefully placed the bottles on each doorstep. 'Morning, missus,' he said cheerfully. 'Want me to take these in for you as you've got your hands full?'

'Thanks Alan. Ron will make you a cuppa if you want one.'

'Nah. I'm a bit behind this morning. What with all that racket with the sirens last night, the cows took a while to round up and get into the dairy to be milked. Skittish they were, and I can't say I blame 'em.'

Peggy nodded and smiled and hurried away. 'Alan Jenkins would talk the leg off a donkey if you let him,' she muttered, as they picked their way over the rubble. 'But he's a nice man and works hard. I hope his cows are all right.'

Sally grinned and balanced the tray as she made her precarious way over the rubble to the knot of men who were trying to clear it and repair the water pipe that was shooting a fountain over everything. She and Peggy were greeted enthusiastically, tea was gratefully drunk, and cigarettes lit as they took a well-earned break.

There were two cups left on the tray and Sally sidestepped a large boulder in an attempt to reach the old man who'd refused to leave his shattered doorstep.

He came from nowhere, knocking into her legs so she lost her balance, the tea tray flying out of her hands to crash on the concrete. Sally teetered and would have fallen hard on to the treacherous masonry if a strong, filthy hand hadn't grabbed her coat and yanked her backwards. She landed in his lap, and into a steely embrace.

'Looks like the tea's gone for a burton, and I was looking forward to that,' he murmured in her ear. She recognised his voice immediately, could feel his arms tightening round her, pressing her back against his chest – but she seemed to have lost the ability to move, and her focus remained on the shattered china and dented tin tray.

'I seem to be making a habit of rescuing you, Sally Turner,' he drawled, his voice deep and pleasant against her cheek, his breath stirring her curls.

'I wouldn't need rescuing if you didn't barge into me,' she replied, trying to wrest herself from his grip.

'How was I to know you were standing in my way?'

'You should look where you're going.' She finally managed to stumble from his embrace, dusted down her coat and angrily turned to face him. The fury died as she became mesmerised by the intensity of those laughing blue eyes sparkling in that dirty, smoke-streaked, ridiculously handsome face.

'Well, I would have,' he replied, dusting himself off and getting to his feet, 'but it's difficult when you're trying to crawl backwards out of a hole.'

She looked at where he was pointing. There was indeed a hole she hadn't noticed before, and it seemed to go beneath the rubble to the basement of one of the ruined houses. 'Do you always have an answer to everything, John Hicks?' she said, cross that once more he'd got the better of her.

'Ah, so you remember my name,' he said, and grinned.

Sally noticed how his smile merely intensified the blue of his eyes. 'Don't let that give you no ideas,' she muttered, the heat rising in her face as she realised everyone in the street was watching them. She bent to pick up the shards of china and the tin tray – she couldn't think straight with him looking at her like that.

'Let me carry this,' he said, taking the tray. 'I don't trust you to get to the end of the street without an accident.'

'I'm perfectly capable . . .'

'I'm sure you are, but I'm the fireman in charge of this area, and my word is law.'

She looked up at him and tried not to giggle. 'You really think you're something, don't you?'

'I have my moments,' he replied. 'Here, take my arm, and watch out for that bit of rusty wire sticking out of the concrete.'

She refused the offer of his arm and carefully picked her way over the rubble. 'I can take that from 'ere,' she said firmly, grabbing the tray and making the broken crockery rattle.

'Before you go,' he said hastily, 'I have something for you.'

'I don't accept presents from strangers.'

'But this is special, and not really a present – and we've met twice, so we're not really strangers now, are we?'

Intrigued, she turned back to him. 'Go on then,' she said, the smile tugging at her lips. 'Show me.'

He reached into the inside pocket of his black uniform jacket and pulled out the colourful head-scarf with a flourish. 'Recognise this?'

She balanced the tray on her hip and reached for it in delight. 'Where did you find it?'

'It had blown across the road. I found it just as you were disappearing round a corner.' He smiled. 'I would have brought it sooner, but I didn't know where you lived.'

She couldn't quite look at him, for the knowledge that he'd carried it with him for at least eight weeks meant he'd hoped to see her again. 'Thanks, ever so.'

'Am I forgiven for manhandling you?'

She nodded shyly, suddenly overcome by the nearness of him and the way his voice seemed to touch something deep within her.

'Then will you let me take you to the pictures tonight?'

'I'm working,' she replied.

'Tomorrow, next night – the week after?'

'I'll think about it,' she murmured, and almost

ran back to the house and up the steps, slamming the front door behind her.

She put the tray on the hall table, stood there for a moment to catch her breath, and then peeked through one of the broken coloured panes at the side of the door. He was standing at the bottom of the steps now, talking to Peggy; as she studied him he seemed to know she was watching him and looked up, smiling straight into her eyes.

'Oh, Gawd,' she breathed, moving swiftly from the window. 'What's 'appening to me? I ain't got a thought in me 'ead worth a light, and me 'eart's going nineteen to the blooming dozen. And all because of some bloke who thinks he's 'andsome.'

She closed her eyes and wrapped her arms round her waist, recalling how it had felt to be held so tightly and safely in his embrace. Could it be that he really liked her, and that this wasn't a game?

'Sal! Sal, where are you?'

Ernie's piping voice brought her to her senses and she hurried to see what he wanted. It was all very well to have these silly moments, but there were more important things to worry about than John Hicks.

Anne and Martin had been with a group of other airmen and their girls, eating supper and dancing to the very good eight-piece band, when the word came from the airbase that there was a flap on. The men left hurriedly in the cars they'd managed to borrow for the night and, deciding she didn't want to stay without Martin, Anne had begun the long walk home.

It had been as dark as pitch outside, with no street lighting and every window blacked out so tightly that not a chink of light showed to help her on her way. The stars had twinkled coldly, but the moon had been only an eyelash curve in the sky.

The sirens had gone off just as she was passing the school and was halfway home. Dithering over whether to make a run for it, or use the public shelter beneath the school playground, her mind was made up for her by the ARP warden, who insisted she used the shelter.

She'd hurried to where the stacks of sandbags shielded the door, and went down the concrete steps to join the residents of the nearby blocks of flats, and hoped it was another false alarm and that she'd soon be tucked up in bed.

Anne helped soothe the children she knew from the classroom, telling them stories and making shapes on the wall with her fingers. Once they'd calmed down, she comforted herself with thoughts of Martin.

They had been courting for several months now, and their feelings for one another had not diminished. They were meant for one another, and soon, very soon, they would be engaged. She'd huddled against the cold brick wall of the shelter, her coat wrapped tightly over the lovely black velvet evening dress Sally had adapted from a cloak they'd found in a basket in the attic. It might be damp and chill down here amongst the crying babies and whining children, but Anne was warm inside, her smile soft and full of affection as she'd recalled their evening together.

Martin had told her he wanted to do things properly – and that meant her meeting his parents before he asked her father for her hand. She'd hugged her delight to her, and done her best to ignore the nervous flutter that always came when she thought about the lunch tomorrow. She wanted so badly to make a good impression, and for them to take to her. Martin had assured her there was absolutely nothing to worry about. His sister and his parents were nice ordinary people who couldn't fail to love her as much as he did. But, try as she might, the niggling doubts would not be denied.

Chapter Seven

'My sister's the last person I need today,' muttered Peggy, as she switched off the Hoover. 'Just look at the place. My kitchen's in a mess and the dust's everywhere.' She eyed the boarding Ron had put over the shattered windows and sighed. 'Let's hope she's got something more interesting to do than come here for tea.'

Sally had already dusted the dining room and cleared away the glass; now she was on her hands and knees scrubbing the ornate tiles on the hall floor. 'It doesn't 'elp 'aving so many people tramping through the place with their muddy boots,' she muttered. 'We must've 'ad 'alf of Cliffehaven through 'ere this morning.'

'At least the Salvation Army people will help those poor souls find somewhere to sleep now their houses are wrecked.'

'Yeah, I suppose a bit of cleaning ain't nothing compared to what 'appened to them.' She wiped the cloth over the scrubbed floor and wrung it out into the bucket.

Anne came down the stairs looking pretty in a neat two-piece suit, carrying her overcoat on her arm. 'I'm sorry I can't stay and help, but Cissy has promised to finish cleaning the upstairs.' She gave a hesitant smile. 'Wish me luck, Mum.'

Peggy kissed her cheek and smiled. 'You look lovely, darling. They can't fail to take to you the minute they see you.'

Anne pulled on her coat, checked the seams in her stockings and touched the sweet little felt hat that had been artfully tilted above one eye. 'You don't think this is too much, do you?'

'You look ever so lovely,' sighed Sally. 'Just like a film star.'

'Martin's been waiting outside long enough,' said Peggy. 'Get on with you.'

After a swift kiss for her mother and a nervous grin at Sally, she carefully stepped over the freshly washed floor and was out of the door.

Sally stood on the step, the bucket of dirty water at her feet as Martin tooted the horn and drove away in his very smart car. Anne might have looked nervous, but it was clear she and Martin were very much in love, and Sally wondered, wistfully, if she would ever know such happiness.

Closing the door, she dismissed all thought of John Hicks. As handsome and charming as he was, he wouldn't want to know her once he realised Sally was committed to raising Ernie. She couldn't expect any man to take on that kind of responsibility.

She carried the bucket through the kitchen and down to the back garden, where she threw it over

Ron's vegetable garden. On her way back to the kitchen she looked in on the three boys, who were playing with a train set they'd laid out on the floor between the beds. 'Where's Ron?'

'In the outside lav with the *Racing Post*,' said Bob solemnly. 'He said not to disturb him until Aunt Doris has gone.'

'It's only three o'clock. She ain't due till six.'

'He's worried she might come earlier if she knows about the gas explosion,' said Charlie. He looked up from the train. 'That's why we're staying down here,' he explained. 'Aunt Doris likes kissing boys, and we hate it, don't we Bob?'

Bob pulled a face and shuddered dramatically. 'Her lipstick feels horrible, but Mum says it's rude to wipe it off straight away.'

'Old Mother Kemp were the same,' grimaced Ernie. 'Yuk.'

Sally left them to it and continued up the steps to the kitchen. Doris sounded an awful woman, and she was glad she would be at work when she arrived.

Glancing at the kitchen clock, she realised she still had half an hour before she'd have to leave. She found a tea towel and got to work drying the cups and dishes that Peggy was stacking on the wooden draining board. The water and electricity had, thankfully, been restored by the engineers two hours ago.

'I'm sorry I broke a couple of these,' she said. 'I hope they weren't good ones?'

'Goodness me, no. Most of this stuff dates back to the Ark.' Peggy finished washing a saucer and added it to the pile. 'I had a nice chat with John Hicks this morning, by the way,' she said airily, fishing in the water for another cup.

'Oh, yes?' Sally tried not to show she was interested.

'Mmm. I've known his family for years,' carried on Peggy. 'He's a nice lad, but what happened to him was terribly sad.' Peggy left the statement to hang between them.

Sally smiled. 'You'd never make a good poker player, Peggy. Go on, you're obviously dying to tell me all about John Hicks.'

'He was married once,' she said. 'Suzy and he were barely out of school – and in hindsight, they probably knew they wouldn't have much time together. Suzy was ill, you see, very ill. She was dead before they could celebrate their first anniversary.' Peggy stared out of the window, her hands deep in the suds. 'Leukaemia, it was. Poor little girl.'

Sally had heard similar stories back home, but they never failed to touch her heart. 'That's really sad,' she murmured.

'Yes. They'd been childhood sweethearts and John took it very badly.'

'That's hardly surprising.' She bit her lip. 'How long ago was this?'

'Four years. They were both only eighteen.'

Peggy continued washing the dishes. 'John's made of sterner stuff than anyone realised, and although he went round like a ghost, he didn't give in like some would have done.' Peggy vigorously scrubbed a pan. 'He was already working for the fire service as an apprentice, and from that moment on he seemed driven to prove himself. He was always the one up the highest ladder, or the first into a burning house – it was as if his own safety didn't matter.'

'He seems all right now,' said Sally, putting the damp tea towel over the rail in front of the range to dry. 'In fact,' she added, 'he's a bit too full of 'imself for my liking.'

Peggy laughed. 'You don't fool me, young Sally. You're smitten, and going by what we all saw this morning, so is John.'

Sally went bright red. 'He don't know nothing about me,' she muttered.

'He knows enough,' said Peggy softly. 'We had quite a chat this morning, and I told him about Ernie, and what a good little mother you are to him. I made it clear that you were only sixteen and I wouldn't have him messing you about, and that if he was really interested in you, then he'd have to accept you and Ernie came as a pair.'

'Oh.' Sally could feel her heart bang painfully against her ribs. 'What did 'e say to that?'

Peggy leant against the sink and folded her arms, her eyes bright with laughter. 'He asked me if it would be all right to call in sometime and perhaps take you both out to tea. I said it was fine by me, but it was ultimately your decision.'

Sally tried to think, but it seemed her brain was scrambled.

'I gave him our telephone number, so I expect we'll hear from him quite soon. What shall I tell him, Sally?'

'Tell 'im . . . tell 'im me and Ernie would like a cup of tea – but it would be better to 'ave it 'ere.' She looked at Peggy, knowing her face was scarlet. 'Now, I gotta go to work.'

'I'll try and get the ingredients together to make a cake,' Peggy called after her as she shot out of the kitchen.

Sally was grinning as she took the stairs two at a time, grabbed the almost-finished dress along with her coat and gas mask, and flew back down the stairs and out of the door.

It was a dreary, cold day, but she hardly noticed as she ran down the street. There was a warm glow inside her, and it felt as if she had wings on her feet, and was floating on a cloud. John Hicks knew her situation, but still wanted to come to tea. Now she knew exactly how Anne felt.

Sally was still smiling as she arrived at the factory and clocked in. If only Pearl was at work today, she could have told her about John and asked her advice on what to wear, and what to do and say. But Pearl was on nights this week, and wouldn't be sitting beside her. Her exciting news would have to wait until the end of the shift when they'd have a few moments to catch up.

She hurried inside and went straight to the girl who'd ordered the dress. Handing over the carefully wrapped brown paper parcel, she waited for her reaction.

'It's lovely,' the girl breathed, holding it up. 'You're ever so clever, Sally. What do you think, girls?'

Sally reddened at their praise. 'I'll do the hem in the break. Stand still a mo, and I'll pin it up to the right length.'

With the women's praise still ringing in her ears, and the dress carefully rewrapped under her arm, Sally hurried to her seat, took off her coat, stowed the parcel on the shelf beneath the machine and sat down. The dress had done the trick and now there were two more customers who had things they wanted altered and brought up to date. Her little business was beginning to really flourish.

She was about to check the machine for sabotage when she realised her cushion was wet, and it was soaking through her skirt. With a gasp of horror, she sprang from the chair and inspected the damage. There was a large, suspiciously yellow patch spreading right across the seat of her light brown skirt. She sniffed the cushion and flinched at the sour reek of urine.

'Oh, do look!' screeched Iris from across the room.

'Sally Turner's wet 'erself. What's the matter, girl, forgot yer nappy today, did yer?'

Sally picked up the sodden cushion between finger and thumb and advanced on Iris, all too aware that everyone was watching, eager to see what would happen.

Iris stood to meet her, hands on hips, malicious smile on her face. 'Ooh,' she said, 'I'm frightened. What ya gunna do, little mouse?'

'Give yer back what's yours,' she replied grimly, and swiped the stinking, sodden cushion right across Iris's face.

Iris screeched and batted it away in horror and disgust. 'You *bitch*,' she shouted, scrubbing frantically at her face with the hem of her cardigan. 'I'll 'ave yer eyes for that.'

Sally stood her ground, even though Iris was sturdier and several inches taller. 'You wanna fight? Come on then. Let's see what yer made of without yer mates to back yer up.'

Iris stopped scrubbing at her face and looked round. She suddenly didn't seem quite so sure of herself. 'I'll still 'ave you,' she growled, her fingers clawed as she took a step towards Sally.

'Sit down Iris,' barked one of the women nearby as she grabbed her arm.

'Let *go* of me you old cow,' stormed Iris, wresting herself from her meaty grip. 'This is none of your bloody business.'

The big woman at the end of the row stood up,

arms akimbo, and gently moved Sally to one side to make way for the others who had risen with her. 'We can make it our business,' she said evenly.

'You don't frighten me.' Iris had a hunted look in her eye despite her words, and she took another step back to discover she was trapped against the end of the table.

The women moved as one to surround her. 'We're sick of you bullying the young ones and getting up to your nasty tricks, Iris. Any more of it and we'll show you how we treat bullies round 'ere.' The big woman was almost nose to nose with her now. 'And it won't be pretty, Iris. I can promise you that.'

'Here, Sally,' muttered one of the women nearby, 'take this and get that skirt off. I'll rinse it through for you.'

Sally took the enormous wrap-round apron and slipped her arms through it before tying it round her waist and stepping out of the skirt.

The skirt was snatched away as Simmons appeared with his clipboard and a thunderous expression.

'What's going on here?' he shouted. 'Why are you women standing about when the whistle went two minutes ago?'

'It's nothing, Mr Simmons,' said the big woman. 'Iris just needed a bit of advice about something, that's all.'

He noticed someone moving among the group. 'Where do you think you're going?' he snapped.

'Lav,' she said, hiding Sally's skirt behind her back. 'I got the runs something chronic.'

'Get on with it then,' he said, his face reddening. He turned to Sally. 'Get back to your own workstation, before I dock your pay,' he roared.

'I need to go to the lav as well,' said Iris.

'Well, you can't. You spend too much time in there as it is.'

With his attention taken up with Iris, the big woman swiftly picked up the cushion by its corner and planted it on Iris's chair.

'Get to work, the lot of you,' Simmons roared, 'or I'll give you your cards.'

Sally scurried back and quickly swopped chairs. There were always plenty to choose from as the Sunday shift was less popular. She looked over to the other side of the room just in time to see Iris leap from her chair with a squeal of anguish.

She smiled as the other women roared with laughter and Iris shoved Simmons to one side as she dashed to the washrooms. Justice had been done.

'I tried to ring you, to see if you were all right,' said Doris, as Peggy opened the front door. 'But of course all the lines were down.' She sniffed and eyed the crater at the end of the road, and the boarded-up windows, as if decrying the untidiness of it all. 'We aren't careless enough to suffer gas explosions at our end of town.'

'That's nice for you,' said Peggy flatly. Doris was almost an hour early, and although she'd had time to wash and change into her new frock, she wasn't nearly ready to put up with her airs and graces.

'I've had to park the car right down the road,' she complained. 'I do hope it will be safe. One can't be sure in this neighbourhood.'

Peggy gritted her teeth and refused to rise to the bait. 'Give me your coat and I'll hang it up.'

'I'd rather keep it on. It's mink, you know, and this house is always freezing.' She stepped into the hallway clutching the mink to her as if afraid it might get tainted by touching anything. 'I do hope you've got some decent sherry for a change. I can't abide that wishy-washy stuff you dish out.'

'There's no sherry,' said Peggy. 'You'll have to make do with tea like the rest of us.'

Her look said it all, reminding Peggy of a disgruntled pug dog that had been denied a biscuit. With a sigh of resignation, she followed Doris, who'd swept into the dining room and placed her expensive leather handbag on the one comfortable armchair. Doris didn't sit in kitchens. She regarded such behaviour as common.

'I see you've got the Singer out again.' Her gaze travelled from the neck to the hem of Peggy's new dress as she peeled off her leather gloves. 'I must say, Margaret, your skills have certainly come on since the last time you tried to make anything. That could almost be shop-bought.'

Doris was the only person in the family to insist upon calling her Margaret, and Peggy suspected she only did it because she knew how much it irritated her. 'Sally made the dress. I'm still hopeless at sewing,' she replied.

'Sally?' The carefully plucked eyebrows rose as she placed the gloves inside the handbag and snapped it shut.

'She's my evacuee,' Peggy explained yet again. 'She and her brother have been living here for two months, as you very well know.'

'I find it difficult to remember things that don't interest me,' she replied dismissively. 'How you can open your home to such dreadful people is beyond my comprehension.' She moved towards the fireplace to regard her reflection in the mirror above it. 'I suppose she's from the East End, and speaks with some ghastly accent that possesses very few consonants and tortured grammar?'

'She's a lovely sweet girl,' murmured Peggy, 'and I won't have you talking about her like that.'

Doris turned from the mirror and eyed the dress again. 'I'm surprised some chit from the East End knows how to sew,' she said, 'but a good dressmaker is a rare find. Send her over to pick up one or two of my cheaper dresses that need altering. If she's good enough, I might even let her work on some of my better things – but not until she's proved herself.'

'Sally's good enough to work on anything,' said

Peggy stoutly, 'but she has enough to do without running all over town after you. If you want alterations done, then you'll have to bring them here.'

Peggy realised she was letting Doris's attitude get to her and took a deep breath. 'She charges the going rate,' she warned. 'I'll not have you trying to get sewing done on the cheap just because she's living here.'

'As if I would.' Doris sniffed delicately and returned to admiring her reflection in the mirror. Carefully taking off her hat and placing it on the table, she patted her freshly washed and set hair with a manicured hand.

'Your hair looks nice,' Peggy remarked, hoping to defrost her sister's attitude.

'Thank you. I had it done yesterday morning.' Her nose wrinkled as she took in Peggy's rather untidy hairdo. 'You should try the salon, Margaret. A fresh shampoo and set would work wonders, and a little tint of colour would soon get rid of that grey.'

Peggy didn't even bother to reply. Doris knew very well she had neither the time nor the money for hairdressers. As for the grey, there were only a few wisps of it here and there and she'd chosen to ignore them – unlike Doris, whose hair was a slightly different colour every time she saw her.

She went to make the tea, adding a plate of biscuits and the last of the sponge cake to the tray before carrying it into the dining room.

Doris was smoking one of her Turkish cigarettes,

and flicking the ash into a glass flower vase she'd taken from the mantelpiece. The fur was draped becomingly off her shoulders to reveal three rows of pearls at her neck, and a dove-grey two-piece suit. She sat in the armchair, slim legs crossed at the ankles, showing off silk stockings and expensive two-tone shoes.

Peggy thought she looked quite at home and far too elegant for her dining room, which only served to make her even more cross. She grabbed the ashtray and rescued her precious glass vase, noting the suit that had definitely not come from any of the local shops. The pearls were a new acquisition.

She felt the familiar stab of envy Doris always incurred – and hastily dismissed it. Her sister might have money and a lovely detached house, but she was married to Ted, who might be a successful shop manager, but still had to be the most boring, self-satisfied and opinionated man on earth. For all his faults, she wouldn't swop Jim for a day of Doris's life.

'Where are the boys?'

'They're out with Ron somewhere,' she said vaguely, knowing full well they were messing about in Ron's shed. But as Doris never went near the back garden, she'd never know.

'I was hoping to see Anne and Cicely, but it appears they too are nowhere to be seen. Really, Margaret, it's not good enough when I've made the journey especially.'

'Anne's gone to lunch with Martin's parents, and Cicely is rehearsing the new show. They knew you were coming, but couldn't change their arrangements. They send their apologies and hope to see you soon.'

Peggy glanced at the little clock on the mantel, and felt a flutter of apprehension. She did hope everything had gone well for Anne. She liked Martin, and was delighted the two of them seemed so well-matched, but it was always nerve-wracking to meet your sweetheart's parents for the first time. She could still remember all too well how Ron and Sybil had been less than friendly when they realised the wedding would have to be a hurried one while Jim was on leave.

Doris's voice broke into her fretful thoughts. 'And where's that feckless husband of yours? I see the damp patch is still in the corner, and those window-frames haven't been painted for years.'

'He's at work.'

Her brown eyes widened. 'Really? How so? The cinema is closed. I saw the notice on the door as I drove past.'

'He had to go in to check on the new projector and make sure he knows how to work it properly before they open again tonight,' Peggy replied briskly. She wasn't about to let her sister cast aspersions on Jim – even though sometimes he wasn't always where he was meant to be.

Peggy poured the tea. She had dug out the best

china, knowing Doris refused to drink from anything else. 'We've been at sixes and sevens today,' she said, handing her the bone-china cup and saucer and offering the biscuits and cake. 'I've yet to make a start on tea.'

'Supper, Margaret. One has tea at four o'clock.' Her disdainful gaze swept over the cake and biscuits before she waved them away. 'I won't have time to stay anyway. I have to chair an important committee meeting of the WRVS tonight.'

Peggy eyed her sister without much affection. The old saying was true, she reflected sadly. You could choose your friends, but not your family.

Doris left an hour later and, before her car had reached the seafront, Peggy's kitchen was invaded by three hungry boys and a thirsty old man. She made more tea, rationed the sugar and milk she put in it and let them loose on the cake and biscuits. She would make a start on the evening meal once she'd had a cigarette and a bit of a sit-down. Doris always wore her out, and she needed a few minutes to gather her senses.

'I see that sister of yours has had the usual effect,' muttered Jim, arriving back from the cinema. 'What's she done now to upset you?'

'It's her high-handed attitude that gets my goat,' she snapped, 'and the way she knows how to wind me up tighter than a clock.' Peggy threw the butt of her cigarette into the coal scuttle and poured him a cup of tea. 'But today really put the tin lid on it.'

'Just like Grandpa's helmet,' chimed in Charlie, who was busy with a colouring book at the table.

Jim softly cuffed his ear, and they grinned at one another before he turned back to Peggy. 'What's she done this time?'

Peggy lit a second cigarette, which was most unlike her, but her nerves were shredded and smoking seemed to calm her. 'You know that girl who cleans for her? Well, she's threatened to sack her unless she tells the billeting officer that she's moved into Doris's spare room. Doris refuses to take in evacuees, or even servicemen, and it's the only way she can get around it without falling foul of the authorities.'

'Is the girl really moving in?'

'Of course not. Doris wouldn't let her in the front door unless she'd arrived to scrub the floors and do the ironing.' She puffed furiously on the cigarette, aware that the three boys were listening to this conversation with avid interest. 'She even had the nerve to say she wouldn't take in Doreen and the girls if they turned up.'

'Why ever not? At least they're family.'

She pulled a face. 'Ted doesn't like his routine disturbed, evidently,' she said scornfully, 'and of course that precious son of hers is working for the MoD, and can't *possibly* risk having his very important – *secret* – work compromised by strangers moving into the house.'

'I've always felt a bit sorry for Anthony. He's a

nice young fellow – a bit shy, but with a hell of a brain on him. It's a pity he's got such a mother. No wonder he's never married.'

'Any self-respecting girl would run a mile at the idea of having her as a mother-in-law,' said Peggy, blowing smoke. 'Bossy is not the word to describe her. Do you know what she had the nerve to say to me?' She didn't wait for him to reply. 'She said that as I already had a houseful of waifs and strays, she didn't think that it would make much difference if I took in Doreen and the girls as well.'

'Has she heard from Doreen then? Is she coming down?'

Peggy shook her head. 'Doris tried telephoning her this morning with no luck, and I tried this afternoon. The lines are still down, and the operator has no idea when they'll be fixed.'

'There's no point in getting all steamed up over Doris,' Jim murmured. 'She'll never change. As for Doreen, well, there *is* plenty of room here, and she'll be guaranteed a warm welcome. Though I doubt she'll want to leave London for too long.'

The anger had left Peggy and now she felt rather deflated. 'Yes, I know, and I'll gladly take them all – as long as Doris doesn't keep poking her nose in and causing trouble. You know how those two fight.'

Jim grinned. 'I do indeed,' he said, 'and it's a sight to see, to be sure.' He gave her a hug and a kiss and left to buy an evening paper.

Peggy finished her cigarette, ordered the boys to

clear the mess from the table before she turned on the wireless for their favourite programme, and went to the walk-in larder to find something to cook for the evening meal. She eyed the bags of sugar with suspicion, and popped them into the empty bread-crock so no-one could see them. If she was caught hoarding such things, they'd all be in trouble.

The sirens went off just as they were about to sit down to mince, cabbage and potato. There was the usual bustle to get everyone safely into the shelter, but fifteen minutes later the all-clear sounded and they were back in the kitchen. The food was luke-warm, but it was eaten with gusto anyway.

The newsreader sounded solemn as they gathered quietly to listen to the wireless after their tea. Russia, in alliance with Germany, had attacked Finland. Barrage balloons were being erected above the more important buildings in London, with more to follow as soon as possible.

He continued with the news that the coalition government were about to debate on the subject of enlistment for, despite the number of men who'd voluntarily signed up for service, it was felt that every man between the ages of nineteen and twenty-seven would be needed to swell the ranks and defeat the enemy. The result of the debate would not be known until the House had conducted a vote. The outcome of this should be declared shortly after Christmas.

They cheered as the newsreader continued with

the rousing news that the notorious enemy ship, the *Admiral Graf Spee*, had finally been hunted down by the British naval ships, *Ajax*, *Achilles* and *Exeter*. Following a fierce battle on the Rio de la Plata (the River Plate), the *Graf Spee* had been blown up and sunk. All three British ships would be returning home for repairs and a hero's welcome.

There was a great deal of discussion about the battle and it all became too much for Mrs Finch, who thought they were still fighting the First World War. She'd begun to fret because she couldn't remember where she'd hidden the pistol her husband, Albert, had given her to protect her honour should the Hun invade while he was away fighting on the Somme.

Peggy had soothed her and made sure she knew what war they were actually fighting before helping her upstairs and into bed. If the poor old duck got any more confused, she'd have to watch her more closely, and Peggy hoped it was just today's unfortunate explosion and the news that were upsetting her and that her mind was unimpaired. She didn't want her going into a home – they were for people who had no-one to care for them, and Mrs Finch was very much a part of her family now.

Peggy poked her head round her bedroom door half an hour later to discover her fast asleep and snoring with the wireless going full-blast on the bedside table. She turned it off and quietly left her to sleep.

Returning to the kitchen, Peggy kept a constant

watch on the clock, wondering where Anne had got to. She hoped the car hadn't broken down on some lonely country road miles from anywhere – it was so dangerous driving about without proper head-lights or streetlamps.

Her own car had been locked away for the dura-tion now petrol was so hard to come by, and she missed the convenience of it. But then there was a war on, and she supposed she'd just have to get used to it, and stop worrying about everything and everyone.

As Sally was still at work, Peggy carried Ernie upstairs a short while later, gave him a bath and tucked him in bed before reading him a story. Anne had told her that his and Sally's reading was very poor, so Peggy had chosen an easy book with lots of pictures and few words, which she let him follow with his finger.

Once he was drowsy, she stroked back his hair, softly kissed his downy cheek, and turned off the main light. She left the door ajar so she could hear if he called out. He hadn't wet the bed in weeks, and seemed happier and far healthier than the little waif she'd first taken in.

Bob and Charlie were at the age when they could bath themselves, though they made a terrible mess, and it took ages to get them settled into bed. Having read them a story, she firmly turned off the light and shut their bedroom door, before returning to the kitchen.

Cicely was having an early night for once and, with Ron playing soldiers in the church hall, Jim and Sally at work and Alex on standby at the airfield, the house was quiet. She finished tidying up and took out her knitting. Bob had worn straight through the heel of his socks; although she'd darned them, he still needed another pair.

She looked up when she heard the key in the front door, and glanced at the clock. It was too early to be Sally. She put down her knitting, expecting to see Anne at any moment. There was the sound of shoes being kicked off, and the rustle of a coat being shed. Then there was a long silence – followed by a muffled sob.

Peggy was out of the chair immediately. She rushed into the icy hall, took one look at her daughter's face and wrapped her in her arms. 'Anne, darling, whatever is the matter?'

'Oh, Mum,' she sobbed into her shoulder. 'It was awful. Simply awful.'

'Come on, darling. Let's get into the warm so we can talk properly.' She steered her into the kitchen and sat her down in the armchair before perching on the arm. 'What happened?' she asked quietly, the girl's heart-rending tears making her want to cry in sympathy.

'Martin and I are finished,' she sobbed. 'It's all over.'

Peggy waited until the storm of tears had ebbed somewhat before she tried to get any sense out of her. 'But he loves you – and you love him. What happened to change that?'

Anne blew her nose and angrily took off her suit jacket. 'His bloody awful family,' she hissed.

Peggy was startled. It was unlike Anne to swear. Something really bad must have happened today, and she was determined to get to the bottom of it. 'You'd better start at the beginning, love, and tell me everything.'

Anne's worst fears had been realised, and she could still feel the debilitating sense of inferiority that his parents had invoked during that torturous lunch.

Her first sight of the long driveway that ran from imposing gates to the even more imposing manor house should have warned her, but she'd allowed her common sense to be drowned with hope. She could still hear Martin blithely talking about the two farms and the pheasant shoot, as he mentioned gamekeepers and gardeners, and pointed out magnificent stables, dense woodland and manicured gardens.

'I knew it was a mistake the minute I saw that house,' she said, her voice rough with tears, as she kept tight control of her emotions. 'Martin never warned me it was a manor house, set on an estate that has been in the family for at least five generations.'

'Good heavens,' gasped Peggy. 'I never realised. He seems so ordinary.'

Anne gave a bitter laugh. 'He's not ordinary at all,' she replied. 'He was educated at Eton and Oxford and followed his father – Air Marshal Black – into the Royal Air Force as a Commissioned Officer. His father has the ear of the War Cabinet, his sister is engaged to some idiot with a title and no chin – and his mother is on just about every committee known to the human race.'

'So's your Aunt Doris,' she replied dryly. 'But that doesn't make her anything special.'

Anne could feel the return of that awful humiliation. It swept over her, making her feel nauseous. She had been greeted coolly by his mother whose first scathing glance had condemned her as 'not one of them' and his father had glared at her from beneath his heavy brows as if she was some poacher caught with a brace of pheasant under her coat. His sister and her fiancé were distantly polite and, after a detached greeting, had proceeded to ignore her.

A parlour maid had taken her coat and hat and, after a stilted, bland conversation over sherry, they'd gone into the dining room. Another maid had served at the table, which had been laid with a confusing amount of cutlery and glassware. She had felt his mother's eyes on her, watching and waiting for her to pick up the wrong piece of silverware. It had made her clumsy, and she'd knocked over a glass of red wine which spread with distressing rapidity over the pristine white linen tablecloth.

'I do know which knife and fork to use,' she said

bitterly, 'but with them watching me I got clumsier and clumsier. The wine went everywhere, and although she said it didn't matter, I caught the look she shot at her husband. It was as if it simply confirmed that I didn't belong at her table, let alone in her house.'

'Oh, Anne, darling. How awful for you. What horrid people.'

'As if that wasn't bad enough they started to interrogate me. They wanted to know where I was educated, where I taught, what my father did.' She fell silent, mortified that she'd been made to feel ashamed of her family.

'Perhaps they were just interested?'

'No they weren't. They simply wanted to make it abundantly clear that I wouldn't be accepted into their privileged, blinkered little world. His mother even managed to mention some girl called Annabelle at every opportunity – and ever so subtly suggest she had high hopes of her and Martin becoming engaged.'

'What did Martin have to say about all this?'

'He was furious,' she admitted. 'He told his parents that he was horrified they had behaved so badly and that, whether they liked it or not, Annabelle and he had long since split, and now could barely stand one another.'

'Good for him,' murmured Peggy.

Anne lit a cigarette and stared into the fire. 'We left halfway through lunch, and Martin was so angry he was driving far too fast. I was frightened we'd have an accident and begged him to stop for a while so he could cool down.'

They had sat in the car without speaking for a while, both too upset to say anything. Anne could barely see through her tears, but she'd been determined to remain calm and in control of her emotions as Martin smoked one cigarette after another in furious silence.

'You obviously had to discuss things,' said Peggy, sitting opposite her and taking her hand. 'I hope neither of you rushed into hasty decisions because of what happened?'

'Martin finally calmed down enough to speak coherently,' she murmured. 'He was full of apology for his family's disgraceful behaviour – and said he'd been shocked at how hostile they'd been. He went on to explain that he and Annabelle had met at Oxford, and both families had hoped they would marry – but it had never been a great love affair, and had soon petered out, and now she was engaged to some boffin at the MoD.'

'I'm very glad to hear it,' said Peggy, 'but I get the feeling that this entire episode will have a lasting effect on both of you.'

'It shook me rigid,' she confessed. 'But Martin's more determined than ever that we should marry. He begged me to ignore his parents' old-fashioned views.' Anne looked at her mother through her tears. 'But how could I, Mum? Girls like me don't marry men like him. I don't fit into their world, and sooner or later it will become obvious even to him.'

'Oh, Anne. I'm so very sorry.' Peggy clasped her fingers. 'But you mustn't let those people make you feel unworthy. You have a great deal to be proud of, and have every right to keep your head high and rise above their snobbery.'

'Easier said than done,' murmured Anne.

'You said it was over between you,' said Peggy. 'Did you mean that, Anne?'

She nodded and blew her nose. 'Martin pleaded with me to reconsider – to take time and think about it, and not rush into any hasty decisions. But it would only delay the inevitable, and cause us both more hurt. I told him it was over – and I meant it.' Her voice broke on a sob.

Anne could still see the devastation in his eyes, could hear him pleading with her – threatening to keep ringing and writing until she changed her mind. She'd been so tempted to give in, and to hell with his damned family. But she knew it could never work. Not ever. 'But I love him so,' she whispered. 'I really do.' The tears streamed down her face. 'Oh, Mum. What am I going to do without him?'

Peggy held her close, murmuring soft words in her ear, rocking her as she'd done when Anne was small. But her mother's words and her embrace couldn't mend her broken heart, couldn't stem the bitter tears, or erase the humiliating knowledge that she wasn't considered good enough to be Martin's wife.

Sally had come in quietly, expecting everyone to be asleep. She'd taken off her shoes and was about to creep up the stairs when she'd heard voices in the kitchen.

About to go in and say good night, she'd frozen outside the door when she'd heard Anne's heart-rending sobs. Through Anne's tears, Sally had heard every word she'd said. And, as she'd listened, she'd felt a chill run through her that dashed the small ray of hope that had burnt so brightly all day.

Anne was the most educated person she knew, with a degree and everything. She spoke nicely, was pretty and had lovely manners, knew how to dress and how to hold her knife properly – Sally had been taking note of all this, and had tried to copy her, but there was so much to learn it was difficult to remember it all. How could anyone possibly think Anne wouldn't make a perfect wife?

Furious that someone as lovely as Anne should be so badly treated, she'd remained in the hallway, tempted to rush in and offer her own comfort. But as she listened to her tale of woe, a dawning sense of dread came over her. If Anne wasn't considered good enough, then what chance did she have of ever being someone's wife? She couldn't read and write very well, her mother was a good-time girl and the family came from one of the poorest streets in Bow.

She thought of John Hicks, and the fledgling hope she'd carried through the day withered and died. He might not be from a posh, wealthy family, but he was educated, talked nicely, and was in a position of command at the fire station. He probably saw her for what he thought she was, and had decided she'd be just the right girl for a bit of fun.

Sally felt the heat of her tears roll down her cheeks. A girl like her wasn't good enough for a man like him – just as Martin's family didn't think Anne was good enough for them. The class system was rigid, the barriers sharply defined, and only trouble could come for anyone who defied those barriers.

As Anne burst into tears again in the kitchen, Sally crept up the stairs, grabbed the coat she used as a dressing gown, and silently closed the bathroom door.

Stripping off the overall and stinking knickers she'd been forced to wear all day, she hung the damp, but clean skirt over the back of the chair and had a strip wash. Using the same water, she laundered the knickers, pulled on the coat and tiptoed back to her room. She dragged the nightdress Peggy had lent her over her head and crawled into bed. It was a long time before she fell asleep.

Chapter Eight

Sally gave Ernie a lick and a promise with the flannel after breakfast and combed his hair, which she noticed could have done with a trim. 'Are you feeling all right?' she asked. 'Only you look a bit pale.'

'Yeah, course I am,' he replied, grimacing as the comb snagged on a tangle. 'Ow,' he protested, 'that 'urt.'

'Sorry, luv, but if you keep wriggling . . .' She eyed him closely. He looked tired, with dark rings under his eyes – but he'd slept well. 'Perhaps I should keep you 'ome today,' she murmured.

'Aw, Sal. It's the last day of term and Mrs Granger said we was 'aving jelly and custard as a special treat.'

Sally didn't want to spoil his fun, but he definitely looked peaky, and that worried her. 'All right,' she conceded, 'but if you don't feel right, you're to tell yer teacher. Promise?'

He nodded, scrambled away from her and bumped his way rather more slowly than usual down the stairs.

Sally cleaned the bathroom, fetched their coats,

and followed him shortly afterwards. Anne had been absent at breakfast, but now she was bustling her young brothers into coats and caps and finding their satchels and gas-mask boxes. Sally noted the swollen eyelids and the wan face and gave her a warm smile of support as she sorted out Ernie and fetched the shopping list and basket from Peggy.

Once everyone was ready, they went down to the basement, fetched the crate cart – which had now been improved with a set of pram wheels that were far more stable – and set off for school, Harvey howling at the gate because he hated being left behind.

'Keep an eye on Ernie, will you, Anne?' she said, as they reached the school gates, and Charlie and Bob dragged the cart into the playground. 'He's not looking too clever this morning.'

Anne dredged up a smile, but it couldn't mask the haunted look in her eyes. 'Of course I will,' she said, 'but I suspect he's just a bit tired with all the excitement of Christmas coming.'

Sally would have liked to express her sympathy for the other girl, but realised that, as she wasn't supposed to know what had happened between her and Martin, it wouldn't be wise. If Anne felt the need to confide in her, then that would be the time to say something. With a wave to Ernie, she fished the shopping list out of her pocket and set off back down the road to the local shops and joined the long queue outside the butcher's.

Two hours later she arrived back at Beach View with three sausages, two chops and a pig's head. There was no sign of Peggy, and the sink was full of dirty crockery, so she dumped the basket on the kitchen table, put the meat in the larder and set about doing the washing-up.

'John Hicks telephoned while you were out,' said Peggy, arriving with an armful of laundry. 'He's coming to tea on Christmas Eve. I thought it would be less awkward for both of you if we all sat down together.'

Sally felt a thrill of pleasure, but firmly tamped down on it. 'I dunno,' she murmured. 'He's a lot older than me, and . . . well . . . What's a bloke like 'im want with a girl like me? We ain't got nothing in common.'

Peggy dumped the laundry on the table. 'Nonsense. John's a nice, ordinary chap who wants to get to know you better. And you're a lovely sweet girl who deserves to have a bit of a life. What's the harm in having tea?'

Sally shrugged and refused to meet Peggy's gaze.

'Did you overhear me and Anne last night?' Peggy put her hand on her shoulder, forcing Sally to look at her. 'Is that what all this is about?'

Sally shrugged again, unwilling to admit she'd been listening – and unwilling to voice the awful doubts that had woken her through the night.

'You silly girl,' said Peggy. 'John comes from a

working-class family, just like you. Having a bit of tea with us is a good way of seeing if you like the look of each other. What happens after that will be up to the pair of you. But if things develop between you and you're taken to meet his family, I can assure you there won't be any of the sort of nonsense my poor Anne had to go through.'

'I dunno,' said Sally again. 'I don't speak proper, even though I've been trying 'ard to change that, and I'm only . . .'

'That's quite enough,' said Peggy flatly. 'John knows who you are and where you come from and it doesn't matter a jot. Now,' she gathered up the laundry, 'I need a hand with this lot. We've actually got a pair of paying guests arriving this evening, and there's a lot to do before they arrive.'

Sally found it impossible to quell the hope and excitement as she helped Peggy scrub the bed linen in the big tub downstairs, wrestle it through the mangle, and hang it on the line. She found she was humming some silly tune as she prepared the room for the guests and decided that Peggy was right. What harm was there in agreeing to have tea with him?

'You look happy today, Sally.' Cissy had kicked off her shoes and was standing on a chair so that Sally could pin the hem of the lovely gown.

'It's nearly Christmas,' she replied. 'And I love Christmas. When Dad was at 'ome, we always had a goose and plum pudding, and a fruit cake with thick white icing swirled on top. It didn't happen every year, of course, but Dad's a good cook, and the smell coming from the kitchen on Christmas morning was always special.'

Cissy grimaced. 'I doubt there'll be much celebration this year,' she replied. 'What with the shortages and the blackout; but Mum's got a dozen plum puddings in the larder she's made over the years, so at least we'll have one of them.' She yawned. 'I'm just looking forward to having a day off. I'm absolutely shattered.'

Sally looked up at her in surprise. 'I thought you loved doing the shows?'

'Oh, I do, but it's exhausting with all the rehearsals and costume changes. We do two shows on Saturdays and Wednesdays, you know, and then there're all the extra ones for the troops.' She grinned, her weariness banished. 'We're doing a special show for the RAF boys on New Year's Eve. It's what the dress is for.'

'You look ever so lovely in it,' murmured Sally wistfully. 'They'll go potty when they see you. I wouldn't mind betting you'll be swamped in admirers.'

Cissy looked delighted at this. Then she bent down and whispered urgently, 'Sally, can you keep a secret?'

She rested back on her heels, looked up into the flushed, excited face, and grinned. 'Of course.'

Cissy stepped down from the chair, checked

the hallway and closed the door. 'I've got a solo spot that night,' she whispered. 'And our director said that Basil Dean and Leslie Henson would be in the audience scouting for talent.'

'Who are they?'

Cissy's eyes widened in shock. 'You don't know?' she breathed, forgetting that not everyone was as involved in the theatrical world as she. 'They're the ones who founded ENSA, and this could be my chance of getting into it.' Her eyes sparkled and her pretty little face took on a dreamy expression. 'Just think, Sally, this time next year I could be a star like Gracie Fields, or even Vera Lynn. She was voted the Forces' Sweetheart two months ago, you know,' she babbled, 'and even goes abroad to entertain the troops. Wouldn't it be wonderful if something like that happened to me?'

'Aren't you a bit young?' Sally said carefully, once Cissy stopped for breath.

Cissy shrugged and got back on the chair. 'I'd have to get Mum and Dad's permission,' she admitted, 'but I'm sure they'll give it. After all, there's a war on, and this is what I'm good at.'

Sally realised the girl was far too excited and wasn't thinking practically at all. She just hoped Cissy wouldn't be too devastated when Jim and Peggy refused to sign the consent form – which they would, she was certain.

Cissy fidgeted on the chair, making it impossible for Sally to continue pinning the hem. 'Oh, Sally,' she breathed. 'Who would have thought it? My life is about to change for ever, and soon all my dreams will come true.'

'You'd better stand still then,' said Sally through a mouthful of pins, 'or else this dress won't be finished in time.'

When Sally arrived for the afternoon shift at the factory, she delivered the last of the clothes she'd altered and mended. With several shillings jingling in her pocket, she sat at her work-station and looked around. There was no sign of Iris, but she could see Simmons bearing down on her with his usual dissatisfied glare.

'Miss Turner,' he snapped. 'A word.'

She looked up at him, her pulse racing. What on earth could she have done to make him so angry? 'Yes, Mr Simmons?'

'It has been noted that you are running some sort of business in company time,' he said. 'It has also been noted that certain of these items have been made from material stolen from company stock.'

Sally was so shocked it took a moment to react. 'I never stole nothing,' she protested, shoving back her chair and standing to face him squarely. 'How dare you accuse me of such a thing? All them clothes I made were out of scraps I bought in the town – and I only do private work at 'ome – never 'ere.'

'Then how do you explain this?' He held up a

jacket that had clearly been made of blue air-force serge.

Sally had become aware of the tense silence surrounding her as she eyed the poorly made garment dangling from his hand. 'That ain't my work,' she said firmly.

'Oh, I think it is,' he said smugly. 'It's obviously home-made, and you're the only one doing that around here.'

She snatched it from him and gave it a swift inspection. 'The seams are crooked, the lining ain't been hand-stitched at the hem or the cuffs, the buttonholes would make a schoolkid blush they're so bad, and the lapels don't even lay flat.' She handed it back to him. 'Where did you get this?'

'Never you mind.'

'Well, I do mind. That ain't my work, and whoever says it is, is lying.'

'I can vouch for that,' said Brenda, glaring through the smoke of the cigarette stuck to her bottom lip. 'Sally would never have made that thing, let alone pinched material from the stock to do it.'

A chorus of agreement went round the factory, and Simmons reddened. 'Be quiet, the lot of you,' he shouted. 'When I want your opinion, I'll ask for it. Get back to work.'

Sally folded her arms and glared at him, determined not to let him see how devastated she was to be accused of theft.

Once order had been restored on the factory floor,

Simmons returned her glare. 'There's no doubt the material came from here – therefore it's stolen. You're the one running a dressmaking business on the side, so it *has* to be you.'

Sally's angry tears were being held back by sheer force of will. 'It wasn't,' she said firmly. 'I'm not a thief.'

'Then prove it, Miss Turner, otherwise you will be dismissed.'

'You can't do that,' shouted Brenda. 'It's only three days to Christmas, and Sally's done nothing wrong.'

'If you don't button it, Brenda, you'll be out on your ear as well,' he snarled.

'I can't prove anything,' said Sally, her spirits plummeting. 'All I can do is show you some of my work so you can compare it to that terrible piece of workmanship, and see for yourself that I 'ad nothing to do with it.'

Almost before the sentence was finished, the things she'd delivered today were being brought to show Simmons.

He glared at each piece before ordering them back to their machines. 'I'll give you the benefit of the doubt this time,' he said coldly. 'But I'm watching you, Miss Turner, and if there is the slightest suspicion that you're up to no good, you'll be dismissed instantly.'

'You can watch all you like,' she retorted, 'but I ain't a thief.' She looked into those emotionless eyes and was tempted to tell him to stick his lousy job.

But being branded a thief made her so angry, she could barely think straight. Besides, she needed the money, and with this hanging over her, she'd never get a decent reference. She sat down and tried to thread the needle, but found to her distress that her hands were shaking and she could barely see through her tears.

'Never mind, ducks,' soothed Brenda when Simmons was out of earshot. 'We can all guess who's at the bottom of it – and, come what may, we'll make sure she gets her comeuppance.'

'But that won't clear my name, will it?'

'We'll see about that,' said Brenda, grimly mashing out her cigarette before getting back to work.

Sally had worked through her shift, eating her sandwiches and drinking her tea at her work-station, unwilling to be the focus of attention – for she knew the accusation was now the only topic amongst the other women.

And yet their sympathy and support was overwhelming, and as she left the factory that night, she was warmed by it. But, as she hurried through the dark streets, she couldn't dismiss the awful shame of being called a thief. It hung about her like a heavy cloud and followed her all the way home.

The house was quiet as she stepped into the hall, and she tiptoed up the stairs. All she wanted now was to climb into bed, pull the covers over her head, and hide from the world so she could at last give vent to her anger and despair.

Pushing open the bedroom door, she was startled to find Peggy sitting by Ernie's bed. All thoughts of her terrible situation fled. 'What is it? What's happened?'

'Don't worry, Sally.' Peggy rose from the chair, a finger to her lips as Sally raced to Ernie's bedside. 'He's asleep, and I don't want him disturbed.'

'What's the matter with him?' she whispered urgently, her gaze trawling the sleeping child for any sign of what could be wrong.

Peggy gently steered her on to the landing. 'He had a funny turn and the school doctor brought him home,' she whispered.

'What sort of funny turn?' Sally's pulse raced.

'He was complaining that his back and hips were hurting and, when he put his weight on his good leg, it gave way on him. He's got a graze on his cheek and a bit of a bump on his head, but neither is anything to get alarmed about.'

'Oh, my Gawd. You don't think the polio's come back, do you?'

Peggy shook her head. 'The doctor says he's just been overdoing things, and that he needs lots of rest. He's given him something to help him sleep, and suggests that we massage his joints every day to try and keep them supple and the pain at bay.'

Sally nodded. 'Yeah, I always gave him a good rub when he were aching. It seemed to help.' She looked at Peggy through her tears. 'You should have come and got me, Peg. Ernie's more important than bloody uniforms.'

'I suppose I should have,' she admitted on a sigh. 'But once the doctor had been, there seemed little point. Ernie wasn't in pain, and he soon fell asleep.' She dug in her apron pocket and brought out two bottles. 'I fetched the prescription from the chemist. He'll have to take these as well as the others from now on. They're to help build up his strength.' She held out the larger bottle. 'This is a special oil to massage him with. Use it sparingly, it's very expensive.'

Sally eyed the bottles, her spirits plummeting further. Ernie's medicines already took a fair chunk out of her earnings; now it looked as if she'd have to work even harder to make any savings. 'How much do I owe you?'

'Nothing,' Peggy said, with a dismissive wave of her hand.

'No, Peggy,' Sally said firmly. 'You've already done so much for me and Ernie, I insist you tell me.'

'Well, all right,' said Peggy reluctantly. 'But you don't have to give it all to me now. There's no rush.'

'I pay me debts, Peg. You'll 'ave it now.' Sally tiptoed into the bedroom, found the jar beneath her clothes in the dressing-table drawer and was about to hand over the coins when she saw the wheelchair. 'What's that doing 'ere?'

'Jim's got a mate at the hospital. It's on loan, so it didn't cost anything.'

Sally glanced down at the sleeping boy, handed the money to Peggy and chivvied her out of the room so they could talk without disturbing him. 'He don't need no wheelchair,' she hissed furiously.

'The doctor suggested it would be a good idea for when he got tired. He has to rest more, Sally. He's been trying to keep up with Bob and Charlie and has been doing far too much lately.'

'Ernie will hate it.' Sally was close to tears again. 'He might only be six, but he's very proud of his independence, and I've encouraged him. That's why 'e won't use his walking stick.'

Peggy sighed. 'If we can persuade him to use it, then perhaps he won't need the wheelchair quite so much.' She bit her lip. 'You see, the doctor explained that he's been putting too much pressure on his joints and the muscles simply aren't strong enough.'

'This is all my fault.' Sally fought the lump in her throat and the welling tears. 'I should've insisted he use the stick, and not encouraged him to do so much. I thought it would 'elp him get stronger.'

'You mustn't think that, Sally. Oh, my dear, there, there. Don't cry.' Peggy drew her gently into her motherly embrace and held her close.

Sally clung to her as the fear, exhaustion and sadness overwhelmed her. It was so good to feel the warmth and comfort of that embrace – so sustaining to know that someone cared, that she wasn't alone any more.

Once the storm was over, Sally dried her eyes and blew her nose. 'Sorry about that, but it all suddenly got too much.' She gave Peggy a watery smile. 'You're a diamond, Peg, and that's a fact.'

Peggy patted her cheek. 'If you need me, I'll be downstairs, and don't be afraid to wake me if Ernie's ill in the night. Just tap on my bedroom door. I'm a light sleeper.'

Sally wished her a good night and crept into her bedroom. Ernie was curled like a puppy beneath the blankets, his thumb plugged into his mouth, eyelashes fanning his pale cheeks. There was a bump on his forehead and a graze on his face, but he seemed to be sleeping soundly.

She washed and changed into her nightclothes and, with the eiderdown wrapped round her to ward off the chill, made herself comfortable in the armchair next to Ernie's bed.

As she watched him sleeping, she realised that – although he was still small for his age – he'd begun to fill out and look healthier, despite tonight's pallor. She knew for certain that it was good fresh air, regular meals and bedtimes that had brought about this change, and she could never thank Peggy enough for all she'd done over the past months. But it was a terrible worry that his joints had become painful again, and that his good leg had weakened, and she prayed the doctor had been right, and that the polio hadn't come back.

She eyed the wheelchair and could remember all too well the weeks he'd had to spend in an iron lung – and the following months when he'd needed nursing at home. Florrie had tried her best, but she'd soon got bored with the endless trips to the hospital, and the sleepless nights when he cried pitifully and would not be comforted.

Sally wearily rubbed her eyes. She had been barely eleven when she'd taken charge of Ernie's wellbeing and, although it had been lonely stuck indoors with a sick child, and she'd missed a good deal of school, it had had its rewards. Like when he took his first faltering steps with the calliper, and the day he ventured out to watch the other kids playing football in the street. The ball had come his way, and he'd kicked it back, earning a shout of praise that made him grin from ear to ear.

That had been the start of his recovery – and she could only hope that this was a minor setback and that he'd soon be riding Ron's shoulders again, and getting up to mischief with Charlie. Any other outcome didn't bear thinking about.

He stirred at three in the morning and she gently lifted him out and sat him on the pot before tucking him back in again. She lay on the single bed, curled round him and fell asleep until the alarm clock went off at six.

'Me legs 'urt, Sal,' he whimpered, as she sat him on the pot again.

'I've got some lovely oil the doctor gave me to give them a rub,' she soothed, putting him back to bed. 'And you'll get breakfast in bed as well, won't that be a treat?'

He nodded, but without much enthusiasm – and then saw the wheelchair. 'I ain't a spastic,' he said. 'I don't need no bloody wheelchair.'

'Language, Ernie. You know you mustn't swear.'

'Well I ain't using it,' he said stubbornly.

'But it'll be just like your crate-car,' she said with a brightness she didn't feel. 'Think about it, Ernie. It'll be all yours, and you'll be able to go everywhere in it, all wrapped up snug and comfortable. You'll be the envy of your mates at school.'

He thought about this for a moment. 'Suppose so,' he muttered. 'But only if I can 'ave flags and stuff on it.'

'I'll see what I can do.'

'They won't call me a spastic, will they? I 'ate it when they do that.'

'Who calls you that?' Sally watched him closely. 'Has someone been bullying you, Ernie?'

He refused to look at her. 'Just a couple of the big boys,' he admitted. 'They laugh and point at me, and when the teacher's not looking, they knock me down.'

'I'll have a word with Anne. She'll sort 'em out.' She brushed back his hair and softly kissed the bump on his head. 'Why didn't you say something before, Ernie? Anne or the headmaster would have stopped it straight away if only you'd said.'

He gave a great sigh. 'I didn't want a fuss,' he said. 'I can stick up for meself.'

'Of course you can.' She kissed him again. 'I'll go and get your breakfast now, so while I'm away, why don't you concentrate on what Santa might put in your stocking this year? Have you made your list yet?'

He shook his head. 'There ain't no point,' he muttered. 'It's always a bit of fruit, some nuts and a couple of sweets. Santa only brings good things when Dad's 'ome.'

'Well,' said Sally, thinking of the presents she'd hidden on top of the wardrobe, 'this year might be different, and you could be in for a surprise.'

'Is Mum coming for Christmas?' His voice was plaintive.

As there had been no word from her since they'd left London, Sally thought this highly unlikely. 'I don't think so, luv,' she said softly. 'It's a long way for 'er to come, and there is a war on, you know. The trains and that are all at sixes and sevens, and I don't think she'd be allowed to get a permit to come down anyway.'

His large brown eyes looked up at her. 'What's a permit?'

Sally took a deep breath. 'It's like a ticket,' she explained. 'And only a very few people are allowed to go from one town to another – especially down 'ere by the seaside.'

'Why?'

'Because Mr Chamberlain said we all got to stay in one place. I suppose it's to keep the spies out.' She closed the door before he could ask any further questions and hurried downstairs to the kitchen to make him a tray of breakfast.

'How is he this morning?' Peggy was busy at the stove.

'Full of questions, and feeling a bit sorry for himself,' said Sally, eyeing the pretty tray and best china.

'This is for the guests,' Peggy explained hurriedly. 'I did warn them that room service was extra, but they didn't seem to care.'

'If those two are married, I'll eat me hat, so I will,' muttered Ron, who was leaning against the sink to drink his tea and getting in Peggy's way.

Peggy laughed. 'Do you want it toasted or fried? They tied the knot at the Town Hall yesterday morning, and have the certificate to prove it.'

'War weddings, eh?' Jim looked over the top of the *Racing Post* he'd been reading at the table, and caught Peggy's eye. 'I remember what they were like.'

Peggy blushed and swiped the tea towel at him. 'Go and find something sensible to do, Jim Reilly. You could make a start by taking this in to Mrs Finch.' She handed him a plate of toast and boiled egg. 'Just make sure you pour her tea, otherwise she'll have it all over everything.'

'Yes, m'lady,' he said, giving a tug of his forelock before taking the plate and teapot.

She grinned at him. 'When you've done that, you can tape the windows again – the ones we've got left. And see if you can get any more plywood in case there's another explosion.'

'B'jesus, it's worse than being in the army. Orders, orders, orders,' he muttered good-naturedly as he headed for the dining room.

Sally set about boiling an egg and cooking toast for Ernie, while Peggy took the other tray to the guests on the first floor.

'Will you be staying home today, Sally?' she asked on her return to the kitchen.

'I'd like to,' she said hesitantly, glancing at Ron, 'especially now Ernie's not quite the ticket. But the thing is, there were a bit of trouble at work yesterday, and if I don't show me face, it won't help me case.'

Peggy eyed her sharply. 'What happened?'

Sally reluctantly told her as she smeared a wafer-thin layer of margarine on the toast and tapped the top of the egg. She still felt so ashamed that she couldn't look at Ron or Peggy. 'So, you see,' she said finally. 'I gotta go in, or they'll think I really did nick that material.'

'Of all the . . .' Peggy plumped down into a chair. 'Of course you must go. I'll come with you if it will be any help.'

210

'No,' she said hurriedly. 'I got to fight me own battles. And I'm determined to clear me name, no matter 'ow long it takes.'

Ron threw the dregs of his tea into the sink and slammed the mug on the wooden drainer. 'If it was up to me, I'd be banging a few heads round that factory. I've never heard such nonsense in my life.' He patted Sally's shoulder and gave her a warm smile. 'To be sure, no-one thinks bad of you here, girl,' he muttered.

'We'll look after Ernie for you,' Peggy said firmly. 'But if you have any more trouble at that factory, then let me know, and I'll be down at Goldman's like a shot to give that Simmons a piece of my mind.'

Sally gave her a hug. 'Thanks, but please don't, Peg. I'm not a kid any more and I'm used to dealing with men like Simmons.'

The words sounded brave, but Sally knew all too well that once Simmons had taken against her, her employment at Goldman's could be terminated at any minute. There were plenty of other jobs to be had, but sewing was what she knew, and what she was good at. She certainly didn't fancy working in a munitions factory.

Ernie ate his breakfast, getting crumbs and egg all over sheet. Sally cleaned him up and then carefully warmed a little of the sweet-smelling oil in her hands and began to gently massage his back and limbs.

He was almost asleep by the time she'd finished, and she gathered up her things and took one last look at him before she left for work. She hated leaving him like this, but had little option if she was to clear her name and keep her job. She just hoped the shift would run smoothly and there were no further upsets – she was too tired to cope with much more today.

Once the overnight honeymooners had gone, Peggy stripped the bed and remade it with fresh linen. They'd been a lovely young couple, and she wished them well, but with him flying Spitfires, and her working as a WAAF at the air-base, they had an uncertain future – but then none of them knew what the next day might bring.

Her thoughts went to Anne and Martin. Was it better to marry in defiance of everything his parents stood for and hope things would turn out all right? Or was Anne wise to break it off? Seeing her daughter's sad little face this morning she didn't think so.

The telephone was ringing as she reached the hall and she picked it up. 'Cliffehaven 329.'

'Mrs Reilly, this is Martin Black. Could I please speak to Anne?'

'Hello, Martin.' This was the fourth time he'd called and, so far, Anne had refused to speak to him. 'Anne's out,' she said truthfully.

'Mrs Reilly, I know what you must think of me,

but I love Anne, and if she'd only let me talk to her, I'm sure we can find some way out of this ghastly mess.'

'I'll tell her you called,' she said. 'But Martin,' she warned, 'don't be surprised if she doesn't ring back. She was very hurt.'

'I know. That's why it's so important I speak to her.' He was interrupted by the pips going. 'Damn, I'm out of coins, and I'll be cut off in a minute. Tell her I'm on duty all over Christmas so I won't be able to see her until the New Year. Please tell her I love her with all my heart, and that I still want to marry . . .' The pips drowned him out and the line went dead.

Peggy put down the receiver and sighed. Love was complicated enough without having to deal with toffee-nosed parents as well as the war. It just wasn't fair.

Sally held her head high as she marched past Simmons and took her place behind the sewing machine. She just wanted to get this shift over and go home to Ernie.

Brenda plumped down next to her. 'Cheer up, ducks,' she said, wrapping the scarf over her rollers. 'I'm calling a meeting with the girls over the tea break. We'll sort something out.'

'I don't want no more trouble,' muttered Sally.

'And there ain't gunna be any,' said Pearl, sitting on the other side of her.

'What you doing here? I thought you was on the lates this week?'

'I was. Then I 'eard about yer trouble and changed shifts.' She grinned. 'We're mates, ain't we? And mates stick together.'

Sally grinned back. It was good to know so many people believed in her and that, regardless of what happened next, she could always count on her friends.

She returned to Beach View feeling much more positive about things. The shift had gone quickly, Simmons had stayed away from her, and the cheerful, warm support of the other women had bolstered her spirits.

The kitchen still held the reminder of the evening meal and the warmth of the fire in the range. 'Hello, Peggy,' she said, taking off her coat. 'How's Ernie been?'

Peggy put down her knitting, poured her a cup of tea, and got the plate of supper she'd been keeping warm off the hob. 'He's been quite chirpy,' she said. 'He had a good long sleep after lunch, then I wrapped him up warm, and Ron and I took him for a ride in his wheelchair along the front.'

Sally held the teacup in her cold hands, relishing the warmth. 'He didn't make a fuss?'

Peggy shook her head. 'Ron warned him that, if he did, he wouldn't take him out with the dog and the ferrets again for at least a month. He was a bit put out about that,' she admitted with a soft smile, 'but his little face lit up when he saw what Ron and the boys had done to make his wheelchair more interesting.'

Sally grinned as she tucked into the stew Peggy had made from the pig's head. 'What did they do to it?'

'The boys had gone down to the gift shop and persuaded Mr Peters to dig out his summer stock of coloured windmills and those little Union Jacks that kiddies stick in their sandcastles. When they got back, they tied them on to the wheelchair and added some stickers they got with their comics.' She shook her head and smiled. 'Charlie even let him borrow his precious Cliffehaven Wanderers scarf as a special treat.'

'Blimey. That's a turn-up. Charlie don't let no-one near that usually.'

Peggy was still smiling as she picked up her knitting. 'He's had a good day,' she said comfortably, 'and is fast asleep now, so you can put your feet up and relax. It's nice to have a bit of company in the evenings.'

Sally sipped her tea, and finished the stew, slowly thawing out from the cold walk home. 'Where are the others?'

'Anne's gone to the pictures with Dorothy. Cissy's in her room sulking. She and Jim had a bit of a set-to over her wanting to join ENSA. He flatly refused to give his permission – and I agree with him whole-heartedly. She's only seventeen.'

'Poor Cissy,' murmured Sally. 'She were that excited. But I'm sure that once she calms down, she'll see you were right.'

Peggy eyed her over the knitting. 'So, she talked to you about it, did she?'

Sally nodded. 'She swore me to secrecy, so I couldn't say nothing – *anything* before.'

'Well, she's had her temper tantrum, slamming doors and stamping her feet like a five year old. If she's meant to be a star on the stage then it will happen – but not until she's twenty-one,' she said evenly.

Sally thought it wise to change the subject. 'I suppose Ron's at the pub?'

'Either that or playing soldiers again.' She put down her knitting and stared thoughtfully into the fire. 'He's been acting a bit mysteriously just lately, and I suspect he's up to something he shouldn't be . . .' She grinned and continued knitting. 'I don't know why that should bother me – Ron's always up to something, and I don't expect him to change the habits of a lifetime just because there's a war on.'

'He's been ever so good with Ernie. Like a real granddad. We never knew ours; he died before we was born, and with Dad away most of the time, it's been 'ard for Ernie not 'aving a man about the place.'

Peggy concentrated on turning the heel of the sock she was knitting. 'Talking of having a man about the place, I'm looking forward to seeing Alex again on Christmas Day,' she murmured. 'Let's hope there aren't any raids and he can get away.'

Sally finished her tea, washed up and stifled a vast yawn. 'I'm for me bed, Peg. Goodnight.' She kissed the other woman's cheek and hurried upstairs.

Ernie was asleep, the wheelchair parked beside his bed. It was festooned in flags, and windmills, and someone had pegged playing cards to the spokes of the wheels so that when it moved, it would make as much noise as a Spitfire.

Sally washed and climbed into bed, snuggling beneath the blankets, her thoughts for once not occupied by Ernie, or the trouble at work, but focused on Christmas Eve. John Hicks would be arriving at about six, and she hadn't decided what she would wear. She still hadn't by the time she fell asleep.

It was raining hard the next morning, and Sally had left Ernie playing cards with the others at the kitchen table while Peggy baked a cake with the last of the eggs and butter, and Mrs Finch knitted something unrecognisable in the chair by the rather dismal fire. The coal was running out and Jim had warned there would be no more until fresh supplies were delivered to the merchant on the other side of town. Ron had immediately set off with a big sack and his axe, promising to bring home some wood.

Work had proceeded smoothly, with no sign of Simmons, which was a relief. When the whistle went for the break, Sally and Pearl were heading for the canteen when Simmons appeared at the door and called Sally back.

'The boss wants to see you,' he said, his gaze not quite meeting hers.

Sally glanced at Pearl and tried to swallow the lump in her throat. Was this the dreaded moment when she'd be given the sack? 'Mr Goldman wants to see me?'

'That's what I said,' he replied impatiently. 'What's the matter with your hearing, girl?'

She shot another glance at Pearl, who gave her a sympathetic smile, and followed Simmons in silence as they headed for the main office.

Marjorie was sitting behind the desk, thumping the typewriter keys as if she needed to vent her fury on something and they were the nearest object. She looked up, glanced at Sally and pushed back her chair. 'I'll let Mr Goldman know you're here,' she said stiffly.

Sally waited nervously, and found she was trembling as she was shown into the boss's office alongside Simmons.

'Sit down Sally,' he said without preamble. 'Mr Simmons has something to say to you.' He glared at Simmons, who cleared his throat before speaking.

'It seems I've made a mistake,' he said, gaze firmly fixed to a point beyond her shoulder.

Sally said nothing. It was obvious he was terrified of Goldman and hated having to admit he'd been in the wrong, but she wasn't about to help him out of this.

'Another woman was responsible for the theft,' he said, 'and she has been dismissed.'

'That isn't an apology, Simmons,' snarled Goldman. 'This girl's character has been put into question, and she has no doubt suffered some distress over your false accusations. You will say you're sorry and damned well mean it.'

'I'm sorry, Miss Turner. Truly.' He looked flustered and Sally actually felt a dart of sympathy for him. 'Please accept that I was merely acting on the evidence I had before me. I shouldn't have believed the worst of you.'

'Thank you,' she said quietly, swallowing the desire to tell him to get his facts right before he started throwing around accusations about innocent people.

'You can go now, Simmons,' rasped Goldman. 'I wish to have a private word with Miss Turner.'

Sally remained poker-stiff in the chair. She didn't like the sound of this at all. What was Goldman up to?

He waited until the door had closed behind the other man and then sat down in his enormous leather chair. 'I've been keeping a close eye on you, Miss Turner – and I must say I was shocked when Simmons told me what you'd been accused of.'

Sally stared at him, unable to think of anything to say.

'You can thank the other women you work with

that your name has been cleared. They suspected who the culprit was and made sure she owned up.'

'It was Iris, weren't it?'

'I'm not at liberty to say,' he replied gruffly. 'It appears the culprit stole quite a bit of material over the past weeks, and has been making these questionable garments and selling them on some market stall. The police are investigating the matter as we speak.'

Sally should have felt more relaxed now her name had been cleared and the culprit brought to book, but she was still wary of Goldman's motives. Bosses had the reputation for taking liberties – and if he expected her to show him more gratitude than she was willing to give, then he'd got the wrong girl.

He lit a fat cigar and puffed on it for a moment before eyeing her through the smoke. 'Your work is exemplary, Miss Turner – as my brother-in-law, Mr Solomon, told me it would be in his letter. Therefore I would like to offer you the position of line-manager. It will, of course, mean a pay rise, but I'm sure you won't object to that.' He gave her a ghost of a smile.

She stared at him, unable to believe she was hearing right. Swiftly pulling her scrambled thoughts together, she smiled back. 'Thanks ever so,' she said breathlessly, 'but will it mean working longer hours? Only I've got me brother to look after and . . .'

'I know all about your circumstances, Miss Turner, and am quite prepared to let you work the same hours as now. But it will mean more responsibility,' he added, his gaze piercing the cigar smoke. 'Are you sure you're not too young to handle it?'

Sally at last relaxed. 'Old head on young shoulders, that's me, Mr Goldman,' she said brightly. 'I won't let you down.'

'I don't doubt it for a minute,' he murmured, the smile lurking again. 'And to make up for the distress you've been caused, you can take tomorrow off with pay, and enjoy your Christmas. Marjorie has your pay packet ready. I'll see you bright and early on the twenty-seventh.'

Sally left the office in a daze, the pay packet snug in her apron pocket. She couldn't wait to tell Pearl and Brenda.

But it seemed her good news had travelled fast, for as she walked into the canteen she was greeted with a round of applause and shouts of, 'Well done, Sal.' Red-faced and laughing, she joined in the celebrations with a cup of tea before they all had to get back to their machines.

Life was full of promise for Sally that evening and, as she walked home three hours later along the slick, wet pavements of a silent, rainy Cliffehaven, she finally felt she belonged.

Chapter Nine

It was at last Christmas Eve and the whole house was scented with festive cooking. Sally had finally managed to have a quiet word with Anne over the bullying at school, and felt some relief that, once school began again, Ernie would be guarded more closely in the playground.

Pearl arrived mid-morning and Anne kept Ernie amused and out of the way while the two girls shut themselves in Sally's bedroom, discussing what she should wear for the tea party. She didn't really have much to choose from, as she'd had little time to make clothes for herself over the past weeks, but by the time Pearl had to leave for work, they'd decided on the lace blouse and fitted navy skirt.

After helping Peggy with the lunch, and making sure Ernie was fully occupied, Sally had returned upstairs late that afternoon to have a bath and wash her hair in the lovely shampoo Peggy had loaned her. Rubbing it dry with a towel, she attempted to bring order to the dark-blonde curls, but, as usual, they seemed to have a mind of their own, and she'd had to resort to the combs again.

Carefully stepping into the freshly ironed skirt,

she smoothed it over her hips and pulled on the blouse which she tucked into the waistband. A navy belt she'd salvaged from a dress went perfectly, the pretty buckle gleaming in the sunlight coming through the window.

It was going to be all right, she kept telling herself, as she hung the navy sweater over her shoulders just like Anne did. The rain had stopped, the sun had come out, she'd wrapped all her Christmas presents – and John Hicks would be here soon.

She gasped in horror as she looked at the clock. He'd be here any minute, and she hadn't done a thing to help Peggy with the tea. Ramming on the sturdy shoes which spoilt the whole effect, she ran downstairs to the kitchen.

'You look lovely,' said Peggy.

'Yes, you do, and I have the perfect earrings you can borrow.' Anne hurried away as Peggy checked on the steaming Christmas pudding and finished dusting the cake with the last of the icing sugar.

'That looks delicious,' said Sally, her mouth watering.

'It's only sponge,' she said ruefully. 'I couldn't find any dried fruit for love nor money, so there won't be a proper Christmas cake this year. Thank goodness I have a store of plum puddings.'

She turned from the cake and dug into a box that was sitting on the kitchen chair. 'I hope these will fit, Sally, but I thought you'd like something a bit more glamorous than those you're always wearing.'

Sally gasped as she pulled out a stylish pair of navy and white shoes. They were of the softest leather, with an elegant heel, and a bow just above the peep-toe. 'Oh, Peggy,' she breathed. 'Are you sure? They look brand new.'

'They were a gift from my sister Doris, last Christmas,' she said, 'but as I don't go anywhere to wear them, they sit in the cupboard untouched. You may keep them if you like.'

Sally couldn't stop grinning. It seemed Christmas had already arrived. Carefully easing her bare feet into the shoes, she discovered they fitted perfectly. 'I feel like Cinderella,' she said, and laughed as she tottered on the heels and had to steady herself.

'As long as that doesn't make me one of the ugly sisters,' laughed Anne, returning to the kitchen. She handed Sally a pair of clip-on earrings. 'They aren't real pearls,' she said, 'and they might pinch a bit after a while. But they're the finishing touch you need for that outfit.'

Sally put on the earrings and studied the effect in the glassed portrait of the King and Queen that hung above the range mantelpiece. 'I look very grown-up,' she breathed.

'You look like a very pretty sixteen-year-old girl who's having a bit of fun for a change,' said Peggy. 'Now, perhaps we can get on and finish putting out the tea.'

Sally rushed to help, carefully balancing on the unfamiliar high-heeled shoes that forced her to move more slowly – and, she hoped, as elegantly as Anne and Cissy. Carrying the plates of sandwiches into the dining room, she thought she'd never seen it look so lovely.

The heavy curtains had been drawn and in the bay window stood a fir tree decorated with shiny baubles and tinsel, its clean, winter-pine smell mingling with the sweet burning apple-wood in the hearth. There was more tinsel draped over the picture frames, and long, colourful paper chains festooned the ceiling. The boys had been busy making them over the past three days.

The mantelpiece had been decorated with holly, candles and trailing ivy – and with three red felt stockings, each embellished by Sally with ribbon that spelled out each boy's name. The sewing machine had been tucked into a corner to make room for two more comfortable chairs, and Ernie's wheelchair was festooned with balloons and yet more silver tinsel.

The six small tables had been firmly wedged together, and were now covered with a crisp white cloth that had crocheted lace at the hem. In the centre was a bowl of artfully arranged holly, mistletoe and ivy. The best china was set out, and there were white paper napkins with pictures of holly on them on each side-plate.

Sally gazed in awe at everything. This would be a real Christmas, with a real family, so very far removed from the ones at home when Dad wasn't around. No wonder Ernie was so excited. 'You've been ever so busy, Peggy. It all looks wonderful, and I'm sorry I haven't been much use today.'

'I didn't expect you to be,' she replied, putting down a plate of scones and rearranging the pots of jam. 'Anyway, I had Anne and Cissy to help, and that was quite enough, what with Jim and Ron getting under my feet.'

She moved the central floral display half an inch to the left. 'Put the cake there, Anne,' she ordered, 'and mind you keep room for the teapot. I'll just go and get the sausage rolls.'

'Sausage rolls?' said Anne. 'How did you get hold of sausage meat, and enough fat for pastry, when you used the last for the cake?'

There was a pink flush to Peggy's face as she avoided her daughter's eyes. 'I swapped a tin of fruit salad for the extra marg with one of the neighbours. Your dad brought the sausage meat home last night along with a nice fat capon. As I needed all of it for the next couple of days, I didn't ask where he got them.'

'Someone mention my name?' Jim strolled into the dining room with Mrs Finch clinging to his arm. He carefully helped her into the armchair by the tree, and handed her the bag of knitting.

'You've been at it again, haven't you, Dad?' hissed Anne. 'If you get caught, you'll have all of us in trouble.'

'Now, then, Annie me darling, don't you be fretting

your pretty head about a bit of sausage and an old chicken. To be sure the butcher was glad to give them in exchange for a couple of hares.'

'If you believe that, you'll believe anything,' muttered Peggy. 'Ron hasn't been out for at least three days, so where those hares were supposed to come from, I don't know.'

'Can I bring these boys in now?' said Cissy plaintively from the doorway. 'Only I'm sick of being stuck down in the basement with them, and they refuse to listen to a word I say.'

Without waiting for permission, Bob and Charlie dashed into the room. Cissy put Ernie carefully on his feet, and gave him his walking stick.

He eyed it with loathing and dropped it to the floor before hobbling over to the tree. His eyes shone as he stared at it in wonderment. 'Cor,' he breathed. 'I ain't never seen one that big before.'

Then he caught sight of the stocking with his name on it over the fireplace, and almost tripped over the rug in his eagerness to reach it. 'Will Santa really come?'

'Of course he will,' said Sally. 'Come on, Ernie, you promised you'd sit still and be good.' She carried him to the wheelchair and plonked him down before handing him a comic.

He eyed her solemnly. 'You look different,' he said. 'And them shoes ain't yours.'

Sally was saved from having to reply by an urgent chorus from the other two boys. 'Can't we have tea yet? Why do we have to wait?'

The demands fell on deaf ears as Peggy made them sit on the floor with their books. 'You'll stay there and mind your manners,' she said sternly, 'otherwise there will be no cake.'

'You look very glamorous, Sally,' murmured Cissy, taking in the shoes and clothes. 'But you could do with a bit of make-up to bring out your eyes. I can do it for you if you like?'

'Oh, I dunno,' replied Sally. 'D'you think I should? Only I feel a bit overdone as it is, and I only got a bit of one of Mum's old lipsticks.'

'Quite right, Sal,' said Jim. 'You've the looks of a film star about you today. You'll not be needing powder and paint.' He shot his youngest daughter a glance, taking in the mascara, rouge and lipstick.

Cissy didn't seem at all put out as she sank gracefully into the other armchair and proceeded to arrange her pleated skirt and pale pink cardigan to her satisfaction. With a cautious pat to her bright blonde head, she turned her attention to the latest *Picturegoer* magazine.

Ron sauntered into the room with a very muddy Harvey. He was still dressed in his poacher's coat and cloth cap, but at least he'd taken off his boots. 'Is the tea ready, Peggy? Sure, and I'm spitting feathers.'

She eyed him in horror. 'Not until you've taken the dog downstairs, got rid of that coat and cap and had a wash,' she said, and sighed with exasperation. 'Honestly, Ron, we've got a visitor coming, and just look at you.'

'I thought it was young John coming, not the blooming King,' he muttered. 'I've known that boy since he was in nappies. He'll not be minding a bit of honest dirt.'

'Well I do,' she retorted. 'Out – the pair of you.' She advanced on them, and Harvey was the first to beat a hasty retreat, Ron hard at his heels.

Sally hurried to fetch the dustpan and brush, and was sweeping up the muddy paw-prints from the rug when the doorbell rang. She scurried back to the kitchen. 'Oh, Gawd,' she muttered, stowing them in the cupboard under the sink. 'I don't know if I can do this.'

Ron's face and hair were wet from his vigorous ablutions at the sink. He reached for the kitchen towel and rubbed himself dry. 'Last-minute nerves, eh?' He chuckled. 'I remember the first time I went over the top. Nerves were jumping so bad I thought I'd pee in me pants, so I did. Did I ever tell you how I got me shrapnel?'

'I see nothing's changed, Ron.' The amused voice came from the doorway. 'Still going on about that war you won single-handedly, eh?' John Hicks stepped into the kitchen, his dark hair glistening with raindrops, the heavy raincoat soaked at the shoulders.

'You're looking well, John, so you are. It's been a while, me boy.' Ron pumped his hand enthusiastically as he grinned up at him.

John's gaze drifted beyond the older man and

settled on Sally with dark blue intensity for a moment before he returned his attention to Ron. 'I've got something for you, Ron,' he said, digging into the deep pocket of his raincoat. 'I hope you're still smoking this rough old stuff.'

'Well, I'll be . . .' Ron took the roll of tobacco and set about filling his pipe. 'I always said you were a good boy, John. God bless your soul.'

Sally saw Peggy scuttle back into the dining room, and watched the scene nervously, waiting for the moment when John could give her his full attention. She didn't have to wait long.

'Hello Sally Turner,' he said, that long-lashed blue gaze settling on her again. 'I brought you something too. Call it an early Christmas present.'

'Oh,' she said nervously. 'You shouldn't 'ave done that. I ain't . . . haven't got nothing for you.'

He dug in another pocket and handed her a square parcel neatly wrapped in Christmas paper. 'I didn't expect you to,' he said lightly, 'but you're not to unwrap that until tomorrow.' He gazed down at her. 'You look lovely,' he murmured.

Sally blushed and couldn't think straight with him looking at her like that. She clasped his gift, longing to open it – but full of remorse that she had nothing to give in return. After a moment of agonising silence, she finally remembered her manners. 'Your coat's soaked through,' she managed. 'Let me hang it up.'

He untied the belt on the navy gabardine

mackintosh and undid the buttons before dragging it off. 'It's a heavy old thing when it gets wet,' he said, draping it over the chair by the range, and rooting about once more in the pockets.

He pulled out a bottle of rum, three candy-striped paper bags, and four small wrapped parcels. 'I feel like Father Christmas,' he said. 'I hope I've remembered everyone.'

'If those are what I think they are,' she said, eyeing the paper bags, 'then the boys will be thrilled. You are kind,' she finished softly.

'I like Christmas,' he replied, 'and I especially like the way your eyes light up with gold flecks when you're smiling.'

Sally heard Ron snort and didn't know where to look. 'Flattery will get you nowhere,' she stammered.

'I have to do something to get you to notice me,' he murmured.

She looked up at him and grinned. 'Oh, I think you've already done enough,' she replied, 'what with pulling me under benches and tripping me up on rubble.'

'Sorry about that, but if you will keep getting into dangerous situations, what's a man to do?'

She had no answer to this and was quite relieved when the moment was broken by Jim's hearty voice.

'Well, John, and it's good to see you.' They shook hands, and Jim's eyes widened as he was handed the rum. He gave a low whistle. 'You obviously have better contacts than me, son. I haven't seen this much rum for months.'

'It was a gift from a grateful householder who had a chimney fire.'

Jim patted the bottle and grinned. 'To be sure and we'll have a good tot of this before the night's out. Come away in and set you down. The others are waiting.'

John glanced over his shoulder and gave Sally a wink as Jim steered him forcefully across the hall and into the dining room. Sally clutched her present and followed them, Ron's clumping footsteps close behind her.

Peggy kissed John's cheek in thanks as he handed her one of the little parcels, and asked after his parents. Cissy and Anne thanked him prettily, and Mrs Finch blushed like a young girl as John handed her the small gift and wished her a Happy Christmas. Bob and Charlie were getting overexcited and demanded to be allowed to eat their sweets immediately.

'All the presents are going under the tree until tomorrow,' said Peggy, gathering them back again and trying to be stern. 'And that goes for yours as well, Sally.'

She realised she'd been clutching the parcel to her chest, and hastily placed the precious gift beneath the sweet-smelling branches as John approached Ernie.

'Hello, Ernie,' he said quietly, hunkering down so they were on the same level. 'You don't know me, but my name's John. And these are for you – but you'd better do what Peggy says, or I'll be in a whole heap of trouble. And we don't want that at Christmas, do we?'

Ernie solemnly shook his head, his large brown eyes fixed on John. He was clearly torn between excitement and doubt. 'Are you Sal's boyfriend?'

'Of course not,' said Sally hastily.

John just smiled and kept his focus on Ernie. 'Not yet,' he replied, 'but I'd like to be.' He leant in a little closer, his voice low. 'I think I'm going to need your help, young Ernie,' he confided. 'You see, your sister isn't at all sure she likes the look of me yet.'

Sally could feel the heat in her face as everybody watched the little scene.

Ernie eyed him closely. 'You look all right to me,' he muttered. His eyes brightened and he grinned. 'Are you really a fireman? Have you got yer engine outside? Can I 'ave a ride on it?'

'I haven't got it with me today,' he replied carefully, 'but perhaps I can arrange for you, Bob and Charlie to visit the fire station and have a go at riding it and ringing the bell. How would you like that?'

'Cor,' breathed Ernie. 'Really?'

'Yes, really,' he replied, swiftly glancing at Sally to make sure she approved. 'But you might have to wait a while, we get very busy sometimes.' He stood and grasped the wheelchair handles. 'Come on, Ernie, let's put those sweets under the tree, and then we can all tuck into what looks like a smashing tea.'

Sally sat on one side of Ernie, John the other and, as the conversation swirled around her, she shot surreptitious glances at him. He was certainly handsome, and had a lovely way with him. Ernie was clearly in the throes of hero worship, and Mrs Finch was actually flirting with him. He seemed very much at ease, and Sally liked the way he kept bringing her into the conversation, talking of things she would know about, asking her opinion and seeming to value it. He was courteous, never overstepping the mark, but when his steady gaze held hers a fraction longer than necessary, she could read something in his eyes that made her feel all trembly inside.

She pondered on all this as she ate the delicious tea and, when the meal was over, she helped clear the table and do the dishes while the three men challenged the boys to a raucous game of snakes and ladders.

'So?' Peggy put the last of the dishes back in the cupboard. 'What do you think of him?'

'He's nice,' she replied softly.

'Yes, he is, isn't he?' Peggy took off her apron and smiled. 'He clearly thinks rather a lot of you too.'

'Really?' Sally felt a surge of happiness that someone as special as John Hicks might actually like the look of her.

'Oh, yes.' She dumped the apron on the table, took John's steaming coat from the chair and hung it on the hook behind the door. 'Now, come on Sally, enough of this idle chitchat. Those boys are going to have to go to bed soon, and I doubt they'll go willingly after so much excitement. I don't know about you, but I could do with a drop of that rum and a few minutes with my feet up.'

One board game had led to another until all the boys were thoroughly overexcited. Peggy called a halt to the proceedings when Bob started accusing Charlie of cheating, and dragged the pair of them downstairs to their beds.

'It's way past your bedtime, young man,' Sally said quietly to Ernie, who'd been fighting sleep for at least the last hour. 'Say goodnight, and thank John for his present.'

'Thanks ever so,' he said. 'Will you carry me upstairs? Sal says I'm getting too 'eavy, and I don't wanna be dropped on me 'ead.'

Sally was about to protest when John hoisted the boy over his shoulder in a fireman's lift and carried him into the hall. 'Which way?'

'Two flights up, middle door.'

John ran up the stairs with Ernie squealing in delight and clinging tightly to John's white shirt. Sally followed more slowly and, when she entered the bedroom, she found the pair of them sitting on the edge of the bed grinning up at her.

'You both look as if you've been up to no good,'

she said, and laughed. 'And don't think you're getting out of having a proper wash just because it's Christmas, Ernie Turner.'

'See,' said Ernie with a grimace. 'I told you she was bossy.'

'Sisters, eh?' He ruffled the boy's hair before getting to his feet. 'I'll leave you to it, Sally,' he said. 'Unless you want a hand?'

'Yeah, yeah.' Ernie bounced on the bed. 'I want John to put me to bed.'

'I think you've had enough excitement for one day,' she said firmly. 'I'll see you downstairs, John.'

Once Ernie was washed, she massaged him, soothing the tender muscles in rhythmic sweeps, calming the little boy until his eyelids fluttered and he fell into a deep sleep.

Kissing him softly, she tucked the bedclothes round his shoulders and crossed the room. She studied her appearance in the wardrobe mirror, and realised with shock that her eyes were shining and her skin glowed. For once in her life she actually looked pretty.

'Probably the effect of that glass of rum,' she muttered. Cross with herself for letting her excitement get the better of her, she snapped off the light, left the door ajar so she could hear if Ernie called for her, and hurried downstairs.

The bottle of rum had been enthusiastically shared as the three men discussed the phoney war that had yet to really show its teeth, and the frustrating lack of information coming from the government. No-one really knew anything, and as the months had passed with little evidence of any real or lasting attacks on the capital, a great many evacuees had returned to London and people had carried on their ordinary lives. It was the general consensus that, despite the awful things happening in Europe and the Baltic States, where their troops were doing sterling battle against the enemy, the British Isles seemed to have been forgotten.

John prepared to leave shortly after Sally came down from seeing to Ernie. He said goodnight to everyone, and Peggy ordered Jim and Ron to get on with drinking their rum and talking nonsense while Sally saw him to the door.

Sally followed him into the kitchen and watched as he wrestled into the thick mackintosh. 'Thanks for everything,' she said. 'It's been ever so nice to get to know you, and Ernie's that excited about your fire engine. He'll be on about it for days.'

'It was my pleasure,' he murmured, as they walked slowly to the front door. 'I'll see if I can get something sorted within the week. It wouldn't be fair to keep him waiting too long.'

Sally reluctantly reached for the doorknob. The evening was over, and she wanted so much to see him again – but, as he hadn't suggested it, she supposed she'd just have to wait until he invited them all to the fire station.

He stilled her hand as she went to turn the door-knob. 'Can I see you again?'

Sally could feel the warmth of his hand, and the tingle that went up her arm. She looked up at him and saw the earnest appeal in his mesmerising eyes. 'If you'd really like to,' she replied shyly.

'Perhaps you'll let me buy you that cup of tea I offered the first time we met?'

'That would be nice.'

He smiled down at her as he opened the door. 'Good night, Sally Turner,' he murmured. 'I'll sleep well tonight and dream of those gold flecks in your lovely eyes.'

She giggled. 'Get away with yer,' she spluttered. 'You do talk soft.'

'I know. Silly isn't it?' He blew her a kiss and ran down the steps into the teeming rain.

Sally could hear his happy whistle long after he'd been lost in the darkness, and she closed the door, daring to dream that maybe, just maybe, she might, after all, have the chance of a less lonely future than she'd always envisaged.

Ernie woke her in the middle of the night, crying because his back and legs were aching. Sally ran down to the kitchen to fill a stone hot-water bottle; wrapping it in a towel, she got him to snuggle up to it while she massaged him back to sleep.

Lying in the darkness, she could hear the church bells calling people to Midnight Mass. It was almost

Christmas Day. She turned off the bedside light and opened the curtains.

The sky was as black as velvet, studded with twinkling stars, and she could see the frost dusting the rooftops like icing sugar. Staring out at the heavenly display, she wondered what her parents were doing. Florrie was probably out dancing, but Dad would be at sea, perhaps looking at the same stars. She hoped he was thinking of her and Ernie, and she wished with all her heart that he could be here for Christmas.

Sally closed the curtains, checked on Ernie and climbed into her bed. There had been no word from him, and she had to hope he was all right. Comforting herself with the thought that Florrie probably hadn't told him where they were, and that he'd come to visit as soon as he could, she closed her eyes and let her mind wander through the day, and the little scene on the doorstep.

With a soft smile of contentment, she was soon asleep.

Christmas Day started with the boys rushing up from the basement to bang on their parents' bedroom door demanding to be allowed to open their presents. Once everyone was awake and dressed, they converged in the dining room with their cups of tea to watch the boys plunder their stockings.

Sally could feel the tears prick as Ernie pulled out a comic, socks and scarf, sweets, marbles and a toy gun. His little face was pink with pleasure, his eyes sparkling despite the disturbed night's sleep. 'This is a smashing Christmas, ain't it Sal?' he breathed, waving the gun and pretending to shoot Mrs Finch.

'Yeah, luv, it's the best,' murmured Sally.

'Can we stay 'ere for ever and ever?'

Sally ruffled his hair and forced a smile. 'Maybe not for ever and ever,' she said softly, 'but for a while yet.'

Peggy must have noticed his little face crumple. 'I know, Ernie,' she said brightly. 'Why don't you and I find everyone's present from under the tree? Then you can help me hand them out.' She took his little hand and Ernie happily went with her.

These people are so good, thought Sally. They've taken us in and given us a real home – loved Ernie and me as if we were their own. I can't bear the thought that one day we'll have to go back to Bow.

'Here we are,' said Peggy, breaking into her thoughts. 'I thought you'd like to open this one first.'

Sally blinked back her tears and carefully unwrapped the pretty paper from the square box John had given her the night before. She gasped with surprise and pleasure as she took out the neat, cream leather bag. It looked expensive and smelled wonderful, and tucked under her arm so neatly, it was as if it had been made for her. On closer inspection, she discovered it was lined with black rayon, and there was a zipped compartment which held a mirror set in a frame of the same leather. His card nestled at the bottom of the bag.

I hope you have a lovely Christmas. Try not to get any bullet-holes in this! Looking forward to seeing you again in the New Year,
John.

Sally rescued the handbag from Ernie's sticky fingers and tucked it beside her in the chair – the feel of it against her hip was the next best thing to actually seeing him.

There were other presents to open and the dining-room floor was soon littered with paper, bits of string and ribbon as each one was admired and cooed over. John had given a bottle of lavender water to Mrs Finch, a powder compact to Cissy, and a pair of gloves to Anne. For Peggy there was a bottle of her favourite lily of the valley perfume. Each of the boys had at least a bob's worth of sweets, which Peggy had to ration, afraid they wouldn't eat the lunch which was already cooking in the kitchen and sending delicious smells all through the house.

Sally opened each gift, the tears blinding her. There was a beautiful pale lilac sweater from Peggy, woollen gloves from Anne, a deep red lipstick from Cissy, and a cosy dressing gown from Ron and Jim which matched the warm slippers from Mrs Finch. 'I don't know how to thank you all,' she said in the lull after everything had been opened, 'but this is the best Christmas I've ever 'ad, and I love you all for making it so special for me and Ernie.'

Peggy sat on the arm of the chair and gave her a hug. 'It wouldn't have been the same without you,' she murmured.

They were interrupted by a furious banging on the front door, which was followed by a lengthy ring on the bell.

'Who the hell's that on Christmas morning?' Jim said crossly. He stomped out of the room and everyone stilled, trying to make sense of the murmured conversation going on in the hall.

Sally dared to hope it might be John but, as Martin Black strode into the room, magnificently heroic in leather flying jacket and boots, she hardly felt any disappointment at all.

'Anne, I had to come. I couldn't leave things the way they were. I had to see you, talk to you, make you realise that I don't care a damn for what my parents think. I want to marry you, and I won't take no for an answer.'

Anne had gone quite pale, now the colour flooded into her face. 'What are you doing here?' she breathed. 'You're supposed to be on duty.'

'The other chaps are covering for me,' he replied impatiently. 'I only have an hour, and we need to talk, Anne. Please?'

'You'll get into the most fearsome trouble,' she said, the tears sparkling on her lashes. 'Oh, Martin, what have you done?'

'I've fallen in love,' he said evenly. 'And I don't care about anything right this minute, but you.' He fell to one knee, dug in the pocket of his flying jacket and held out a diamond ring. 'Will you marry me, Anne? Will you make me the happiest man in England?'

Sally thought it was the most romantic thing she'd seen outside the cinema, and waited, almost as impatiently as Martin, for Anne's answer.

Anne clearly didn't have the same sense of romance as Sally. 'Get up,' she hissed, shooting a glance at the others and reddening further.

'Not until you give me your answer.'

She shook her head and backed away from him. 'Then, I'm sorry, Martin. The answer is no. I won't be rushed into this.'

Sally could see by his expression that he was devastated by her turning him down, and she felt a deep pang of pity for him.

'But you'll think about it? You won't just finish things between us? I couldn't bear it if you did, Anne.'

Her stance softened and she smiled. 'I'll think about it, I promise,' she murmured. 'Now please get off your knee; you look very silly down there surrounded by wrapping paper.'

He suddenly seemed to realise they had an enthralled audience, that it was Christmas morning and he was probably making a complete ass of himself. He rose shamefacedly to his feet, clutching the peaked air-force officer's hat under his arm.

'I'm sorry for breaking in like this so early on Christmas morning,' he said to the room in general. 'But I had to see Anne. I can't sleep, can't eat – don't have a sensible thought in my head.'

He took Anne's hand and made her blush again as he kissed her fingers. 'This very special, beautiful lady is the only one for me, and I'm determined that one day she will accept my ring and be my wife.'

'Then you've got some talking to do – in private,' said Peggy. 'Come on you lot, you can help me in the kitchen. Alex should be here soon, so when he comes, Cissy, bring him straight in to me. We don't want him seeing Martin when he's not supposed to be here.'

'Are we playing charades?' Mrs Finch trilled. 'How lovely. But what's the play? I don't recognise it.'

Peggy gave an exasperated sigh. 'Jim, stop trying to look like an outraged father and help Mrs Finch out of her chair.'

'Oh, dear,' chirped Mrs Finch, as Jim carefully hoisted her to her feet. 'Is the game over already?'

'No, bless you,' muttered Jim. 'I'm thinking it's only just started.'

The telephone rang and Peggy rushed to answer it. Her face lit up and she settled in for a long chat. It was her sister Doreen.

Sally gathered up her gifts and wheeled Ernie into the kitchen. She thought Martin was extremely dashing, just like Clark Gable whose photograph she'd seen in Cissy's film magazines – and he and Anne made the perfect couple. Now Anne had decided to give him a second chance, the New Year looked brighter than ever.

Chapter Ten

The New Year of 1940 brought Sally's first kiss. It had happened beneath the mistletoe that hung over the front door of Beach View, and she'd forgotten her shy awkwardness, giving herself up to the sweet and unfamiliar sensations that raced through her. He'd looked into her eyes then, and asked if she'd be his girl – and of course she'd said yes.

But while Sally and John were falling in love, and Anne and Martin were finally preparing for their wedding, the world around them was a far darker and more menacing place. Martin's squadron, which included Alex and his Polish comrades, was flying ever more missions into Europe. Two million men between the ages of nineteen and twenty-seven were called up, along with the unemployed. February had brought terrible storms all over the country making it even more difficult to get supplies through, or travel anywhere and, in April, Denmark and Norway were invaded.

In May there was a change of leadership in Parliament, and Churchill took the helm of a coalition government and made his first broadcast speech in the House of Commons. Like everyone else in the country, Sally and the family at Beach View sat by the wireless and listened in awe as he offered his blood, toil, tears and sweat to the cause of defeating the advancing enemy.

The heart-stopping news that Paris had fallen and France had surrendered was swiftly followed by the fall of Belgium and Holland. The enemy guns could now be heard across the Channel. Invasion was suddenly a very real possibility.

Sally came out of the factory, tired and dispirited. Her position as line-manager had proved harder than she'd expected and, at the end of every shift, she was wrung out. Things had gone well to begin with, but as the weeks had gone on and she'd had to be rather firm over sloppy sewing, bad time-keeping, pilfering and too much gossiping during work, a few of the women had taken umbrage.

Their numbers weren't large, but their whispering campaign had begun to wear Sally down – now they didn't bother to lower their voices when they discussed her youthful lack of experience in management, and the fact they thought she was getting ideas above her station. It was even suggested she'd only got the job because she was Goldman's favourite, and there was a lot of sniggering and elbowing as she made her regular trips to the office with the work-sheets.

She knew she should ignore them – there always

had to be someone who was the focus of gossip, and she'd accepted the challenge of trying to keep them in order – but it was wearing to be constantly criticised, especially as she knew she was doing the job well.

Work was frequently disrupted by false alarms, but productivity was up, Goldman was pleased with her, and even Simmons gave his grudging praise when he saw the day's output. At least she could rely on the majority of the women, especially Pearl, Brenda and Edie, a sweet, shy girl from Croydon who'd arrived in January, and was billeted with Pearl at the elderly couple's house north of town.

'Would the lady like a lift?'

She'd been so deep in thought she hadn't noticed him waiting outside the gates on his motorbike. The weariness fled at the welcome surprise. 'My dad said I shouldn't accept lifts from strange men,' she chuckled.

'And my mum told me not to pick up girls on street corners,' he replied, his handsome face creased in a smile. 'But I'll risk it if you will.'

She still blushed when he looked at her like that. 'Go on then, but I've got to get straight back, cos Anne's due for her last fitting.'

'You're a clever girl, Sally Turner, and I'm a lucky man.' He hesitated for a moment as if he was about to say something else, then smiled and carefully placed the spare helmet over her head.

As Sally waited for him to fasten the buckle

beneath her chin, she breathed in the scent of him. It was such a manly smell – of good woollen cloth, Brylcreem and Lifebuoy soap. He moved closer, his lips softly tracing kisses over her cheeks and nose before they lingered tantalisingly on her mouth.

She gave herself up to the kiss, swept away in the delicious sensations he was arousing.

'Are you sure you have to go straight home?' he murmured against her lips.

She gently pulled away from him. 'I'm certain,' she replied softly. 'Anne's wedding's only three weeks away and there's still a lot to do. Parachute silk isn't the easiest fabric to work with, you know.'

He heaved a sigh, gave her a swift hug and helped her clamber on to the back of the motorcycle. 'You have no idea what you're doing to me, Sally Turner,' he groaned. 'I don't get to see you nearly enough, and when I do, you're always rushing off somewhere.'

'I know, and I'm sorry,' she replied, cupping his cheek with her hand. 'What about we go to the pictures tomorrow night? I'm sure Peggy won't mind looking after Ernie.'

'I can't,' he said, his gaze fixed to a remote spot over her shoulder. 'I've got to go somewhere.'

She frowned. 'Anywhere nice?'

'I can't really say.' He took her hands, his expression earnest. 'Sally, you've got to trust me, all right? There's something I have to do, but I'm not allowed to tell anyone about it – not yet anyway.'

She was still frowning as she regarded him suspiciously. He was behaving very strangely, and it was unlike him not to be open with her. 'All right,' she replied hesitantly. 'We can go to the pictures the night after.'

He rammed on the helmet and took a moment to fasten it under his chin, his gaze still not meeting hers. 'I don't know, Sal. I might be away for more than one night.'

She eyed him suspiciously, the chill growing inside at his obvious reluctance to tell her the truth. 'You're beginning to sound like Ron. He's been disappearing for two or three days at a time as well, and refuses to tell anyone where he's been.' She eyed him keenly. 'Peggy thinks he's finally managed to nab Rosie Braithwaite at the pub. You ain't playing me false, are you?'

'I wouldn't do that, Sal,' he said urgently. 'I thought you knew me better.' He leaned closer, his voice low and urgent. 'This trip has nothing to do with any damned woman,' he hissed. 'But it's hush-hush and I can't say anything.'

Startled by his fierceness, she regarded him warily. 'It sounds a bit much,' she murmured, 'like something out of one of Ernie's comics.'

'I suppose it does,' he replied, anxiously. 'But I promise you Sal, when I get back I'll tell you everything.' He kissed her firmly, their helmets clashing. Then he climbed on to the motorcycle, told her to hang on, and drove down the road.

Sally clung to him, her cheek pressed against the soft wool of his coat, her heart banging painfully against her ribs. There was something going on in Cliffehaven – she and Peggy had felt it all week; had even discussed it this morning – and it looked as if John was part of it. She closed her eyes, hating the secrecy and fear, longing for this awful war to be over – and praying that whatever it was that was taking him away would see him return to her safe and unharmed.

When they'd pulled up outside Beach View, Sally took off the helmet, but remained clinging to him. 'I'm sorry I didn't trust you,' she said. 'Please be careful, John. I couldn't bear it if anything happened to you.'

He swung off the bike and pulled her to him in a tight embrace. 'No-one and nothing will stop me coming back to you, Sal. I promise.'

After a long kiss goodnight, he tore reluctantly from their embrace and climbed on to the motorbike. Sally stood on the steps and waited until the sound of it faded into the distance. She had to believe he would return to her – and that their fledgling romance was meant to flourish in the ashes of a war that must be won.

Sniffing back the tears, she opened the door. Her worries over John were instantly muted by the unfamiliar and therefore frightening sound of angry voices in Peggy's kitchen. She froze.

Jim's roar of anger was followed by Peggy's plea

for him to calm down. Then came the sound of a man's voice she couldn't identify. It was calmer than Jim's but edged with barely controlled fury. Stung into action by the need to protect Peggy, she hurried into the room.

Cissy and Anne were sitting warily at the kitchen table. Peggy was in her usual chair by the range and Ron was standing helplessly by as the two big men stood in the middle of Peggy's kitchen shouting each other down. It was clear that all three men were related, and Sally realised this must be the brother Jim hadn't spoken to since being demobbed after the previous war.

'You're not welcome in this house, Frank. Get out.' Jim was almost nose to nose with his brother, who stood like a rock, refusing to be intimidated.

'I'll go when I've said my piece and not before.' Frank exchanged glare for glare, his fists curling at his sides, his eyes flashing with anger. 'You always were a hot-head, Jim, but this time you need to actually listen for a change instead of running off at the mouth.'

'I've done listening to you,' Jim bellowed. 'Get out, before I throw you out.'

'Why don't the two of you sit down and talk like civilised human beings instead of yelling at each other?' said Ron, shoving himself between them. 'You're brothers, for God's sake. Isn't there enough fighting in this world without you tearing into one another?'

'If you all don't stop shouting this instant, I'll put the lot of you in the street,' snapped Peggy. 'The children are asleep and I don't want them waking to the sight of you at each other's throats.'

She saw Sally hovering in the doorway and waved her into the kitchen. 'I apologise for their behaviour, Sally, but it seems my husband and his brother have forgotten their manners.'

Sally edged into the room and slid on to the nearest kitchen chair beside Anne, who immediately grasped her hand and gave her a nervous smile. But Sally found little comfort in the other girl's gesture – she'd seen too many fights in her life, and hated them; but to see such anger in this particular kitchen shocked her to the core.

'You don't apologise for me, Peg,' snarled Jim. 'This is my house, and I'll do what I want.' He threw himself into a chair, legs sprawled, arms tightly folded as he glared at his brother. 'You've got five minutes to tell me why you're in my kitchen before I boot you out,' he growled.

Frank lifted his chin, his stance square and determined. After a glance at his father, he began to speak. 'Since the war started I've lost most of my fishing crews. Two of the big trawlers have been taken to be used as minesweepers, and my four sons – along with all the other lads, have joined the Royal Naval Reserve. I've had to haul up and store all but two of the smaller boats because all I have left are three old men and a boy to run them.'

'I don't want to hear your hard-luck stories,' rumbled Jim. 'Get to the bloody point.'

Frank took a step towards him, his expression grim. 'What I'm about to tell you is top secret, so I want your word you'll say nothing outside this room.'

Jim sneered. 'You're just a fisherman, Frank – not some high-ranking boffin from the MoD.' He snorted derisively. 'Top secret, my arse.'

'I think you should listen to your brother, Jim,' said Ron, quietly. 'There are things going on in Cliffehaven you know nothing about.'

Jim stared at his father, his tone caustic. 'And I suppose you've got an ear to it all, eh, old man?'

'I know more than you give me credit for,' he retorted. 'Frank wouldn't be here if it wasn't important, so hold off the aggression and listen to him.'

Jim snorted again and fidgeted in the chair. 'Go on, then. Spit it out. I'll not be telling anyone you and Da have gone soft in the head.'

Frank got everyone's assurance to keep his secret, and Peggy firmly closed the door to the basement. 'Walls have ears,' she said, 'and so do small boys.'

She signed to Sally to shut the door into the hall then returned to sit on the edge of her seat by the range. 'I know something's up – there's been a strange atmosphere in the town all week, especially down at the fishing station. What's it all about, Frank?'

'Every seaworthy craft of a certain size in the south of the country has been commandeered by the government for a special mission,' he began. 'From private motorboats to pleasure steamers, decked-in luggers and open fishing punts, they're being taken up the coast. The local fishermen still working their boats are all going, and I plan to be one of them.'

He had everyone's attention as he turned to Jim. 'But it will be dangerous out there, and I can't take old men and boys with me. I need you to crew the *Seagull*.'

'I haven't been in a fishing boat for years,' Jim retorted. 'I'd be no use to you.'

'You know the boat as well as me, Jim. After all, we use to fish her together when we were lads.'

'That was when I could trust you,' muttered Jim, holding his gaze evenly and without affection.

'I'll go with you,' said Ron, eyes shining at the prospect of an adventure. 'To be sure I taught you all I know, and an old sea-dog never forgets.'

'No, Dad,' Frank said firmly. 'Not this time.'

'I'm as strong as you, and tougher than Jim who's got soft sitting in that projection room every day. I know the sea and everything it can throw at me, and—'

Frank silenced his father with a heavy hand on his shoulder. 'I admire your courage, Da,' he said quietly, 'and I have no doubt you're as fit and strong as a butcher's dog. But I won't be having your safety to worry about – things could turn very nasty out there, and I'll need me wits about me.'

'Oh, my God,' breathed Peggy. 'You're going across the Channel, aren't you?'

Frank hesitated and then nodded. 'We have to rendezvous further up the coast before dawn tomorrow.'

'But the Channel's mined,' gasped Sally. 'You could all be killed.'

'You mustn't go – either of you,' said Peggy. 'I won't allow it.'

'We'll have the navy escorting us,' said Frank. 'It will be as safe as it is sitting in a shelter during an air-raid.'

'But . . .'

Frank's expression hardened. 'Our men are trapped with no way of escaping those beaches unless we do something about it, Peggy. The boats are their only hope. I have to go.' He turned back to his younger brother. 'What about it, Jim? Are you coming – or do I have to find someone else?'

Jim eyed him in silence for a long, tense moment. 'I've got a job to keep as well as fire-watch and warden duties. How long will we be away?'

Frank shrugged. 'I can't honestly say. But I'm sure Peg can tell your boss something to keep him sweet until you get back.'

Sally saw Jim glance at Peggy, that fleeting look expressing his mixed emotions. She saw the tears in Peggy's eyes and the fear as she waited to hear his answer. Anne and Cissy had the same haunted look in their eyes – and she knew it reflected her own terror. Could it be that John's mysterious absence had something to do with this fleet of fishing boats and pleasure craft?

'Is John Hicks going with you, Frank?' she blurted out.

'I have no idea, but as his uncle is a fisherman, it's likely.'

Sally could feel the hammer-blows of her heart against her ribs and was certain everyone could hear them in the deathly silence of that kitchen.

'I'm sorry, Peg,' Jim muttered. 'I can't stay here while our men need rescuing.' He turned back to Frank. 'You've got your crewman, Frank, but don't expect me to talk to you.'

'I doubt there'll be much call for conversation,' Frank replied grimly. 'Get your things together, Jim. We have to leave within the hour if we're to catch the tide.'

Sally took in the scene through her tears as Frank followed Jim out of the kitchen. Peggy was trying very hard to be brave, but as she bustled into action and set Cissy and Anne to making flasks of tea while she made fish-paste sandwiches, she began to crumble.

Anne and Cissy immediately rushed to her side and helped her into her chair. Sally stifled her emotions, took the knife and continued to make the sandwiches as the three of them huddled by the meagre fire and sobbed. She wanted to cry too, but tears wouldn't do John or the others any good – she just had to keep her fears tightly locked in and do her best to remain strong for all of them.

'I'm sorry, Peg,' said Frank, returning in sea boots, the thick waterproof coat and sou'wester slung over his arm. 'But I didn't know who else to ask. The *Seagull* isn't the easiest boat to crew in a swell, and Jim knows her foibles.'

'I know them too,' muttered Ron. 'I don't see why I can't come.'

'Da,' sighed Frank, 'someone's got to stay here and look after the women and kids. They need you more than ever now.'

'But Jim hasn't been in that boat for years,' protested Peggy, her face streaked with tears. 'Isn't there *anyone* else you could take instead?'

He hunkered down in front of her and took her hands. 'There's no-one I could trust more with the *Seagull*, Peg. He'll soon remember how to handle her – and we have the trip along the coast to get him used to the feel of her again. He won't have forgotten. He needs to do this, Peg, please try and understand.'

Peggy was about to reply when the air-raid siren began the terrible whine that soon rose to an ear-splitting crescendo.

Sally put her fears aside and raced upstairs to collect Ernie. Wrapping him in his blanket, she soothed his tearful complaints at having been woken for the third night running. She hurtled down the stairs to the kitchen where Anne, Cissy and Peggy were gathering blankets and all they might need for the next few hours.

Ron and Frank had already gone down to the basement to get the other boys, and Jim marched in, resplendent in corded trousers, thick sweater, waterproof coat and boots, carrying a sleepy and disorientated Mrs Finch.

There was no panic as they turned off the lights and trooped out of the back door and down the path to the Anderson shelter. They had become inured to spending nights within its cold damp walls, and this familiar routine was strangely comforting.

With Mrs Finch settled in her chair, Peggy lit the primus and heated milk for cocoa. It was one of the anomalies of the war that the milk and newspapers were delivered every day, regardless of what had happened the night before.

Sally kept Ernie on her lap and tried to make herself as small as possible in the tight squeeze of so many people. Cissy and Anne sat either side of their parents, the two boys on their laps. Ron kept Harvey firmly against his chest, wrapped in the folds of his poacher's coat, and Frank sat edgily by the door, clearly impatient to be away to his boat.

Searchlights raked the sky and the wailing siren mingled with Harvey's anguished howls.

'You should have put that animal down months ago,' shouted Frank over the din.

'I've had to let the ferrets go already,' Ron yelled back, 'and that was enough. Harvey hates the siren.

When it stops wailing, so does he.' He ruffled the dog's ears and earned a lick on his face which he dried on the animal's fur.

Sally held Ernie close as she remembered the day Ron had released his precious ferrets. He had asked her to go with him on that awful morning eight weeks ago, and she would never forget the anguish in the old man's eyes as he'd been forced to face the fact that Cleo and Delilah were suffering.

He'd waited until everyone was out before he shut Harvey in the shed. As Sally watched, he'd taken Delilah and Cleo out of their cage, stroked them lovingly and given them some bread and milk before tucking them in his cavernous coat pockets. Their long walk up into the hills had been silent and thoughtful, accompanied only by the mournful cries of the gulls and the sweet-scented smoke coming from his pipe.

He'd chosen a spot by a ring of gorse where there were plenty of rabbit scrapings and burrows. She had sat on the springy grass beside him, the salt wind in her hair as he took the animals one by one from his pockets. He'd murmured to them as he'd stroked the soft pale fur of their bellies, and whispered his goodbyes as he'd gently put them down.

There were tears in his eyes as he watched them scurry into the nearby rabbit holes, but he said nothing as he helped Sally to her feet and began the long journey home.

Sally had walked silently beside him, knowing

this was not the time for talk. But it seemed only natural to take his gnarled, rough hand in hers to offer tacit comfort and sympathy.

'Thank you, me darlin',' he'd said softly, squeezing her fingers. 'I knew you'd be the one to understand.'

And she had understood, for Delilah and Cleo were as much a part of him as the landscape. They had been his companions and his children – and now he'd had to say goodbye to them for ever.

She could feel the tears prick as she dipped her chin, resting it on Ernie's head as she saw how Jim and Peggy were holding fiercely to their children, how Anne and Cissy were trying so hard to be brave for their mother's sake, and the way Ron was regarding his sons, the love and fear for them doing battle in his eyes.

Her thoughts turned to John, to her father – and even to Florrie. Would she ever see them again? At this very moment she couldn't believe any of them would survive, and she huddled in the flickering shadows of the hurricane lamp and waited for the enemy to come out of the skies.

The sirens stopped and the ensuing silence was deafening. Frank held his watch up to the meagre light and grimaced. 'We've got to go, Jim.'

'Now?' Peggy put her hand over her mouth. 'But the all-clear hasn't gone, and there's a curfew for the boats. No-one's allowed out after dark – it isn't safe – you could be mistaken for the enemy.'

'The curfew's been lifted tonight, Peg, and we'll be all right for a while,' said Frank. 'Got your things together, Jim?'

'In the hall.' He took Peggy and the girls into his arms. 'I'll be back before you know it,' he murmured. 'Please don't cry.' He gently thumbed the tears from Peggy's cheek before ruffling his sons' hair. 'Look after your mother and do as she tells you.'

'Where are you going, Dad?' they chorused.

'Well, now,' he said, with forced cheerfulness and a wink. 'I'm going with your Uncle Frank on a wee adventure, and I'll tell you all about it when I get home.'

He stood and gave Ron's shoulder a squeeze. 'I'm leaving you in charge,' he said softly. 'Look after them for me, Da.'

Frank hugged his father, said goodbye to everyone else, and left the shelter. With a nod to Sally and a soft touch to Ernie's head, Jim followed him into the night.

Sally held Ernie close as the boys badgered Ron and Peggy with questions. The tears were blinding her and her heart felt as if it was being crushed by an iron hand. Jim and Frank were going into the unknown, braving the channel and the mines, heading for France and into the jaws of the enemy guns. And, if John was with them . . .?

She closed her eyes and tried to shut out the images of what might happen – but they remained with her.

When the all-clear finally sounded, they struggled, aching and stiff with cold, out of the Anderson shelter and into the dawn.

They silently trooped indoors, thankful that no raid had come, but weary of the nightly disturbances.

'I'll put the kettle on,' said Peggy, then sank defeatedly into her chair. 'I forgot to fill the kettle, and there's no water. The fire's gone out and . . . and . . .' She burst into tears.

Cissy and Anne rushed to her, and the boys were on the verge of tears themselves as they witnessed this unsettling behaviour from a mother they'd never seen cry before.

'I'll light the fire,' muttered Ron. 'You boys go and get some wood from the shed. But mind how you go.'

Bob and Charlie took another worried look at their mother and then hurried downstairs, still in their nightclothes and slippers.

Sally took Ernie upstairs to get him washed and dressed, but her thoughts were of John, Jim and Frank, and suddenly she was overwhelmed by it all. The dangers had never seemed so real before, but now they were stark and terrifyingly close.

'What is it, Sal? Why you gone a funny colour?'

'Nothing,' she said hurriedly. 'I'm just a bit tired from spending all night in that shelter. Come on, let's get you sorted, and then I can see about breakfast.'

* * *

The morning was spent cleaning the house while Ron kept the boys occupied in the vegetable garden. Sally realised she wasn't the only one who needed to be busy so she didn't have time to dwell on what might be happening out in the Channel, for Peggy, Cissy and Anne set to work cleaning as if their lives depended upon it.

It was her day off from the factory, and come mid-afternoon the housework was done.

'Come on, Anne,' Sally said. 'We need to do the last fitting so I can finish your dress in time.'

'I don't feel very much like dressing up,' Anne replied, her brown eyes huge in her wan face. 'Martin's probably out there now giving air-cover to the boats. How can I possibly even think about dresses and weddings and—?'

'Because he'll be coming home expecting you to marry him in three weeks' time,' said Sally firmly. 'And you can't do that in a dress that ain't – that *hasn't* been finished.'

'But what if—?'

'That's quite enough of that,' she said sternly, realising she was beginning to sound like Peggy. 'We all got to get on with things, Anne. It's the only way we're going to win this bloody war.' She took Anne's arm and firmly steered her into the dining room and shut the door.

Anne stood and gazed out of the window. 'You're right of course,' she murmured. 'I'd be letting Martin down if I give in to such defeatist thoughts.'

Sally opened the trunk she now used to store her needlework away from the dust, and pulled out the dress, which she'd covered in a muslin sheet. There had been much discussion over what Anne should wear for her wedding, for even a day-dress would now mean handing over at least seven clothing coupons. Wedding dresses were as rare as hen's teeth and would have cost a fortune if one could have been found, so most girls opted for something borrowed, or the uniform of the service in which they served.

Then Jim had come home with the parachute silk a few weeks ago. He'd refused to say where he'd got it, as usual, and as there had been no enemy airmen parachuting into the town, and the stores at the airfield were under lock and key, it was thought wiser not to ask any more questions.

She felt the slithery weight of it on her arm as she drew away the muslin sheet, and knew it was the finest thing she'd ever made. 'Close the curtains, Anne,' she said softly. 'You don't want half the street seeing you in your Liberty bodice and knickers.'

The room was plunged into darkness, and Anne switched on the light before stripping to her underwear. She slipped her feet into the white high-heeled sandals her Aunt Doris had lent her, and held out her arms so Sally could carefully slide on the dress. 'It's cold,' she muttered with a shiver.

'Silk is always cold at first,' said Sally through a mouthful of pins. 'It'll soon warm up.'

The tiny buttons would fasten the dress from neck to hip, and it was important she got it just right, otherwise it would hang awkwardly. She smoothed the material over Anne's hips and adjusted it at the shoulders and neck. They had all lost weight over the past months, due to shortages, stiff rationing and the sheer energy used in getting through each day, so it wasn't surprising she had to take it in at the waist again.

'I couldn't get the right buttons,' she mumbled through the pins, 'but at least I found a dozen all the same size, if not the same colour.' She rooted in the box on her sewing table, and took out a handful. 'As you can see, I've started to cover each one with the same silk as the dress, so no-one will ever know.'

'You are clever, Sally. I would never have the patience, or the skill, to do something like this.'

'And I couldn't be in a classroom all day with those kids,' she muttered, as she pinned the back where she wanted the buttons and buttonholes to be. 'I'd end up throttling them.'

'I doubt it,' murmured Anne. 'You've endless patience with Ernie.'

'He's me – *my* brother,' she said. She finished pinning the back of the dress and stood behind Anne as they admired the effect in the cheval mirror that Peggy had brought down from one of the bedrooms.

Anne's dark hair and eyes were a perfect foil for the shimmering silk. The dress had a scooped neckline and cap sleeves, and fell from the close-fitting bodice into a waterfall of silk that would float around her ankles when she walked. To emphasise her tiny waist, Sally had stitched in a false belt at the front, which she'd decorated with scraps of lace, seed pearls and sequins to match the embellishment on the sleeves.

Sally gazed at her creation and wondered if she'd ever have the chance to wear such a beautiful dress – to look so regal, to feel so assured of being loved by the man she adored. Then she caught sight of her own reflection and realised she could never look as elegant or beautiful as Anne – and that although she was in love with John, that was no guarantee he loved her enough to ask her to marry him. She looked away from their reflections. She wasn't quite seventeen anyway, so she was being silly to dream of such things.

Anne seemed to read her thoughts. 'It'll be your turn one day,' she murmured.

Sally gave a great sigh and tried to extinguish the hope that burnt so brightly. With so many uncertainties at the moment, it wasn't wise to try and see into the future. 'You look ever so lovely,' she said instead. 'Like a princess.'

Anne grinned with delight. 'I feel like a queen,' she replied, swirling the skirt, and almost tripping over the hem.

'Stand still before you tear the silk,' said Sally hastily. 'I need to pin the hem and, once that's done, I can get on and finish it.'

* * *

The boys were just settling down to listen to *Children's Hour* when the doorbell rang. As Sally and Anne were doing their best to put together an evening meal from Spam, whiskery potatoes and dried eggs, Peggy went to see who it was.

Sally could hear the voices in the hall, but couldn't make out what they were saying. At least it didn't sound like the telegraph boy with a dreaded brown envelope.

Peggy returned to the kitchen with a hesitant smile. 'That was Miss Ormiston from the Billeting Office,' she said. 'It looks like we've got another couple of waifs and strays to look after, though how on earth we can make that food stretch to so many, I don't know.'

Sally turned to greet the new arrivals, gasped in amazed horror and forgot her determination to speak nicely. 'Pearl, Edie?' She took in the dirty clothes, the tear-streaked faces and the two bulging, filthy pillowcases they carried. 'Oh my Gawd,' she breathed. 'What 'appened to you?'

Pearl swept back her tangled hair with a dirty hand. 'The 'ouse went up while we was at work last night,' she said, stifling her tears. 'The silly old bugger 'ad a big box of grenades he'd kept after the last war, 'idden in the cupboard by the chimney. The fireman said they musta deteriorated and got over'eated and blew up. The poor old dears never stood a blinking chance.'

Edie nodded dumbly. She wasn't given to talking

much at the best of times, but now she seemed too traumatised to say anything.

Pearl pointed at the pillowcases. 'This is all we could salvage,' she said, her voice breaking. 'The clean-up crew said it were too dangerous to look for anything else.'

Sally put her arms round both of them, sat them down and poured cups of tea that resembled dishwater. The leaves had already been used several times, but at least it was hot, and there was milk to help it go down.

Peggy returned to washing lettuce under the tap. 'You can both have the room next to Sally's,' she said. 'There's only a double bed in there, so I hope you don't mind sharing.'

'That's blindin' Mrs Reilly,' said Pearl, blowing on the tea. 'I could sleep anywhere tonight, I'm that tired.'

'Did you manage to salvage your ration books?'

They shook their heads. 'Sorry, Mrs Reilly, but they went up with the 'ouse. Mrs Whatsit from the Billeting place gave us some temporary cards to be going on with though.' Pearl reached into her coat pocket and pulled them out. 'It could be a while before we get the proper ones.'

Once the tea had been drunk, Sally showed them upstairs and helped to make the bed, find towels and teach them how to use the gas boiler in the bathroom without losing their eyebrows.

Pearl was distraught as she tipped the contents

of the two pillowcases on to the floor. 'All our lovely things are gorn,' she wailed, 'and look what's 'appened to me best dress, and Edie's new jacket.'

Sally eyed the bedraggled bits of cotton and gathered everything up. 'A bit of a wash and they'll all come up lovely,' she soothed. 'You'll feel better once you've had a bath as well. I'll be downstairs in the kitchen when you've finished.'

'I 'ope Mrs Reilly don't mind us turning up like this,' said Pearl.

'She's glad to have you, I'm sure,' she said softly, 'but she's got things on her mind at the moment, so she's not quite herself.'

Pearl and Edie looked at her questioningly, but it was Pearl who spoke. 'Mr Reilly's brother's a fisherman, ain't 'e? Have they gone over – you know – over there? Cos my Billy's dad's gone, and 'is mum don't know what to do with 'erself, so I can guess what she's going through.'

'I think John has as well,' she admitted, 'and with Martin in the RAF, none of us are thinking straight at the moment.'

'Oh, Gawd, Sal. Where will it all end?' Pearl burst into tears again.

Sally rushed to comfort her. 'We gotta keep strong, Pearl,' she murmured, close to tears herself. 'We just gotta for their sakes.'

An hour later, everyone had finished tea and cleared away. The boys had been put to bed and cigarettes had been lit as they sipped weak tea and sat by the wireless, fearfully waiting to hear the news.

It was the twenty-sixth of May, and the armada of little boats had been escorted by naval gunships through the minefields of the Channel to Dunkirk and the beaches of northern France. As the gunships gave covering fire, the RAF flew above those little ships as they headed for the shallow water and the hundreds of thousands of men stranded on the beaches. There was order amid the mayhem as those men awaited their turn to wade through the water, past fallen comrades, to reach their rescuers.

As Sally listened, she could only pray that they would all come home safely. But none of them realised they would have to wait another nine agonising days before there was any news of their loved ones.

Chapter Eleven

The following days dragged by, their fears tormenting them as they went about their daily lives and pretended nothing had changed. There had been no word of their men, and the news that several ships had been sunk and hundreds had been killed didn't make the waiting any easier.

Sally found she couldn't concentrate on anything, and earned a rare reprimand from Mr Goldman over allowing some careless sewing to get passed, which sent her back to her machine in tears. Tears that were duly noted by her friends and enemies alike, and she'd had to dredge up every ounce of will to make light of them and reinforce her position.

Then the longed-for telephone call had come from the Lifeboat Station. The local boats had returned to the rendezvous point and were now making their way home.

Pearl told her to look out for Billy's father's boat, the *Pelican*, and Edie wished her luck before they went off to work. Sally had taken the day off, promising Mr Goldman to work a double shift the following day to make up for it. It was a sunny June day and she'd washed and ironed her sprigged cotton frock with the white Peter Pan collar and cap sleeves, taking a cardigan to keep off the chill wind that still blew in from the sea. With brightly coloured combs in her hair and a dash of lipstick, she felt quite pretty, and hoped John thought so too.

Mrs Finch remained at the house, promising to put the kettle on the minute she heard the key in the door. She had no wish to intrude on what was clearly a private reunion.

It was quite a family outing, with Harvey pulling eagerly on his leash as Peggy and Ron led the way to the seafront. Anne and Cissy followed with the boys, whilst Sally pushed Ernie in his flag-festooned wheelchair. The boys were also armed with flags and kept running on ahead, which made Harvey pull even harder on the lead. Ron had to yell at them to come back and walk properly as Harvey was in danger of strangling himself.

There was already a crowd waiting impatiently by the Lifeboat Station, and the WRVS had set up a canteen, doling out cups of tea and rather stale biscuits for a farthing. Armed with tea, biscuits and cigarettes, the adults perched on the low wall that divided the promenade from the road, and settled down to wait. The boys wheeled Ernie along the strip of promenade to inspect the gun emplacements and annoy the soldiers with their endless questions, but they returned some time later with sticks of chewing gum, which they shared with everyone except Ron, who complained it got stuck in his false teeth.

Almost two hours later a great cheer went up and they were on their feet, craning to catch sight of the first boat. It was the *Minerva* and, with a sigh of disappointment, they jealously watched the joyful reunion of the *Minerva*'s crew with their families.

Next to come in was a large motorboat, swiftly followed by the pleasure steamer that, in peacetime, had taken tourists on trips around the bay. And then the *Seagull* came round the headland, and Peggy pushed her way through the melee to stand on the shingle at the water's edge.

Sally watched with tears in her eyes as Jim jumped down and swept Peggy into his arms and kissed her passionately. Then she laughed as they were swamped by their children, the boys clinging to him like monkeys, the girls showering him with kisses as Harvey leapt up and tried to lick everyone. Ron, who was not a man to show his emotions in public, stood by his side and kept patting his shoulder, as if to confirm he was not a figment of his imagination.

Frank clambered down and tied the ropes firmly to the posts sticking out of the shingle. Then he threw his arms round Ron and held him in a tight embrace until a pretty, fair-haired woman shoved through the crowd and flung herself into his arms. Sally guessed it had to be Frank's wife.

The *Pelican* chugged round the headland, smoke belching from the stack into the blue sky. Sally saw the men on board and sighed gratefully. At least

Billy's father and uncle had returned safely, even though one had bandages round his head, and the other wore a sling.

Sally watched the celebrations, her gaze returning repeatedly to the headland for sight of another boat. But when it came, her spirits ebbed once more, for it beached on the shingle with no sign of John among the exhausted and battered crew. She realised then she didn't even know the name of the fishing boat John had sailed on – or even if it had come from this harbour. She wanted to ask Peggy, but the family were still celebrating, and she didn't want to intrude on such a private moment.

Frantic now, she impatiently waited for the celebrations to calm a little and went to Frank, who still had his arm round his wife. 'You said you knew John Hicks,' she began.

His happy grin faltered and he regarded her warily. 'That's right,' he replied. 'You're Sally, aren't you?'

She nodded. 'What boat is he on? Did you see him?'

Frank took his arm from his wife's shoulders and rammed his hands in his pockets, clearly uneasy. 'He was on the *Little Nell* with his dad, his uncle and two cousins,' he said hesitantly. 'I saw them when we left, but it was such chaos out there, I don't remember seeing them again.'

'But he's all right, isn't he? He *is* coming back?' Sally's fear was threatening to overwhelm her, the tears ready to fall, her heart feeling as if it was being squeezed by a giant hand. Then she looked into his eyes and saw something that made her go cold. 'What is it?' she whispered. 'What happened?'

'I'm sorry, Sally,' Frank murmured. 'I heard the *Little Nell* was sunk.'

'Sunk?' she stammered. She covered her mouth with her fingers, blinking up at him through her tears. 'Are you sure?'

He placed his hands on her shoulders to steady her. 'According to what I heard, Sally – and this isn't gospel – it went down the day before yesterday.' His grip tightened as a sob escaped from her and she swayed towards him. 'But that's not to say John and the others weren't picked up by someone else. We managed to fish out the crew from the *Jenny*, just like many others rescued other crews. I'm sure they're fine, Sally.'

She wanted desperately to believe him, but something in his eyes told her he didn't believe it himself. 'How can I find out what happened to them?'

'No doubt someone in charge will know. You could try the harbour-master at Dover, I suppose.' He swiftly looked over the dwindling crowd on the beach. 'I don't see any of the family here,' he said. 'But that's not necessarily a bad thing,' he added hastily as she sobbed more loudly. 'Every boat has its own mooring, and if they *were* picked up, they could be anywhere along the coast by now.'

'I have to find him,' she managed through a throat constricted by tears.

'Here's Peggy,' he replied, clearly relieved for the support. 'She knows the Hicks family better than me.'

Peggy put her arm round Sally as Frank quickly explained the situation. 'I've got their number at home,' she said to Sally. 'I'll ring when we get back.' She turned back to Frank. 'Would you and Pauline like to come back with us for a cuppa?'

He shook his head. 'Thanks, Peg, but I'm going home to me bed, where I'm planning on staying for at least a week.'

'Thanks for bringing Jim back safely.'

He nodded curtly, put his arm round Pauline's shoulders and walked away.

'Oh, dear,' sighed Peggy. 'It looks as if the rift between them hasn't been mended. I was so hoping this might bring them together.' She gathered her thoughts and took Sally's hand. 'Come on, let's get you back and make that call.'

The walk seemed to take for ever, and yet Sally was almost reluctant to arrive at the familiar front door – for Peggy's telephone call might tell her the worst news, and she didn't know how she could bear it. On the other hand it could be good news – that John had been picked up and was safe somewhere. This thought lightened her step but, as she followed Peggy into the hall, the optimism fled again.

Peggy didn't even take off her hat before she grabbed her address book and riffled through the pages. Dialling the number, she listened to it ringing at the other end for what felt like a lifetime. Then she put the receiver down. 'Betty must be out,' she said, 'probably over at her sister's – but she's not on the telephone. I'll try again later.'

Sally didn't know what she felt, her emotions were so mixed. There was relief at putting off the evil moment, fear that it could only be bad news, and a burning, desperate hope that John was all right and, even now, was making his way home from some distant harbour.

She helped Ernie out of the wheelchair, took his hand and followed Peggy as she made for the kitchen. Hearing Jim's voice filling the silence, they tiptoed into the room and sat next to one another.

He was drinking the last of the Polish vodka that Alex had given him at Easter. His voice was low, without a hint of bravado – just a terrible weariness that coloured his words and made the scenes he described come frighteningly to life.

'The weather turned bad, with high winds, thick fog and heavy waves; but the noise was the worst thing. What with the machine guns from the beach, the planes overhead and the gunfire from the destroyers that escorted us, you could barely hear yourself think.'

He paused, took a sip of vodka and grimaced. Whether it was from the burn of it going down his throat, or the images that haunted him, none of them knew.

'There were thousands upon thousands of men trapped on the beaches,' he said softly, his gaze distant with the memories of what he'd seen. 'Apart from our troops, there were Frenchies, Aussies, Canadians, Belgians.'

He was silent for a long moment before continuing. 'We got in as close as we dared, the machine-gun bullets ripping into the *Seagull*, sending shrapnel flying everywhere – it was a miracle neither of us got hit. They poured off the beaches, wading through the water that was soon thick with the bodies of their comrades – so thick that they were being trampled underfoot.'

The silence in the kitchen was deathly. They could all see and hear the terrible images he'd conjured up.

'It was like the Somme all over again,' he rasped. 'They were being mown down even before they could reach us. The poor bastards never stood a chance.'

Peggy didn't even admonish him over his language as she perched on a chair, her face ashen, eyes fixed to him, wide with horror.

'We dropped anchor and hauled as many as we could into the *Seagull*.' His haunted gaze sought his father. 'But there were too many, Da – we couldn't take them all, and the boat was shipping water and in danger of capsizing as they clung to her sides, pleading to be let on board. We had to force their fingers off her planking, and leave them in the water, so we could take the lucky ones to the Navy destroyers that waited further out.'

Peggy moved to sit on the arm of his chair, her hand softly settling on his shoulder.

Jim's voice was lower now, broken with emotion. 'Then we went back – and back again until we lost count. On and on it went through the night and into day after day, after day. The sea was red with blood, and we could hear them screaming for help – but there was nothing we could do; there were just too many.'

He looked at Ron, his face a mask of pain. 'There had to be almost a thousand craft out there, naval and civilian, but we couldn't save them all, Da. We couldn't possibly save them all.' Jim's face crumpled as he buried his face in his hands, the deep, agonising sobs filling the little room with his heartbreak.

Peggy wrapped him in her arms and held him as he wept. The boys crept towards him and clutched his legs as Ron surreptitiously wiped his eyes and Mrs Finch sobbed into her handkerchief. Anne and Cissy sat dumbly, their tears running unheeded down their faces as they watched their big strong father cling to their mother, curling into her like a wounded, terrified child.

Sally felt chilled to the bone, for the images Jim had painted were all too real, and her fear for John was overwhelming. She gathered the wide-eyed

Ernie close, needing his warmth and weight in her arms – needing the solace in this, her darkest hour.

'Did the Germans hurt Uncle Jim?' he asked, his voice wavering on the edge of tears.

'No, love,' she murmured, 'but he's hurting inside cos of everything he saw – and sometimes that's even worse than a bullet-wound.'

Ernie rested against her and closed his eyes. 'I don't like it when he cries,' he murmured. 'It makes me hurt inside too.'

Sally kissed the top of his head and cuddled him. 'I know,' she whispered, feeling the same terrible pain.

'Come on, Jim,' murmured Peggy. 'You're exhausted. Let's get you to bed.' She turned to the girls. 'There's a bit of mince for tea. Do what you can while I see to your father.'

The mood was broken and, glad to have something to do to dispel the awful thoughts, Sally and the girls dried their tears and began to prepare the evening meal. Peggy's larder was still well stocked with the bottled fruit, jam and pickles she'd made the previous summer and autumn, but there was only a handful of mince and two sausages to share among them all – they had to be creative.

Ron collected onions, potatoes and tomatoes from the garden, and cut some parsley and chives from the box he'd made to fit beneath the basement window at the front of the house. His tiny herb garden was flourishing, but the tomatoes were his pride and joy, brought on beneath sheets of glass close to the side garden wall where the sun shone for most of the day. He saved every last drop of used water to keep them and all his vegetables alive.

There was no fat, so Sally dry-fried the mince, chopped sausages and onions while the potatoes boiled. Anne made a sauce with the tomatoes, adding the parsley and chives, some pickled cabbage and a pinch of salt to give more flavour. There was no pepper – it had long since run out and was now affectionately called white gold by the beleaguered grocer whose shelves were becoming emptier by the day.

Cissy laid the table before helping Mrs Finch unravel a particularly large knot in her knitting. The old lady was quiet for once, her expression sad and thoughtful, and Sally wondered if she was remembering the last war, and the husband she'd lost at Ypres. Jim's descriptive storytelling must surely have conjured up such memories.

The girls worked silently, keeping their thoughts to themselves as the boys disappeared into the basement to play with their train set. But none of the usual bursts of laughter came from down there – it seemed they were all affected by the terrible events of the past week.

Jim didn't come downstairs for the evening meal, and Peggy assured them he was fast asleep and would probably stay that way until morning. He was exhausted.

'I tried that number again, Sally,' she said a while later. 'Still no reply. I'm sorry, dear.'

Sally nodded and helped Anne clear the dishes and tidy away while Peggy put the boys to bed. In an attempt to dispel the terrible dread, she made a game of carrying Ernie upstairs for his wash. They had become used to having a nightly bath, and Ernie always looked forward to it, but they were encouraged to save water now, so they bathed once a week in the few inches allowed, Sally climbing in after Ernie had finished. Tonight it would be a lick and a promise with a damp flannel for both of them, and a few drops of water in a mug to rinse their toothbrushes.

Having massaged him with the last of the oil, she wrapped him in his pyjamas and snuggled him into bed. She sat in the chair and waited for him to fall asleep, wondering if he'd have nightmares. She could hardly blame Jim, but his description had been all too graphic, and she knew without a doubt that she'd have a disturbed night because of it.

The news was about to start as she returned to the kitchen and, with a nod of welcome to Pearl and Edie who'd just come in and were eating the warmed-up plates of food, she settled down to listen. Silence fell as the deep, well-educated and familiar voice came from the wireless and into the room.

Operation Dynamo had been a resounding success due to the bravery of the Royal Navy, the RAF, and the many civilians who'd risked their lives to bring the men home safely. They had rescued almost six hundred thousand men from the beaches of Dunkirk, Cherbourg, Saint Malo, Brest and Saint Nazaire.

But in his speech to the House of Commons that afternoon, Churchill had tempered his praise for this success by saying that, although huge numbers of men had been rescued, and the bravery of the rescuers was in no doubt, it had been a 'colossal military disaster' – and that wars weren't won by evacuations.

There had been a huge number of casualties, and the British Expeditionary Force had had to abandon vital heavy armour and equipment that would be needed in the coming months. With over five thousand dead, Dunkirk reduced to rubble, two hundred and thirty-five vessels and one hundred and six aircraft destroyed, the consequences of this evacuation could not be yet determined.

Sally saw how Anne paled, and held tightly to her hand. 'Martin will ring when he can,' she whispered. 'He's probably being debriefed and can't get away.'

'I know, but . . .' She didn't need to say any more, and Sally squeezed her fingers in empathy.

The news ended with a speech from Prime Minister Churchill, who darkly warned the nation to brace itself for another blow. 'We are told that Herr Hitler has a plan for invading the British Isles,' he said in that now familiar, gravelly voice. But the prime minister's message to Herr Hitler was resolute. 'We shall defend our island, whatever the cost may be. We shall fight on the beaches; we shall fight on the landing grounds; we shall fight in the fields and in the streets; we shall fight in the hills; we shall *never* surrender . . .'

They stood as one and cheered, bolstered by those fine words and the determination behind them, fired up with patriotism and the spirit that would take them to victory.

But as they went to their beds that night, the euphoria of the moment subsided. They didn't doubt that the cost of victory would be high – but were they strong enough to pay it when it demanded the ultimate sacrifice of losing their loved ones?

Ernie cried out in the night, the nightmares waking him. Sally took him into her bed, and discovered that by giving him comfort, she found solace in the warmth of the little body pressed so tightly against her. But her dreams were troubled, the images of John fighting for his life in a sinking boat too powerful to sustain restful sleep.

Startled awake by the alarm clock, there was an instant when she couldn't remember the horrors – and then they returned, stark and terrifying to haunt her throughout the day.

Clambering out of bed, she got Ernie ready for school and then dressed for work before carrying him downstairs for a breakfast of thin porridge and toast. Oats were hard to come by, but the local baker had taken on five new workers, and now the ovens were going through the day as well as the night all the while he could get the flour. Another delivery was expected on the Saturday train, and already his order book was full.

The telephone rang and Anne and Sally jumped to answer it. But Peggy got there first, smiled and handed the receiver to Anne. 'It's Martin,' she said, 'he's safe.'

Sally swallowed her disappointment that there was no news of John, and returned to the breakfast table. But her appetite was gone and she gave the rest of it to Ernie.

'Once the boys are at school, I'll go over and see if Betty's in, or if her neighbours know anything.' Peggy patted her hand. 'I know it's terribly hard, dear, but I'm sure . . .'

'I know,' murmured Sally, listening to Anne's happy voice in the hall. 'If Martin's come through, then I'm sure John has. It's the not-knowing that's so hard,' she confessed.

The factory was buzzing with the news of Operation Dynamo as Sally, Pearl and Edie walked in. It took some time for everyone to settle, and although there was still too much chatter over the machines, Sally decided to ignore it. She didn't have the heart to say anything – didn't really have the heart for anything today.

It was almost the end of the shift when Sally saw Peggy bustle through the door. Her hands stilled and her mouth dried as she abandoned the khaki trousers she was working on and slowly got to her feet.

Peggy was arguing with Simmons. Now she was pushing past him, walking purposefully down the long aisle in the centre of the room as the machines quietened and then fell silent.

Sally couldn't tell by her expression what news she had – but she wasn't smiling. She found she couldn't breathe, and as her legs threatened to give way, Pearl had to grab her arm to steady her.

'It's not bad news,' said Peggy, as soon as she was in earshot, 'but it's not particularly good either.' She reached Sally and took her hands. 'I managed to catch Betty before she went back to her sister's place. John's alive, but he's been injured and will have to stay in hospital a while – but Betty told me the doctors are sure he'll make a full recovery.'

'Oh, thank God,' breathed Sally, the ready tears blinding her as she all but fell on to her chair. 'Thank God he's alive . . . I thought . . . I was sure . . .'

Peggy wrapped her arms round her and held her as the cocktail of pent-up fear and enormous relief finally boiled over into heaving sobs. When the storm was over, she dried her eyes and gripped Peggy's hand.

'What happened to him? Is he very badly injured? Can I visit him in hospital?'

'The *Little Nell* took a direct blast from the enemy guns. John and the others were blown off her and into the water. John has shrapnel wounds to his back and face, his leg is broken in two places and his shoulder was dislocated. He was one of the lucky ones and got picked up within minutes of the *Little Nell* going down.'

She fell silent, her expressive face mournful. 'His father and one of his cousins were never found,' she said quietly. 'The other boy and his uncle escaped with just a few bruises and scratches, and will be sent home today.'

Sally stared at her in horror. 'Does John know about his father?'

Peggy shook her head. 'He's heavily sedated, but he'll be told once he comes round enough to fully understand.' Peggy took out her handkerchief and blew her nose. 'Poor Betty is beside herself. She and Stan were childhood sweethearts, you know, and her sister's boy was only fifteen. I can't imagine what they must be going through.'

'Can I go and visit John?'

'No, my dear, only Betty is allowed to travel to Dover. You'll just have to wait until he comes home.'

'But he will make a full recovery?'

'So Betty tells me.'

'That's enough chit-chat,' boomed Simmons. 'You're not even supposed to be here, madam, and you're keeping Miss Turner from her work.'

Peggy had the light of battle in her eyes as she faced Simmons. 'You really are the most *obnoxious* little man, aren't you?' she said in her most scathing tone. 'Don't for one *minute* think you can bully *me*, Simmons. I'll leave when I'm ready – and not before.' She held his gaze, and he was the first to look away.

There was a smattering of applause and a few whistles of encouragement from the surrounding women. Simmons went scarlet. 'Get out of my factory,' he hissed.

Peggy raised her eyebrows. 'It's not *your* factory,' she retorted, 'and I'll be having a word with Mr Goldman before I leave. I can't imagine *what* he was thinking when he hired you.' With that, she jammed her handbag under arm, hitched the gas-mask box over her shoulder and strode away, head high, seemingly unaware of the admiring looks from the other women and their low murmurs of approval.

She hadn't quite reached the door to the office when Simmons caught up with her and barred the way.

Sally and the others watched and silently cheered her on as Simmons made what was clearly a grovelling apology, escorting her away from the office and off the premises.

'Blimey,' breathed Pearl. 'Who'd have thought sweet, kind, lovely little Peggy could be such a tartar?'

'I suspect she has more in common with her sister than she cares to admit,' laughed Sally. 'If you want to witness a real harridan at work, you should meet Doris. When she's in full flow, she's enough to scare even Hitler.'

'Perhaps we should send her, and others like her, across the Channel as our secret weapons,' said Brenda, lighting a cigarette. 'There's nothing like a woman on her high horse to scare the living daylights out of bullies.'

Sally sat down that evening and, with Anne's help, wrote a letter to John. Her spelling was improving, as was her handwriting, but she still had difficulty with the thin nib that splattered ink everywhere and left far too many blots on the paper. The finished article looked as if a spider had crawled across the page.

She deliberately kept the letter short, for she didn't really know how to express her deep feelings for him, and if someone had to read it to him, she didn't want him to be embarrassed. Instead of telling him how much she loved him, she sent her condolences for his terrible loss, and told him of her relief and joy that he would soon be well enough to come home. Finishing with a brief regret that she couldn't visit him, she signed it *with love from Sally* and added two kisses at the bottom.

Sealing the envelope, she dropped it in the letterbox at the bottom of the street. All she could do now was wait for his reply and hope he'd recover quickly so they could be together again.

There was still no reply from him three weeks later, and as there was no way of finding out how he was,

Sally had to tamp down on the frustration and get on with things in the firm belief that he would write when he could. But at night she fretted, her thoughts and dreams jumbled and disturbing, leaving her emotionally drained.

As Anne's wedding day dawned with the promise of sunshine, Sally knew she must put her worries aside and help to make this a special day. With determined cheerfulness, she joined in the chaos as the girls battled to get five minutes alone in the bathroom before they got dressed in their finery.

The car had been taken out of storage and off the four piles of bricks. Jim and Ron had bolted the wheels back on and spent several hours polishing the bodywork and chrome to gleaming perfection before filling it with enough precious petrol to get them to the church and back.

The three boys complained bitterly about having to wear their school uniform on a Saturday. But, as it was the only decent set of clothing they possessed, their complaints were ignored. Ernie's wheelchair had been decorated with strips of coloured ribbon, and Sally had added a few sprays of forsythia blossom to mark the occasion. The chair would go in the boot of the car in case Ernie got too tired, but it seemed he was determined to use the walking stick. Ron had lovingly carved a dog's head in the handle, and Ernie was suddenly quite happy to be seen with it.

Sally had put her worries aside, finding solace in

the hard work of getting the three bridesmaids' dresses finished in time. She'd just put the finishing touches to her own dress when the doorbell rang yet again. It was Anne's friend Dorothy from Cliffehaven Primary, arriving flushed and excited from her honeymoon. She and Greg, her Canadian soldier, had married three days before, and Dorothy was to be Anne's matron of honour.

Cissy was doing everyone's make-up and hair, bossing them about so much that she was finally banished from Anne's bedroom by her mother. Sally got Ernie dressed in his freshly pressed blazer, shirt and short trousers, while Ron polished shoes over a piece of paper on the kitchen table. Jim was sent to the nearby hall to check that the tables had been laid properly with all the food their neighbours had kindly donated for the occasion, and that the decorations were tasteful. Mrs Finch sat like a tiny empress in a comfortable chair in the hall so she could watch the fun until it was time to leave.

The doorbell rang again, and Sally answered it to find Doris on the doorstep. She was resplendent in a silk suit, the fancy hat tipped forward so the brim almost covered half her face. The ubiquitous fur was draped round her shoulders, despite the warm June day. 'Ted is waiting in the car,' she said. 'I hope everyone is ready. Time is getting rather short.'

'I'm coming,' called Peggy, making her way carefully down the stairs in her high-heeled shoes. The navy and white suit looked very smart with the dinky little white confection of netting and papier-mâché flowers that perched on her freshly styled hair. The outfit was finished with white shoes, bag and gloves, and Sally thought she'd never looked so elegant.

'Right,' Peggy said, determinedly, 'let's get every-one in the car. It'll be a tight squeeze, but the boys can sit on laps.'

'No boy is sitting on me,' said Doris. 'Do you have any idea how much this suit cost?'

Peggy shrugged dismissively as she chivvied Ron and the boys ahead of her. 'It's a good thing you've got a big car then,' she muttered, as she stepped outside and regarded the gleaming Bentley.

'Cor,' shouted Ernie. 'We going in that?'

'Yes, you are,' said Doris, hastily forestalling him from stroking the bonnet. 'And I'd appreciate it if you didn't touch anything or scratch the leather.'

Ernie eyed her solemnly. They'd had run-ins before. Then he gave her a huge grin. 'I like yer 'at,' he said, before ducking into the car. 'It 'ides yer face.'

Ron snorted, Doris went pink, and there was a flurry of giggles as the boys piled into the back seat. Sally tried to look stern, but it was impossible. The look on Doris's face was just too comical.

Once everyone was settled, they were waved away until they were out of sight. Pearl and Edie pushed through the little gathering on the steps and, clutching their hats, ran down the pavement to catch the bus. Billy was home on leave, and would meet them at the church with his best mate, Tom.

Cissy had raided the theatre's wardrobe for the bridesmaids' dresses, and Sally had adapted them to suit the occasion. The sequins and beads had been carefully removed from the tight-fitting bodices of the long ballet dresses which she'd dyed candy pink, or blue, or lavender. Using the frothy netting from another eight dresses, she'd dyed them to match, adding enough layers over the muslin underskirt so they couldn't be seen through. They reached mid-calf to show off slender ankles and shoes that had been dyed to tone with the dresses. Each of them carried a single rose donated by a neighbour whose garden continued to flourish despite the lack of rain.

Sally stood in the hall with Dorothy and Cissy waiting for Anne. When she emerged on the landing and came slowly down the stairs clutching Jim's arm, there was an audible gasp of admiration.

Anne was radiant, the borrowed veil falling in a cloud about her lovely face from the glittering comb fixed in her dark hair, the lovely dress shimmering as she moved. Her skin was lightly tanned from the early sun, pearls gleamed at her throat and in her ears, and her eyes sparkled with the kind of joy that could only come from a woman in love. She carried a bunch of roses that matched her dress, the thorns carefully removed by Sally, the stems wrapped tightly in the last scraps of the same silk.

There were tears in Jim's eyes as he gazed in awe at his lovely daughter, and Sally felt a huge lump in her throat. She missed her dad more than ever these days and it was at times like this that the longing to see him again was almost unbearable.

'You look very lovely, my dear. A truly beautiful bride.' Mrs Finch got carefully to her feet and handed her a jeweller's box. 'Please accept this little gift, Anne. You're such a sweet girl, and you deserve something extra-special on this happiest of days.'

As Anne opened the box there was a loud gasp from Jim. The brooch was in the shape of a sprig of flowers – but these were no ordinary blooms, for the petals were diamonds, the heart of each flower a dark green emerald.

As Anne drew it out of the box, the diamonds shot fire around the hallway and the emeralds glowed as green as the deepest sea. 'It's absolutely stunning,' she breathed, watching the spectrum of colour dart against the faded paint on the walls. 'Quite exquisite.' She reluctantly put the brooch back into the box and handed it back. 'Thank you so much, Mrs Finch, but I can't possibly accept such a generous gift.'

Mrs Finch firmly pressed the box back into her hand. 'My husband gave this to me on our wedding day,' she said, 'and he would approve of me passing it on.'

'But it's—'

Mrs Finch waved away her protest, clasped

Anne's fingers round the box, her own gnarled hands covering them. 'Your family have taken me in and looked after me as one of their own,' she said softly. 'My sons and their families have deserted me, and you have become the daughter I never had, the daughter that I feel blessed to know. This was a token of my husband's love – now it is my token to you. Please take it, Anne.'

Anne drew her into a gentle embrace, kissing the soft cheek. 'Thank you so very much,' she murmured. 'I will think of you every time I wear it, and I'm honoured you regard me as a daughter.'

Mrs Finch gently moved from the embrace and sat down as Dorothy helped pin the brooch to Anne's dress where it glittered with icy fire. 'There,' she breathed, 'I knew it would look perfect.'

Jim took Mrs Finch's hand and kissed it. 'To be sure, me darlin', that's the finest gift I've ever seen.'

'Get away with you, you rogue,' she replied with a smile, as she gently patted his cheek. 'I've heard enough blarney from you to last a lifetime, so enough of this. We have a wedding to attend.'

Sally realised they were all damp-eyed and getting far too emotional. 'Come on,' she said, after clearing her throat and glancing at the hall clock. 'We don't want to be too late at the church, and poor Martin must be having kittens by now.'

The ancient church of grey stone and flint had stood in the valley behind Cliffehaven since Saxon days.

Surrounded by trees, it serenely watched over the rolling hills and pastures where sheep and cattle had grazed for centuries. As the car drew up to the lychgate and they climbed out, the bells were ringing out their joyful melody.

Dorothy and Cissy fussed with the dresses and flowers while Sally helped Mrs Finch along the cinder path to the church porch where the verger was waiting to escort her to her seat. She waited on the steps as the rest of the wedding party approached.

Jim drew Anne to a halt at the bottom of the stone steps that had been worn by generations of feet. He turned to Anne and kissed her cheek. 'My beautiful girl,' he murmured, as he almost reverently adjusted the veil so it drifted over her face. 'I wish you happiness and all the love in the world on this special day.'

Anne clasped his fingers, sharing a moment of silence with him before she turned to the three girls. 'Are we all ready?' At their nods, she took a deep breath and tucked her hand into the crook of Jim's arm. 'Then you can start the music,' she said to the verger, who was hovering in the porchway.

The rousing organ music soared to the ancient rafters as they entered the candlelit church and slowly made their way down the worn flagstones and past the paintings of The Stations of the Cross that lined the walls above the dark wooden pews. The golden eagle glowed above the polished oak of the lectern and the little light in the tabernacle on the altar seemed to beckon as they approached the carpeted steps where the priest waited in glorious robes of red and gold.

Pearl was radiant as she sat next to Billy, who looked very dashing in his Royal Navy uniform. A man of medium height with fair hair and blue eyes, he was looking at Pearl with such tenderness, Sally wondered if there would be an engagement announcement before too long.

Martin and his best man – who sported a magnificent handlebar moustache – were very handsome in full dress uniform, and Sally watched as Martin stepped from the pew to greet his bride. Sally saw the adoration in his eyes and briefly wondered if anyone would ever look at her in such a way.

She hastily pulled her thoughts together as she realised she and the other bridesmaids were being regarded by some snooty-looking woman in the second pew. There were three other people sitting beside her and Sally wondered who they were. Their clothes looked expensive, the furs and hats even more magnificent than Doris's.

She glanced at Doris, who was giving them the evil eye on the other side of the aisle, and bit down on her smile. It seemed that at last Doris had been outshone.

Their vows were made, the register signed, and the glorious music once again soared to the rafters as

Anne and Martin went arm-in-arm back down the aisle. They stopped to greet their guests, shake hands and kiss cheeks; then it was out into the sunshine for the photographs which would be taken by Mr Walters, a retired reporter from the local newspaper.

'Who are they?' muttered Sally to Ron, as the rather stately group of four stood to one side of the milling guests looking distinctly uncomfortable.

'Martin's parents, his sister and her fiancé,' he muttered round the stem of his pipe. 'Stuck-up lot, if you ask me. Could barely give Jim and Peggy the time of day when they were introduced.'

'But it's wonderful they came,' said Cissy, who'd been listening in to the conversation. 'I mean, it shows they've given their approval, doesn't it?'

'I wouldn't count your chickens, girlie,' he mumbled. 'People like them don't approve of much at the best of times. I pity poor Anne having a mother-in-law like that.'

The three of them watched as Martin approached his family with Anne, who was looking amazingly calm and self-contained. He carefully kissed his mother and sister, shook hands with his father and the other young man, and kept tight hold of Anne's hand as she bore their polite, but faintly patronising, congratulations.

Ron chuckled. 'There's no use you getting cross on Anne's behalf,' he said to Sally. 'That girl can handle Doris, so she can certainly deal with that mob of snobs.' He puffed on his pipe. 'She won't let them spoil her day, you'll see.'

And he was proved to be right. The only sign of friction had come in the churchyard when Doris and Martin's mother realised with horror that they were wearing identical shoes. This tricky situation was soon resolved by Doris ordering Ted to return home to fetch a second and more exclusive pair she'd bought in Paris before the war. The fact that they were agonisingly tight and difficult to walk in was something Doris would never admit.

The wedding party finally moved from the church to the community hall that was only a short walk from the house. Martin's family didn't stay long, for which everyone was grateful – including the groom – and the party lasted well into the night.

Sally noticed that Pearl and Billy had been absent for quite a while, and then she saw them coming into the hall, hand-in-hand, with eyes for no-one else. Her suspicions were confirmed when Pearl rushed over to her a short while later and flashed the small diamond ring on her finger.

Sally leapt out of her chair and hugged her. 'It's about time,' she said and laughed. 'So, when's the wedding?'

'We're getting a special licence,' Pearl breathed. 'So it'll be within the week while Billy's on leave.' She glanced across at Anne. 'Do you think she'd lend me her dress?'

'You'd better ask her, but I'll have to take up the

hem – you're at least three inches shorter.' She smiled and kissed her cheek, wanting to be excited and happy for her, but deep inside the heartache twisted like a knife.

It seemed everyone was getting married, and here she was alone, not knowing if John would ever come home – or even if he really loved her. She plastered on a smile and joined in the celebrations, but every now and then she thought of John, and the anxiety swept over her like a great wave, and she had to go outside for a breath of air.

Anne and Martin left just before nine to drive to the little country hotel where they would spend the one and only night of their honeymoon before he had to return to base. They left the hall, the numerous cans tied to the car's rear bumper making an almighty racket as everyone poured into the street to wave them off.

'Oy,' shouted Warden Wally Hall, red with anger, moustache twitching. 'Shut that door – or turn off that blooming light. Don't you know there's a war on?'

He was greeted with a raucous rendition of 'Colonel Bogey' before the men swept him up and carried him on their shoulders back into the hall. His temper was soon soothed by several bottles of beer and a large plate of food.

Sally felt as if she was back in the East End, and it made her long for her dad – he would have been in his element. There was a lot of noise, the men were getting louder as the drink supplies dwindled; the food was copious, if not a little strange – someone had donated a bunch of carrots, which sat incongruously beside a plate of whelks and winkles and a tin of broken biscuits. The wedding cake was sponge and only one tier, but each tiny piece was devoured slowly and with much appreciation. Cake was a rare treat these days.

There was music too, a group of Irishmen who played piano, fiddle, fife and drum and soon had them all dancing. Sally was whirled on to the floor by the best man who danced with more vigour than expertise, and was then snatched away by Billy's friend Tom into a mad kind of jig that left her breathless. By the time the party was over, Sally was pleasantly exhausted.

Jim and Ron swayed arm-in-arm down the pavement, their voices raised in a joyous but drunken version of 'Danny Boy', as Peggy carried Charlie, and Cissy tried to disguise the fact that Bob had been at the beer. Mrs Finch was flushed with the effects of at least three glasses of sherry, and had fallen asleep in Ernie's wheelchair, so Sally carried him on her hip as she pushed the chair along the pavement. Pearl and Billy had slipped away some time ago, and Edie was going to a nightclub to dance the rest of the night away with Tom. Dorothy had gone home with her new husband.

'I don't think it would be wise to get either of the men to carry Mrs Finch upstairs tonight,' said Peggy, wincing at the loud singing coming from the kitchen. 'Let's put those two armchairs in the dining room together and make her a nest. She'll be quite comfortable.'

Once the old lady was settled with blankets and pillows, Cissy took the wilting Bob and Charlie down to their basement room and tucked them in. Sally was about to carry Ernie upstairs when Peggy stopped her.

'You've got a letter, Sally,' she said. 'It must have come by afternoon post.'

Sally looked at the unfamiliar writing and hope ignited. 'Do you think it's from John?'

'Well, no-one can tell you that until you open it,' she said, and laughed. 'Go on, put that boy to bed and enjoy your letter. I'll see you in the morning.'

Sally carried the sleeping child upstairs, woke him enough to use the lavatory and climb into his pyjamas, and then tucked him in bed.

She made sure the blackout curtains were tightly shut before turning on the bedside lamp and picking up the precious letter. Taking a deep breath, she carefully opened it and began to read.

Dear Sally,
I'm sorry I've taken so long to reply to your
letter, but until now it has not been possible. As
it is, I am dictating this to one of the nurses who
has been looking after me so well. My right arm
is in plaster, so I can't write it myself.

*My mother and I thank you for your
condolences. The loss of my father and young
cousin has hit our family hard, and we appreciate
your kind thoughts.*

*My injuries are such that I may be in hospital
for several more weeks yet, and the doctor has
advised me that I will have to go through a short
term of recuperation and physiotherapy before I
will be fit to return to work. It is unlikely that I
shall be home much before next Christmas.'*

'Oh, no,' Sally breathed. 'It's far worse than Peggy
thought.' She returned to the letter, a little put-out
at the stilted way it was written, but accepting he
couldn't get too romantic when someone else had
to write it.

*My mother has taken Father's death very hard,
and being the only son, it is my duty now to pay
the bills and look after her. As it is still uncertain
whether I can continue my job with the fire-
service, it will be vital to find other employment.
Because of this, I must ask you not to write
again, or hope that we can have any kind of
future together.*

Sally stifled her sobs with her hand as she curled
in the chair. The pain was deep, cutting her like a
knife. He didn't love her.

Time ticked by and she finally had the courage

to finish this awful letter. The words were blurred, but that didn't soften their cruelty.

> *I'm sorry, Sally, but I hope that one day you will understand why it is so necessary, and forgive me for any pain I might have caused you. What we had was very special, and I shall carry the memory of it always – but as the weeks have passed and I can see things more clearly, I realise I haven't been fair to you.*
>
> *You're a lovely girl, Sally, but you are very young, and I blame myself for any false hope I may have given you. One day, God willing, you will make some lucky man a wonderful wife – but it won't ever be me.*
>
> *Keep safe, sweet Sally,*
> *John.*

Sally crumpled the letter in her fist, crawled into bed and smothered her heart-rending tears with the blankets. The agony of knowing he didn't love her – had probably never loved her – was almost too much to bear.

Chapter Twelve

'It feels odd without Pearl and Edie in the house,' murmured Peggy. Like Anne and Mrs Finch, she was sitting in a deckchair on the only patch of back garden that hadn't been planted with vegetables. It was a hot August day and they were shelling peas and slicing beans.

'Yes, I quite miss Pearl's chattering. I wonder how Edie's getting on in Wiltshire? I never had her down as a country girl, but at least she's got her mother and sister with her. It must be a relief to know they've escaped Croydon now the real bombing's started.'

Peggy continued slicing beans. 'At least Pearl still visits. I think she gets lonely in that little house with Billy away, and it's nice to have her here.' Her hands stilled and she stared across the garden. 'She's asked Sally to move in with her, you know – and although I'll miss her and Ernie terribly, I've encouraged her to make a fresh start. I think it's a good thing. I worry about that girl, I really do,' she finished on a sigh.

'Yes, she seems to have lost her sparkle since she got that letter from John.'

'I suspect he broke things off. It can be the only explanation.'

'Poor Sally,' Anne sighed. 'I do feel for her. It's been almost two months, and yet I still catch her crying in some corner where she thinks no-one can see.' She slit the pod and thumbed the peas into the bowl with some asperity. 'I'm surprised at John letting her down like that. He seemed really taken with her.'

'I agree. And that's why his ending things doesn't feel right.' Peggy finished slicing the beans and put down the bowl. Adjusting Mrs Finch's sunhat so she wouldn't get sunburnt as she dozed, she leant back in her chair. 'I've tried contacting his mother, but the neighbour told me she'd gone down to Devon and rented a place there while he's in the convalescent home. She has no idea when they might get back.'

She sighed and sank lower in the deckchair. 'The officer in charge at the fire station wasn't much help either – but I got the feeling he knows more than he's letting on.'

'It sounds as if his injuries are worse than we thought,' murmured Anne.

'I wondered that,' she replied, turning her face to the sun, relishing its warmth. If she closed her eyes to the bomb-damaged garden wall and the missing roof of the house next door, it could almost be like a normal summer. 'But with no-one to ask, we'll have to wait until he gets back to find out what really happened.'

'After listening to Dad's horror story, it's a miracle anyone survived Dunkirk. But with the terrible bombing over the past week, it feels as if we're all living on a knife-edge – especially those of us with sweethearts in the Air Force.'

Peggy regarded her daughter through her lashes. The girl still had the glow of a woman in love, but she knew she was finding it hard to be living at home still, never knowing when she might see her husband again. 'When do you expect him to get leave?'

'I have no idea,' sighed Anne. 'His squadron are on constant alert, and they're flying almost daily missions. When he does have leave he's so fired up and impatient to get back to the airfield, I wonder why he bothers – but he's exhausted, Mum, and spends most of his leave asleep.'

'Poor man. They must all be under a terrible strain now the bombing raids have increased and the shipping in the Channel is coming under fire.'

Anne nodded. 'It's not just the men who are stressed,' she replied, softly. 'Every time I hear the planes take off, I wonder if it's Martin, and if I'll ever see him again.'

Peggy grasped her hand. She had no words that could comfort her daughter, even though she longed to take away the awful anxiety she could see in her eyes. This war had a lot to answer for.

'It was nice to see Alex again the other night,' said Anne, breaking the silence and changing the mood. 'He seems less intense somehow; perhaps it's because he's been given a squadron to lead and finally feels he's a real part of the action – instead of being stuck on base, training the young ones.' Anne blinked in the sunlight, her eyes suspiciously bright. 'And they are young, Mum, so very young, with only a few hours of flying time under their belt before they're sent out into the thick of it.'

Peggy had no intention of letting the conversation deteriorate into sadness again. 'Alex was certainly more cheerful over supper – but I suspect that had something to do with the vodka he brought.' She chuckled. 'Jim and Ron were absolutely legless by the end of the evening, but his gifts of sugar, butter and flour were a godsend now the rationing is getting even tighter – and I can understand that they all needed to let off some steam.'

'He and Martin get on very well, and Martin says the Poles are the bravest, most daring pilots he's had the privilege to fly with.' She smiled. 'They seem to lead charmed lives, but they have the most awful prangs – and with so few aircraft available, Martin wishes they wouldn't be quite so gung-ho.'

'I didn't like to spoil the mood the other night by asking about Alex's family. I don't suppose Martin knows if he's had any further news of them?'

'I asked Martin, and he said there'd been no post for Alex since that last awful letter from his sister.

But those who still have contacts inside Poland say that things have reached crisis point.'

'Then we must make sure he knows he has a home here, and people who care for him. Tell Martin next time you see him, and make it clear that Alex is welcome at any time – although I'm sure he already knows that.'

Anne was about to reply when they heard the latch click on the back gate. 'Granddad must be back from his hunting trip,' she muttered. 'Let's hope he's got a pheasant, or something for the pot, or we'll be eating vegetable soup again.'

But it wasn't Ron who stepped into the back garden. It was someone quite different, and it was clear right from the start that things at Beach View were about to change – and not for the better.

Sally loved being in the hills with Ron and the boys. She'd found freedom in the vast expanse of empty land, and a sense of well-being which came with the salty wind that blew from the sea even on the warmest days. Out here in these great rolling hills and deep valleys, Sally had found an inner peace, and discovered a side to her that she had never suspected she'd possessed. For here she felt at home – at one with the grandeur.

It hadn't always been so. The first time Ron had persuaded her to join them she'd been wary of that emptiness, of the feeling of isolation and danger that seemed to lurk in the dark thickets and spiny gorse. And yet, guided by Ron's knowledge and calm education, she'd gradually begun to understand and appreciate that this wild, empty land was not only beautiful, it could enchant and provide.

Now the crowded, poor streets and alleyways of Bow were a world away, and she wondered if she could ever return there – could ever survive the smog after breathing such clean, clear air, and feeling so free.

She tramped purposefully up the hill in the old dungarees she'd cut down to fit, the hessian sack of firewood heavy on her back. Her leg muscles no longer complained and her breathing was steady. These regular outings after the long stints at the factory were making her strong, and her mirror told her she'd been tanned by the sun and looked healthier than ever. But the sadness inside lingered, and she tried not to think of John – yet every now and then she wondered where he was, and whether he ever thought of her.

'It's not a race,' muttered Ron, who was striding along beside her, Ernie on his shoulders, two brace of poached pheasant hidden in his pockets and a hare in his hand. 'Take time to look around you, Sally. You never know what you might be missing.'

He nodded towards Bob and Charlie, who had smaller sacks of twigs and were racing ahead of them, Harvey at their heels. 'Their only thought is for their tea,' he said, 'but at that age they're always hungry.'

She grinned at him, hitched the sack more comfortably over her shoulder and slowed her pace. She was hungry too, but the pleasure of taking in her surroundings made her forget that hunger as she gazed about her. Because of Ron, she and Ernie could now name most of the wild flowers that grew in the windswept grass – could recognise rose-hips, sloe, elderberry and blackberry, and distinguish the different calls of the birds, from the creaky-gate cry of the pheasant to the melody of the song thrush. They collected berries now it was summer, and Ron had carefully taught them which mushrooms to pick last autumn. Nature's larder provided many a treat – and it was all free.

In the spring, Ron had taken her and the boys to watch fox cubs and badgers at play, and very early one morning he'd led them to the edge of a silent glade, where they'd sat entranced as a magnificent stag had warily led his doe and fawn to drink from a dew pond. They were sights and memories that would stay with her for the rest of her life.

As they breached the final hill before home, she heard the rapid hammer-drill of a woodpecker along with the soft coo of the wood pigeons. In a world of turmoil, this countryside she had come to love was an oasis of peace, and she would always hold a special place in her heart for this old man who so generously shared it with her.

She turned her thoughts to Pearl and their plans for the following weekend, when Sally would move out of Beach View and into the little terraced house Billy had inherited from his grandfather. She was excited at the prospect, hoping that a change of scenery would help her to forget John and get on with her life. Her home-dressmaking business could flourish in Pearl's front parlour, they could share the care for Ernie; and when Billy came home on leave, Peggy had assured her she could always return to Beach View for as long as she wanted. For someone who'd had so little before she'd arrived in Cliffehaven, Sally felt blessed.

The sack seemed to grow heavier the nearer they got to Beach View and, as Ron lifted Ernie down and the boys pushed through the back gate, she gratefully took it from her back and dragged it into the garden.

'Blimey, Sal. You look like some gyppo. What you done to yerself, gel?'

Sally froze in shock as the heavily made-up peroxide blonde rose from the deckchair and smoothed away the creases in the garish red and orange summer frock that clung to every curve. 'Mum?' she managed, hitching the dungaree strap back over her shoulder. 'What you doing here?'

'Well, that's nice, ain't it? I come all the way from the Smoke, and all I get is "what you doin' 'ere?"' She folded her arms, the plastic bracelets clacking on her wrists. 'Ain't yer even gunna say hello, then?'

'Mum, Mum.' Ernie was struggling to reach her.

'I knew you'd come,' he yelled, as he hobbled towards Florrie, flung his arms round her hips and buried his grubby face in her frock.

'Hello, luv,' she cooed, patting his shoulder and kissing the air above his head. 'At least someone's glad to see me,' she said, her accusing gaze aimed at Sally.

'You took your time getting here,' retorted Sally. 'It's nearly a year since we left, and neither of us has heard a thing from you since.'

'I 'ad things to do,' she said airily, 'and you know I don't find writing and stuff easy.' She grimaced as Ernie sniffed and buried his head deeper into her side.

'You could have got someone to write a card for you – you could even have telephoned. I put the number on my letters. Didn't you get them?'

'Course I did, but I ain't got time to mess about reading letters and making phone calls. There's a bloody war on, or 'adn't you noticed?'

'Did you send our address to Dad? Have you seen him?'

'He ain't been 'ome much,' she said rather vaguely. 'But 'e knows where you are, right enough.' Florrie prised Ernie's dirty hands from her hips with a look of disgust. 'Go and 'ave a wash, mate. You're filthy, and this is a new dress.'

Ernie's little face collapsed with disappointment. 'But I . . .'

'Just do it, Ernie.' Florrie's blue eyes flashed and

314

the bright smile disappeared as her red lips formed a thin line and she nudged him away.

'There's no need to talk to him like that,' Sally said grimly as she steadied him.

''E's my kid. I'll talk to 'im any way I want.' She examined the damage to her frock and brushed at the smears of dirt on the material.

'It's a pity you didn't remember he was yours when we left London,' retorted Sally. She smiled at Ernie, who was now hovering by the basement door. 'Go and wash, love, then come back to me for a cuddle.'

'You're making that kid soft,' said Florrie. 'He's far too old to be 'aving cuddles. What is he now – eight, nine?' She sniffed derisively. 'Still a skinny little runt. All this sea air ain't done much for 'im, 'as it?'

'He's only just seven,' Sally replied evenly, her anger firmly controlled. 'He's thin because he's not been well – but on the whole he's far healthier than he ever was back in Bow.'

'If you say so.' Florrie sat down in the deckchair. Crossing her legs, she revealed a good deal of shapely thigh and the tops of her stockings. She shot a glance at Ron. 'Ain't you gunna introduce me then? That old geezer looks like 'e's about to 'ave an 'eart attack at the sight of a decent pair of legs.'

'The name's Ronan Reilly,' he said with a glower, 'and I've seen more tempting bits of meat on a butcher's block.' He grabbed the sacks of kindling and stomped off to his shed where Bob and Charlie were watching with avid interest.

'Well, of all the . . .'

'You asked for that,' said Sally, biting down on a smile. Ron's judgement was pinpoint accurate as usual – he'd take no nonsense from Florrie.

Sally pulled the scarf from her hair and mopped her sweaty face before stuffing it into the pocket of the dungarees she always wore when Ron took her up into the hills. 'If Dad knows where we are, why hasn't he come to see us?'

'How should I know?' Florrie smoked her cigarette with fierce intensity. 'He ain't 'ome that often, and it's difficult to get down 'ere,' she said less aggressively. 'I got no idea where 'e is at the moment – but I think 'e's on the convoys.'

Sally felt a stab of disappointment. She'd been hoping for news of her father, but Florrie was clearly not interested in anyone but herself. She eyed the empty deckchairs and sat down. 'Where is everyone?'

Florrie squashed the cigarette butt beneath the toe of her high-heeled sandals, the tarnished ankle bracelet glittering in the sun. 'Peggy took that old biddy indoors, and Anne's getting some drinks.' She folded her arms and eyed her daughter steadily and without approval. 'You've changed,' she said flatly, 'and what's with all the posh talk? You ain't my Sal no more.'

'I stopped being your Sal that day you couldn't be bothered to come to the station to see us off,' she said evenly. 'And yes, I've changed. There's nothing wrong in trying to improve myself.'

Florrie snorted. 'Improve yerself?' she sneered. 'Where's that gunna get yer, eh? Some poxy job in a factory, and a room in this dump.'

'It's not a dump,' she retorted. 'Peggy's given me and Ernie a real home, and shown us more affection in the last year than you ever have. Compared to our place in Bow, this is a palace.'

'You're an ungrateful little cow,' snarled Florrie. 'Me and yer dad did the best we could, but it ain't easy tryin' to manage without a man in the 'ouse 'alf the time and a sick kid to bring up.'

Sally was about to remind her that it was she who'd brought up Ernie, when he came out of the basement and hesitantly approached them. Keeping her anger well hidden, she lifted him on to her lap and held him close. 'What are you doing here, Mum?' she asked again.

'I got bombed out, didn't I? 'Ad to move in with a friend.' She lit another cigarette, studiously avoiding Sally's gaze.

Sally had a fleeting image of that street lined with tenement houses, the factory and the gasworks looming over them. 'How bad was it?'

Florrie shrugged. 'Bad enough. 'Alf the bleedin' street's gorn. We was lucky we was all in the public shelter, else we'd 'ave all copped it. The gasworks

317

went up along with the factory – so I was out of work as well as on the bleedin' streets.'

Sally could imagine the devastation, despite having seen only a glimpse of it here in Cliffehaven. 'Solomon's has gone?'

'He's setting up down 'ere with Goldman. They've bought the place next door evidently, and that's why I come down. I gotta job there.'

Sally's spirits plunged further. 'That's where I'm working,' she said softly. 'Goldman made me line-manager.'

'Blimey.' The blue eyes regarded her without affection. 'Comes to something when me own daughter gets to be management – talk about changing sides.' She narrowed her eyes. 'I 'ope you don't think you're gunna lord it over me, gel, cos I won't stand for that.'

'I'll make sure you're in a different section,' she said hastily. 'It won't help either of us once the other girls know we're related. They'll think I'll be doing you favours.'

'I don't need no favours from you,' she said with a sniff. 'Solly's promised to set me up nice and tight in the cutting department where I can earn some decent money.'

'But you ain't – aren't a cutter.'

'I been learning.' Her gaze was flat, her expression determined.

Sally eyed her as her thoughts raced. She'd always suspected Florrie had a thing going with Solomon

– it had often been the cause of the rows between her parents. 'Was it Solomon who took you in when you got bombed out?'

'He's got a big 'ouse,' she replied matter-of-factly. 'With 'is wife living with 'er sister in Scotland, it seemed a shame to let all them rooms go to waste.' She looked Sally in the eye. 'I moved into the spare room and paid rent like any other lodger.'

Sally almost laughed. She knew her mother far too well, and it was ludicrous of Florrie to even attempt such a ridiculous lie. She eyed the suitcase and gas mask that were standing beside the deck-chair. 'Where are you planning to stay?'

'Well, 'ere of course. Peggy said I could 'ave the room next to you. Solly gave me some money to pay for the weekend, and once the Billeting Office opens on Monday, he'll sort out the government grant and such-like.'

'Me and Ernie are moving out at the end of next week,' said Sally. She saw the glint in Florrie's eyes and hastened to put her right. 'My mate, Pearl, got married recently; as her Billy's away at sea, she asked me to move in to the spare room with Ernie.'

'Are you really staying, Mum?' Ernie breathed. 'You ain't gunna go off again?'

'Not just yet, luv.' She glanced coolly at Sally. 'I was 'oping we could be a real family again, but it seems yer sister 'as other plans.' She shot Ernie a smile. 'Wouldn't you like to stay 'ere with me and Sal instead of going off?'

Ernie eyed her thoughtfully and then shrugged. 'Dunno,' he muttered.

'I might even take you for a paddle on the beach,' she said, as she dug in her big white plastic handbag for her powder compact and lipstick.

'They got mines on the beach, Mum,' said Ernie. 'We ain't allowed down there or the bombs will blow us all up.'

'That's nice, luv,' she murmured, distracted by her reflection in the compact mirror and the need to add more lipstick.

Ernie looked up at Sally in confusion. 'Does Mum want us to get blown up, Sal?' he hissed.

'Of course she doesn't. She's just not listening properly, that's all.'

'Why?'

'Because that's the way she is,' said Sally flatly. 'Why don't you go and help Bob and Charlie with the kindling?'

'All right,' he said with a huge sigh. 'I know when I ain't wanted.'

Sally grinned at him and handed him the walking stick. 'Get on with you,' she said fondly, 'and stop feeling so sorry for yourself. Look, Harvey wants you to go and play with him.'

Snapping the compact and lipstick away in the large bag, Florrie eased back into the deckchair and closed her eyes. 'This is like being on 'oliday,' she sighed. 'Mind you, I 'ad one 'ell of a journey down. The lines were up, and we 'ad to get off and on bleedin' buses every five minutes. I thought I'd never get 'ere.'

Sally was quite shocked to discover how her mother's voice and language grated on her. Even Pearl's accent had been smoothed out over the past months, and she had become used to the softer, rounded tones of Peggy and her family.

'How did you find Beach View?'

She gave a chuckle. 'I met a really nice bloke outside Cliffehaven Station who gave me a lift, otherwise I'd've 'ad to walk, and that suitcase ain't 'alf 'eavy.'

'Trust you to find the one man in Cliffehaven who has a car and doesn't mind ferrying you about,' muttered Sally.

'It's a knack I learned years ago, Sal. Wouldn't 'urt you none either.' She cast a sneering glance over Sally's dungarees, wellington boots and cotton shirt. 'Not that any bloke would look at you twice in that get-up. You've let yerself go, Sal, and that's a fact, otherwise I'd've asked you along for drinks with 'im tonight at the Mermaid. He's bound to 'ave a mate.'

Sally inwardly shuddered at the thought. Florrie usually got very drunk when out with her men-friends, and it was embarrassing to watch. 'I can't go out, anyway,' she replied, 'there's Ernie to look after, and I've got a lot of sewing to finish.'

Florrie didn't seem at all put out by this as she lifted her face to the sun and closed her eyes. 'This is a lovely sunny spot,' she sighed. 'I might even get a tan now I'm at the seaside.'

Peggy came out of the house carrying a tray of mismatched glasses, with Anne following closely behind with a jug of cordial. These were set on the low stool.

Florrie opened one eye and stared resentfully at the cordial. 'I thought we was 'aving proper drinks,' she muttered. 'I don't suppose there ain't any chance of a beer? Only I'm parched.'

'I keep the beer for the men,' said Peggy firmly. 'It's the cordial or water.'

'What about a cuppa?'

'Sorry. I'm down to the last few leaves, so I'm rationing it for breakfasts.'

Florrie heaved a very deep sigh and closed her eyes again. 'Then I suppose I'll 'ave to 'ave the cordial.'

Sally shot an apologetic glance at Peggy, who shrugged and poured the cordial into the glasses. Ron and the boys took theirs to a sunny spot by the tomatoes where they sat on strips of sacking and helped prick out the cabbage seedlings that would soon be planted in the vegetable plot.

Ernie seemed quite happy, so Sally turned her attention back to Florrie, who was now leaning back in the deckchair as if she was on holiday at some smart hotel, waiting to be served refreshments. 'How did you get a permit to cross into this restricted zone, Mum?'

'Solly knows some bloke at the Transport Office,' she murmured. 'I think 'e laid it on a bit thick about me being bombed out, and that me kids were down 'ere and such. But it worked, and 'ere I am – out of London and away from them bombs.'

She sat up as Anne handed her the glass of cordial. She took a sip, found to her surprise that she liked it and took another. 'London's on fire, you know,' she said to no-one in particular. 'Them Germans are flying over nearly every day now.'

'It's not much better down here,' replied Peggy dryly. 'We've had raids too, and a great many tip and runs. Didn't you know that the newspapers are calling this part of the south coast Bombers' Alley?'

Florrie's blue eyes widened. 'Solly said it would be safe 'ere,' she breathed. 'That's why I agreed to come.'

'He was obviously misinformed,' said Peggy.

'But the kids are still 'ere, ain't they? They wouldn't let 'em stay if it were that dangerous.'

'Our school nearly got bombed the other day,' shouted Ernie from across the garden. 'It was exciting, cos we 'ad to go into the shelter under the playground and we could 'ear the planes and everything.'

'See?' said Florrie. 'Even Ernie ain't scared. I can't see what all the fuss is about.'

Anne lit a cigarette and regarded Florrie with uncharacteristic coolness. 'A lot of the local children have already been evacuated, along with most of the ones who came down from London. The class-rooms are almost empty, and soon it won't be viable to keep the school going. The bombing so close to the school was a warning to all of us that it isn't safe any more.'

'But your boys are still 'ere.' Florrie glanced across at Bob and Charlie who were helping Ernie to water the vegetable plants. 'And Sally's been talking about moving in with a mate. It don't sound that urgent to me.'

'It might not seem urgent to you,' said Peggy. 'But Jim and I have been talking seriously about sending them all away until things quieten down. And yet we've heard some of the evacuees' stories, and we can't make up our minds what to do for the best.' She heaved a deep sigh. 'It's all a bit of a dilemma really – especially now Sally's making plans to start afresh at Pearl's.'

'I don't see why. If it ain't safe, then they gotta go. My kids done all right with you, why shouldn't they be all right somewhere else?'

'We were lucky Peggy took us in,' said Sally. She lowered her voice so the boys couldn't hear what she was saying. 'No-one wanted Ernie,' she said quietly, 'and the lady from the Billeting Office said he'd have to go to an orphanage. If Peggy hadn't come along when she did, we'd have had to get on the next train back to London, because there was no way I was leaving Ernie in some home.'

'It were a good thing you didn't,' she replied. 'It's

been 'ard enough to cope without you and 'im getting under me feet.'

'Don't worry,' said Sally. 'I don't expect you to look after either of us. We've managed very well without you.'

'Oh, that's nice, ain't it?' Florrie looked to Peggy and Anne for support, found she didn't have it, and glared at Sally. 'I'm still yer mother. You got no call to be rude.'

'And you've no right to call yourself a mother,' hissed Sally, her emotions finally getting the better of her. 'You haven't seen or written to us since we left, and yet you haven't asked about Ernie's health, or how I've been coping – you could hardly force yourself to give him a proper hug and kiss. So don't you *dare* come down here and start pretending you care.'

Florrie slammed the glass on to the stool and sat forward in her chair. 'You ain't too big to get a good slap, my girl,' she growled. 'You wanna watch yer mouth, or I'll shut it for yer.'

'I wouldn't if I were you,' Sally retorted. 'I'm bigger and stronger than I was a year ago, and not afraid to hit you back.'

'I think it would be better if we discussed this once the boys are in bed and Jim is home,' said Peggy calmly.

'I'm off out tonight. Got a date at the Mermaid.'

'Isn't your children's safety rather more important than a date with some man at the Mermaid?' Peggy's face was a mask of dislike.

'Well, of course it is,' Florrie blustered. 'But 'e was ever so kind, giving me a lift and all, and I can 'ardly stand 'im up, now, can I? It would be rude.'

'Rude or not, I think it's your responsibility to be here when we discuss Sally and Ernie's well-being.'

Florrie took a long drink of cordial as if stalling for time. 'I don't see that's any of your business,' she replied finally. 'If Sal wants to go swanning off with Ernie to some countryside hell-hole, it's up to 'er.' She put down the glass, glanced at her watch and gathered her things. 'I'd like to see me room now,' she said. 'Time's getting on, and I need to change out of this frock. I don't want to be late for that drink.'

'I'll show you the way,' muttered Sally, her face red with shame as she caught Peggy's eye.

Florrie hadn't changed a bit, and in a matter of half an hour had managed to upset everyone that Sally held dear. As she led the way up to the top floor, she knew she had hardened her heart enough to withstand all Florrie could throw at her, but she resolved to safeguard innocent little Ernie, for she suspected his mother was about to break his heart all over again.

Sally was very quiet as she helped Anne and Peggy in the kitchen. She went into the dining room and laid the table, her gaze repeatedly returning to the sewing machine in the corner and the pile of sewing she had still to do. She was exhausted rather than being exhilarated from her trek across the hills, and all she really wanted to do was go to bed and shut out the world until morning. But there was the evening meal to get through first.

Florrie came downstairs almost an hour later in another tight-fitting frock. She had done her hair in a new style and had freshened her make-up. She cornered Sally in the dining room while the others were in the kitchen.

'I don't know what you got planned for Ernie, but let me tell you straight, Sal. I ain't going nowhere with 'im. You understand?'

'Oh, I understand perfectly,' she replied.

Florrie raised a finely plucked eyebrow. 'Don't you get sarky with me, my girl. I got things planned so, as you seem to think you're in charge of Ernie, then you can get on with it. I got a life to lead, and 'aving 'im on me tail all the time ain't gunna help.'

'I see. So it doesn't matter about me and my life then?'

'You ain't old enough to 'ave the sort of life I'm aiming for,' said Florrie in an angry hiss, 'and I ain't gunna let you and Ernie spoil it.'

Sally frowned. 'How exactly could we spoil it?'

'Solly's promised to marry me once the war's over and 'e can get a divorce, but 'e's already warned me he won't take on Ernie.'

'Haven't you forgotten you're still married to Dad?'

'Not for long,' she said dismissively. 'The divorce papers are already going through.'

Sally stared at her, numb with shock.

'Don't look at me like that,' snapped Florrie. 'Me and yer dad were over years ago. I only stayed with 'im cos 'e was earning good money.'

'Does Dad know you're divorcing him – or are you just going to present him with the papers the next time he comes home on leave?'

'He knows right enough,' she said bitterly. 'He were the one to file the papers in the first place.' She grabbed Sally's arm, her long nails digging into her flesh. 'But you keep that to yerself. I don't want Solly finding out it weren't me what started the divorce.'

'But if he's named on the petition, he'll find out soon enough.' She wrested her arm from her mother's grip and massaged it.

Florrie's gaze drifted. 'He ain't. It were another bloke altogether.'

'Well, well, and who do we have here?' Jim strolled into the dining room and looked appreciatively at Florrie from head to toes.

Florrie's smile switched on like a light bulb. 'I'm Sally's mother,' she simpered. 'You must be Jim.'

'Indeed I am,' he said with a wink. 'Sure, and you're not old enough to be the mother of Sally. Why you're far too young.'

'I can tell you're full of the Irish blarney, Jim,' she said with a giggle. 'You are a one.'

'Well now, I've always found that a pretty woman likes to receive a compliment.'

'Get away with you,' she said, lightly tapping his arm.

'When you've quite finished,' snapped Peggy from the doorway. 'Tea's ready.'

'I was just welcoming our new—'

'I know exactly what you were doing, Jim Reilly. Go and help your father in the kitchen.' She turned her furious gaze on Florrie. 'Are you staying for tea?'

'Why not? I am paying for it after all,' replied Florrie, her gaze never wavering beneath Peggy's glare.

'Then you'll respect my home and my family by not flirting with my husband, or bullying your daughter.' Peggy folded her arms. 'You can sit at the end of the table next to Ernie.'

Sally didn't say much during the meal; the conversation round the table was stilted, the atmosphere charged. Jim and Ron ate in silence, Peggy glared down the table at Florrie, and even Mrs Finch was unusually quiet as the boys chattered to one another.

Cissy had no real idea of what was going on as she'd only just arrived home, but she'd clearly decided to try and lighten the mood by chattering on about her day and the show she was rehearsing that evening. 'I like your hairstyle,' she said to Florrie. 'Is that the latest fashion in London?'

'It's called the Victory Roll,' she replied. 'It's ever

so easy to do. You just roll it back at the sides, and up at the back, 'olding it in place with pins or, if you 'ave one, a snood. A lot of girls stuff wadding in the rolls to make 'em look thicker.'

'I'll give it a try when I get back tonight,' murmured Cissy.

Florrie smiled slyly as Peggy glowered at the other end of the table. 'It sounds ever so glamorous being on the stage – someone told me once I should give it a go, cos I look like Dorothy Lamour.'

Peggy snorted and Sally bit her lip, not daring to catch her eye.

'It's not as easy as people think,' replied Cissy. 'We do revues in the theatre most nights, and of course there're the shows for the forces. Any spare time is taken up with costume fittings and rehearsals. Sally's been an absolute brick when it comes to the costumes. We don't know what we'd do without her now our usual wardrobe lady has gone off to join the Wrens.'

'Really?' Florrie eyed Sally thoughtfully. 'I didn't realise you'd come on so much since yer gran taught yer.'

'You weren't interested, so I didn't bother to tell you.' Sally put her knife and fork together on her plate and helped Ernie scrape off the last bit of meat from the bones.

Cissy looked from Florrie to Sally with a frown, and decided to fill the awkward silence. 'What I'd really like to do is join ENSA – but Dad won't give his permission and I have to be twenty-one before I can join without it.'

'You can't blame 'im for that,' laughed Florrie. 'Some of them shows ain't worth seeing – and I should know, I've been to plenty.' She left most of the meal on the plate and pushed it to one side. 'Do y'know what ENSA stands for in London?'

'Entertainments National Service Association,' said Cissy.

Florrie gave a shriek of laughter that made Sally cringe and Mrs Finch shudder. 'Every Night Something Awful. And that about says it all when the fat lady can't sing, the one on the piano can't play, and the comic ain't funny.'

'That's only the small shows,' said Cissy defensively. 'I want to be in the big ones with people like Gracie Fields, Arthur Askey, Tommy Trinder and George Formby.'

'Only famous people get into them,' said Florrie, careless of Cissy's feelings. 'I'd stick to what yer doing, luv. You'll probably find a nice rich stage-door Johnny before too long, and won't 'ave to bother with prancin' about in some draughty town hall.'

Sally broke into the frosty silence before Peggy could give vent to the palpable rage that stormed in her eyes. 'Aren't you going to be late for your drink at the Mermaid?'

'Gawd, yes, and I don't even know where it is.'

'Down the road, turn right into King Street. It's

the third pub on the left,' muttered Ron. 'Make sure you shut the door properly on your way out.'

Florrie shoved back her chair, picked up her cardigan and handbag and, with a cheery wave, left the dining room. The front door slammed with such force it rattled every window in the house.

'I don't usually speak ill of people,' said Mrs Finch quietly into the ensuing silence, 'and I'm sorry if it upsets you, Sally, but that woman is trouble.'

'I've known that for years,' Sally replied, 'and I want to apologise to you all for her behaviour. You've all been so good to me and Ernie, and I can't tell you how ashamed I am.'

'It's not you who should be apologising,' said Peggy, as she gathered the plates together. 'It's unfortunate she's your mother, but then we all have our crosses to bear.' She shot an accusing glare at Jim.

'You should keep an eye on that one,' said Mrs Finch, with a sage nod of her head. 'She's up to no good.'

Once the dishes had been washed and put away, Sally carried Ernie upstairs. When he was in bed, she massaged his back and legs, and then opened one of the storybooks Anne had lent her and they both slowly and carefully read it together.

Ernie's eyelids grew heavy and Sally gently tucked him in and kissed his soft cheek.

'Is Mum coming back?'

'Yes, love, but you won't see her until tomorrow now.'

'I dunno if I want 'er 'ere,' he muttered sleepily. 'I liked it before she came.'

'You and me both,' she muttered under her breath. 'Well, we won't let her spoil things, will we? Auntie Peg will still look after you when I'm at work, and Grandpa Ron will still take us for walks on the hills – and soon we'll be moving in with Pearl. Won't that be lovely?'

'I love Grandpa Ron,' he murmured, falling deeper towards sleep. 'And I love you too, Sal. You won't ever leave me, will you?'

'Not if I can help it,' she whispered as he finally fell asleep.

She sat beside the bed for a long while, her thoughts troubled. She had tough decisions to make but, as the silence filled the room and the sky darkened, she knew in her heart that she had no real choices at all. Ernie needed her and, no matter what, she would stick to her promise and not desert him.

As she reached the bottom of the stairs she heard Peggy talking in the kitchen.

'It's tough for all of us, but poor Sally has the worst of it. I heard that mother of hers flatly refusing to have anything to do with Ernie, let alone go with him to Wales or wherever they send our children. But I know Sally well enough to accept that she'd have changed her plans and gone with him, regardless of what that woman said.'

Her voice broke. 'It breaks my heart, it really does. That poor little girl has made a good life for herself here, and she'd be leaving her work, her friends, and her little sewing business behind and having to start all over again. It's just not fair.'

Sally bit her lip and blinked back the tears as she hurried into the room. 'Please don't worry about me, Peggy, I'm tougher than I look, really.'

'But you're only just seventeen,' snapped Peggy, still thoroughly put out by everything. 'Of *course* I worry about you.'

'Oh, Peg,' she sighed, putting her hand on her shoulder. 'Please don't make this harder than it already is. You see I can't let Ernie go alone, I promised I'd never leave him.'

'It's an awkward situation for everyone,' said Jim. 'I don't want me boys going off to strangers, but none of them are safe here any more. The bombing is getting more frequent and we've been lucky so far – I'm scared that if we leave it much longer, our luck will run out.'

Sally had to accept her plans to go and live with Pearl would have to be delayed. Ernie had to come first. 'If Jim and I can persuade the billeting people to let us travel together, and perhaps get accommodation in the same town, then I can keep an eye on the boys for you. If there's any trouble, I can sort it out straight away.'

'You'd do that?' Peggy's eyes were moist as she grasped Sally's fingers. 'Oh, Sally, you are a good girl. But what about all your plans to move in with Pearl?'

She kissed Peggy's damp cheek. 'I can do that when the war's over,' she said softly. 'You've been more of a mother to me than Florrie ever was, and if I can do this for you, then I'll feel that in a small way I'm repaying you for all you've done for me and Ernie.'

'But how long would you all have to be away?' sighed Peggy, mopping her tears.

'For as long as it takes to win this bloody war,' muttered Jim.

'I don't like the thought of my boys growing up without me,' said Peggy. 'What if it's years before they can come home? They might not even recognise us.'

'Now you're talking daft, woman,' growled Jim. 'If the boys have a chance of growing up at all, it won't be here with us. We have to let them go, Peg.'

'Doesn't anyone have any relatives the children could go to?' piped up Mrs Finch. 'Only, it seems to me that would be far safer than entrusting them to strangers.'

'There's an ancient aunt in Dublin, but I wouldn't leave a dog with her, let alone my boys,' growled Ron. 'The rest of the Reillys are scattered over America and Australia - which isn't any help at all.'

'My dad's got an older sister. I think she lives in Somerset, or somewhere down in the west, anyway. I only met her a couple of times, and she was really nice.' Sally grinned for the first time for hours. 'She and Florrie took one look at each other and the hatred was instant. You could literally see their hackles rising. Poor Dad, he didn't know what to do – it was ever so funny.'

'I don't suppose Florrie would have her address, then?' said Jim.

Sally shook her head. 'I could write to Dad, but the letter might take weeks to reach him. If he's not part of the Atlantic convoys, then he could be anywhere.'

Further discussion was interrupted by the wailing siren, and they swiftly went into what had become a nightly routine. Weighed down with children, blankets and pillows, they trekked down the garden path. Searchlights pierced the darkness hunting for enemy planes, the warning siren so shrill it rang in their heads as they entered the tomb-like dankness of the Anderson shelter.

Peggy lit the lamp, settled Mrs Finch in her deck-chair, and swathed the boys in blankets. Ron and Jim got out a pack of cards and Sally opened a comic so Ernie could look at the pictures. They'd probably be stuck in here for an hour or so, and they'd become inured to the nuisance of it all.

The silence was deafening as the siren stopped shrieking. And then they heard it, and all eyes looked to the ceiling, following the ominous sound. The mighty, deep and continuous roar was unmistakable. It was the sound of hundreds of enemy planes coming from over the sea. 'Oh, my God,' breathed Peggy. 'This is really it, this time, and my girls are out there in the middle of it.'

'They'll be in a shelter, Peg. Don't you be frettin'.' Jim put his arm around her shoulder and kissed her cheek. 'They know the drill, darlin', they'll be quite safe.'

'But this is a proper raid,' protested an ashen faced Peggy. 'Just listen to how many enemy planes there must be.'

'Hush, now,' he murmured, 'or you'll be worrying the boys.'

Peggy wiped her eyes and turned to Bob and Charlie, gathering them into her arms and holding them close.

The crump of heavy artillery and the sharper 'ack-ack' of the anti-aircraft guns on the cliffs joined the steady, menacing drone, and through the gap between the door and the arc of corrugated iron, Sally watched the great white searchlight beams hunting them, finding them, pinpointing them and starkly revealing the vast numbers that flew above them. It was an awesome, terrible sight.

Despite her own terror, Sally put her arm round Ernie, whose eyes were wide and frightened. 'It's all right,' she murmured in his ear, as she pulled him on to her lap and rocked him. 'We're all here, nice and snug and safe in our cave.'

The mighty explosion rocked the earth beneath them, making it tremble. It reverberated in their heads and through their bodies, making them all cry out.

Harvey began to whimper as a second explosion swiftly followed. It was much nearer this time, and had them cringing and clinging to each other, wondering if the next would kill them all.

Sally buried Ernie's head into her chest and closed her eyes, but she could hear more explosions in the distance, could hear the sound of tumbling masonry and shattering glass nearby, could smell burning, and hear the urgent clanging bell of the fire engines.

And still the heavy-bellied drone of the enemy planes continued. On and on it went, filling the very air around them and making the corrugated iron shudder as Harvey shivered and cringed, and Ron tried to comfort him.

The guns boomed from the cliff-tops and along the seafront, searchlights strafed the skies, and ambulance and fire engine bells added to the cacophony.

Sally prayed for it to end as she held Ernie and tried not to panic. She glanced at the others and realised they too were making a brave show for the children's sakes. Yet, as she looked at Mrs Finch, she couldn't help but giggle. She was fast asleep and snoring fit to bust.

Harvey had clambered into Ron's lap and buried his nose deep beneath his coat – from this questionable place of safety, he, thankfully, had stopped howling.

And now they could hear the lighter, quicker buzz of Spitfires and the throaty roar of the Hurricanes.

Their eyes turned heavenward again, their spirits rising.

'Come on me boys,' yelled Jim. 'Show 'em what we're made of!'

They sat and listened, prisoners in this iron shelter, hostages to whatever was happening outside.

'I can smell smoke,' said Peggy, suddenly alert. 'Oh, Jim, you don't think it's us, do you?'

He opened the door a fraction and looked out. 'I can't see anything much over our roof, but I'm guessing it's a couple of streets down from us,' he muttered. 'The fire brigade is already on to it.'

'Oh, those poor people,' muttered Peggy. 'I do hope it isn't too bad.'

Sally continued to rock Ernie, finding it gave her comfort to feel his solidity and warmth in her arms. This was her first experience of a real air-raid, and she was terrified, but looking at Peggy's calm, sad face and the stoicism of Ron and Jim, she took heart.

As the brave little Spitfires and Hurricanes tried to push the invaders back out to sea, they sat listening to the dog-fights overhead and silently cheered their brave boys on. It seemed to last for hours, and every time they heard the deathly whine and crump of a fallen plane they prayed it wasn't one of their own.

'They're probably heading for London,' muttered Peggy. 'I do hope Doreen and the kids are safe in a shelter somewhere.'

'Probably down in Cannon Street Tube station,'

replied Jim, 'though the thought of being trapped underground with hundreds of strangers doesn't bear thinking about.'

'I know, Jim.' Peggy held his hand. 'After what you went through last time, that's understandable.'

'He wasn't the only one to get buried in a trench,' said Ron scornfully. 'His brother almost died in one when it caved in.'

'You'll not mention his name, Da,' Jim growled.

'Frank's my son too, and I'll talk about him whenever I want,' fired back Ron. 'What happened to make you both so bitter?'

'I'll not be talking about it.' Jim wrapped his thick coat more firmly round him and crossed his arms. 'Leave it, Da. This is not the time.'

'When is the time, then, Jim? Tell me that. After I'm dead and buried – after we're all killed in this damned war?' He chewed furiously on his unlit pipe. 'I would have thought your shared experience of going to Dunkirk might have knocked some sense into you. But it seems you're still as pig-headed as ever.'

'That's enough, the pair of you,' said Peggy. 'What's done is done, and if neither of them wants to talk about it, Ron, then there's nothing you can do to alter things.'

'Hmmph.' Ron stroked the dog who'd almost crawled inside his coat. 'It comes to something when brother fights brother and their father can't mention their names. What the hell was the first war all about? What good did it do? It was supposed to be the war to end all wars – now look at us. Cowering in this bit of tin while men kill each other in the skies above our heads. We never learn. Never.'

'I know, Ron, I know,' soothed Peggy.

'And all because men have too much pride to say they're sorry. Too stiff with it to admit they've done something wrong. If I go to me death before you boys make it up, I'll never forgive either of you.'

Jim's face broke into a grin. 'And what will you be doing after you're dead, Da? Haunting us?'

'That's for me to know and you to find out. I could bang your heads together, so I could.'

It was clear the tense situation had got to them all, and they sat in a long silence after that, listening to the battle going on overhead.

And then the guns stopped. The searchlights pierced an empty sky and all that could be heard were the shouts of men and the crash of masonry and breaking glass.

'The planes have gone,' said Bob. 'Can we go back indoors?'

'Not until the all-clear.' Peggy rammed a woollen hat over his ears and found another for Charlie. 'Is Ernie warm enough? I've brought another sweater.'

'He's fine, thanks, Peggy.' She smoothed back the hair from his forehead and kissed him. 'He's almost asleep now the noise has stopped.'

Peggy smiled and nodded at Mrs Finch. 'He's not the only one,' she murmured.

They waited for what felt like hours in the shifting, flickering light of the hurricane lamp. And then the bombers returned – dropping the last of their loads on Cliffehaven so they were light enough to outrun the British planes that pursued them over the Channel.

Half an hour after that, the welcome sound of the all-clear sounded and they clambered, cold and exhausted, from the shelter into a dawn filled with thick smoke and the stench of burning. Ash floated like confetti, charred paper drifted in the light breeze, and they soon discovered there was no electricity or water.

They all sighed gratefully that the house was still standing, but the garden wall had taken a hit and collapsed, along with the shed. The outside lav stood in solitary splendour among the debris of its walls and roof. A tree had come down on the house behind them, telegraph poles had fallen like ninepins, and the chimney on the house opposite had toppled and taken half the roof with it.

Peggy left Jim in charge of Bob and Charlie and hurried off to check on the neighbours. There were several elderly people living nearby, and Peggy had taken it upon herself to keep a close eye on them.

Sally carried Ernie upstairs and put him to bed.

'Where's Mum?' he asked sleepily.

Sally felt a stab of guilt – she hadn't given Florrie a thought all through the raid. 'She's down in the town with her friend,' she replied softly. 'She'll be back later.'

'D'ya promise?'

Sally gritted her teeth. 'She'll turn up, Ernie. You can bet on it.'

Once he was asleep, Sally went back downstairs and on to the pavement. The thick stench of burning filled the dawn, and she could see the orange glow of fire in the distance. Their own terrace of houses seemed to have escaped the worst of it, but no doubt a copious amount of tea would be called for to cater to the men clearing the rubble and the ambulance drivers and firemen – as well as any neighbour Peggy could find who needed a bit of help, or others needing the comfort of a kitchen and a good gossip. And that was all before the cleaning up began in the house.

Sally sighed deeply and headed for the kitchen. Her shift began at one this afternoon. It was going to be a very long day.

Chapter Thirteen

Florrie appeared later that morning, dishevelled and clearly in a foul mood. Without a word to anyone, she staggered up the stairs and slammed her bedroom door.

Sally was just thankful she hadn't brought some awful man home with her, and that Ernie was still asleep, so couldn't witness Florrie's less than sober state. As she finished the dusting, Sally wondered how long it would be before Mr Solomon realised just what he'd taken on with Florrie.

She went to wake Ernie at lunch time, and he threw back the covers. 'Where's Mum? I wanna see Mum.'

'She's asleep, luv, and you know she doesn't like being woken up.'

'But I wanna see 'er,' he insisted.

'Well, you can't.'

'I ain't washing till I do,' he said, folding his arms and glowering.

Sally swept him up, none too gently, and carried him along the landing, thanking her lucky stars that Florrie had indeed come back and on her own – she didn't dare think what she could have done if that hadn't been the case.

'Don't you *dare* make a sound,' she whispered in his ear, 'or we'll both be for it.' She opened the door just enough so that he could see the mound under the covers, and hear Florrie's snoring.

'Right,' said Sally, having shut the door, '*now* will you get washed and dressed?'

He nodded and tucked his head beneath her chin as she carried him to the bathroom. 'That was 'er, weren't it?' he asked.

'Of course it was, silly,' she said, as she tried to tickle him out of his doleful mood. 'Who else snores like that? Eh?'

He wriggled and giggled and it took some time to get him washed and into his clothes. Having taken him down for his lunch, she ran back up and prepared for the day, her thoughts on Florrie, and the thing that had been worrying at her since her arrival. She came to the conclusion that if she didn't do something about it now, she might live to regret it.

She went to the dressing-table drawer and took out the jar of money. Peggy had already opened a bank account for her, and the passbook showed a healthy balance – but there was at least another five pounds still in the jar which she'd been saving to put towards her keep at Pearl's. She wouldn't have time today to go to the bank, but first thing tomorrow morning, she'd pay the money in.

But where could she hide the jar and the passbook until then? Everywhere seemed too obvious until she looked up. Dragging the chair over to the wardrobe, she put the passbook in the jar and pushed it as far back as she could, and checked to see if it was visible from anywhere in the room.

Sick at the thought that her mother might stoop so low, but suspecting she was quite capable of it, Sally put the chair back, checked the room was tidy and went to wake her.

She tapped nervously on the door and got no reply, so she opened it a fraction and wrinkled her nose as she peeked into the darkened room which stank of fags and cheap perfume.

'Mum? Mum, you've got to wake up. You're going to work this afternoon and lunch is on the table.'

The bedcovers moved and, with a groan, Florrie flung her arm over her face. 'Tell Goldman I'll come in later. I've got an 'eadache.'

'Mr Goldman's very particular about good time-keeping,' she replied, switching on the light which made Florrie burrow beneath the covers. 'It won't look good if you're late on your first day.'

'Bugger off,' growled Florrie, throwing a pillow at her. 'Solly will smooth things over with Goldman.'

Sally realised she was wasting her time and shut the door and went downstairs. 'She won't be down for lunch,' she said to Peggy.

'Got a hangover, has she? I saw her coming in.'

Sally reddened with shame. 'I'm sorry she's upset everyone. I feel horribly responsible.'

346

'Don't be silly,' replied Peggy. 'You can't help it if she's your mother, and no-one is going to blame you for what she does.'

'They might not,' she replied with a watery smile, 'but she's only staying here because of me. Perhaps, once I've gone, she'll go too.'

'Perhaps,' said Peggy. She poured tea and became businesslike. 'It's only dried eggs, but there're tomatoes and a bit of fried potato to go with it, so eat up.'

Sally had little appetite, but she tucked in, knowing how wrong it would be to leave anything on the plate now the rationing was so restrictive.

Peggy eyed her thoughtfully. 'Isn't Florrie supposed to be working today?'

'She's going in later,' mumbled Sally. 'But she probably won't get out of bed until tea time.'

'What time are you finishing today, Sally? Only the Billeting Office shuts at five, and I'll need to make an appointment.'

'I'll meet you there at four thirty,' she replied, pouring a second cup of tea, and trying not to show the emotions that were welling inside her. 'I'm sure Goldman won't mind as it's so important.'

'Then I'll make sure Jim gets there in time. He's on the late showing tonight. But I can't promise I can get an appointment; there's bound to be the usual endless queue, and we'll probably be stuck there for hours.'

Having kissed Ernie and quietly warned Peggy

not to leave Florrie alone with him, Sally left for the factory.

It was a bright, breezy summer day, the sea and sky an innocent blue, with no hint of the horrors that had taken place during the night. But, as she walked the familiar route to the factory, she was made all too aware of how dramatically the landscape of Cliffehaven had been changed over the past week.

She carefully picked her way over and around the piles of rubble, dodging burst water pipes and hissing electricity wires that the teams of workmen were trying to repair. The graceful terraces of Victorian and Edwardian houses had been defaced by the rubble-filled gaps between them. Garden walls had disappeared, pavements had been torn up, and telegraph poles were felled like trees, their wires draped across shattered roofs and toppling chimneys. Shop windows were boarded, electricity cables and water pipes laid bare in the gaping holes where even more men worked to repair them. The end of one road had been shut off completely so the army could defuse an unexploded bomb, and in another, a huge bulldozer was slowly dismantling a house that was threatening to fall and demolish the two beside it.

She was almost at the factory when she saw Pearl coming the other way. With a wave, Sally hurried towards her and then came to a horrified standstill.

'Bloody hell,' breathed Pearl. 'Will you look at that?'

Sally stared at the vast pile of rubble that had once been the two blocks of flats that overlooked the primary school. They had collapsed like a pack of cards right across the playground, and effectively sealed the entrance to the vast public shelter beneath it. If the attack had come during the day, the children playing there would have been killed, or buried alive in that shelter.

She shivered, and the terrible dread of what might have been grew stronger as she watched the men desperately digging at the still-smouldering mountain of rubble to clear the entrance. 'It would be a miracle if anyone's still alive,' she breathed.

'If the kiddies had been playing in that yard,' murmured Pearl, 'it don't bear thinking about.'

'That's why I'm taking Ernie away,' said Sally. She turned to her friend and took her hand. 'I'm sorry Pearl, but I can't move in with you – not yet. The boys have to leave Cliffehaven, and I've promised Peg and Jim I'd look after them.'

'But all our plans . . .'

'They can keep,' she said softly. 'But it's too dangerous here for the boys now and, as Ernie can't travel alone, I have to be with him.'

'But you can't,' breathed Pearl. 'What about your job, and your sewing? What about Peg and Jim and Ron? What about me?'

'Don't make this any harder than it already is,'

she pleaded. 'I've already had me mum on me case, and she's not helped a bit.'

Pearl crossed her arms, her eyes stormy, her tone acidic. 'If your mum's turned up, then why can't she take Ernie?'

'I wouldn't trust her to look after him properly,' said Sally with some asperity. 'At the first whiff of a bloke with a stuffed wallet, she'd be off.' She forced a smile and hugged her friend. 'I'll keep in touch, I promise,' she breathed. 'And, who knows? This war could be over in a few months and I'll be back and moving in with you before you can blink.'

'But, Sally, I don't want you to go.'

'Look at that, Pearl.' She pointed to the devastation in the playground. 'I have to go. Please try and understand. He's all I got, and I have to keep him safe.'

Pearl gave a deep sigh. 'I know. But I'm going to miss you, Sal. And that's a fact.'

Sally took her arm. 'Come on, we're not doing no good standing here gawping. We're going to be late for work.'

'That's if the factory's still standing,' muttered Pearl. 'You never know, Hitler might have done us a favour by blowing it up – Simmons along with it.'

'Nah, no such luck,' said Sally, as they reached the gates and found the building hadn't been touched. 'The new one's all right as well.' She pointed to the enormous red-brick building that stood on the next corner. There were men putting up the 'Goldman and Solomon Clothing Factory' sign above the gates.

'I didn't realise they'd expanded,' said Pearl. 'Someone's obviously making a packet out of this war. Shame it ain't us.'

They went inside, clocked in and headed for their machines.

'Miss Turner,' shouted Simmons from the far end of the factory.

Sally wasn't prepared to conduct a conversation from one end of the factory to the other, neither was she going to scurry back to see what he wanted. She waited until he came stomping to her work-station.

'Where's Mrs Turner?' He was breathing heavily, and his face was red.

'She's not well. She'll come in later and do a different shift. I can only stay for three hours, and all. I have to go to the Billeting Office.'

'That's not good enough,' he snapped. 'You women can't just pick and choose what shift you're going to do. It messes up my schedules.' He took a deep breath and hugged his clipboard, his cold eyes magnified by the thick lenses in his glasses. 'What's the matter with her?'

'Women's trouble,' she said shortly, knowing it would shut him up.

He went puce and couldn't look at her. 'I'll have to inform Mr Goldman of her absence. This is most irregular – especially as this is her first day.'

'You do that.' Sally took off her lightweight jacket and sat down. Simmons was still hovering. 'Is there something else, Mr Simmons, only I need to get on?'

'Is it true that Mrs Turner is your mother?'

There was a glint of something in his eyes which Sally didn't like, and she coolly returned his stare. 'It is. Why? Is it important?'

'Mr Goldman and Mr Solomon seem to think so. What's so special about your family, Miss Turner? First you get a letter of recommendation from Solomon which gives you a raise in salary and a management position, and then your mother is assigned straight to the cutting tables. She has no proper experience, and I've been told by Mr Solomon that she will have to be supervised, which means taking someone off a more important job to make sure she doesn't make costly errors. What's going on, Miss Turner?'

'I have no idea,' she said on a sigh. 'Why don't you ask my mother when she comes in? I'm sure she'll be delighted to put you in the picture.'

He eyed her belligerently then turned away and started harrying two latecomers.

Sally pushed her chair into the table and grimly checked her machine. Florrie hadn't even bothered to show her face yet, but already she was causing trouble – and Sally wished with all her might that she'd stayed in London.

* * *

It was two o'clock and Peggy had finally finished cleaning the downstairs. She was about to begin on the bedrooms when Florrie appeared on the landing dressed in a tight skirt, high-heeled shoes and an almost diaphanous blouse. To Peggy's mind she didn't look at all as if she was on her way to work – unless it was on a street corner. 'Lunch is over,' she said curtly. 'I've put some bread and marg under a plate for you in the kitchen. The tea's stewed and rather weak, but you can warm up the pot on the range.'

'I'll eat in the factory canteen,' said Florrie through a vast yawn. 'Where is this flamin' factory, anyway? Sally ain't left no note or nothing.'

Peggy told her. 'Ernie's playing out in the back garden if you want to see him before you go to work,' she added.

'Nah. I'm running late as it is. I'll see 'im tonight.'

Peggy watched her run down the stairs to the hall, and winced as the front door slammed behind her. 'I wish to God I could get rid of her,' she muttered crossly, 'but as she's Sally's mother, I suppose I'll just have to put up with her. But the minute Sally leaves, that woman's out of here.'

'Talking to yourself, me darling? First sign of madness, you know.' Jim wandered out of the bathroom freshly shaved and looking very handsome.

'Is that right?' she retorted. 'I'll tell you what, Jim Reilly, it's not my sanity you should be worrying about – it's my rapidly decreasing patience. If you flirt with that woman again, she won't be the only one on her backside in the street.'

He grabbed hold of her and gave her a resounding kiss. 'I love it when you get all jealous and fiery,' he said with a grin. 'How about a bit of a cuddle while the house is quiet?'

'Get away with you,' she said, pushing against him. 'You can't get round me like that. I know you too well.'

'But Peg, you know you're the only woman for me.'

'I'm the only one who's had to put up with you for over twenty years,' she replied, trying hard to maintain her tetchiness and not giggle.

'And to be sure, my love, we'll still be together another twenty.' He kissed her again. 'Are you sure you don't want a cuddle?'

'Quite sure. I've got work to do.'

'Oh, well, I suppose I can't win 'em all,' he said without rancour, as he headed for the stairs.

'I've made an appointment at the Billeting Office for four thirty,' she called after him. 'We're meeting Sally there, so don't be late.'

'I'll do me best,' he said, his voice fading as he headed into the kitchen.

The telephone rang in the hall. 'Will someone answer that?' shouted Peggy.

'I've got it,' called Anne. 'Hello?' Her eagerness dwindled. 'Oh, hello, what can I help you with?'

Like Anne, Peggy had hoped it was Martin. They

hadn't heard from him for over a week now, and she knew how much Anne was fretting. His blasted family didn't help either – they hadn't seen or heard from them since the wedding. Not that she minded much – they were unpleasant people – but it would have been nice if they could have shown Anne some support during these difficult days.

She kept herself busy by scrubbing the bathroom, muttering to herself about the way men never cleaned up behind them and left damp towels and dirty socks on the floor instead of putting them in the laundry basket.

She'd just finished when Anne caught up with her outside Mrs Finch's room.

'That was the headmaster,' she explained. 'The blocks of flats next to the school took a direct hit and the debris fell right across the playground, effectively cutting off the entrance to the underground shelter. The work crews have been digging for hours, and they've at last managed to get everyone out.'

'Thank goodness it wasn't term-time,' breathed Peggy. 'When I think of all those children who could have been playing there . . ..' She sat on the nearest stair, her legs threatening to give way.

'I know,' soothed Anne, as she sat beside her, 'at least we were spared that.'

'What about the people from the flats?'

'They were all in the shelter. There were some minor cuts and bruises and a couple of cases of hysterics, but they came out virtually unscathed. But the school didn't escape completely. Two of the classrooms will have to be demolished, and the assembly hall's been flattened.' Anne gave a deep sigh. 'With so many of the children having been sent away, and more following every day, it won't make much difference. The headmaster is closing it down for the duration. I'm out of a job.'

'Oh, Anne, what will you do now?'

'Well, I have been giving it a lot of thought,' she admitted. 'You see, it was inevitable the school would soon close once the raids became more frequent, so I started thinking about how I could do my bit for the war effort.' She took a deep breath. 'I went to see the recruitment officer the other day, and there's a place for me in the Observer Corps. I'll have to go on a training course to begin with, but I can start whenever I want.'

'What will that entail, Anne? You won't be in any danger, will you?'

'No more than I was in that school.' She smiled, her eyes bright with an excitement Peggy hadn't seen for a long time. 'I'll be tracking aircraft in some underground bunker in the cliffs, making sure Martin and the rest of our boys know where to find the enemy.'

'Will it mean you having to leave home?'

Her smile faded as she took her mother's hand. 'Well, that's the thing, Mum. You see, I'll be living in the female quarters close to the shelter, so I'll always be on call during an emergency, and can carry out my duties without having to make the long journey each day.'

'But when will we see you?'

'I'll come home whenever I can, I promise.' She gave Peggy a hug. 'But I'm looking forward to it, really I am, Mum. And it isn't as if I've never left home before. I was at university for three years.'

'I know, but with everything going on, I like to keep my family close. What with the boys having to be sent away, and Sally leaving, and now you planning to move out . . .'

'I know it feels hard at the moment, Mum. But it won't be so bad, really it won't. Please try not to worry.'

'I worry about all of you,' Peggy muttered. 'But then I'm a mother, and that's what we do.'

Anne held her in a tight embrace for a while, and then gently drew her to her feet. 'I'm taking Mrs Finch to the library,' she said. 'Why don't you leave the housework for once and come with us? We might even manage to get a decent cuppa at the WRVS canteen they've set up in the High Street.'

'No, you go on. I need a little time to think quietly and try to get used to things. But as you're going to the shops, see if there's any tea been delivered – and we need more bread as well.'

Anne left with Mrs Finch, and Peggy continued cleaning. It was a task she could do in her sleep and gave her time to mull over all that had happened in the past two days. She came to the conclusion that there was very little she could do about anything, regardless of how vulnerable and uncertain that made her feel. The house would feel so empty when they were gone, but she would probably worry even more about them once they were out of sight.

She finished hoovering the top landing and headed for Florrie's bedroom. Opening the door she stood there in furious silence, taking in the spilled powder on the carpet, the squashed cigarettes in the hairpin dish, and the lipstick and mascara smeared on her good pillowcases. The whole room stank of stale drink, cigarettes and cheap perfume, and she flung the window open to let the fresh air in while she made the bed and swept up the talcum powder.

Florrie had flung shoes, underwear and dresses everywhere and, in the end, Peggy lost her patience and simply gathered everything up and dumped them in the middle of the bed in an untidy heap.

Closing the door behind her, she hesitated for a moment before peeking into Sally's room. It was as she'd suspected; Florrie had been through the wardrobe and drawers, leaving everything strewn about as if a whirlwind had passed through. Sally would never have left it like that.

But what worried her more was the jar of money Sally kept in her dressing-table drawer. There was no sign of it, or the passbook for the bank. A few frantic minutes of searching finally revealed where she'd hidden it, and Peggy gave a deep sigh of relief as she pushed it even further back until it almost touched the bedroom wall.

Peggy quickly folded the discarded skirts and blouses and hung up the dresses as her thoughts whirled. Had Sally suspected her mother might help herself to those savings? Should she advise the girl not to leave money in her room? Should she have taken the money herself and hidden it until Sally got home?

It was another terrible dilemma, and she hoped her fears would prove unjustified. The last thing she needed was a thief in the house – the atmosphere was deadly enough.

Thoroughly overwrought, she shut the door and stomped downstairs. The cup of tea and cigarette she was longing for would have to wait a few more minutes.

Reaching the hall, she unlocked the small wall cupboard and eyed the rows of tagged keys that hung inside. It had been a long time since any door had been locked in this house, but she couldn't risk Florrie helping herself to anything else. She returned upstairs and locked every door but Florrie's.

'That'll spike her guns,' she muttered crossly, and headed back to the kitchen, the keys snug in her apron pocket.

It was almost three o'clock and the house was quiet now everyone had gone out. She could see Ron and the boys were still happily occupied in the garden and so she sank into her favourite chair by the unlit range and put her feet up.

The tea was horribly weak, but there was still just enough flavour to take the edge off her anger, and she lit a cigarette and blew the smoke out on a long sigh. She had an hour before she had to get changed to go to the Billeting Office, and she was determined to enjoy the peace and quiet for as long as it lasted.

Ten minutes later she was startled by the heavy knock on the front door. 'Now what?' she said crossly, ramming her feet back into her slippers. She opened the door and her impatience fled. 'Hello, Martin, what a lovely surprise. Anne's out, but she shouldn't be long.'

'Hello, Peggy,' he replied, taking off his air-force hat. 'It's not really Anne I've come to see – though I was hoping to, obviously.'

He looked uncomfortable, which was most unlike him, and Peggy felt a chill of foreboding as he stepped into the hall. 'What is it, Martin?'

'I'm sorry, Peggy. This isn't a social call.'

She closed the door and they stood drenched in the sunlight that poured through the taped windows. She swallowed the lump in her throat as she suddenly realised the only possible reason for his coming today. 'It's Alex, isn't it?' she said fearfully.

He nodded. 'He was shot down last night over the Channel during the raid on our convoy. There were three positive sightings of him going into the water – and a fishing boat picked up his body at first light this morning.'

Peggy sat down with a bump on the hall chair. 'Poor Alex,' she said, the tears streaming down her face. 'He wanted so much to do his bit – and I so hoped, so very much hoped that he . . . that he . . .' She pulled a handkerchief from her cardigan sleeve and blew her nose.

Martin stood awkwardly in front of her. 'I'm so sorry, Peggy. He was a fine chap and a first-rate pilot as well as a good friend. He'll be sorely missed by everyone.'

'Yes, I can believe that,' said Peggy softly, remembering his melodic voice, his dark, troubled eyes and his broken English – and the day he'd asked her to explain the English money. It had been the same day he'd shown her the picture of his family. She dabbed her eyes. 'I suppose there's no way of contacting his people in Warsaw?'

'No. Poland is in such a mess, it's impossible – and none of us knows where to start looking for them, even if they have survived.' He squatted before her and took her hand. 'He thought of you and Jim as his family, Peggy, which is why he asked me to give you this in the event of his death.'

Peggy took the envelope and stared at her name scrawled across it in black ink. Like the man, his writing was strong and carefully controlled, with just a glimpse of his passion in the artistic curls on each capital letter. 'I'll read it later,' she murmured.

'Thank you, Martin. It can't have been easy for you to come here today.'

'He was my fellow officer, and you were the only family he had. I was proud to have known him.' He took a slip of paper from his jacket pocket. 'The funeral has been arranged at the church where Anne and I were married. I hope you don't mind, but I thought it was where he might find peace at last. The details are all on there.'

Peggy read them before she stood and patted his cheek. 'Thank you, Martin . . . Now go and find Anne,' she murmured. 'She's only down the street at the shops or in the library.'

'Will you be all right?'

'I'll be fine.' She watched him hurrying towards the shops and then, feeling weary and battered and suddenly every one of her forty-three years, Peggy shuffled into her bedroom and quietly closed the door. She sank on to the soft bed she'd shared with Jim since their honeymoon and stared out of the window, beyond the back garden and up to the blue sky that seemed to mock her with its clarity and its emptiness.

She sat there, unaware of time passing, as she remembered the man who had so briefly and tragically entered their lives. Then, finally, she turned her attention to the letter. There was something small and hard inside and, as she opened the envelope, a gold chain and medallion fell into her lap.

She gathered it up and stared at the sweet-faced

Madonna etched in the worn gold. On the other side was something written in Polish, which she couldn't understand – but it was clear the medallion and chain were of the finest gold, and that both had been treasured. She held it in the palm of her hand, feeling the gold warm to her touch as she began to read his last words.

My dear Mrs Reilly,
You gave me a home and shared your warmth and love with a stranger who was in great need of such comfort. I have felt that you have become like my family, and I hope that you will remember me always with affection – for I have great affection for all of you, and can never repay your kindnesses.
As you are reading this, I am no longer with you – perhaps finally at peace in the loving arms of those who were lost to me in this world. But I ask one thing more of you, my dearest Mrs Reilly. Would you keep the holy medallion safe until it is confirmed that none of my family have survived the terrible things that are happening in Poland? I have prayed to God that Anjelika or Danuta may find their way to you – but I am thinking God cannot hear our prayers through the gunfire and mortar shells of this war.
But perhaps the words on the back of the medallion will bring comfort to you as they did to me. Translated from the Polish, they read, 'Holy Mary, Mother of God, pray for us.'

*I leave you in the hope that you will remember
me with kindness, and I pray that you and your
family will come through these dark days without
harm. For Jim and Ron, my friends, there is a
case of vodka hidden in the cupboard under the
stairs. Ask them to please remember me when
they take their first drink.*

*With the greatest of respect and affection, I bid
you goodbye,*
Aleksey.

Peggy sat with the letter and the medallion in her
hand, the tears drying on her cheeks, and it wasn't
until she heard the little clock on her dressing table
chime four, that she realised how long she'd been
there.

Sally had kept an eye out for Florrie all day, but it
was now four o'clock and there was still no sign of
her. She could only suppose she was still sleeping
off the previous night's drinking, but Goldman
would be furious, and she didn't like to think of
the row that would ensue when Florrie did finally
show up.

She said goodbye to Pearl, and hurried into the
town. The streets had been cleared enough for the
trolley-bus to wend its way through, but it meant
having to clamber over the rubble that had been
piled on the pavements. There was little point in
wearing her smart shoes any more, and she was

glad of the old ones which didn't matter if they got a bit more scuffed.

The Billeting Office was busy, with a long line of people waiting outside. Sally nudged her way through with apologetic smiles, and finally saw Peggy and Jim sitting in one of the long rows of wooden chairs in the main office.

'I came as quick as I could,' she said, as Jim gave up his seat for her and perched on a nearby windowsill.

'You needn't have rushed, dear,' said Peggy. 'We've at least another half-hour before it's our turn.' She delved into her string bag and brought out a bottle of elderflower cordial and a packet of sandwiches. 'I thought you might need something to keep you going.'

'Thanks, I'm starving.' Sally bit into the sandwich and munched happily on the Spam and tomato sauce. 'Is Ernie all right?'

'He's with Dad,' said Jim. 'They've all gone down to the fishing station to try and get something from today's catch.' He glared out of the window and folded his arms. 'I expect they're all round Frank's right this minute, drinking tea and having a fine old time listening to his stupid stories.'

'Now, Jim,' said Peggy softly. 'There's no need for that. The boys have a right to know their uncle, and Ron needs to see his son now and again.'

He continued to stare belligerently out of the window and said nothing.

'Did Mum go too? Only she never showed up for work.'

Peggy frowned. 'She left around two. She was planning to eat in the factory canteen. Are you sure you didn't miss her?'

'That's hardly likely, Peggy. Florrie's not someone *anyone* could miss.'

'Mmmm. Well, if she's not careful, she won't have a job to go to at this rate.'

Sally chewed on the sandwich for a while. 'I don't think she's that bothered,' she said finally. 'She seems to have it in her head that Mr Solomon's going to divorce his wife and marry her.'

'I would have thought Florrie was far too sharp to fall for that line,' sniffed Peggy. 'She's a fool to believe such nonsense, because it will never happen. His wife comes from one of the richest Jewish families in this county, and she's the one holding the purse-strings, believe you me.'

'How do you know so much about Mr Solomon?'

'He's married to Goldman's sister, and Goldman is chairman of the local Trader's Association that Jim and I belong to. Goldman's wife is a fountain of gossip. Mrs Solomon knows what he gets up to, and when she thinks he's playing away, she tugs on those purse-strings and he comes running back as fast as his fat legs can carry him.'

'Mr and Mrs Reilly, Miss Turner?' The middle-aged woman was thin and dressed entirely in grey, which did little to enliven her pale, lined face and the dull eyes which regarded them imperiously. 'I'm Miss Fforbes-Smythe,' she said in her upper-class voice. 'Follow me, please.'

Miss Fforbes-Smythe was clearly a bitter old spinster with nothing better to do than boss people about, and Sally didn't dare catch Peggy's eye as they went into a small office that smelled faintly of unwashed clothing, disinfectant and, incongruously, lavender water.

They sat down before a large desk as the woman settled herself behind it, perched the half-moon glasses that hung from a chain round her neck on to her sharp little nose, and opened a folder. 'I understand you want to have your children evacuated as soon as possible,' she said.

'That's right,' said Jim. 'It's not safe for them here any more.'

'Quite.' She gave him a wintry smile. 'Unfortunately there are a great *many* parents in this county who suddenly feel the same way. It's a shame no-one thought to take the government's advice much earlier. It makes our work *so* much harder when people don't do as they're told.'

Jim opened his mouth to give a sharp reply, and Peggy quickly butted in. 'I'm sure it does,' she said, 'but you're doing such a sterling job here, I'm sure you'll rise to the occasion.'

'We will have to, Mrs Reilly,' she replied, without a glimmer of emotion. 'Now, we are currently sending our children to Wales. I see you have two boys aged nine and almost thirteen.' She glanced up from the folder and peered at Sally over the spectacles. 'And you, *Miss* Turner, have a son of seven.'

'He's my brother,' Sally said flatly.

The greying eyebrows lifted fractionally as the dull eyes regarded her. 'Really?'

'Yes, really.' Sally's voice was low and filled with anger.

'I can only go by the information I have, Miss Turner.' The woman returned to the folder and shuffled through the papers. 'Oh, yes. Ernest. It seems there has been some error in the paperwork that came down from London.'

Sally waited for an apology, but there was none forthcoming.

The woman took off the glasses and began to polish the lenses with a pristine handkerchief steeped in lavender water. 'I understand you wish to travel with your brother, Miss Turner? It's highly irregular. You can't expect the government to fork out on train fares willy-nilly for just *anyone*, you know.'

'They paid my fare down here – what's changed?'

'There is a war on. Every penny has to be spent wisely – and you are now seventeen, and not eligible for such arrangements. I assume you have paid work?'

'I'm at Goldman's, and if you won't pay the fare, then I will. Ernie ain't – isn't going away on his own.'

'Her brother has had polio, and can't get about easily,' said Jim, his voice tight with anger. 'Sally has to travel with him, and I know for a fact there's a government grant to cover her fare. She's kindly offered to look after our boys as well, so we'd be grateful if you could arrange for all four of them to be accommodated in close proximity.'

'I doubt I can arrange that,' she said, placing the glasses precisely on her nose, and tucking the handkerchief into her sleeve. 'We have lists of willing householders who will take the children in, but it's highly unlikely anyone will want a seventeen-year-old girl and a spastic boy.'

'He's not a spastic,' snapped Sally.

'None of us like that term,' said Peggy coldly, 'and if you can't keep a civil tongue in your head, then I shall make a complaint to your supervisor, Florence Wren – who happens to be a close friend.'

There was a deathly silence, broken only by the loud ticking of the clock on the wall.

Sally stared at that clock, determined not to let her angry tears spill. It was happening all over again, and this beastly old trout was about as sympathetic and helpful as a fox in a hen-house.

'I apologise if I have caused any ill-feeling,' Miss Fforbes-Smythe said stiffly. 'But it's almost impossible to place crippled children – even if they are accompanied by an older sibling.'

'I can work and pay my way,' said Sally. 'Ernie's no trouble.'

'I can vouch for that,' said Jim. 'The wee girl here works hard, and that wee boy is no bother at all.'

The woman eyed him over her glasses for a long moment, and then wrote something in her folder. 'All I can promise is that they will travel together and go to the same village. What I *cannot* do is guarantee they will be billeted close to one another, or that there will be accommodation suitable for Ernest. It will depend very much on the individuals who have kindly offered their homes for the duration, and it is out of our hands.'

'And what do I do if no-one will have us?'

'Then you must consider what is best for Ernest.' She looked at Sally coolly. 'I believe he was offered a place at the orphanage which you turned down when you arrived here in Cliffehaven?'

'My brother is *not* an orphan, and I'm *not* leaving him in a home.'

'I think you're being rather hasty, Miss Turner. Ernest will be well provided for in a children's home where they will understand his needs – which will leave you free to pursue your work without hindrance.'

'He's never been a hindrance, and hell will freeze over before I dump him in one of them places,' she snarled. 'If no-one will take us, then I'll sort something out myself.'

'That, of course, is your prerogative, but I warn you, the Office for Children's Welfare take a very dim view of such things. After all, you are not yet twenty-one, and therefore still classed as a minor in the eyes of the law. There would have to be an inquiry into what is best for Ernest, regardless of your obvious concern for him.'

Sally fell silent. The last thing she needed was the welfare people poking their noses into her business. She'd had a few run-ins with them before back in Bow, but luckily Florrie had managed to persuade them that she hadn't left an under-aged child in sole charge of her frail son. But it had been touch and go several times, and she just hoped there were no records from the London welfare office in that file.

Peggy clutched her handbag and sat forward. 'If it comes to any inquiry,' she said, 'then I will apply for legal guardianship of both of them.'

'That's entirely up to you,' Miss Fforbes-Smythe said with a distinct lack of interest.

Peggy's jaw became firm, her gaze hardening. 'You said they were going to Wales. Where in Wales?'

'It's a fairly small farming community called Llanbister.'

'And when would they have to leave?'

'In about a week's time.'

'A week?' Peggy shot to her feet, her body trembling with fear and anger. 'But that's too long. Anything could happen in a week – look what they did to the school last night. Much more of that and Cliffehaven will be flattened.'

Jim grabbed her hand and gently sat her down again.

'There are no trains until then,' said Miss Fforbes-Smythe, unmoved by Peggy's outburst. 'The raids over the past few days have destroyed miles of track, and once they're repaired, the service personnel will have exclusive use of the trains for the first three days.'

'But surely, children are more important?'

'Not in this instance,' she replied. 'There are several thousand service personnel stranded on the south coast who need to get back to their bases. It's imperative to the war effort that we do all we can to help them achieve that.' She took off her glasses again and pinched the bridge of her nose. 'Which is why it would have been wiser to follow the government directive on evacuation in the first instance.' She paused to let her admonition sink in. 'So, do you still want me to book places on the first available train?'

Sally and Peggy looked at one another. 'We have no other choice,' said Peggy.

Miss Fforbes-Smythe gathered several leaflets and handed them across the desk before turning once more to her folder. 'That is the list of requirements for each child. Please make sure they have everything on that list and limit their luggage to a case each.'

They took the lists and scanned them quickly, and Sally saw they were the same as the one she'd got in London.

The woman behind the desk had got into her

stride now she had forms to fill in, and she looked quite animated. 'I will need each child's name, date of birth, home address and, in your case, Miss Turner, your London address as well as your billet here. I will also need to see your identity cards.'

They duly handed them over, gave her the details, and waited in silence as her pen scratched across the official-looking form.

'They will have to have medical checks, of course. We can't risk the spread of diseases.' She glanced at Sally over her glasses. 'I take it you are registered with a local doctor?'

'It's Dr Brown in the High Street,' said Peggy. 'He's our family doctor.'

'I will need you to sign these consent forms.' She handed them to Jim before turning to Sally. 'I see we already have your mother's signature on the form for when you left London. I see no reason why that would not still hold as you are travelling with Ernest.'

'And Sally's train fare?' said Jim.

'I will make sure she is fully covered for that.' Miss Fforbes-Smythe checked her notes. 'I see you are connected to the telephone service, which will make it easy to notify you of the train's departure. Please make sure your children are ready to leave at very short notice. We cannot always guarantee the time-table, but the train will leave promptly at the allotted time, so don't be late. It won't wait for you.'

* * *

The summer's sun was low in the sky as they finally left that awful office. Peggy pulled on her gloves, adjusted her hat and tucked her handbag under her arm. 'I don't know about you two, but I could do with a large whisky and soda.'

'You'll be lucky to get a beer,' muttered Jim. 'Come on, girls, let's go to The Anchor and see if Rosie's got a decent drop under the counter.'

The pub had stood in the narrow street for eight hundred years. It leant precariously over the pavement, the great black beams running like arteries between the whitewashed walls. Inside it was warm and noisy, the cigarette smoke hanging in a pall several inches from the ceiling.

Peggy and Sally found a seat by the enormous inglenook fireplace where a bunch of dusty dried flowers had replaced the burning logs. This was Sally's first time in The Anchor, and she looked about it with interest as Jim went to the bar.

Heavy dark beams crossed the sway-backed ceiling that was brown with hundreds of years of nicotine-staining. The tiny, diamond-paned windows had been covered in tape and were further protected by the outside shutters. The flooring was made from bricks that weren't very evenly laid, and over the bar were row upon row of pewter tankards. There was an out-of-tune upright piano being played in one corner, where a group of soldiers were singing enthusiastically, and a group of girls in the smart uniforms of the WAAFs were gossiping and flirting with the soldiers in another. She could understand now why Pearl and Edie liked coming here. The atmosphere was warm and friendly and, as yet, no-one had had too much to drink. It was a world away from the East End pubs where no decent woman would dream of going.

Jim leant on the bar, flirted with Rosie, and disappeared through a side door. He came back with three glasses and a bottle of whisky under his coat. 'She hasn't any soda, but she's bringing over a jug of water,' he explained, quickly pouring each of them a hefty measure and hiding the bottle again. 'You've got the old man to thank for this,' he said with a grin. 'Rosie's obviously got a soft spot for him – this is his special bottle she keeps out the back.'

'I didn't even realise he liked whisky,' said Peggy.

'Don't knock it, Peg. It's nectar compared to the beer they serve in here.'

Sally watched as Rosie sashayed from behind the bar with the jug of water. Her skirt was tight, the heels were high, the blouse revealing a magnificent cleavage. Such an outfit on Florrie would have made her look like a tart, but Rosie possessed a warmth in her voluptuousness that made her soft and rather endearing. No wonder Ron was smitten.

'Nice to see you, Peg,' she said with a broad, friendly smile as she put the jug of water on the low table. 'It's not often we see you in here.'

'We've had a bit of a day,' she replied, 'so we thought a nip of whisky might cheer us up.'

Rosie eyed Sally. 'I hope you're eighteen, darlin', otherwise . . .'

'Had her birthday only last week, to be sure, Rosie,' said Jim, with a sly wink.

'I just bet she did,' Rosie said, and laughed. 'You and your dad are as bad as each other. I wouldn't trust either of you.' With that, she sashayed back to the bar and began to wipe down the highly polished oak, her magnificent bosom moving gently and provocatively beneath the thin cotton of her blouse.

'Ach, she's a fine-looking woman, so she is,' said Jim, his gaze fixed admiringly on that blouse.

'Put your eyes back in, Jim,' laughed Peggy. 'They're in danger of dropping into your whisky.'

Chapter Fourteen

Sally wasn't used to drinking alcohol, and found she didn't like the taste, and although she'd tipped most of it into Jim's glass and watered down the rest, she still felt light-headed as they strolled back to Beach View. She was thirsty now and looking forward to a nice cup of tea.

As they stepped into the hall and shed coats and hats, Sally noticed that Peggy seemed unusually subdued. But then she didn't feel too bright herself now that her departure from Cliffehaven had become a reality.

She followed Peggy into the kitchen and found everyone was home except Florrie. The boys were listening to *Children's Hour* on the wireless and gave scant attention to their arrival. Anne was putting the finishing touches to a fish pie, and Ron was cleaning the sink where he'd gutted the fish, gathering up the heads, scales and bones in a bucket to put on the compost heap. Mrs Finch was wearing white cotton gloves and a large apron, busily cleaning her small collection of silver on the table.

'Have you seen Florrie?' Sally asked Cissy, who was poring over a film magazine.

'No, sorry.' She shot a glance at Ernie and kept her voice to a murmur. 'How did you all get on at the you-know-where?'

'We'll tell everyone our news once the boys' programme has finished,' said Peggy. 'Did you manage to get any tea, Anne? I'm gasping.'

'We did, and the kettle's almost boiled. Sit down, Mum. You look all in. Was it awful at that office?'

'I've met more pleasant people,' she muttered. 'Did Martin find you?'

She nodded. 'He caught up with us in the grocer's queue. Mrs Finch stayed in the line while we went for a quiet chat. You've got her to thank for the tea.' She lowered her voice. 'I haven't told anyone about Alex,' she whispered. 'I thought you'd want to do it.'

Peggy just nodded, her face drawn and pale as she lit a cigarette and made a concerted effort to relax.

With the tea poured and the fish pie in the oven, they sat in near silence until the story-time came to an end.

Peggy waited until she had everyone's attention. 'It has been a bit of a day,' she began, 'and there are several very important things we have to tell you.' She glanced at Jim for moral support as he knew what was coming. 'Martin came earlier with some very sad news.' Her voice broke and she took a deep breath as Jim took her hand. 'I'm really sorry to have to tell you this, but Alex was killed last night defending the convoy in the Channel.'

378

'Such a gentleman,' said Mrs Finch, sadly. 'How awful to think we'll never see him again. He had such lovely manners.'

'Ach, the poor wee man,' sighed Ron. 'He was a fine fellow, so he was. We'll miss him, won't we Jim?'

'Aye, that we will, Da. That we will.'

'Then you'll be pleased to hear he's left you a case of vodka under the stairs. He asked that you remember him as you take your first drink.' She saw the light in Jim's eyes and forestalled his hasty retreat to the hall. 'There are other important matters to discuss before you and Ron get stuck into the vodka,' she said firmly. 'And you've got work in an hour, Jim, so you need to keep sober.'

'What can be more important than giving Alex a decent wake?' said Jim.

'Security,' she replied, and reached into her knitting bag for the keys she'd hidden there earlier. 'I've decided it's time we all kept our bedrooms locked – even during the day. With the raids going on, we're out of this house far too much, and anyone could easily get in.'

She eyed Mrs Finch's silver twinkling on the table. 'We might not have much, but what we do have is precious. I would hate to think of someone stealing it.'

'So that's why Anne and I couldn't get into our rooms earlier,' said Cissy. 'You might have warned us, Mum.'

'I didn't really think about it until this morning,' she replied, checking the tags and handing them out. 'I suggest you keep the key with you at all times, and not leave them lying about. Can you remember to do that, Mrs Finch?'

She nodded and tucked the key away in the handbag that rarely left her side.

Peggy leant back in her chair and smiled at Anne. 'Now that's settled, I think Anne wants to tell you her news.'

Sally tried to listen as Anne excitedly revealed her future plans, and the boys cheered at the news of the school closure, but she was finding it hard to concentrate. Peggy had avoided looking at her as she'd talked about locking the rooms – and had certainly not met her eye as she'd handed her the key. She could feel the heat of shame building in her as the only possible reason for this became clear. Florrie had been up to her old tricks.

Had Peggy caught her – what had she taken? The thought of that jar of money made her feel quite sick. But she couldn't go rushing off now in the middle of things, it would be too obvious, and Peggy had been so careful not to reveal her true reasoning behind this sudden urge for security.

Sally sat at the table, the key clasped in her sweating hand, the weight of its implication burning into her skin.

Jim's voice roused her from her dark thoughts. 'Peg and Sally and I have finally done what we discussed the other night, but I'm thinking it would be wiser if we didn't go over it now.' He glanced meaningfully at the boys who had returned to their comics, bored with the adult conversation. 'It will be hard enough as it is, and might take some time, so I think we should do it quietly and in private.' His dark gaze settled on Sally. 'Are you all right with that – or would you prefer we do it together?'

'It's probably best I do it,' she murmured, glancing at Ernie who was busy colouring in his picture book. As Jim had said, it would be hard to disrupt him again – hard to make him understand they would have to leave this warm, homely place and go to live with strangers. She wasn't looking forward to it at all.

The delicious fish pie was received with relish, and everyone groaned in exasperation as the siren howled before they could finish it.

'Jim,' said Peggy, as he hurried back from the hallway swathed, incongruously, in his thick coat, 'wrap that silver in this tea-towel and put it in this box. Everyone take your plates with you – I'm not letting Hitler ruin the fish pie as well as everything else.'

They trooped into the garden and got settled as Ron went back for Harvey. The dog still hated the sirens, and had to be forcibly dragged down the path until he smelled the fish pie – then it was a job for Ron to keep up with him.

'Will you get that flea-bitten animal out of me

dinner?' Jim tapped Harvey's nose as it investigated the plate.

'He hasn't got fleas,' muttered Ron, pulling the dog away and making him sit under the bench. Ron quickly ate most of his food and left just enough on the plate for the dog to lick it clean.

'That's disgusting,' snapped Peggy, as the enemy bombers droned overhead and the guns began to boom. 'I wish you wouldn't let him do that – it's unhygienic.'

'It'll save on the washing-up,' retorted Ron with a grin, 'and what's a few germs compared to that lot?' He looked up as the droning bombers continued their flight.

Sally giggled as Harvey slumped on the floor at Ron's feet and proceeded to snore. It was the same every air raid. The banter would go back and forth, the determined cheerfulness covering their fears, Harvey at the centre of everyone as Mrs Finch fell asleep and the boys chattered. Sally knew she would miss this so much she could hardly bear to think about it – but Ernie had yet to be told of their plans, so she must keep her emotions under control for his sake.

She became aware of Jim nudging his father, and of the old man softly chortling as Jim opened the large coat to reveal the bottle of vodka he'd liberated from the cupboard under the stairs.

'I don't know why you thought it necessary to wear that great coat, Jim Reilly,' shouted Peggy above the clamour. 'It was obvious you couldn't resist the vodka, so why bother trying to hide it? D'you think I was born yesterday?'

He looked sheepish. 'Not at all, me darling – not at all.'

'Then I hope you brought enough glasses for everyone so we can drink a toast to Alex?'

Jim drew out the two tumblers and couldn't quite meet her gaze. 'I didn't t'ink you'd be wanting any,' he said. 'You usually screw up your face and call it poison.'

Peggy brought the teacups from the box. 'In this instance, I'm prepared to make an exception.'

They raised cups and glasses, and Jim made the toast.

> 'May the winds of fortune sail you,
> 'May you sail a gentle sea,
> 'May it always be the other man,
> 'Who says the drink's on me.'

He drank the vodka down in one. 'God love your soul, Alex, and may you be flying with the angels tonight.'

The level on the bottle of vodka had been lowered quite substantially by the time the all-clear finally sounded two hours later, and it was with some difficulty that they managed to get Ron and Jim out of the shelter. It was decided they could both sleep in the cellar so their snoring didn't disturb the rest of the house. The boys would go in with Anne and Peggy.

Sally carried Ernie upstairs. Unlocking her bedroom door, she gently laid him on the bed and pulled the blackout curtains before turning on the light. He was fast asleep, so she carefully stripped him to his underwear and tucked him in.

Once she was certain he wouldn't wake, she got the chair and looked for the precious jar. Her fingers trembled as she reached for it, and she frowned as she discovered it had somehow slid further back and was now out of reach. But at least it was still there – the room looked as tidy as she'd left it, and there was no evidence that Florrie had been through her things. If she had, the room would have been a tip, for Florrie was the untidiest person she knew.

With a deep, grateful sigh of relief, she replaced the chair and began to hunt through the drawers for a clean blouse to wear for work the following day.

Her hands stilled as she realised her best skirt had been folded neatly in the drawer instead of being hung in the wardrobe, and the lovely sweater she'd been given for Christmas was in with the blouses. She knew in that instant that Florrie *had* been in her room, and that Peggy must have tidied up behind her.

She sat there for a long time staring at that skirt and sweater, the shame flooding through her at the thought of Peggy knowing Florrie had no qualms about rooting through other people's things. Had she gone into any of the other rooms? Sally felt beads of cold sweat run down her back at the thought.

'What's the old saying?' she whispered. 'Like mother, like daughter, that's it. Now none of them will trust me ever again – especially after that to-do at the factory. No wonder Peggy couldn't look me in the eye when she handed out those keys.'

Sally waited for an hour after she'd turned off the bedside light before she crept across the room and opened the door. The house was silent but for the groans and creaks of the timbers and the faint gurgling in the water pipes. She tiptoed to Florrie's room and tried the door. It was unlocked, so she stepped inside and pulled the curtains.

Switching on the light, she looked at the pile of clothes and shoes in the middle of the bed, and the make-up and cheap jewellery strewn across the dressing table. Then she turned her attention to the chest of drawers. Her heart was thudding against her ribs and she was finding it hard to breathe as she eased out the bottom drawer. The cavity beneath a bottom drawer had always been a favourite hiding place of Florrie's, and Sally prayed with all her might that she wouldn't find anything as she steeled herself to look.

Her prayers had come to nothing, and her hands trembled as she took out three of Mrs Finch's lace-edged handkerchiefs, and one of Anne's good blouses. There was a belt of Cissy's too – the one with the glittering buckle that was her favourite, and an almost unused lipstick she'd bought from Woolworths only the other week.

Sally felt such a rage it was like a huge mass growing inside her as she placed the stolen things on the bed. She used that rage to remain focused as she continued her methodical search through the rest of the drawers and the wardrobe – and when she was certain there was nothing else that shouldn't be there, she swept the pile of Florrie's clothes off the bed and sat down to wait.

The town-hall clock had just struck two when she was woken from her doze by the sound of stealthy but unsteady footsteps on the landing. She climbed off the bed and prepared herself for the coming confrontation.

Florrie's make-up was smudged, and she was drunk. 'What you doing in 'ere?' She shut the door none too quietly, kicked off her shoes and slung the handbag onto the bed.

'Keep your voice down,' hissed Sally, 'or you'll have the whole house awake.'

'I asked wot you was doin' in 'ere,' mumbled Florrie.

'Looking for the stuff you nicked from other people's rooms.'

Florrie's bleary gaze settled unsteadily on the things Sally had placed on the dressing-table stool. 'I was only gunna borrow them for a bit,' she muttered. 'What's all the bleedin' fuss about?' She staggered to the bed and sat down.

'You didn't borrow 'em,' Sally hissed. 'You bleedin' well stole 'em, and I won't 'ave it. These are good people.'

'Yeah, yeah, yeah. Me 'eart bleeds.' Florrie took a whisky flask out of her handbag and took a swig. 'So, whatya gunna do about it, then, Miss Goody Two-shoes? Miss Mealy-mouth-butter-wouldn't-melt? Call the rozzers?'

'I'd bloody well like to,' she growled, 'but it's shame enough me mother can't keep 'er thieving 'ands to 'erself, let alone have the rozzers all over the gaff.'

Florrie snorted and tried to focus on Sally. 'You ain't so posh now, are yer?'

Sally was beyond caring what she sounded like. 'Where you been all day?'

'None of your bleedin' business,' she slurred, taking another drink from the flask.

Sally grabbed it, screwed the lid tight, and tossed it under the bed. 'It is my flamin' business when Simmons starts asking me questions about ya – insinuating you and me got something special going on with Solomon and Goldman.'

'Well, I 'ave, ain't I? Solly and me, we're gunna get married.'

'In yer dreams. Solomon's married to 'is wife's money. He ain't gunna look at you twice once she finds out what he's been up to.'

'And who's gunna tell 'er?' Florrie's expression was belligerent as she struggled to get off the bed, found she couldn't keep her balance and fell back again. 'If I 'ear you been flapping your gob about me and Solly, it'll be yer eyes, girl. And that ain't no threat, it's a bleedin' promise.'

Sally regarded her with the coolness of someone who had long since stopped caring. Florrie's mascara and eye-shadow were streaking down her face to mingle with the smudged lipstick. Her blouse was buttoned up wrongly and the bra it revealed was grey and grubby. Florrie was thirty-five, but she looked a decade older.

'You disgust me, do you know that?' she murmured without emotion. 'Take a long, hard look in that mirror before you pass out, and try for once to see what I see.'

Florrie tried to focus on her reflection in the dressing-table mirror, but soon gave up. 'You ain't no bleedin' oil painting yerself,' she spat. 'No wonder you ain't got no bloke.'

'I'm not like you,' Sally whispered furiously. 'I don't need some bloke to leech off – some chancer to buy me drinks, and take me to bleedin' 'otels.' She jabbed Florrie hard in the shoulder, making her almost topple over. 'You 'ad a decent man, but you treated 'im like dirt – and now it's too late. Dad won't never want you again.'

Florrie's face crumpled and she began to sob, the large tears making an even worse mess on her face.

'I only married 'im cos you was on the bleedin' way. That's the story of me life,' she wailed. 'I never 'ad no chance of nothing.'

'Shush,' hissed Sally. 'Keep it down.'

Florrie eyed her mournfully, but at least she'd stopped wailing. 'I ain't 'ad a proper life,' she sobbed. 'Bleedin' tied down with a man I couldn't bleedin' stand, and a flaming kid wot never shut up crying.' She swiped the back of her hand under her nose and sniffed hard. 'You was a pain in the arse as a kid – and then, just to put the tin lid right on it, I 'ad Ernie.' She gave a harsh cough of laughter through her tears. 'What a bleedin' joke that was.'

'I didn't find it funny,' replied Sally coldly. 'And neither did Ernie, or Dad.' Florrie was getting maudlin, as she always did after drinking too much, and Sally was bankrupt of patience. If Florrie thought she could wring one morsel of pity out of her with this act, then she was very much mistaken.

'But I only wanted a bit of fun, Sal – don't yer see? Surely there ain't no 'arm in that?' She collapsed on to the pillows and howled.

Sally realised she'd have the whole house awake in a minute. Pulling the covers over Florrie, she knew from experience that the only way to shut her up was to treat her like a child. She grimaced as she smoothed the over-bleached hair from her hot forehead and caught the rank odour of her unwashed body. 'Yeah, all right,' she said softly. 'You go to sleep now. Everything's fine, everything's lovely. There, there.'

Florrie was asleep within seconds, and Sally turned her on to her side and wedged her there with the spare pillow. She took her cigarettes and matches in case she started a fire by trying to smoke when she woke up, and then collected the hankies, belt, lipstick and blouse.

Creeping out of the room she clicked the door shut and hesitated on the landing. She didn't want to take these things into her room in case Peggy saw them and thought she was the thief. But what to do?

She stood there for some minutes in the dark, and then crept downstairs to the kitchen. She could hear the snores coming from the basement as she unfolded the handkerchiefs and blouse and mixed them in with the rest of the laundry in the basket. The belt was left hanging over the back of a chair, and the lipstick placed in view on the dresser. It was the best she could do to cover up Florrie's pilfering, and she just hoped it wouldn't raise any more questions.

It was almost three in the morning by the time she collapsed into bed. Florrie had to go – and soon. But how on *earth* did she get rid of her?

'Because of the raid last night, things haven't been settled,' said Peggy, as she poured tea and handed round the cups at breakfast. 'So Jim and I thought it might be best if we do it all together. What shift are you working today, Sally?'

'I'm not due in until one.' She was exhausted, both mentally and physically, after the trauma of the previous night, and could barely think straight. 'I agree with you,' she said, glancing at Ernie. 'It'll be best to get it over with in one go.'

'What you on about, Sal?' Ernie eyed her over the teacup.

'You'll find out soon enough,' she said, and ruffled his hair.

'That's what grown-ups always say,' said Charlie, with all the wisdom of an eight year old. 'They never really tell you anything.'

'Where's Mum? I ain't seen 'er for ages. She ain't gone, 'as she?'

She noted the bewilderment in his eyes and made an effort to keep her voice low and soothing. 'She's asleep upstairs,' she replied. 'You'll probably see her later on.'

'I wish I could stay and help,' said Anne, 'but I have my first full interview with the OC this morning. Once I know when the training course begins, I'll have a better idea of when I'll be moving out.'

Sally saw how Peggy's smile faded and her eyes darkened. She was going to find it very tough once everyone had gone, and she wished with all her heart that it didn't have to be so.

Ron and Jim weren't exactly bright-eyed and bushy-tailed this morning, but they nursed their hangovers with cups of tea, and told the boys not to make so much noise as they argued over their plans for the day.

Sally ate the toast and drank the tea, waiting on tenterhooks for someone to mention the mysterious disappearance of their belongings. But as one by one they left the table to prepare for the day without saying anything, Sally felt as if a great weight had been lifted from her shoulders.

Once breakfast was over and the kitchen put to rights, Anne and Cissy left to go their separate ways, and Mrs Finch took her library book into the dining room. She liked to sit by the window in the sunshine and watch what was happening in the street.

The three boys were playing a game of snakes and ladders on the kitchen table when Peggy caught Sally's eye and signalled it was time.

'Now boys,' she said brightly. 'I've got a real surprise for you all. You're going with Sally on a holiday.'

'Where? Why? For how long?' The chorus of questions came in a mixture of anxiety and excitement.

'Well now,' said Jim. 'You'll be going on a train with lots of other boys and girls, and Mam and Sal will make you a picnic to eat on the journey. It'll be quite a long journey, so we'll put in some of your favourite comics and toys as well.'

Ernie looked at Sally with accusatory eyes. 'Are we going away for very long?'

'I don't know how long we'll be away,' she said truthfully. 'But Bob and Charlie and me will be going with you, so you don't have to worry.'

'Will it be like last time?' he persisted. 'With them fat women bossing us about?'

Sally tried to make light of it. 'There're always fat women telling us what to do, Ernie. It's their job. But that doesn't mean you can't enjoy yourself.'

'What about Mum? Is she coming too?'

'No, love. She's got to go to work.'

'That's what you said last time, and she didn't come for ages and ages – and when she did – she . . . she . . .' He burst into tears.

Sally gathered him up, noting that Charlie was about to cry too. 'Listen, Ernie, it's not like before. This is a holiday with Bob and Charlie and me, and we're going to have lots of fun.'

'Yes,' said Peggy, putting her arm round her two boys. 'You'll be going to Wales where there's mountains and rivers and lots of farms to explore. You'll see forests and cows and sheep, and might even be allowed to help the farmer with his chickens. How about that?'

'Why aren't you coming, Mum?' Charlie's voice was still quavering with doubt, even though his eyes had lit up at the thought of being on a farm.

'Because, my darling, I've got this place to look after. And then there's Cissy, and Anne, and Mrs Finch to take care of.'

Ernie sniffled. 'Will I be allowed to take me

wheelchair – and what about Bob's train set – can we take that too?'

'Well, now,' said Jim, 'I reckon that chair of yours will fit nicely in the guard's van, but your granddad and me will be looking after that wee train set till you come back. It might be too big to put in a case, and could get broken – and that wouldn't be good, would it?'

All three boys eyed him solemnly, but it was Bob who spoke. 'We're being evacuated, aren't we?'

'Yes, son,' said Jim. 'Most of the other children have already left, and your mam and me decided it was too dangerous for you to stay any longer.' He drew both his sons into his embrace. 'We love you and don't like sending you away,' he said softly. 'But we have to keep you safe.'

'When will we be going?' Bob's voice was steady, his expression calm and accepting as he held Charlie's hand.

'Quite soon,' said Peggy. 'We don't know exactly because the train lines are up, but we'll have to start packing this morning so we'll be ready when it's time.'

'What about Daddy?' said Ernie, wiping his nose on his sleeve.

Sally winced and gave him a handkerchief. 'I told you before, Ernie. Don't do that.' She took a breath. 'I'll write to Daddy and tell him what's happening once we know where we're staying.'

Peggy became businesslike. 'Right, let's find those

lists and see what we're going to pack. Jim, get up in the loft and find some suitcases. Ron, take Harvey outside, he's blowing off and it stinks.'

The three boys collapsed into giggles as a shame-faced Harvey was dragged out of the kitchen, his tail between his legs.

Sally eyed Peggy thankfully as the atmosphere lightened and they began to discuss the list, and what could be added to make the boys' time away less harrowing.

The morning passed quickly as clothing was brought downstairs to be washed, mended or ironed. A list was made of things which would have to be bought, and Peggy dug out some of Charlie's old shoes and pyjamas for Ernie. The heat of summer meant travelling in shirts, shorts, socks and sandals, but they also had to think about the coming autumn and winter. A pile of sweaters, blazers, wellingtons and mackintoshes were added to the growing mound of clothing on the table.

Sally helped with the washing, before setting to with a needle and thread to sew on buttons, turn collars and darn socks. Jim polished shoes as the boys argued over which books and games to pack.

It was a hectic morning, and Sally was up and down the stairs a dozen times before it was time to leave for work. She hesitated outside Florrie's bedroom door and decided to leave her to sleep it off. She was in no mood for any more confrontations. Grabbing her jacket and gas-mask box, she picked up the string bag holding a flask and sandwiches, hurriedly kissed a cheerful Ernie goodbye and was running down the street.

She was already late, and Simmons would no doubt give her an ear-bashing – but as she would have to hand her notice in to Goldman this morning, she didn't really care.

Simmons didn't say anything as she scurried past him. Perhaps he'd realised finally that it would be wasting his breath. Pearl and Brenda were at their machines, already halfway through their shifts when she sat down beside them.

'How did it go with the kids?' shouted Pearl over the clatter of machinery.

'All right, I think,' she replied, swiftly feeding the material beneath the needle. 'Ernie doesn't seem too upset now he knows me and the others are going too.'

'Where's Florrie? Ain't she supposed to be on this shift with you?'

'She's sleeping off her night out,' said Sally grimly. 'I'm not responsible for her, and if she gets the sack, maybe she'll go back to London.'

'When are you going to tell Goldman you're leaving?' asked Brenda, the fag bobbing at the corner of her mouth.

'During my break.' Sally concentrated on her work, her thoughts flitting from Ernie to Florrie, to Peggy and the boys – and to the journey ahead.

She was dreading it – dreading a repeat of what

happened to them when they'd first arrived in Cliffehaven. And although she'd told that Miss Fforbes-Smythe she was quite capable of making her own arrangements, she didn't really know where to start. She couldn't afford a hotel or guest house, and even if she did manage to find a room somewhere, the money she'd saved would soon be eaten away by rent and food and Ernie's medical care.

She finished the trousers and snipped off the loose cotton, her thoughts elsewhere. She suspected there wouldn't be any work like this in Wales, and that she'd probably end up with the land army girls, or on the production line of a munitions factory – neither of which appealed in the slightest. But needs must, and if that's what it took to make sure Ernie was safe and well looked after, she would do it.

The siren went off fifteen minutes later and everyone trooped into the vast shelter that had been built behind the factory. They sat and smoked and gossiped and tried to read magazines in the dim light as the clatter of gunfire and the roar of plane engines went on above them.

It was an hour before the all-clear sounded, and by then they'd had enough of being underground and quite happily returned to work.

Sally worked fast and efficiently until it was time for her break. Pearl was going off shift and planning to spend the rest of the day browsing round

Woolworths for new make-up, and perhaps treating herself to an ice-cream from the dairy.

Sally approached Simmons who was standing in the corridor by the office. 'I need to speak to Mr Goldman.'

He eyed her through the thick lenses of his glasses. 'If it's about Mrs Turner, then you're wasting your time. She was sacked an hour ago.'

The news was hardly surprising, but it had other connotations which didn't bode well. Florrie's position here was guaranteed by Solomon – had he tired of her already, or had his wife found out and he'd dumped her as fast as he could? There would be the most fearful row when she got home, because Florrie was bound to blame her.

'She was still in bed when I came to work. Does she know she's been sacked?'

He smirked. 'Oh, yes. She came swanning in three hours late, and was headed off by Mr Solomon at the staff entrance. I didn't hear everything he said to her because he shut the office door, but I couldn't fail to hear him telling her she was never to put a foot in this place again. She was yelling fit to bust, and stormed out ten minutes later calling him all the names under the sun.'

Simmons grinned. He was clearly enjoying himself. 'Your mother does possess a vast and colourful vocabulary, doesn't she?'

Sally could just picture the scene, with Simmons's ear glued to the door as Florrie and Solomon tore into each other, and her spirits rose and ebbed as she thought of the different consequences of such a falling-out.

She pulled her ragged thoughts together, determined not to encourage Simmons's voyeuristic streak further. 'My request to see Mr Goldman has nothing to do with Mrs Turner,' she said quietly. 'It's personal.'

His lip curled as he eyed her. 'If you tell me what it's about, I'll see if he's available. I should think both Solomon and Goldman have had enough of the Turner women today.'

'If I wanted you to know my business I wouldn't have asked to see Mr Goldman. Are you going to see if he's in, or do I do it?'

Simmons hesitated, eyed his watch and fidgeted with his clipboard. 'Wait here,' he muttered.

She stood in the corridor outside the office, her pulse racing. It was clear Solomon had dumped Florrie – but without work, what would she do for money? Florrie had expensive tastes, and although she'd no doubt find some other fool to feed her gin and fags . . .

'Oh, Gawd,' she breathed, as she had a sudden very nasty thought.

She dug frantically in the pocket of her dress. The key to her room was still there – but had she remembered to lock the door this morning?

Now those chaotic few hours returned to haunt her. She hadn't locked the door because she'd been in and out of the room all morning – by the time she'd had to leave for work she was already late and in such a hurry she'd forgotten. The precious jar was still on top of the wardrobe – along with the passbook.

Sally leant against the wall and closed her eyes as the chill ran through her. 'Please,' she whispered. 'Please, please don't let her find that jar.'

'Go and wait in the outer office,' said Simmons, bustling past. 'He'll see you in a minute.'

Sally pushed away from the wall and found that she was unsteady and almost blinded by the fear that swept through her.

'Are you all right, Miss Turner?' Marjorie stopped thumping the keys on the typewriter.

'I'm fine,' she lied, sinking into the first chair she came across.

'Well you don't look it,' she said, pouring a glass of water from a jug on her desk. 'Drink this before you either faint or throw up. I've had enough dramas from your family this morning.'

Sally sipped the water, but her heart still thudded and she felt sick. All she could think about was that jar.

'Miss Turner. Please come in. I understand you wish to see me on a personal matter?'

Sally followed him into the office and took the chair he indicated. There was, thankfully, no sign of Solomon. She made a concerted effort to focus on the reason for this interview. 'I've come to hand in my notice, sir,' she said.

'I hope this has nothing to do with the unfortunate scene with your mother,' he replied. 'You're a good worker, and an honest one, too. It would be a great shame to lose you.'

'That's very kind of you to say so, sir, but this has nothing to do with Florrie. You see, I'm leaving Cliffehaven.' She calmly told him about evacuating the boys, and the likelihood that she wouldn't be returning for the duration. 'I'll be sorry to leave, sir. I've enjoyed working here.'

'I wish you luck, Miss Turner. It can't be easy having to look after your brother in such circumstances.' He smiled, his great jowly face creasing up like a pug dog's. 'I admire your courage and fortitude, and I'll make sure you have a good reference to take with you.'

'Thank you, sir. I would appreciate that, and I'm sorry if this leaves you in the lurch.'

'When will you be leaving us?'

'Probably by the end of the week. There's no set date until the trains are running again, but I'll work right up to the day I have to go.'

He stood to show the interview was over, and shook her hand. 'It has been a pleasure knowing you, Miss Turner, and should you ever be in need of a job again, my door is always open.'

Sally spent the rest of her shift fretting and, with still an hour to go, she couldn't wait any longer. Grabbing her things, she didn't bother to explain to

Simmons, and raced through the pitch-black streets for Beach View.

The house was silent as she stepped into the hall. The kitchen and dining room were deserted, with no tell-tale sounds of Cissy's music, or the boys' chattering coming from the basement. Peggy and Jim must have taken the boys to the cinema. They'd been promising this treat for some time, and as the boys would be leaving Cliffehaven soon, it was no surprise they'd chosen tonight.

She slowly climbed the stairs, reluctant to reach her room, but knowing she must. She steeled herself to open the door, and stood there numb with shock. The wardrobe was open, the drawers yawning – her clothes were scattered everywhere.

With fear squeezing her heart, she climbed on to the chair and frantically searched the top of the wardrobe. Her money and passbook were gone.

Sinking to the floor she burst into anguished tears of despair.

Chapter Fifteen

Sally didn't know how long she'd sat there on the floor but, as the tears dried, the anguish turned to such anger she was shaking with it. She left her bedroom and opened Florrie's door. The room still stank of her sickly perfume, but the drawers and cupboard were empty. Florrie had gone. 'You bitch,' Sally breathed. 'You absolute bitch.'

She returned to her room and slowly began to pick up her clothes. It was soon clear that Florrie had taken her best skirt, her favourite blouse and the lovely sweater Peggy had given her at Christmas. But the loss of those expensive navy and white shoes was the final straw. The bitter tears over her mother's betrayal fell silently down her face as she carefully folded her things back into the drawers and hung up her remaining jacket and two skirts.

Once the room was straight again, she went to wash her face and brush her hair, but as she stared at her wan reflection in the bathroom mirror, she felt a stab of fear that made her go cold. She raced down the stairs and into the dining room. The trunk was still there by the machine – but had Florrie taken her pick of the clothing Sally had laboured over for other people?

She knelt in front of it, and sighed with profound relief. A sturdy padlock had kept Florrie's thieving hands at bay – and she knew she had Peggy to thank for that. But how shaming it was; how utterly awful that Peggy had thought to do it at all.

It just proved to Sally that she'd known what Florrie was capable of, but had this knowledge tainted the trust and love she'd been so certain of before today? Had it brought back memories of the accusations of theft at the factory? Her name had been cleared then, but would the doubts now be setting in?

Sally slowly went into the kitchen and put the kettle on the hob. As she waited for it to boil, she came to the conclusion it was a good thing she was leaving; for now, every time Peggy looked at her, she would see Florrie and wonder. She made the tea and took it upstairs. They would no doubt soon be home, but she didn't yet have the courage to face them.

She was curled up on her bed when Peggy found her a short while later. 'Sally? Oh, Sally, I was hoping to get home earlier, but the picture overran, and we could only walk at the same pace as Mrs Finch.'

Sally scrambled to her feet and hastily swiped away the remains of her tears. 'She's gone, Peggy. Cleared off and taken half me clothes and all me money.'

'I had a feeling she might,' she replied, 'but the money's safe. She didn't take that.'

It was as if a great beam of light flooded the room as Sally stared at her. 'But the jar's gone – how . . .?'

'I took it,' she said hastily. 'I was going to do something about it yesterday and it's been worrying me ever since. I came up after you'd gone to work, found your door unlocked, and decided to put the jar in the floor-safe in my room.'

'Oh, Peggy,' she said, her voice hitching on a sob. 'Thank you, thank you. I'm so sorry you've 'ad all this trouble. I feel so ashamed.'

Peggy wrapped her in her arms as she sobbed. 'You have absolutely nothing to be ashamed of,' she soothed. 'I'm just sorry you had to go through all this. That's why I wanted to get home earlier, so I could explain what I'd done with your money before you discovered it was missing.'

Sally gently withdrew from Peggy's embrace and blew her nose. 'I can never thank you enough,' she said, unable to meet her eye. 'But it's a good thing I'll be leaving soon, cos then you won't 'ave to keep locking doors.'

'That's quite enough of that,' said Peggy sternly. 'I have always trusted you, Sally, and I'm shocked you should think I'm so shallow as to believe you are anything like your mother. This is your home – will always be your home, even when you leave to start an independent life, as Anne is doing. So don't you *dare* think otherwise.'

A spark of hope ignited. 'You mean it?'

'I never say things I don't mean,' she said, bristling. 'Now, dry those eyes and sit down for a minute to catch your breath. A few bits of clothing can soon be replaced, so there's no real harm done.'

'But she took them – those – lovely shoes you gave me, and the sweater. I could never replace those.'

'I've got a wardrobe full of Doris's cast-off shoes, and I can always knit another sweater. Come on, Sally,' she said with a soft smile, 'cheer up, love. Worse things happen at sea, and at least she didn't make off with all your sewing. Ron found that padlock in his shed, and the key's quite safe.'

'Oh, Peg, Ron and the others don't know about her, do they?'

'They didn't need to know anything. We all love you and have absolute faith in your honesty, so why taint it with Florrie's actions?' She gave a little sigh. 'You see, I heard you and Florrie last night, and saw you going downstairs with the things she'd filched. I so wanted to say something then, but it was clear you were already very upset, and I didn't want to make things worse.'

Sally slipped her arm round her waist as they both sat on the bed. It was so good to know this lovely woman and her family really did care about her and Ernie. 'How am I going to explain to Ernie that Florrie's done a runner?'

'Tell him the truth. I don't think he'll be too upset,'

said Peggy. 'He's hardly seen her since she arrived, and from the little he's said, I think he rather wishes she hadn't come at all.'

Sally nodded, accepting Peggy was right. 'But where could she have gone? She got the sack today, so Solomon won't take her in.'

'She probably headed straight for the station and the first train out.'

'But the trains aren't running.'

'Actually,' said Peggy, 'they are. I had a call from the Billeting Office this afternoon. You and the boys will be leaving the day after tomorrow.'

'So soon?' she whispered.

'That's why we thought we'd go to the pictures as a last treat for the boys. It turned into quite a family outing. Anne made it back from her interview in time, Cissy didn't have a show tonight and Mrs Finch decided she didn't want to be left behind. We even bumped into Pearl in the town and she joined us.' She gave a soft chuckle. 'Only Ron was absent. He decided to sit and watch Rosie Braithwaite instead of *The Wizard of Oz*.'

'I wish I could have come too,' she murmured.

'We'll all go when you come back home – and that's a promise. Now, come on, Sally, wash your face and brush your hair. Everyone's downstairs, and with only two nights left before this family is cast to the winds, we must make the best of them.'

It was a warm, happy evening, despite the knowledge it would be one of their last together for what could turn out to be a long time. The three false alarms which had them scurrying back and forth across the garden hadn't helped much, but it wasn't until Sally was getting Ernie ready for bed that he asked about Florrie.

'She's gorn, ain't she?' he said, as he grimly withstood the wet flannel that was being energetically scrubbed round his neck and ears.

'Yes, love. She's gone back to London.'

'Didn't she like it 'ere?'

'Not really. I think she missed her mates back in Bow.'

'She don't like us, either, does she?' Ernie's brown eyes studied her closely. 'Cos she never come to play with me. And I 'eard you and 'er 'aving a row last night.'

Sally was shocked he'd overheard and didn't quite know how to answer him. 'Families always have rows,' she said, drying him off. 'Me and Mum never really got on, but I'm sure she likes us really.'

'Well I don't like 'er,' he said with a grimace. 'She ain't cuddly and nice smelling like Aunt Peg. I'm glad she's gorn.'

Sally gave him a hug. She hadn't been fooled by his brave words – he was bitterly disappointed in Florrie, and her leaving him again after such a fleeting and unsatisfactory return had been a bitter lesson for them both.

She put him to bed and read him a story. When he was asleep, she pulled on a cardigan and went back downstairs. The house was quiet now everyone was in bed, and she slipped out of the front door into the night. She was exhausted, but knew she was far from sleep, and the soft, salty air and the sigh of the sea against the gravel were calling her.

It was a beautiful night, with a million stars twinkling against the velvet black of the heavens. There was a bomber's moon, shedding its glow over Cliffehaven's roofs and empty streets, gilding the destruction and chaos into an almost magical landscape.

She reached the seafront, having avoided being accosted by wardens or watchmen, and although she knew she shouldn't be wandering about on her own, it was good to breathe in the clean air, and to have time to let her thoughts wander as she drank in the essence of Cliffehaven.

As she instilled the sights and scents into her heart, she knew these memories would sustain her all the while she was away, for she would miss this place much more than she'd ever missed Bow. It was here that she'd discovered what a real family was; it was here that she'd come to learn that life could be better if only she took the time and effort to improve her speech, and to learn to read and write. It was also here that she'd experienced her first kiss, and the heartbreak of losing the man she'd thought had returned her love.

Staring out at the water that glistened like silk beneath the moon's glow, she pulled her cardigan more firmly over her chest. His name still echoed in her heart, but soon she would be leaving and they would probably never meet again. How strange and unsettling life was – how uncertain the future.

She strolled along the seafront, heading for the fishing station. Nothing moved down there, for a strict curfew forbade night fishing. She stood and looked at the *Seagull*, remembering the day she'd returned, battered but unbowed, from Dunkirk, and how Jim's heart-rending story had touched them all.

Not wanting to think of such things, she turned quickly away, only to realise there was someone lurking in the nearby shelter. She experienced a stab of unease. It was clear he'd been watching her for – as she'd turned – he'd swiftly dodged back into the shadows.

She looked behind her and into the distance, her unease turning to fear. Apart from the soldiers manning one of the big guns several hundred yards down the prom, she was quite alone. 'Who's there?' she called, her voice cracking.

The figure shifted in the shadows.

She trembled and her mouth dried. He looked big and bulky, his shoulders strangely hunched. He was clearly up to no good. She glanced towards the distant gun emplacement. If she made a run for it, she'd have to get past him first. She gathered every ounce of courage. 'Show yourself,' she ordered, 'or I'll scream for help.'

He slowly emerged from the shadows, and Sally saw he was indeed a tall man, made bulky by the long overcoat he was wearing, his shoulders hunched as he leant heavily on the crutches. His face was in shadow, hidden beneath the brim of his hat.

'What you doing, scaring the living daylights out of people?' she demanded, her fear making her angry. Crippled or not, he had no right to frighten her like that.

He stood there for a heartbeat of time, his chin sunk into the collar of his coat, his face in deep shadow. And then he turned and slowly moved away from her, his progress hesitant and ungainly.

Sally's pulse stopped racing as she saw how difficult it was for him, and she wished she hadn't been quite so sharp. Like her, the poor man had probably only been out for a bit of fresh air and some quiet contemplation.

She was about to head back to Beach View when his foot caught on a rough edge of broken pavement. He tried to keep his balance, but the crutch clattered to the ground and, with a loud oath, he hit the concrete.

Sally rushed to his side. 'Let me help you,' she breathed.

'I don't need your help,' he snarled. 'Go away Sally. Just for the love of God leave me be.'

She stared at him in disbelief as he scrabbled for the fallen crutch. 'John?' she breathed, touching his shoulder. 'John, is it really you?'

'Of course it bloody well is,' he snarled, shrugging off her hand and grabbing the crutch. He tried getting to one knee, battling desperately to keep his balance and haul himself up. The crutch lost purchase on the broken concrete, and skittered away and, with a deep, agonised groan, his knee gave way and he crashed to the ground again.

She instinctively rushed to help.

'Go away,' he hissed. 'I don't want you seeing me like this.'

She had been consumed by a cocktail of love, sadness and shock, but she swiftly gathered her wits. 'Don't be stupid,' she retorted. 'You need help.'

'No, I don't,' he insisted, struggling to sit up.

'Well I'm not leaving you here on your arse in the middle of the night,' she said crossly. She grabbed his arm and put it over her shoulder. 'But you've got to help me, John, you're too heavy to lift on me own. Can you put your weight on your good leg?'

'That's just it,' he snapped. 'I don't possess a good leg.'

'Then do the best you can,' she replied, trying her hardest not to let him see how shocked she was by his helplessness. 'I'll count to three. Ready?'

His expression was stormy as he nodded.

He wasn't as heavy as she'd expected, but even so, Sally almost buckled as he leant on her and hauled himself to his feet. She steadied him, aware that he was glaring down at her almost defiantly, and concentrated on retrieving the crutches.

'Thanks.' He rammed them under his armpits. 'Sorry to be a nuisance,' he mumbled. 'Good night.'

'Oh, no you don't, John Hicks.' She barred his way, hands on hips, glaring up at him. 'You owe me an explanation, and I'm not moving until I get one.'

'There's nothing to say,' he replied, refusing to meet her angry gaze. 'You can see how things are. One leg's made out of tin, and the other's been broken so many times it's got more metal in it than a Lancaster bomber.'

'Is that why you wrote that horrid letter? Because you didn't think I'd want any more to do with you now you're injured?'

'That's about the size of it,' he said evenly. He looked at some distant point over her shoulder. 'You're young. You'll get over it.'

She slapped his face, the sound of it echoing along the silent seafront – shocking them both. 'How *dare* you think so little of me?' she snapped.

He looked at her then, his dark blue eyes delving to her very soul as they stood beneath the stars.

There were messages in his eyes she couldn't read, and a sense of helplessness and sorrow in his expression that made her want to hold him and tell him everything would be all right. That she loved him no matter what – and that together they could get through this.

413

But he broke the spell and looked away, the small muscle working in his jaw. 'I don't love you, Sally. I'm sorry if you got the wrong idea, but there it is. Whatever we had has gone, so just accept that and get on with your life.'

'You don't mean that,' she said softly. 'You did love me, I know you did – and I loved you too. She stepped closer and breathed in the familiar scent of him, yearning to feel his arms round her, his lips against her mouth. 'I never stopped loving you, John,' she whispered, tentatively cupping his cheek with her hand. 'Please don't break my heart all over again.'

He flinched from her touch and edged away. 'Stop it, Sally, you're making a fool of yourself.'

Sally took a step back, shocked by his vehemence.

But he seemed determined to hurt her, determined to twist the knife. 'I don't love you; I never loved you. It was just a bit of fun, and never meant to be anything more. Go home to Beach View, Sally, and forget me.'

She didn't want to believe him, couldn't believe him – and yet there was such coldness in his tone, and his face looked as if it had been hewn from the same concrete that lay under their feet. She reached out her hand to him, but he stood there like a rock, unmovable and impenetrable. 'I don't want to forget you,' she said, on the verge of tears. 'This can't be goodbye, John. It just can't.'

He looked down at her, holding her gaze with the coolness of someone who didn't care. Then, without another word, he turned away and headed towards the other end of the promenade.

Sally watched him through her tears and noted that his shoulders were hunched more than ever, his progress slower and even more laborious. The hope burned in her that he'd change his mind, that he'd know she was praying for him to turn back to her. But he continued down the promenade and never looked back.

She felt the tears roll hot down her face as she stumbled from the seafront and began the long climb towards Beach View. Seeing him again had brought her love for him flooding back, and in the moment when he'd looked into her eyes, she'd thought he'd felt the same way. But what a fool she'd been to ever believe someone like John could ever love her – how naïve to think she might have meant more to him than just a bit of fun. Dear, God, how it hurt.

Her dreams that night were troubled, her emotions soaring and ebbing as if she was on a giant roller coaster at the fairground. But, as morning dawned and she prepared for her last day at Beach View, she decided she wouldn't mention John and their encounter on the seafront, for it would achieve nothing.

Determined to keep up a cheerful front and not make things even harder for everyone, she washed and dressed and even put on mascara and a dash of lipstick. If bravado was going to get her through the day, then so be it.

It seemed Peggy had come to the same conclusion for, although her greeting was cheerful as she sat at her usual place at the breakfast table, her smile didn't quite reach her reddened eyes. She turned her attention quickly to cutting up the Spam fritters for Ernie. 'Will you be going in to work today? Only there's the packing to finish, the last-minute shopping, and a hundred and one things I've probably forgotten.'

'I'll ring the factory in a minute and warn them I'll only be in to collect my wages, drop off the sewing and say goodbye to everyone. It shouldn't take long, and then I can help you.'

She looked at Ernie who was happily chewing his fritters and slurping his tea. 'How about coming with me, Ernie? You could meet Brenda and the other girls, and see where I've been working.'

He screwed up his little face as he thought about it. 'Can I go in me chair? And can we buy another flag on the way? Only Harvey's eaten me best one.'

'I think that could be arranged,' she replied with a smile. 'Now finish your breakfast, and drink your tea without making that horrible noise.'

The three boys raised their eyes to the ceiling and tutted. 'Sisters,' they chorused with the exasperation of long-held experience.

* * *

It was a beautiful day, but the rubble and the bonfires that sent spirals of black smoke into the clear sky seemed to echo her mood as she pushed Ernie down the road. This would be the last time she would make this journey – the last time she would look in these shop windows and stand in the long queues outside. She tried not to, but she searched the crowds for a sight of John – of course he was nowhere to be seen.

Having collected her wages and Goldman's reference from Marjory, who'd unbent enough to give Ernie two of her custard cream biscuits, they went into the factory to say goodbye and hand over the sewing.

Simmons awkwardly ruffled Ernie's hair. 'We'll be sorry to see you go, Miss Turner.' He cleared his throat. 'You can say goodbye to everyone in the canteen.'

As the whistle went, the women poured into the canteen, the noise of their wishes drowning the radio programme blaring from the wall speakers. Sally handed over the parcels of sewing and slipped the money gratefully into her pocket as Ernie was hugged and kissed and cooed over.

Brenda almost swamped Sally in her embrace. 'Now you take care, Sal. Those Welsh are a funny lot. If they give you any trouble, you come back to us. We'll see you right.'

Pearl shoved her way through the crush and threw her arms about her. 'I'm gunna really miss you, Sal,' she said, her blue eyes swimming with tears. 'Just remember there's a place at my house for yer anytime you want it.' She gave her a watery smile. 'It gets a bit lonely rattling about in it on me own, and I don't really want to take in some lodger I don't know.'

Sally hugged her back. 'I'll miss you too, Pearl. Stay in touch, won't you?'

'Course I will. In fact, I think I'll come over after tea and say goodbye properly. I'm about to make a complete show of meself 'ere.'

'You know you're always welcome at Peggy's,' she murmured. 'I'll see you later.'

It took a while for Sally to extricate herself and Ernie from the crush and, with a last sad wave goodbye, they left the factory as the whistle went for the return to work.

Ernie kept the basket on his lap as they set off for the shops. Peggy had given them a list, and it could be some time before they would reach home, as the queues outside every shop snaked along the pavement.

They eventually managed to buy most things on the list and had even found a new flag for Ernie's chair. They were making their slow way past The Anchor for the last time when Sally noticed a uniformed man in the distance waving his hat about.

She frowned and looked behind her, but no-one was waving back. He was waving more frantically now – and running towards them. With a thrill, Sally suddenly recognised that rolling gait and realised who it was.

'Dad!' yelled Ernie. 'Dad! It's Dad.'

Sally's joy swept all the sadness away as she hurried towards him. Harold Turner was as handsome as ever in his naval officer's uniform, his tanned face and light brown hair unchanged since she'd seen him last. She'd waited and hoped for so long to see his wonderfully familiar and reassuring sturdy figure and seaman's swagger that she could hardly believe that, at last, he was here.

'Daddy, oh, Daddy,' she said, the tears and laughter mingling. And then she and Ernie were in his strong embrace, clinging to him, never wanting to let go of him again as he kissed their faces and held them tight.

Harold eventually swung Ernie up, rested him on his hip and put the peaked hat on his head, where it fell over his eyes. 'It looks as if the sea air's done you some good, son,' he said, his brown eyes twinkling as he adjusted the hat. 'You're almost too heavy to lift now.'

He looked at Sally and held her to his heart. 'As for you,' he breathed, 'you've turned into a beautiful young woman. I can hardly believe you're the same little girl who stood on the doorstep and waved me off almost two years ago.'

'I'm just so glad you're here,' she murmured, breathing in the wonderful, comforting mixed scents of soap and saltiness that were so much a part of him. 'I've missed you so much, Dad.'

'I've missed the pair of you, too.'

'Are you staying, Dad?' Ernie clung to his neck, the brown eyes, so like his father's, desperate with hope. 'You ain't gunna go with Mum, are yer?'

'I'm not going anywhere without you for a while,' he replied, 'and certainly not with your mum.' He looked at Sally. 'I've got three whole weeks' leave. My ship was hit during the attack on the convoy the other night. She's in dry-dock for repairs.'

'Our friend Alex was killed in that,' said Ernie. 'He was a Spitfire pilot and very brave.'

'They all are, every last one of them,' Harold replied softly. 'We lost three ships that night, along with a great many good men.' He shook his head as if to be rid of the gloomy thoughts. 'Come on, you two. Peggy's got the kettle on, and I managed to tuck away a few treats in my kitbag.'

'You've already seen Peggy?' Sally gazed up at him, loving the way his eyes creased in the corners when he smiled.

'It was the first place I went after getting off the London train yesterday.' He laughed. 'Everyone was out, so I waited a bit, and then booked into The Anchor. I slept late, so missed you when I went back this morning.' He grinned. 'That Rosie Braithwaite's a bit of all right, ain't she?'

'Careful, Dad,' she warned, returning his smile,

'you could be stepping on toes there. Granddad Ron's got his eye on Rosie.'

'Yeah, so he told me. Quite a card is Ron. In fact,' he said, taking the wheelchair and steering it with one hand while he kept Ernie tethered to his hip with the other, 'I like the whole family. You and Ernie fell on your feet there, girl, and no mistake.'

'We very nearly didn't,' she said and, as they ambled along the street, she told him what had happened.

He mulled this over as they approached the house. 'Then I hope she sees what I've got to propose as a small token of my regard for her.'

'What sort of proposal?' Sally looked up at him and frowned.

'I'll tell everyone later,' he murmured.

'What? What is it? Have you got 'er a present?' shouted Ernie. 'Have you got me and Sal a present as well?'

Harold twisted his finger in his ear and winced. 'Blimey, son, you don't 'alf have a pair of lungs on you. Yes, I've got presents for everyone, but they're to be shared and no nonsense.'

He stepped aside and waited for Sally to unlock the door, then pushed the wheelchair into the hall and parked it in the dining room. 'Everyone's in the garden,' he said, heading for the kitchen. 'It's too nice a day to be indoors.'

Sally hurriedly put away the shopping and followed him down the basement steps.

Peggy had ordered Ron and Jim to take the kitchen table outside, where she'd covered it in a colourful cloth, and dressed it with the best china and a vase of flowers she'd picked from next door's abandoned garden. Mrs Finch was setting out the glasses and napkins, happily chattering away to Peggy, who was only giving her half her attention as she quietly organised the girls. Cissy had the day off because the Woolworths building was so damaged it was no longer safe, and Anne was making the best of her last two days home before she left for the women's barracks and the start of her training.

As Harold appeared carrying Ernie and his enormous kitbag, Peggy smiled. 'It's only a bit of salad for lunch,' she said, 'but I did manage to find a bottle of wine at the back of the larder, and of course there's the vodka.'

Harold set Ernie down and grinned as he opened the kitbag. 'I think I've got something in here to liven things up.' He pulled out a bottle of rum and two bottles of wine. 'Courtesy of the merchant navy,' he said with a wink.

Everyone's eyes widened as these were swiftly followed by a roll of strong-smelling sausage, and an even stronger-smelling box of cheese which had come from a French sailor he'd met in the naval quarters in Tilbury. Digging deeper into the kitbag, he pulled out tins of ham, salmon, sweet biscuits and a ginger sponge cake. These were followed by a bag of oranges, a tin of golden syrup, and an enormous packet of dried fruit.

Peggy was almost in tears as she looked at the bounty spread before them. 'Dried fruit,' she breathed, 'and oranges. We haven't seen an orange for months.'

'Just don't ask where I got 'em,' he said, tapping the side of his nose and winking.

'You're a man after me own heart, so you are,' said Jim, clapping him on the shoulder.

'Quite,' said Peggy, snatching up the tins and bags of fruit as if someone was threatening to take them from her. 'I'll just put these away,' she muttered, before hurrying indoors.

Harold grinned at the boys as he opened a side pocket in the kitbag. 'There's a couple more bits and pieces, but I don't expect you'd be interested in these, would you?' He paused just long enough to heighten the suspense before pulling out bags of liquorice bootlaces, toffees, humbugs and sherbet dabs. He laughed uproariously as he was swamped in small boys, and had to hold the bags of sweets high above his head.

He caught Peggy's eye as she hurried back to see what all the shouting was about. 'I think we'd better ration these, or you won't be eating your lunch.' He doled out two sweets each before handing the rest to Cissy, who took them into the house and hid them.

As the sun shone into the garden and everyone tucked into the delicious food, Sally's gaze repeatedly turned to her father, reassuring herself that he really was here, that she could touch his sleeve and listen to his voice, and know he'd never forgotten her or Ernie.

The meal was a raucous affair as Harold told tales of his adventures at sea, the rum being shared between the men as the women sipped the wine. Not to be outdone, Jim spoke of the awful trip to Dunkirk. The mood immediately sobered, but Ron livened things up again by telling them how he *really* got wounded in the First World War.

It was a tale they hadn't heard before, which wasn't surprising, for it turned out that Ron had been squatting in the bushes with his trousers round his ankles when a nearby shell exploded. The shrapnel had been deeply embedded in his bottom, and he'd had to suffer the indignity of the surgeon pulling out each piece as his mates looked on and fell about laughing.

He eyed them belligerently as the tears of laughter ran down their cheeks. 'It wasn't funny,' he muttered. 'I've still got some in me back, so I have. You wait until you get shrapnel up yer arse – then see how you like it.'

A fresh gale of laughter went round the table, the boys collapsing into giggles. 'Ron,' Peggy spluttered, holding her sides. 'Mind your language.'

He grimaced, but couldn't quite extinguish the mischievous glint in his eyes as he looked round the table. 'If a simple word like "*arse*" makes you all laugh, then perhaps I should use it more often.

To be sure, I haven't heard this family so happy for a long while.'

Once the laughter had subsided, they settled down to enjoy the summer's day. The sun was hot, the mood mellow as they relaxed and simply enjoyed one another's company.

It was Harold who broke the small silence that had fallen between them as the alcohol, good food and heat began to take effect. He hitched Ernie to a more comfortable position on his lap. 'Peggy, I have a proposition to make. You see, I didn't just come here to see my kids, I came to take them to safety – and I wonder if you would allow me to do the same for your boys?'

'But it's all arranged, Harry.' Jim shifted in his chair and lit a cigarette. 'They're off to Wales in the morning.'

'I know, but I'm sure it can be unarranged.' He looked round the table at the wide-eyed children and the curious adults. 'I have an older sister, Violet, and she lives in Somerset. I managed to telephone her from London last night, and she's happy to take them all.'

'But she couldn't possibly have known about my two,' said Peggy with a frown. 'Won't it be a bit much?'

Harry grinned. 'Not at all. Vi loves kids, and as I'd had a couple of letters from Sally, telling me all about you, I took the liberty of asking her if she'd take Bob and Charlie as well. She just laughed and said "the more the merrier", and asked when we were planning to arrive so she could air the rooms and get them ready.'

'That's very generous of her,' said Peggy, hesitantly.

'I didn't think you ever got my letters,' said Sally. 'Why didn't you write back?'

His smile was warm, his eyes teasing as he patted her cheek. 'It's a bit difficult when I didn't know where you were, Sal. You'd forgotten to put your address on them.'

'But Mum knew it. I told her to tell you.'

'I didn't find that out until I came home on my last leave and found the letter you sent when you first got here.' He must have seen the question in her eyes, for he quickly reassured her. 'I only had forty-eight hours, so I didn't have time to get down here. When I tried to telephone, I was told all the lines were down.'

He put his warm, rough hand over hers as it rested on the table. 'Never mind, love, I've found you now, and I'll never let you slip away again – either of you.'

'Does your sister have children?' asked Peggy.

'Three daughters, but they've all married and left home.' Harold carefully filled his pipe and passed the pouch to Ron. Soon, the sweet smell of good, rich tobacco drifted in the warm air. 'Vi's one of nature's diamonds,' he continued. 'She was a nurse in the first war when she met her husband,

and now, sadly, she's a widow. But she runs that dairy farm as well as her husband ever did. There's an elderly cowman still on the place, but she's been allocated three land girls to help her now the young farm-workers have joined up. It's a big place, with a rambling old farmhouse, and lots of barns and sheds. A perfect playground for three boys.'

'Has she got chickens?' piped up Charlie. 'Will she let us feed them and collect the eggs?'

'She's got chickens, ducks and geese, and on the pond at the bottom of one of the paddocks, she's even got a pair of swans and some moorhens.' He smiled at Bob who was watching him thoughtfully. 'There's a wood, too, and behind the house there are hills just like the ones here. I suspect a big lad like you will soon find plenty to do. She might even let you learn to drive the tractor.'

Bob's eyes lit up and he smiled. 'That would be smashing,' he breathed.

'Can Harvey come too?' Ernie was patting the dog's shaggy head and attempting to keep his nose from the sausage on the table.

'Harvey's all right where he is,' rumbled Ron. 'He and I have been together so long, we'd neither of us feel comfortable apart.'

Harold eyed Harvey and grinned. 'There's always three or four dogs about the farm. I'm sure at least one of them would like to keep you company, Ernie.'

'What do you think, Jim?' Peggy's eyes were bright with hope.

'I'm thinking it's the answer to our prayers, even though Miss Fforbes-Smythe will probably have us all shot at dawn for messing up her arrangements.'

They all laughed as Peggy did a wonderful impression of her and explained to Harold who she was. 'When would you be leaving?' Peggy was suddenly serious, her eyes once more revealing the heartbreak of having to send her children away.

'I've managed to get train passes for tomorrow afternoon,' he replied. 'I thought it best to get them away from the coast as soon as possible now invasion has become a very real threat.'

Peggy swallowed and blew her nose rather fiercely. 'Of course,' she managed, her voice breaking. She took a deep breath. 'Do you think I could telephone Vi? Only I'd like to make sure she's quite happy about all this, and to thank her for her kindness.'

Harold looked at his watch. 'She'll be out in the fields at this time of day. I'll ring her after dark when she's sure to be indoors.'

The boys left the table and were soon engrossed in a game of marbles as the adults discussed their plans. Harold turned to Sally a while later, and took her hand. 'Fancy showing your old man this countryside you wrote to me about?'

'I can't think of anything I'd like more,' she replied warmly.

* * *

428

The sea was sparkling with sun-diamonds as they breached the hill and found a soft hummock of grass on which to settle. From their viewpoint, they could look down at the crescent-shaped bay and the little town that sprawled from the seafront and into the surrounding countryside. They were silent as they caught their breath and drank in the scenery, content and at peace in each other's company.

Harold finally pulled a small package out of his pocket. 'Happy birthday, love. I'm sorry I missed it, and there was no card this year.'

She untied the ribbon and opened the little box. There, nestled in a bed of cotton wool, was a heart-shaped locket on a matching gold chain. 'Oh, Dad,' she sighed. 'It's beautiful.' She kissed his cheek. 'Thank you. I'll treasure it always.'

He fastened it round her neck and gave her a kiss. 'Seventeen already, eh? My how time flies.' He re-lit his pipe and, with a sigh of contentment, leant back on his elbows. 'I'm glad Ernie doesn't seem too upset by Florrie letting him down again,' he said quietly.

'How did you know she was here?'

'Maisie from downstairs,' he replied. 'The minute we docked I went back to Bow and found half the street was missing. It didn't take long to track Maisie down and discover where she'd gone. When I found out Solomon had relocated here as well . . .' He was quiet for a moment. 'Did she tell you about the divorce?'

Sally nodded. 'The only thing worrying her was the thought of Solomon finding out she'd been carrying on with someone else.' She gave a rueful smile. 'Unfortunately, I suspect he did find out – which was why she left Cliffehaven in a hurry.'

Harold sighed deeply. 'Yeah, I caught sight of her at the station, and have to confess I ducked out before she saw me. As for Solomon; he's a fool – but even he doesn't deserve to be saddled with Florrie.'

She stared at her father's grim face. 'Was it you who told him?'

'I wanted to, but I didn't in the end. I'm not a vindictive man, Sally, and although Florrie has had her own way for too long, and I was sick of being made to look a fool, I'd had enough of trouble.'

'He must have seen her with that man she picked up at the station,' she murmured.

Harold stared out at the view, the smoke drifting lazily from his pipe. 'When Peggy told me what she did to you, I almost wished I had spiked her guns. It was unforgivable to steal from you and ignore Ernie the way she did – but that's Florrie. Selfish to the end.'

'What do you think she'll do now?'

'Probably get some other mug to look after her,' he replied, brushing the grass from his sleeves as he sat up. 'But don't let's talk about her. I want to hear what you've been doing over the past two years.'

Sally told him how much she loved Peggy and

Ron; told him about Ernie's need to be massaged regularly, the visits to the doctor, and the very real proof that decent food and a steady routine in fresh air was giving him the strength to fight the ongoing effects of the polio.

Harold was silent as she described the long walks with Ron up here in the hills, the work at the factory, her friendships, and the fact that her little home-dressmaking business was flourishing. 'Of course I'll have to put everything on hold until I can get back,' she finished wistfully.

'You don't have to go to Vi's you know,' he said quietly, his dark gaze settling on her. 'She's quite capable of looking after him.'

'When Mum left, I promised Ernie I would never leave him again,' she replied. 'I can't break that promise.'

'But if you could, would you choose to stay here?'

She nodded, shamed by the thought she could even consider breaking her promise. 'I love it here,' she said simply.

'Peggy said you were planning to move in with your friend Pearl before it was decided to evacuate the boys. If you stayed, would you still do that?'

'Her husband's on the minesweepers, so he's rarely home, and there was room for me and Ernie. We'd even planned to turn the front parlour into my sewing room so I could continue with my work. But then the bombing got so bad, there was no choice but to get Ernie to safety.'

'You didn't answer my question, Sally.' He put his fingers beneath her chin and gently forced her to look him in the eye. 'Would you move in with Pearl if you didn't leave for Somerset?'

She couldn't lie to him, couldn't deny the yearning that tugged at her heart. 'Yes,' she said softly.

He chewed the stem of his pipe and gazed beyond the sea to the horizon. 'And what about this young man of yours? John Hicks, isn't it? You've not even mentioned him.'

She knew she was blushing as she eyed him. 'You and Peggy certainly covered a lot of ground this morning, didn't you?'

'She simply told me what I wanted to know,' he said evenly.

'John made it perfectly clear last night that he wants nothing more to do with me,' she blurted out. 'So you can forget about him.'

His gaze sharpened. 'So, you've seen him then?' He regarded her for a moment. 'But you didn't tell Peggy, did you, Sal? Why?'

She blinked in the bright sunlight. 'There was no point,' she mumbled. 'John made it absolutely plain he didn't love me – had never really loved me, even before he went to Dunkirk and got injured.' She sniffed, scrabbled for the handkerchief in her sleeve and blew her nose. 'It was all a romantic dream of a silly young girl, and I feel embarrassed at having made such a fool of myself.'

He put his arm round her shoulders. 'Falling in

love is foolish,' he agreed, 'but we all do it. There's nothing to be ashamed of.' He waited until she was more composed. 'How bad are his injuries?'

'He's lost half of one leg and the other one is held together with metal. He has to walk with crutches, and it's very obvious he hates having to rely on other people, and loathes the fact that he's not as fit and strong as he was before Dunkirk.'

Harold was thoughtful. 'Tell me exactly what happened last night, Sally – word for word, and leave nothing out.'

Her voice faltered as she haltingly described the scene. 'I thought at first everything would be all right,' she said finally, 'but then he suddenly turned cold and angry – not just with me, but with what had happened to him, and the world in general.'

'What made you think he still loved you?'

'It was the way he looked at me. His eyes . . . his eyes seemed to reach right to my heart – just like they had before . . . before . . .' She angrily rubbed away the tears and hugged her knees. 'I wanted him to look back when he walked away, but he just kept on going.'

'You know, Sally, I never had you down as a quitter.'

'I'm not,' she retorted. 'But even I know when I'm beaten.'

'Do you love him, Sally?'

She nodded, furious that she couldn't stop the tears rolling down her face.

'Are you prepared to take him on, even though his needs will be greater than ever now he has those injuries?'

She nodded again.

'Then I suggest you go and find him and tell him that. I think you'll be surprised at how very wrong you've been.'

She eyed him sharply. 'Wrong?'

Harold took a deep breath. 'He's very angry, Sally. Angry because he's not fit and healthy and capable of doing what he used to do. He's angry at the world – at the war – and at the way fate has changed everything he's ever known. He's trying to protect you, as well as himself, because he's terrified you'll go back to him out of pity. And the only way he knows to make certain that you don't do that is to push you away.'

The great surge of hope that swept through her was swiftly dammed by the fear that it was false. 'How do you know that? You've never met John.'

'I know men like him,' he said sadly. 'Good shipmates who'll never go to sea again. They all share the same fear, and they hide it in anger, using it to keep loved ones at a distance because they simply couldn't bear to see pity in their eyes. But if the bond is strong, they soon discover it can never be broken, and that's when they start to really heal.'

He paused and stared into the distance. 'You see, it's not just limbs that are shattered in this war, but hearts and minds – and they take longer to heal when it seems no-one else cares or understands.'

Sally digested her father's wisdom. 'I don't know, Dad,' she said eventually, the doubts and fears clouding her ability to think clearly.

'Are you afraid you don't love him enough to take on the demands of a man battling to overcome his disability?' He took her hand. 'You're still very young, Sally, and I suspect this John is your first love – which is always a powerful emotion. But this is not a decision to take hastily. It's a huge responsibility, and no-one would think the worse of you if you left things as they are.'

She shook her head. 'I know all that – but no, I'm not afraid of the responsibility. I'm afraid he was telling me the truth, and that he never loved me at all.'

'Well,' he said, getting to his feet. 'The only way you're going to find that out is to ask him.'

Sally stood and gazed out at the horizon where the calm blue sea met an azure sky. 'I'll sleep on it,' she said finally. 'I'm exhausted from everything that's happened over the past few days, and not thinking clearly at all.'

'If I can persuade Ernie to go to Somerset without you, will you stay here?'

She touched the locket and nodded, unable to speak.

He pulled her into his arms. 'My brave girl,' he

murmured. 'You really have been through the mill, haven't you?'

She felt the anguish melt away as she buried her face in his chest and heard the steady beat of his heart. Her dad was home, if only for a few hours; but she'd needed the solace of him, the wisdom and love he always gave so generously. And it was as if she'd been given new strength and new hope to face whatever may lie ahead.

He drew away from her finally and tucked her curls behind her ears, gently thumbing away the last of her tears. 'You deserve to have your own life, Sal. With Ernie in Somerset, you can take all those responsibilities you've shouldered for so long and set them aside.'

He silenced her protest with a soft finger over her lips. 'Vi will look after him as if he was her own, and it's time you enjoyed being young and carefree – even if there is a war on. Walk into the future with pride, Sally Turner, and know that you've more than earned every step.'

'You promised you'd stay with me,' said Ernie, glaring at Sally. 'You said so, and now you're trying to get out of it – just like Mum.'

Ernie, I didn't—'

'Hush, Sally. I'll sort this,' said Harold. He held Ernie against his knee. 'Now, Ernie, don't be unkind to your sister. I'll be coming with you to Auntie Vi's, and I'll be staying until I have to get back to my ship. You're such a big boy now, surely you don't need your sister to blow your nose every time you sneeze, do you?'

'Suppose not.' He kicked moodily at the table leg.

Harold caught Sally's eye, his silent message clear. Don't let this display of childish behaviour change your mind. 'I tell you what,' he said, 'why don't you give it a good go? Bob and Charlie will be there to keep you company, and Auntie Vi's a whizz at baking cakes, and letting little boys get mucky in the farmyard. I'll stay with you for as long as I can and show you round the place – perhaps even take you all up into the hills like Ron does now. We won't have Harvey, of course, but I'm sure Vi won't mind if we take one of her dogs instead.'

'Well . . .' Ernie was warming to the idea but still reluctant to give in completely. 'Will Sally come and visit?'

'With the trains and the bombs and everything else, she can't promise, Ernie. But I'm sure she will at some point.'

'I tell you what,' Sally cut in. 'I'll send you a postcard and letter every week, and when I've got a few spare pennies, I'll even send you a parcel.'

'All right,' he said, unwilling to express the excitement that now shone in his eyes. 'I suppose you can stay 'ere. At least then you won't be able to boss me about no more.' He hobbled away from them and joined the other boys without a backward glance for his sister.

Sally met her father's gaze and smiled wistfully. 'He took that well,' she said, dryly.

'He's a kid,' he replied. 'Just because he can be bribed with cards and parcels, doesn't mean he doesn't love you as much as I do. Whatever happens in the future, you're never to forget that.'

Pearl joined them after tea, and she and Sally made themselves comfortable in the deckchairs so they could enjoy the balmy summer's evening while Harold bathed Ernie and put him to bed. Harold had made quite an impression on Pearl, but Sally had yet to tell her she was staying, and she was bubbling with her secret.

'I found a letter on the mat when I got in,' said Pearl. 'It's from Edie. She's well, and enjoying working as a land girl. Who would have thought it, eh? And she's met some farmer at one of the local dances, so it looks like she's settled right in. I doubt she'll ever come 'ere again for a visit.' She gave a deep sigh. 'It's gunna be lonely down 'ere once you've gone an' all.'

'I don't think it'll be that bad,' said Sally, unable to keep it to herself any longer. 'I'm not going to Somerset, Pearl – so is the offer of that room still on?'

The blue eyes widened and she flung her arms round Sally. 'Of course it is. Oh, Sal. I'm so glad you're not leaving. When can you move in?'

'I was thinking about the end of the week. Peggy will need time to adjust to the boys leaving, and Anne will be going the day after tomorrow. I want to stay a few days just to make sure she's all right.'

Pearl nodded. 'Good thinking, Sal. She's been so wonderful to all of us – like a second mum, really, so I'll pop in too. It's the least we can do for 'er.'

'I told her she could visit us any time, and promised we'd call in at least once a week to keep up with the news of the boys. I hope you don't mind?'

'Course I don't, silly. I still think of this place as 'ome, even though I don't live 'ere no more.' She became thoughtful. 'Peggy's gunna find it strange with an empty house.'

Sally laughed. 'It won't be empty for long. She's already been on to the billeting people, and there are four nurses arriving next week. She'll have plenty to keep her busy.'

'She'll have a full-time job keeping an eye on Jim and Ron with all those young women in the house,' laughed Pearl. 'Still, if I know Peggy, she'll keep a tight rein on both of them.' She fell silent and plucked at a loose thread on her cotton dress.

'What's the matter, Pearl?'

'I dunno if I should tell you this,' she said reluctantly, 'but I saw John Hicks today, and 'e's—'

'I know he's back,' Sally cut in, 'and I know about his injuries. I still love him, Pearl, and as soon as I can, I'm going to make him admit he loves me.' She went on to tell Pearl what had happened the previous night, and how her father had wisely advised her to clear the air.

Pearl frowned. 'Are you sure, Sal? It's a big decision.'

'I've never been so sure of anything,' she replied, and smiled joyfully. 'But don't worry, Pearl, I'm not about to rush into anything. We both need time to get to really know one another first.' She stood and tugged her friend's hand. 'Come on, let's go indoors. I want to spend some time with Dad before he leaves tomorrow.'

Chapter Sixteen

The entire family caught the trolleybus to the station the next afternoon, and even Harvey was allowed to travel if he kept still between Ron's legs – which he didn't, of course: there were far too many interesting smells to sniff and people to greet.

The train was already waiting at the platform, the steam billowing from the smoke-stack as servicemen and -women clambered aboard and knots of tearful families made their fond farewells. The station echoed with the cries of children, the hiss of steam and the slamming of train doors. Piles of kitbags and suitcases had to be circumnavigated, and Ron grabbed Harvey just as he was about to cock his leg on one of them.

Peggy tightly gripped the boys' hands as she slowly made her way through the chaos. Her dark eyes were enormous in her pale face, but it seemed she was determined to be stoic and not let them see just how hard it was to let them go.

Ron kept the dog on a tight leash as Jim and Harold loaded the cases and kitbags into the carriage and took the wheelchair to the guard's van. He pinched the boys' cheeks and ruffled their hair, promising to look after Harvey and their precious train-set as Harvey enthusiastically licked their faces. Anne and Cissy kissed them before Peggy swamped them in her embrace.

'Now, you be good for Vi,' she murmured to Charlie and Ernie, 'and remember to wash properly and leave a clean plate at mealtimes. I will write to you every week, and as soon as I'm allowed, I'll be coming to visit.'

Charlie looked up at her, his little face working as he tried not to cry. 'Will you come very soon?' he asked plaintively.

'As soon as I can, I promise,' she assured him, her face stiff from the effort of controlling her emotions. She turned to Bob, who was trying so hard to be brave and grown-up about leaving. 'Try not to grow too quickly,' she said, her smile faltering. 'Sally's already let those sleeves down twice.' She softly kissed his hair. 'And take care of the young ones for me, Bob, there's a good boy.'

'I'll look after them, Mum,' he said solemnly. 'You don't need to worry.' He kissed his mother and gave her a swift embrace before ducking his chin and turning to grasp Charlie's hand. Without looking at his mother again, he determinedly watched the stoker shovelling coal into the yawning mouth of the fire beneath the train's boiler.

Jim grabbed all three boys and held them tightly for a moment. 'I'll see you soon enough; now you be good and do as Vi and Harry tell you. All right?'

They nodded and he reluctantly let them go.

Sally gathered Ernie to her heart and held him close. 'Have lots of fun, luv, and the next time I see you, I want you to be nice and fat and strong.' She kissed his little face and looked deeply into his eyes. 'Me and Peg will come and visit as soon as we can. I promise.'

'I know yer will, Sal,' he replied. 'I love yer, you know?'

She could only nod as her father gathered her to him and kissed her cheek.

'I'll come to see you on my next leave,' he murmured. 'Don't worry about Ernie, he'll be fine.' He smiled down at her. 'Good luck, Sal, and remember – there *will* be blue skies over England again. This war can't last forever.'

He kissed her again and then swung Ernie into his arms. 'Come on, son,' he said softly. 'Let's get this adventure started, shall we?'

Jim put his arm round Peggy. Anne and Cissy held hands and Ron chewed the stem of his pipe as Harvey howled and tried to reach the boys. Sally could barely see through her tears, and she flinched as her father slammed the carriage door. The sound of it echoed through the station like a gun-shot.

The guard blew his whistle and they moved as one towards the open window and the beloved faces. The train's great iron wheels began to turn and the thick white smoke and steam filled the air as they walked alongside the carriage, touching hands and faces, calling out a few last words as they had to run to keep up.

As the train picked up speed, Sally and the Reilly family were soon stranded at the end of the platform. They waved and called out, but it was impossible to know whether they'd been heard, for the train taking that precious cargo was rapidly moving around the bend – and out of sight.

They stood in silence as, at last, the tears could fall. Peggy collapsed against Jim, and Anne took Sally's hand. It was a sad and defeated little group that slowly left the station and made its way back to Beach View.

Three days had passed since Harold and the boys had left, and now Anne was firmly ensconced at the OC barracks, it felt stranger than ever for Peggy not to hear their voices, or to have their things littering the house. Anne had promised to return home as often as she could and, despite her sadness, Peggy had acknowledged to Sally that Anne had done the right thing, for her face had been animated, her spirits high as she'd been driven away by Martin.

It worried Sally that Peggy was still pale, with dark shadows beneath her eyes, but she seemed to use her sadness to bolster her determination. She moved about the house with her usual bustling, organising the men, helping Sally to pack, fussing over washing and ironing, and preparing the rooms for the new lodgers. It was almost as if she was afraid to stop – because then she would have to face the stark fact that her family had been torn asunder.

Sally had stayed until the Saturday to keep her company; the nurses were due to arrive the following day. She stood in the bedroom she'd shared with Ernie for almost a year and took one last, lingering look before she closed the door and took her cases downstairs. Pearl's father-in-law was coming for her in his van, and he would be here in a few minutes.

She kissed Jim and Ron goodbye and patted Harvey, who seemed as bewildered as the rest of them at the rapidly emptying house. Then she turned to Peggy and embraced her. They had talked long into the night since the boys had left, and now she was leaving, there didn't seem to be anything left to express – except her heartfelt thanks.

'I'm not far away,' Sally said, 'and I promise to call in every week. Thank you for everything,' she murmured, battling with mixed emotions.

Peggy sniffed and dabbed her eyes. 'You wouldn't think a person could cry so many tears, would you?' she said with a watery smile. She patted Sally's cheek. 'Good luck, my dear. I hope everything goes well with John.'

Sally linked arms with her and went into the hall as the horn was tooted outside. 'I'm going to see him tomorrow,' she replied. 'I'll let you know how things are when Pearl and me come over on Sunday.'

Peggy quickly opened the front door and called down to the man in the van. 'Can you come in for a minute? Only I've got something heavy that needs taking with you.'

Sally frowned as the burly fisherman ran up the steps and Peggy showed him into the dining room. 'Jim will give you a hand,' said Peggy, nudging her reluctant husband forward.

'Peggy,' breathed Sally, as the two men heaved the sewing machine down the steps and into the back of the van. 'Are you sure about this?'

'When was the last time you saw me using that thing?' retorted Peggy. 'You'll make far better use of it than I will, and there's no point in it sitting here gathering dust.'

'Oh, Peg, you're a diamond.' Sally hugged her hard, grabbed her cases and ran down the steps before she spoilt it all by bursting into tears.

Clambering into the van, which stank of fish, she wound down the window and leant out. 'I'll see you on Sunday,' she called, as the engine growled into life and the gears were clashed.

As the van trundled down the hill and headed for the line of terraced cottages at the far end of the promenade, Sally leant back in the seat and gazed at the sea. She wasn't leaving home for ever – just making her way in the world like any other much-loved daughter. The knowledge that Peggy and the Reillys would always support and encourage her gave her the strength to look eagerly to the future, and walk towards it with self-assurance.

The terraced house stood in a quiet street that

looked over rooftops to the fishing station. There were two bedrooms, the parlour, bathroom and kitchen, with an outside lav in the pocket-handkerchief back garden.

It hadn't taken long to unpack her cases and organise Pearl's front parlour into her sewing room, and when she was satisfied, she and Pearl took two deckchairs into the garden and raised their cups of tea in a toast to friendship and new beginnings.

Peggy had steeled herself against the silence of that empty house as she'd watched Sally being driven away. She'd discovered that if she kept busy and didn't think about things too much, she could cope. But Sally's leaving had hit her hard, and she closed the front door with the sense that, by doing so, she'd brought a chapter in her life to an end.

The arrival of three nurses on her doorstep a couple of hours later had the house ringing once again with voices and hurrying footsteps, and Peggy welcomed the sounds and the need to cater for them all. They seemed very young as they donned their uniforms and hurried down the street to the hospital – but then, thought Peggy, everyone seemed to look young these days.

She'd stayed up to greet the fourth nurse, a Staff Nurse Brown, but when she still hadn't shown by the time the last bus had gone, Peggy went to bed.

She lay there fretting for a while before Jim put his arm round her and kissed her ear. 'You and your chicks,' he murmured fondly. 'Talk about a mother hen. How's about a bit of attention for this old rooster before the air-raid sirens go off?'

'Jim,' she giggled, snuggling against him. 'You are a caution.'

Peggy had left Jim in the house to wait for Staff Nurse Brown, while she went to the church with some flowers for Alex's grave. She found a strange sort of comfort, sitting there in the late summer sun, telling him everything that had happened. She supposed it was because she didn't have to hold back on her thoughts and emotions as she did with the living.

On her return to Beach View, there was still no sign of the missing nurse, and Peggy telephoned the Billeting Office and was assured she was still coming. She decided she should learn some patience and get on with her day. The girl was obviously held up somewhere – which was hardly surprising, since she was coming from Hereford.

Peggy was in the kitchen preparing the tea when she heard the knock on the front door. 'That must be her,' she said, whipping off her apron. 'She's probably been ringing that bell for half an hour. I asked you to fix that weeks ago, Jim Reilly,' she said crossly, as she hurried into the hall.

Opening the door, she discovered a thin, dark-eyed and exhausted-looking young woman on the doorstep with a battered suitcase. 'You must be Staff

Nurse Brown. I was getting worried you'd never make it through.'

The young woman frowned and shook her head. 'I am a nurse, yes, but I am not Staff Nurse Brown. I am here to find my brother. My name is Danuta Chmielewski.'

'Oh, my dear,' breathed Peggy, the tears springing in her eyes. 'Oh, you poor child, come in, come in.'

Sally had woken that morning and greeted her day off with a smile. Pearl had already left for the factory, so she took her time in the bathroom and dressed carefully. Leaving the house, she tucked the door key in her handbag, shouldered the gas-mask box, and set off for the quiet, tree-lined street where John lived with his widowed mother.

It was a sturdy house of two storeys with a bay window overlooking the small square of neat front garden. Pushing through the gate, Sally took a deep breath as she walked up the path to the front door and pressed the bell.

Mrs Hicks looked flustered as she kept the door almost closed and peeped round it. 'I told you when you telephoned that he didn't want to see you,' she said quietly. 'I'm sorry, dear, but it really won't do you any good, and the doctor says he mustn't get upset or agitated.'

'Please, Mrs Hicks. I know what he said, but you see I don't think he really meant it. I won't upset him, but I have to see him, I just have to.'

The door was begrudgingly opened wider. Betty Hicks looked careworn, but her hair was freshly washed and her cotton frock was covered in a neat floral pinafore. 'Well, don't say I didn't warn you,' she muttered. 'He's being particularly awkward today.'

Sally stepped into a sundrenched hall that smelled of furniture polish and roses. Her pulse was racing, her hands were clammy and her tongue felt as if it was glued to the roof of her mouth.

'Who is it?' shouted John from somewhere at the back of the house.

'You've got a visitor,' his mother called back.

'I told you, Mum. I don't want any visitors.'

Sally and Betty Hicks exchanged glances. 'This one refuses to leave, so you'd better make yourself decent,' she replied. She tilted her head in the direction of his voice. 'He's in the kitchen,' she murmured. 'I'll leave you to it.'

'Well,' shouted John. 'You can tell whoever it is to bugger off. I don't want to see anyone.'

Sally took a deep breath and stepped into the kitchen. John was sitting on a chair and morosely staring out through the glazed doors that opened on to the back garden. He was in his pyjamas and didn't look as if he'd washed or shaved for days.

'I'll bugger off when I'm ready and not before,' she said firmly. 'But I'm not surprised you don't want visitors. You look a fright.'

He stared at her in disbelief and hastily pulled

the dressing gown over his pyjamas. 'What the hell are you doing here?' he asked rudely.

'Waiting for you to offer me a cup of tea.' She dumped her bag and gas-mask box on the table. 'I've had quite a walk from Arden Terrace, and it's a warm day.'

'Then you've wasted your time. There's nothing here for you Sally. Go away.'

'Not until I've had a cuppa.' She reached for the kettle, checked the water level and lit the gas-ring. Ignoring him, she searched for the pot and cups and saucers. Finding a bowl full of sugar, she set it aside with the milk, and fetched the packet of biscuits from her handbag.

'I don't want any tea.' His tone was petulant.

'Then I won't make you any.'

'I don't want you here, either. Go away.'

She turned from the stove, folded her arms and looked at him. 'You know, John, you're beginning to sound like Ernie. At least he's got the excuse of being only seven. What's yours?'

'Are you blind as well as deaf?' His dark blue eyes flashed with something Sally couldn't translate. He yanked up the pyjama trouser legs, exposing a horribly mangled and scarred left leg which was held together with long metal rods and vicious-looking screws – the right leg had a tin prosthesis bound to the knee with thick leather straps.

'And your point is?' She returned his gaze steadily.

'It's tin,' he snapped, giving it a hard rap with his fist.

'So? At least you'll never suffer from woodworm.'

He burst out laughing.

'That's more like it,' she said softly, turning away to make the tea. Her hand wasn't quite steady as she carried everything to the table and sat down. 'Now you seem in a better mood, perhaps we can talk?'

His eyes held hers for a long moment. 'I've already said everything, Sally. You're wasting your time.'

She poured two cups of tea, added sugar and milk and pushed one towards him. 'It's my time, John. I can do with it what I please.'

He swept the cup and saucer aside and slammed his fist on the table. 'Go away. Leave me. Bugger off. I don't love you. Don't want you. Never want to see you again.'

She took the hammer-blows of his words like a boxer reeling from punches as she watched him closely and finished the cup of tea she didn't really want. John couldn't look at her and, despite his cruel words, there was desperation and terrible loneliness in his eyes that made her yearn to reach out to him, to take him in her arms and make everything all right again.

But she said nothing as she cleared up the mess on the floor. When she finished, she gathered her things and stood looking down at him. His chin was sunk to his chest, his shoulders slumped.

'You win,' she said quietly. 'It was nice knowing

you, John. I hope the leg heals soon and you can go back to work.'

She was trembling as she went into the hall. Was she making the worst mistake of her life? She gathered all her courage, forcing herself to believe she was doing the right thing. Looking up, she saw his mother's worried face as she peered down from the landing – but Sally signalled for her to stay there and say nothing. She opened the front door and slammed it shut, then stood in the hall and held her breath as she listened.

The first sob was deep and heartbreaking. The second was deeper and cut her to the quick – but still she remained in the hall. His voice drifted out to her, broken with his tears and anguish. 'Oh, Sal, Sal,' he wept.

Sally dropped her things on the hall carpet and moved swiftly and silently back into the kitchen.

John was slumped over the table, his face buried in his arms, the sobs wracking his frame as he repeatedly whispered her name.

Moving to his side, she put her arms around him. 'I'm here, John,' she murmured against his cheek. 'I'll always be here.'

'Oh, Sal,' he groaned, as he turned to wrap her in his arms and bury his face in her neck. 'I do love you, of course I do. But I have nothing to offer you – not any more.'

'I only want your heart,' she said, kissing away his tears. 'The rest is easy.'

He raised his head and looked into her eyes, searching for the truth. 'Are you sure? Can you really love someone like me?'

'Why not?' She stroked back his hair and cupped his face. 'You're still my John, aren't you? I wouldn't care if you had two tin legs as long as you loved me.'

'Of course I love you, Sally Turner. I've loved you since that first day you nearly got yourself shot.' He tentatively moved closer, his lips seeking her mouth.

Sally's tears mingled with his as their lips met. In that moment they re-forged the bond they had so nearly broken, and took their first hesitant steps into the future. They would be faced with many trials and tribulations, but together, they would overcome them all. For it was a bond that would endure and strengthen for the rest of their lives.

We'll Meet Again

Lily Baxter

How can their love survive?

It is April 1939 and unaware that the German war machine is advancing towards the Channel Islands, seventeen-year-old Meg Colivet and her sister are enjoying a holiday in Oxford with their aunt. Here Meg meets charismatic German undergraduate Rayner Weiss and the couple fall passionately in love. But all too soon, Britain is at war with Germany, Guernsey has been occupied and Meg's family home requisitioned by the German army.

Meg insists on remaining with her father, determined to help save her beloved island from the ravages of war. And then she finds herself face to face with Rayner – now a German officer – once more and her life is thrown into turmoil as they risk their lives to meet in secret. As the conflict in Europe intensifies, basic provisions become scarce and soon the people Meg loves come under threat. Torn between her love for Rayner and her duty to her family and the island she grew up on, a heartbroken Meg has a terrible choice to make . . .

arrow books

THE POWER OF READING

Visit the Random House website and get connected with information on all our books and authors

EXTRACTS from our recently published books and selected backlist titles

COMPETITIONS AND PRIZE DRAWS Win signed books, audiobooks and more

AUTHOR EVENTS Find out which of our authors are on tour and where you can meet them

LATEST NEWS on bestsellers, awards and new publications

MINISITES with exclusive special features dedicated to our authors and their titles

READING GROUPS Reading guides, special features and all the information you need for your reading group

LISTEN to extracts from the latest audiobook publications

WATCH video clips of interviews and readings with our authors

RANDOM HOUSE INFORMATION including advice for writers, job vacancies and all your general queries answered

Come home to Random House

www.randomhouse.co.uk